A Man with FAULTS

LORY LILIAN

D1559310

Oysterville, WA

ALSO BY LORY LILIAN

RAINY DAYS

REMEMBRANCE OF THE PAST

HIS UNCLE'S FAVORITE

A PERFECT MATCH

SKETCHING MR. DARCY

THE RAINBOW PROMISE

A MAN WITH FAULTS

ISBN: 978-1-68131-016-9

Cover design and layout by Ellen Pickels

Special thanks to Margaret Fransen and Ellen Pickels
for their support and assistance in publishing this book.

Chapter 1

The room was silent, cold, and dark. Two candles burned to their ends, and the chamber fell into starker darkness. Only a gleam of light found its way around the heavy curtains.

Sometime later, the door opened, its sound shattering the quiet; a man stepped in tentatively. From the armchair by the large wooden desk, a shadow moved slightly.

"Sir…I am deeply sorry for interrupting you…"

"And yet, you did," the answer came sharply.

"Yes…no…forgive me. I brought a note from the countess, regarding Miss Darcy."

The servant looked around, undecided, then finally approached the desk and put down the piece of paper in an awkward hurry.

"Sir, it is cold here…and so dark…"

"And? Is it of any use to me that you point out the obvious? Or do you wish us to spend the morning in needless chatter?" The voice turned more severe, and the shadow seemed to move.

"No…I will light other candles," the servant said quickly, attending to the task without waiting for approval.

"Leave them on the fireplace. I do not need light."

"Very well, sir. May I bring you some food? It has been a full day since your previous meal."

"Wilson, leave me alone—now!"

"As you wish, sir. Would you like to send any response to the countess?"

"Tell her I am fine with whatever she decides. Now leave!"

The door closed again, and the chamber returned to its previously dark silence. The candles, burning now vigorously, were the single sign of life. But they could bring no warmth to the room or to the heart of the man who suddenly left his seat and began to pace.

Fitzwilliam Darcy filled his glass with brandy, took a gulp, and then threw the glass into the empty fireplace.

What answer could he possibly send to the countess?

He was surely in no position to make decisions regarding the most important person in his life. Not after all his previous failures. Not after he escaped and abandoned her precisely when she needed him most. He was in no position to make decisions regarding anyone else—including himself —since every previous decision was unfortunate and disappointing. And he could blame no one but himself. He had been a fool—a weak character with a shallow will—forgetting his principles, his education, and his duty.

For more than four months, he had despised himself, laughed at his folly, and dreaded his weakness.

Everything he knew about himself, everything others expected of him, and everything he had been taught meant nothing after that horrible day at the Parsonage. He had made a complete fool of himself and put his pride and sense aside, placing his heart on a plate before a woman who ripped it apart.

Everything he believed about *her* proved to be wrong, as was everything he believed about himself.

He had been as certain of her feelings as he had been of his own, but events had shown him to be a simpleton. She not only rejected him, but she cast all the blame on him. More hurtful than her words was the expression of disgust on her face. She treated him with disdain, as though he were the last man in the world she could ever marry. And indeed, for her, he was. *"Your arrogance, your conceit, and your selfish disdain of the feelings of others…"* She accused him of ruining her sister's happiness and, even worse, of being responsible for Wickham's "misfortunes"! That was as ridiculous as it was untrue!

How could he ever consider her witty and bright? She was just like the other silly girls who fell for that scoundrel's charms. And Darcy had asked for her hand in marriage. What did that say about his own wit and intelligence?

She refused him, bashed him, accused him—and yet, he continued to be the same pathetic fool. He spent the night writing to her, explaining, justifying his actions, and revealing his—and his beloved sister's—most painful secrets. Then he waited for her, wandering in the grove on a windy, cloudy morning. She finally appeared, and he handed the letter to her. She took it, but moments later, she ran after him and tore up the pages in front of him. The wind blew away the scraps of paper and carried with them his words, his thoughts, and his torment.

She cared not for any of those things and wished to hear nothing from him. She declared she did not trust him and refused to listen to his arguments.

That new rejection was a slap in the face and broke the last remnant of his self-control. He remembered staring at her, unable to move, fighting the claw that tore at his head and heart. And she ran away from him without a single glance.

He left Kent the same day with Colonel Fitzwilliam, and he remembered little of what happened next. His mind was invaded by her words, her gestures, her expressions—no room for anything else—and his state had not changed since then.

In the next two months, he secluded himself from his friends, his family, and his own sister. He carried a pain so deep and overwhelming that it almost paralysed him. He felt ashamed, guilty, and angry. And full of resentment towards himself—and towards *her*.

Lost in his own selfishness, preoccupied with feeling sorry for himself, and bearing a grudge against what had happened, he never considered for a moment the effect of his behaviour on those around him, especially on the kindest, most loving, and loyal person in his life.

His world was shattered the morning he found Georgiana unconscious, the life almost drained from her thin body and her room enveloped with the pungent smell of opium.

Her pallor, her stillness, and her coldness filled the nightmares that invaded his sleepless nights and tormented his already unsettled mind. Nobody knew what happened to Miss Darcy, and while she eventually recovered, she pretended to remember nothing. But doubt seared Darcy's chest as he suspected his beloved sister had attempted to take her own life.

What could have pushed her to such extreme action? Why would she have wanted to leave him forever? He could only imagine. And how was it possible that he suspected nothing? How could he be completely blind to his sister's suffering? How could he be preoccupied with his own self-deception while unaware of his sister's despair?

The dreadful thought that she might be tempted to do it again frightened him and caged him in fear and agony. He would do anything to protect her, but he did not know how.

Georgiana became more restrained and shy than before, and he felt he was becoming a stranger to her. She spoke little to him and only smiled politely; she seemed unwilling to increase the bond between them. She refused to talk—not only of the past but also of the present and future. She avoided their friends and family—just as he did. While he spent most of the time in his library, she engaged herself in music, playing all day long. They barely met at breakfast; at dinner, they were like polite, well-behaved acquaintances.

Their lives and their home turned colder as the summer progressed. Both avoided the sun, light, warmth, and joy of the season. The siblings were trapped in their sadness and loneliness.

And, while he cared little for himself, he felt the blame for his sister's distress and hated himself for it. Likewise, though to a lesser degree, he blamed and hated Miss Elizabeth Bennet.

Darcy startled when the door opened once more—this time without any notice—and an elegant figure, preceded by the superb scent of flowers, approached his desk.

He took her hand and kissed it.

"My lady…"

"How are you, my dear nephew? Still sitting in the dark?"

"No…not quite…I just finished some papers for my solicitor."

"Liar," she replied lovingly, gently caressing his cheek. "I just came to see you briefly. I am taking Georgiana for a walk in the park. Will you not join us?"

"I cannot," he answered hastily. "But I am certain you will have a lovely time. Are you going to Hyde Park?"

"No…she does not favour it today. Too crowded and too many acquaintances."

"I see. Where then?"

"The same small park we have visited the last two weeks. Georgiana seems to enjoy it. It is very lively but not too noisy. And no chance to be bothered by annoyingly familiar faces."

He smiled bitterly. "So Georgiana hides herself from our friends and family and prefers the company of strangers. At least I am not the only one whose company she avoids."

"Nonsense, my dear. She does not avoid you. I have rarely seen a more loving and devoted sister. I believe she is a little intimidated by you. You can be quite frightening at times," the lady teased him.

"If only I could be a proper brother for Georgiana as she deserves. But I am afraid I have failed and disappointed her."

"Such a thing to say! I agree you have been in a poor mood lately; you must improve your manners. So I am leaving now before you manage to ruin my day. We shall see you again later. Will we have the pleasure of your company for dinner?"

"Of course. I wish you both a most pleasant day, Aunt."

The door closed, leaving the delicate scent in the air and a little smile on Darcy's face—which vanished an instant later.

ELIZABETH FINISHED HER CUP OF TEA, LISTENING TO THE CHILDREN'S HAP-py voices. Her Uncle Gardiner had left for his business immediately after breakfast, and she enjoyed a few peaceful moments with her aunt.

"Is it safe for you to leave your bed?" Elizabeth inquired while pouring more tea.

"Do not worry, my dear; I am much better. Besides, three weeks in my room is too much to bear. I feel I took advantage of you."

"Not at all, I assure you. I do little else but play with my cousins. In fact, we are ready to go to the park—which is as delightful for me as it is for them."

"Are you certain they are not too tiresome?" her aunt inquired, and Elizabeth laughed.

"Not at all. Mama would tell you that, at their age, I was much wilder. Both Edward and Elinor are well behaved and very sweet. Even our new acquaintances said so."

"I am glad to hear that. Elinor speaks often of 'Miss Anna.' She seems quite fascinated by this young lady."

Elizabeth laughed.

"The children are especially fascinated with the little white dog and the blue kitten that the two ladies carry with them every day. But Miss Anna is a lovely young lady indeed. The day Edward ran into her, she was nothing but gracious and accepted our apologies with kindness."

"And you still do not know her identity?"

"No—in fact, we do not speak much. She introduced herself as 'Miss Anna,' and she addresses me as 'Miss Lizzy'—as she heard the children call me. She obviously wishes to keep a sort of secrecy, and I have no intention of inquiring further. But we do know her companion is a countess, and their gowns are clearly fashionable and expensive. They always have two maids following them and a large carriage waiting. They do not fit well in our small park, yet they have come every day for more than a fortnight."

"What a lovely mystery," the elder lady said with a smile. "I am glad you have someone your own age to exchange a few words with."

"Oh, I think she is most likely Lydia's age. But her manners are impeccable, and every time she expresses her opinions, they are sound and well argued. She seems highly educated, and her manners are faultless. And I say all these things without knowing her well. I hope my first impression does not prove to be wrong."

"Hopefully not; you are usually a good judge of character. Is the countess of the same age?"

"Oh, no—she seems to be rather Miss Anna's grandmother or a great aunt. But she is still a very handsome and elegant lady. Her features are perfect; surely, she was a great beauty."

"Now you make me even more curious—I hope to join you in the park soon. Lizzy, I cannot tell you how grateful I am for your help. How could I possibly repay your kindness? Not only that we did not take you on the trip to the Lakes as we promised, but we put our entire household on your shoulders." Mrs. Gardiner lowered her eyes and her voice. "I would not imagine that a sudden miscarriage could be so painful...in so many ways..."

They were both tearful, and Elizabeth kissed her aunt's cheeks.

"I am happy that you feel better, and it is my greatest pleasure to spend time with you, whether in London or at the Lakes. The company matters much more than the surroundings."

"Thank you, my dear; I promise we will compensate with a longer trip next year. But dearest, are *you* well? I did not fail to notice that you have not been yourself lately. Your eyes betray you, my darling. Is there something that troubles you? May I be of any use?"

She forced a laugh. "I assure you there is no need of concern for me, Aunt. If I am not myself at times, it is only because I am thinking of Longbourn.

I am still a little worried for dear Jane. But I am pleased that she writes me so often, and I know everything is at peace—except for Kitty's complaints of not having been invited to Brighton with Lydia."

"Lydia will most certainly have an exciting summer this year. I wonder how she will behave on her return. She will surely be bored by the steady life in Meryton."

"Yes, I am afraid the more she gets, the more she demands. I hope and pray that she will become wiser as she grows older."

The two Gardiner children—Elinor, seven years old, and Edward, eight—rushed into the drawing room, hugged their mother, then hurried Elizabeth to the park.

She took their small hands, smiling at them, while she tried to escape the guilt of deceiving her aunt. Other reasons for distress troubled her frequently in the last four months—and Mrs. Gardiner knew her too well to miss it.

In all that time, Mr. Darcy's proposal and her own reaction to it had kept her awake countless nights. The tumult of her mind had been painfully great—and it was little diminished.

She still wondered whether it were true that Mr. Darcy—a man whom she thought only to look at her to find a blemish—had proposed to her. That he had been in love with her for so many months—so much in love as to wish to marry her—seemed as incredible now as it was that day at the Parsonage.

It was gratifying to have inspired unconsciously so strong an affection from such a man whose education and intelligence she could not but admire despite her dislike of him.

But on the day of the proposal, his abominable pride, the shameless avowal of his intervention between Jane and Bingley, and the careless manner in which he had mentioned Mr. Wickham had defeated any other feelings and brought out the worst in her.

In a perturbed state of mind, she had spent the rest of that afternoon, crying and struggling. She had retired early, refusing dinner, and the night brought even more turmoil. She could not recover from the surprise of what had happened, and it was impossible to think of anything else. She was grateful when dawn first appeared, so she had dressed in a hurry and escaped to the solitude of nature, directly towards her favourite walking path.

The sun was up when she had been shocked to see Mr. Darcy—waiting for and then approaching her. Was he there for her? Did he have more to say? She had looked at him hesitantly, prepared to apologise for her own rudeness if he expressed similar regret. But he only handed her a letter, his manners as cold and haughty as ever, barely looking at her. He asked her to do him "the honour of reading that letter," but his voice indicated that he demanded assent rather than asked for it. He wished something from her, and he expected her to obey. Nothing had changed.

She took the letter and only had time to read through it briefly. After such a long time, she still remembered vividly a few words that cut her soul and raised a storm in her mind—words that hurt and offended her so that she was unable to control herself or to continue reading more than a few minutes.

"The necessity must be obeyed, and further apology would be absurd … that total want of propriety of your three younger sisters, and occasionally even of your father … to preserve my friend from what I esteemed a most unhappy connexion. … persuade him against returning into Hertfordshire … on this subject I have nothing more to say, no other apology to offer … George Wickham was my father's godson … the vicious propensities—the want of principle … a life of idleness and dissipation …"

With amazement did she understand that he believed justification to be in his power without being affected by shame or guilt.

Her anger hastily overcame her reason. How dared he attempt to excuse his rudeness by putting the blame on dear Jane and Mr. Wickham? Was Jane guilty for Darcy's destroying her happiness? Was Mr. Wickham to blame because Darcy had ruined his life? What a horrible man! He deserved no consideration from her, and she would surely not waste another minute of her time reading his falsehoods. And she would let him know that she was not someone to trifle with.

She had found herself running after him, calling his name, and holding him responsible for offending her and her family once again. She ripped the letter and threw the pieces at him—and the wind took them and spread them throughout the wet, rainy grove.

A light summer rain had started, and she still recalled the cool drops on her face. Till presently, she could not forget his hurt expression: the raindrops on his face like heavy tears and the apparent shock as he glanced at the scraps of paper stolen by the wind.

She never regretted refusing Mr. Darcy's proposal. But as the days and weeks passed and she thought of it repeatedly, she began to repent that she did not read the letter to its end. She painfully tried to remember what else she had seen—letters, words, sentences melted together—and while she knew they were there, she could not distinguish them.

He had taken the trouble to fill two pages and the back of the envelope. Surely, he considered it to be worth the effort. How could she destroy it instead of putting it in her reticule for later consideration? Surely, she was not in her right mind that day.

He had no excuse for separating Jane from Mr. Bingley. No gentleman could ever hope for a more beautiful, sweet, kind, generous, and perfectly behaved wife than Jane. Mr. Bingley was lucky to have won her affection. Then how was it possible that he allowed his friend and sisters to intervene so easily? Did Mr. Bingley deserve Jane's affection? Would Jane truly be happier with him?

Regarding Mr. Wickham, her thoughts were equally varied. Although she had no motives to change her opinion of him, her observations became keener and more objective once she returned from Kent.

Rather often, she remembered her father's mocking comments about him as well as Jane's advice for prudence in believing his words. And eventually, she realised that, although she had no reason to doubt him, she had no reason to trust him from the beginning either.

Rumour said Mr. Wickham was banished from the company of Miss King and their engagement had been broken by the young lady's uncle. While many others took Mr. Wickham's side and considered it an injustice, Elizabeth wondered about the inducement of Mary King's family to take such drastic measures.

Elizabeth also discovered that Mr. Wickham had made his past story with Darcy universally known in town although he had declared to her that he would not expose it publicly out of consideration for his late godfather. Was it acceptable for a gentleman and an officer to change his thoughts and his resolutions so easily?

The first time Elizabeth met Wickham after her return to Longbourn was at a small party in Meryton. He asked her about her visit to Rosings, and she mentioned the presence of Colonel Fitzwilliam. She was surprised to see him somehow uneasy and suddenly wondered how she forgot to ask the colonel about Mr. Wickham.

Wickham had then turned the conversation towards Mr. Darcy.

"I would imagine he behaved reasonably well in the presence of his aunt. His fear of her has always operated, I know, when they were together; and a good deal is to be imputed to his wish of forwarding the match with Miss De Bourgh, which I am certain he has very much at heart."

"Are you certain of this?" she asked to test his honesty, and Wickham reinforced his statement.

"Without doubt. I have known Darcy for a lifetime, and nothing about him is strange to me."

At such a statement, Elizabeth stepped back, staring at him as if seeing him for the first time. The falsehood was impossible to ignore and suddenly affected everything he had told her before.

Wickham attempted to change the subject, but she would not allow herself to be engaged in conversation, so he apologised and approached other ladies in the room.

Elizabeth studied him thoroughly the entire evening and observed traits she had missed before. He had a tendency to flirt with the young ladies, starting with Colonel Forster's wife and ending with herself. He never spoke of books, or plays, or anything of consequence. He seemed always to be accompanied by Denny and two other officers younger than he was but never by older fellow officers. And she admitted that she knew nothing of his previous life, nor could she remember a single proof of the goodness of his character.

In the following weeks, Elizabeth rarely saw Mr. Wickham, but she thought of him often. She also gave much consideration to Mr. Darcy, Mr. Bingley, and Jane's obvious suffering. There were three gentlemen, all with goodness and mischief, affecting their lives two by two.

Who was right and who was wrong in the accounts of Mr. Darcy and Mr. Wickham? Where did one man's blame stop and the other's fault begin?

And who was more responsible for Mr. Bingley's separation from Jane: the named gentleman himself or his friend Mr. Darcy?

Mr. Darcy seemed to be present everywhere and all the time. And the more she thought of him, the more she realised that she might have been somehow wrong in judging him, but neither was he a man without faults —quite the contrary.

Time and distance—and the certainty that she would never see him again—shadowed part of Elizabeth's tormented thoughts regarding the gentleman. However, her sleep, her spirit, and her entire life were never the same again after that day at the Parsonage.

Summer had brought the welcome departure of the regiment but also Mrs. Forster's invitation for Lydia to join her and Mr. Bennet's ready acceptance.

Elizabeth had argued with her father about allowing Lydia to leave alone, but she met no success in changing his mind. Mr. Bennet was only too happy to be left in peace, so he approved and encouraged his youngest daughter's journey, teasing his favourite about her unreasonable worry. One less nagging person around his library for the entire summer was a most pleasant thought, and Mr. Bennet rejected further discussion on the subject.

ELIZABETH AND HER TWO COUSINS ENTERED THE PARK AND IMMEDIATEly noticed the presence of Miss Anna and the countess. They greeted each other politely; then Elizabeth sat on an available nearby bench. From the countess's lap, a white bundle of fur jumped and ran towards the children, who laughed and hugged it tenderly.

"Oh, Didi, I missed you," Elinor cried, caressing the small Dandie Dinmont terrier, who answered with countless kisses.

"I believe she missed you too," the countess replied. Miss Anna's countenance remained unmoved; only her eyes showed a trace of amusement.

From a small elegant basket in her lap, filled with a pile of silky fabric, a small grey-blue head appeared and tried to look outside. Miss Anna gently petted it, holding it delicately but firmly.

"I believe he would like to play too," Elizabeth said with a smile.

Miss Anna seemed to struggle to reply. "I am sure he does, but I cannot allow it. He is so restless; I can hardly find him when he hides in the house."

"Indeed, the name 'Mist' suits him very nicely," the countess intervened.

While Edward played with Didi, Elinor approached and curtseyed elegantly, addressing Miss Anna.

"Did Mist sleep well last night?"

"Yes, he did." The young woman smiled.

"And did he eat properly? He is very little yet and needs good food and rest," the girl explained.

Miss Anna's smile brightened.

"I assure you I am taking good care of him. You must not worry."

Elinor was content and leant to caress the kitten, placing a soft kiss on the small, silky head.

"He is beautiful," Elizabeth murmured. "I have never seen a kitten of such a wonderful colour."

"This breed is very rare in England; it is called Chartreux. I looked for a special gift for G…for Anna…they are both very special beauties," the countess added, and the young lady turned instantly pale then crimson.

"Aunt, please…" She shyly objected to the compliment in front of a stranger.

The countess laughed, and Elizabeth smiled, careful not to increase Miss Anna's uneasiness. The countess caressed her niece's hand.

"I hope Elinor and Edward do not disturb you," Elizabeth said as the children became louder, running and shouting in their play.

"Not at all…they are only joyful, and joy is never disturbing," Miss Anna answered.

Another hour passed in polite conversation and the happy voices of children. The sun was burning stronger, and the day became very warm at noon. They all prepared to leave, Elinor and Edward reluctant to abandon their fun.

As she rose from the bench, Miss Anna's foot slipped, and she dropped the little basket. She cried and hurried to pick it up, as did the two servants. Their hasty movements scared Mist, who looked around frightened, then ran towards the nearest tree and climbed up until he found refuge among the leaves. From there, he carefully watched his mistress, who panicked, barely holding in her tears.

"Mist, please come down," Miss Anna begged, together with Elinor and Edward. The servants apologised as if it were their fault while the countess seemed equally embarrassed and worried.

"What should we do, Aunt?" Miss Anna asked while Mist climbed a bit higher.

"Go and fetch the footman," the countess addressed one of the maids. "Tell him to tie the horses and come quickly. He can climb the tree and take Mist down."

Elizabeth looked at the young woman who appeared as frightened as Elinor and Edward at the notion of losing the little kitten then glanced around at the almost empty park.

"Your ladyship, we should not delay longer; Mist might run higher or even fall. Let us be quick. I believe I can bring him down. Miss Anna, do you have some treats to show to him—to keep him busy? I will try to climb from the other side of the tree. It is only the third branch; I should reach it easily."

Both ladies stared at Elizabeth in shock. "Miss Lizzy, you cannot…it can be dangerous. How could you?"

Before the countess finished, Elizabeth had already lifted her dress and petticoat enough to climb the tree trunk and touch the first branch. The ladies and children watched her in complete astonishment, and Miss Anna finally remembered to stretch her hand with some treats towards Mist. The kitten showed curiosity and interest, taking a step lower towards its mistress.

A couple of minutes were enough for Elizabeth to grab Mist and pull him to her chest, petting him to calm his trembling little body. She then gave him to Miss Anna, who held him in a tender embrace. Elinor and Edward unanimously cheered their cousin.

"Lizzy, you are a hero," Edward declared ceremoniously. Elizabeth laughed as she returned safely to the ground, trying to arrange her dress and bonnet.

"Miss Lizzy, that was quite extraordinary," the countess approved.

"How can I thank you? I am so grateful…" Miss Anna intervened with no little emotion, but Elizabeth stopped them both.

"Everything is fine now; let us talk no more of it. Just promise me you will never tell my mother about this, or I shall never have a moment of peace regarding my improper behaviour. It is fortunate that there are no acquaintances around," Elizabeth joked to avoid further praise. She felt rather embarrassed for her unladylike gesture but also content for bringing joy back to her companions. Surprisingly, she found herself wondering what Mr. Darcy would have said had he seen her climbing trees in a public London park.

With more expressions of gratitude, the two ladies—together with Didi and Mist—departed, promising to meet again the next day.

On their walk home, Edward and Elinor could not stop chatting about the bravery of their cousin, and they continued long after they reached the house. Even later, at dinner, they related to their father—several times—how Mist was in danger of almost dying, and Lizzy had saved him.

Chapter 2

In the evening, Darcy observed that his sister was more animated than usual. As was their custom in the month since the countess returned to Town, all three had dinner together. But unlike other evenings, more conversation and smiles complimented the excellent courses.

"I am glad to see you both in such lively dispositions," Darcy said.

"Well, we did have quite an exciting and pleasant day. We met a lovely young lady with two children in the park a couple of weeks ago, and today she did us a great favour."

"What do you mean?"

"Oh, Brother," intervened Miss Anna, "I dropped Mist, and he escaped, hiding in a tree. He almost fell. I was so frightened that he would run away and be lost forever. And Miss Lizzy just climbed the tree and brought him down..."

Miss Lizzy? Darcy thought, startling as the name bored into his mind. He quickly drank some wine, scolding himself for his silly reaction at the mere mention of a name that brought him many painful memories. Surely, there were dozens of young women in London who bore that name.

He tried to speak calmly. "Miss Lizzy? So she is a Miss, not a Mrs.? And she climbed the tree? Quite a peculiar choice, I would say."

His voice, trying to conceal his distress, sounded harsher than he intended, and his sister paled slightly, worrying that he disapproved.

"Peculiar but efficient," the countess answered. "I say—I was quite impressed. We were all crying around, but she found a way to solve the problem. Lovely, spirited young lady."

Darcy's thoughts spun in his mind again. Unwanted memories filled his head as he considered that the "Lizzy" he knew would also climb a tree to save a kitten.

He clenched his teeth, breathing deeply and fighting his recollection and the weakness he hated so much. He was certain he hated *her*, that he despised everything about her, that he loathed even the idea of having a glimpse of her ever again. Then how could he be such a complete fool, such a ridiculous, witless man that a mere story brought back such vivid images of her?

He finished his wine and filled his glass again.

"My dear, would you favour me with some music, please?" he begged his sister, whose disconcerted expression he completely missed.

Miss Georgiana Darcy would never refuse her brother's request, but her heart was heavy as she realised how little he was interested in what she had to say. He could not be troubled with such fatuous stories; she would not repeat the mistake. She started to play, glancing at him from time to time.

Didi jumped on the countess's lap, while Mist found a comfortable spot to rest on the settee.

During the next week, Elizabeth met Miss Anna and the countess in the park every day.

By the beginning of August, less than a month since they first met, their acquaintance had improved considerably, and they talked about their likes and dislikes and preferences in literature, music, or theatre.

"My niece is very proficient at the piano," the countess said proudly.

"My aunt is very kind; I am not certain how proficient I am, but I do love music," Miss Anna answered shyly.

"I love music too, but I cannot pretend to any proficiency with it," Elizabeth replied with a smile. "I was not disciplined enough to practise as much as I should have, and I suspect I do not possess any particular talent either."

"I am sure you are as good as any other young lady," the countess offered. "It is laudable that you can be so accurate in judging your own talents. Few people are able to do that. So you do not play much but surely read quite a lot—your extensive knowledge proves that. And you can climb trees—reasonably enough."

Elizabeth laughed. "And I really enjoy walking and spending time outdoors. I have measured my father's estate by foot more times than I can remember. I inherited my passion for books from my father, but it is still a family mystery as to where I got the inclination for wandering about the fields. My mother has been struggling for years to censure my unladylike habits."

Both Miss Anna and the countess laughed discreetly.

"So your father owns an estate? You seem to be close to him," the latter inquired.

"Yes, he owns a modest estate. And it is true—we are very close," Elizabeth answered warmly.

"You seem kind and gentle with the children too," Miss Anna added.

"I confess I am fond of my cousins, as well as my uncle and aunt. I shall miss them dearly."

"Oh, will you leave soon?" Miss Anna asked, and Elizabeth looked at her with warmth. The young woman seemed affected by the news.

"In about a fortnight. I plan to be home the middle of August. My family misses me—especially my older sister, Jane."

"Oh…you have sisters…" Miss Anna whispered. She immediately forced a smile and replied politely, "I can imagine you are all eager to be together soon."

"Indeed, we are. But I did enjoy my stay in London exceedingly. And I feel grateful and honoured for the privilege of meeting you both and spending such wonderful time in your company," Elizabeth said with heartfelt and genuine seriousness.

"As did we," the countess answered. "We would like to see you again when you next visit your relatives, would we not, Anna?"

"Yes—I would like that very much…very much indeed."

"As would I," Elizabeth accepted heartily.

"Well, I shall give you my direction, Miss Lizzy, and we shall welcome any word from you whenever you wish," the countess intervened.

"Thank you, your ladyship," Elizabeth replied without attempting to conceal her delight.

That such ladies—whose means and situation in life were easy to guess —showed great interest in maintaining and deepening their connection with her was equally surprising and flattering.

She took it as a sign of their approval of her manners, but she was aware that their opinion might change once they discovered her uncle was in trade.

On the other hand, the location where they had met—the small park near Cheapside—must have been an indication that her family was not an illustrious one. And yet, neither the countess nor Miss Anna seemed bothered by a situation that in the past had raised so many disapproving glances and offensive comments from Miss Bingley, Mrs. Hurst, and Mr. Darcy.

Elizabeth wondered whether the two ladies were of less consequence than she believed or they were the kindest and least prejudiced members of the ton that had ever existed.

On their way home, the countess saw with an easy heart that her niece wore a large smile on her lovely face.

"Aunt, I was wondering…should I tell Miss Lizzy my real identity? I feel uncomfortable in having avoided the subject for such a long time. I believe she is trustworthy."

"My dear, it is your decision. And I confess I find your secrecy a little strange; it is not as if you have anything to hide. We cannot deny that Miss Lizzy's company was a delightful and unusual occurrence, and surely, you cannot suspect her of having ulterior motives to exploit our friendship. From what she told us, she is a gentleman's daughter, and I can hold nothing against her."

"True. I think I shall tell her very soon…one of these days. I find Miss Lizzy's presence so refreshing! She makes me laugh! And she is so bright and brave. I have never met a lady like her."

"I can see you enjoyed your time, dearest. Indeed, Miss Lizzy has been a lovely companion for you."

"Do you think William would approve of her?" Miss Anna glanced hopefully but uncertainly at her aunt. The countess caressed her hair.

"I cannot see why he would not. Besides, if you really like something or somebody, I shall stand behind you anytime. You are old enough and wise enough to make your own decisions, and we must trust them."

The young woman lowered her eyes, and her face paled.

"You know that is not true, Aunt. I have been nothing but childish and reckless lately. I know I do not deserve to be trusted."

"Oh, my dear, do not be so harsh on yourself, I beg you," the countess whispered, gently embracing her.

Deep, heavy silence was the only answer.

On the third day of August, Darcy prepared himself for dinner as usual. He had no interest in either the food or conversation, but he had promised himself to dedicate a couple of hours to his sister every day—and evening was the most appropriate time to accomplish it.

For the last six weeks, Georgiana had spent most of her time with their great aunt, Lady Amelia Hardwick. His sister even had her own apartment in her ladyship's house—only three buildings from the Darcy residence.

Darcy hardly approved such an arrangement, but he did not dare contradict his sister or forbid her anything. He knew too well that his behaviour had been wanting, and he felt incapable of offering comfort, so he was only grateful—although worried and pained—that Georgiana found the tranquillity and the support she needed in their aunt.

He was also puzzled at the ladies' preference to travel across Town in search of a small park when Hyde Park was large enough to offer them all the diversity they needed.

The notion that his sister had formed a sort of attachment with a stranger —a young woman whose identity was mostly unknown—also worried him and made him struggle between trusting his aunt and stepping forward to decide for himself.

Georgiana spoke daily about their new acquaintance, and Darcy's heart squeezed every time for a reason he could barely understand. He suspected it was the name "Lizzy" that stirred the turmoil in his mind; therefore, he felt unable to approach the situation as he normally would have done.

The circumstances were peculiar, and he was inclined to put an end to such an odd friendship. One moment he considered his concern natural and just; the next moment, he doubted his reasons for doing it. Georgiana appeared to improve every day, and her smile was the best proof. Did it really matter who was responsible for that happy result? Since the countess was always with her, why worry about her being in any danger at all?

His greatest fear was that his sister might be deceived again and that she would have to bear another disappointment. She was not yet strong enough to withstand such a battle. But could he protect her from everything and everyone—and mostly from the dangerous enemy that was her own heart and mind?

Darcy needed only a few minutes to reach the countess's town house. From the main hall, he heard the enchanting sound of music; Georgiana was practising.

He silently entered the music room. Inside, the countess was enjoying the performance while Georgiana was playing with a rarely seen smile on her face.

A few minutes later, Miss Darcy rose to greet her brother. He kissed her hand then accompanied both ladies to the dinner table.

"Did you have a good day, Brother?" Georgiana inquired as dinner was served.

"As usual, my dear. I had a meeting with Mr. Sinclair, and I spent an hour at the club. And you?"

"I received a letter from Lady Matlock, which I answered. They are having a lovely time at their estate—as always. She invited us to join them, but I told her it was unlikely. I am not even certain about our plans for Pemberley yet. You know, first I regretted staying in town these months, but now I am quite pleased. We met Miss Lizzy again today. She said she would leave Town soon to return home, but I trust we will meet again in the future. Perhaps we can keep up a correspondence. We did not talk about that, but maybe we will have a chance tomorrow. Oh, she is soooo amusing, Brother. I laugh several times whenever we meet."

Darcy listened as his sister chatted, with a surprise he could not conceal. It was entirely uncommon for her—not only in light of recent events but also for Georgiana's usual nature.

He suddenly became worried, and a strange coldness gripped his chest. He glanced at their aunt. The countess seemed perfectly at ease, wearing a slight smile.

"I can see you are quite animated about your new acquaintance. Would you not tell me more about her? What is her name? Where does she live? You mentioned she is taking care of her little cousins but nothing more. Is her family in trade? Can we confide in her?"

"Her father is a gentleman; he owns an estate," Georgiana explained in a low voice as if attempting to protect her new friend from her brother's mistrust.

"We do not know any more about her than she knows about us," the countess intervened, "but it was enough for us to spend a few delightful hours together, which is precisely what we intended to do. Let us not be too serious about this."

"I could not ask her for further details since I concealed my identity. It would have been rude to do so," Georgiana explained to justify the rather peculiar situation.

"But, my dear, will you not tell me why you chose to do so? Why would you pretend to be someone else?"

"I do not pretend to be someone else, Brother. I just did not reveal my name. I apologise for upsetting you. I know you disapprove."

"I do not disapprove, dearest. It just saddens me that I cannot understand why you are ashamed of the Darcy name."

Georgiana paled, and she seemed unable to breathe. "I beg you not to say that, Brother. I believe it is the Darcy name that should be ashamed of me. I cannot...forgive me, I...I am sorry..."

Darcy leant towards her and took her hands in his. "My beloved sister, it is I who am sorry for bringing up this subject. I had no right to do so...forgive me for disturbing you. Please feel free to do whatever you like. I wish only to know you are well and happy. Please do not trouble yourself so..."

He kissed her hands, and she barely managed to contain her tears.

"I thank you, Brother...I am well. Forgive me for giving you so much trouble. There is nothing I can do to repay your kindness to me..."

"Oh, for Heaven's sake, let us eat!" The countess's mocking scold and her apparent severity reminded the siblings about proper manners during dinner. "What is wrong with you both? This should be a time of relaxation and enjoyment. I am three times your age, and I seem to be the most lively and joyful one here! What shall I do with you? You are my only blood relatives, but you are very unlike me!"

Their attention turned towards the tasteful food, but no subject of conversation brought up by the countess could alleviate Georgiana's sadness or Darcy's worried countenance. The evening progressed slowly and ended rather early with Georgiana playing for them. But the earlier joy and liveliness seemed lost in her performance, and the sound of music fell heavily on their hearts.

DARCY COULD NOT DECIDE WHETHER TO RETURN HOME. IT WAS A WARM summer night, lit by the stars. His steps took him down the street towards Hyde Park, hastily as if he were eager to reach some destination. But he had no place to go and nobody to see. The Matlocks had long since left London for the summer; the colonel was with his regiment. He realised that, except for his close family, there were no other people whose company he could enjoy in times of need and distress. It was entirely his choice and for what he thought to be his comfort. He loathed large gatherings, and there were few people he truly liked and trusted. He often felt relieved to be allowed his solitude. But at times—although rarely—the solitude turned into empty loneliness.

Bingley, his trusted friend, seemed too busy to see him—or simply wished to avoid him, just as his own sister did. And why would he not—why would they both not? Darcy was certainly in the habit of ruining everybody's good mood; that was a well-known truth.

Just like Georgiana, Bingley had not been himself that entire year. Months had passed since they returned from Hertfordshire, but the amiable man who resided at Netherfield seemed to remain there because Darcy never saw him again.

After his painful argument with Elizabeth in Kent, he wondered several times whether he had been correct in his judgement regarding his friend and Miss Jane Bennet. From Elizabeth's heated anger and her tearful eyes as she spoke of her sister, he could easily guess that Miss Bennet was not as indifferent to his friend as he presumed. As for Bingley, his changed temper and unwillingness to attach himself to any other young lady were proof of his broken heart.

Darcy's intervention affected two apparently honest and faultless people. Had he made that decision for Bingley's benefit or for his own comfort? Was it a desire to break any connection between himself and Miss Elizabeth Bennet? Was it possible that he had ruined his friend's happiness out of his own weakness and cowardice?

He walked along the paths, oblivious to other visitors enjoying a stroll in the park despite the late hour. Elizabeth certainly would have enjoyed walking in the park after dinner. But would she? His own folly made him laugh with disdain. When would his preposterous thoughts become reasonable again? Surely, he did not know what Elizabeth liked or disliked. He had made a fool of himself without even learning his lesson.

He did not even know his own sister's likes and dislikes; even worse, he was incapable of carrying on a single conversation without upsetting her. If not for their aunt, Georgiana would be lost—and he would have lost her forever.

Amelia, Countess of Hardwick, was the youngest sister of Darcy's grandmother on his father's side and only eight years older than the late Mr Darcy. She had been married twice to two exceedingly wealthy and titled men, but she had not been blessed with children of her own. Being again widowed at the age of sixty, she had decided to retire to her estate in Derbyshire, far from the tumult of London, and had spent the last three years there. A large number of relatives from her husbands' families visited her regularly, and she still ruled everyone and everything around her. Once a great beauty, admired by peers and royals, she was still proud of her handsome features, which did not at all betray her age.

The Darcy siblings were her only blood relatives, and Lady Hardwick's attachment to them was as strong as a mother's would be. Her estate was situated only a one-hour ride from Pemberley, and she had always been part of the Darcys' life. After Lady Anne tragically and painfully passed away, followed by George Darcy several years later, the countess was the greatest comfort to the two siblings. Meanwhile, young Fitzwilliam Darcy, exceedingly skilful in the management of his estates, also took responsibility for her ladyship's several properties.

Once she learned of her niece's precarious emotional state, the countess abandoned her resolution and returned to London, becoming Georgiana's closest companion. So much faith did the girl have in her aunt that she willingly confessed to her the attempted elopement with George Wickham and everything that followed.

Darcy himself trusted his aunt enough to share with her the rest of the story about Wickham's demands and betrayal. He was grateful for the countess's support with Georgiana, but the tighter the bond grew between the two, the more Georgiana seemed to drift away from him.

And no matter how painful the revelation might be, he slowly became selfishly content with the situation as it gave him time to deal with his personal struggles and immerse himself in solitude.

So deep was Darcy in his musings, that he ignored the length of his ramble. It was unsafe to be alone in the middle of the park at that time of night, but he did not mind. He slowly turned back, concluding that the silence, the dark, and the isolation suited him.

It was after midnight when he finally entered his house. He dismissed the doorman for the night and retired to his apartment. His valet was waiting, hurrying to greet him.

"You may go to bed, Watts. I shall ring for you in the morning when I need you."

"As you wish, sir. I just want to inform you that Mr. Clayton came to talk to you. He said he had some urgent news that could not wait until morning. I took the liberty of hosting him in one of the guest rooms until your arrival. What should I do with him?"

Darcy was taken by complete surprise and hesitated to offer an answer. He was already tired and spent by his own emotions, but he knew he would not be able to rest. Besides, his curiosity was stronger than the impropriety of the hour, even more so as he could guess the subject of the extraordinary news.

"Please bring him here; I will see what he has to say and be done with this so we can all find some rest."

Several minutes later, as Darcy removed his coat and filled a glass with brandy, Watts brought in a gentleman of middle age, wearing on his face the signs of exhaustion. He apologised several times for intruding at such a late hour until Darcy stopped him by offering a drink and a seat.

"I thank you, sir; I have some important news, and I wished to deliver it without delay."

"It must be something most extraordinary since you could not wait until tomorrow morning. News that is shared at midnight would worry anyone."

"Sir, you are paying me to inform you about anything uncommon related to George Wickham, and that is what I am doing," Mr. Clayton answered, stepping forward as if to disclose a secret.

"Yes, but you usually send me the reports express. What could be worth discussing at midnight? What did the scoundrel do this time?"

"A day ago, Mr. Wickham abandoned his regiment—he eloped," said Mr. Clayton solemnly.

Darcy's eyebrows rose in puzzlement.

"Eloped? Should you not say that he deserted? I cannot say I am surprised. Since he was unworthy of any other honourable occupation, it was expected he would not excel in the militia. What else?"

"His elopement brought some great disturbance among the other officers. Colonel Forster takes personal responsibility in finding a reasonable resolution."

"I can well understand the colonel's anger; such an incident might affect the reputation of the entire regiment. Fortunately, Wickham's new wretchedness has little effect on us."

Darcy was more curious than truly interested. Since Wickham's attempt to deceive Georgiana, Darcy had done everything in his power to keep track of his steps. He could not forget what happened when he neglected Wickham's life and plans for three years. It had been his fault, and Darcy was determined never to repeat it.

"Do you have suspicions about his new location? I would feel more at peace if I know where he is."

"I have, sir. He and the young lady are staying at the —— Inn."

"Young lady?" The late hour, the second glass of wine, and his enduring fatigue made Darcy's mind less keen than usual.

"Yes, sir. The young lady with whom he eloped. She was staying with the colonel's wife. A Miss Bennet from Hertfordshire."

Darcy looked at the man, narrowing his eyes to better see him. He heard the words, but his mind rejected their meaning. He must have heard wrongly; surely, this was not possible. It must have been either the most pathetic joke or an absurd misunderstanding. He took a seat, then rose and opened the window widely; the room had become so warm that he could not breathe.

"Are you sure about the name? Is it absolutely certain? Who was the source of your information? This is not something to be easily discussed; a mere mistake might ruin a young woman and her family's life forever." Darcy's voice turned colder and sharper with every word, and Mr. Clayton took a step back, suddenly worried that he upset the gentleman somehow. He cleared his voice.

"Yes, sir...the young lady is the daughter of a gentleman from Hertfordshire. Colonel Forster already travelled there to inform the family himself. It is said that the young lady followed him from Meryton, a small town where her family lives. It seems they had an attachment when the regiment was camped in Meryton."

Darcy listened as if in a nightmare. Each sound, each word was as a knife cut to his head and heart. The bad dream turned into a frightening reality. He had no doubt about which "Miss Bennet" the man meant. Only one of them had bonded with Wickham from the moment they met. Only one of them had raised Wickham's interest and become enchanted with him. And only one of them had thrown the paper in his face when he tried to reveal the truth to her.

She was the one to whom he foolishly became attracted. She was the one who refused him with deep anger and disdain but readily accepted Wickham, the one who ignored the needs of her family and the prospect of being able to offer them a life of comfort and safety, and the one who abandoned her sisters and her parents to elope with the man she loved so passionately that nothing else mattered.

The mere thought made him nauseous, and he rubbed his temples with heavy fingers. How would it feel to be loved in such a way?

He then threw his glass into the empty fireplace. He was surely out of his mind. Certainly, he could find nothing acceptable in such an unreasonable feeling, in such a condemnable gesture. Even more so, while her feelings must have been strong to provoke such an irresponsible decision, could Wickham's feelings be sincere? Did he truly feel such a deep attachment towards Elizabeth?

He might have—just as it happened to him. Darcy, too, had made a reckless decision when he proposed to her against his duty, his family, his own common sense, and wisdom. Why would Wickham—who had nothing to lose—act differently?

Darcy paced his room until dawn. The notion that Elizabeth could abandon her entire life and family, bond forever to Wickham, lie in Wickham's arms, and choose him against all reason was a burden he could not carry, and he felt it would crush him the moment he sat down.

And he knew it was his fault again; had he exposed Wickham from the very beginning, had he showed some interest and respect for the feelings of the people in Meryton, had he not intervened to convince his friend against his own feelings, perhaps this would not have happened.

But all that was in the past now, and he knew his rest and his peace were gone forever.

Dinner at Gracechurch Street was pleasant as always. It ended rather early, and Mrs. Gardiner, as well as the children, retired for the night. Elizabeth and her uncle moved to the library, enjoying a glass of wine and a cup of tea while spending time in conversation and reading.

Mr. Gardiner asked for a little music, and Elizabeth played for him and then shared with him the conversation about Miss Anna's proficiency at the pianoforte.

Mr. Gardiner showed increased curiosity about the two ladies who had become Elizabeth's friends. They speculated about their identity, and Mr. Gardiner expressed his hope that there were at least one or two handsome gentlemen in their family who might become as interested in Elizabeth as they were.

Elizabeth laughed and begged her uncle not to even mention such a possibility to her mother, or she would never hear the end of it.

It was rather close to midnight when they were startled by voices at the entrance. Before either had time to see what was happening, the door opened, and Mr. Bennet barged in, followed closely by Colonel Forster.

Both gentlemen wore tormented expressions on their faces, and there was no doubt that the situation was grave.

THE PRESENCE OF THE COLONEL—ALMOST A STRANGER TO THE FAMILY —frightened Elizabeth. She hurried to her father, who leant against the settee in a visible state of exhaustion.

"Papa, are you hurt?"

"No, my dear, I am fine…as fine as I can be. It is about Lydia. She eloped from Brighton…with our 'friend' Wickham."

Astonishment left both Elizabeth and Mr. Gardiner in silent disbelief. The extraordinary announcement sounded like thunder in Elizabeth's mind, raising a storm of thoughts and questions without answers.

"Papa, what are you saying? How can this be? Lydia? With Mr. Wickham? It must be a mistake," Elizabeth cried. "Sir, are you certain?" she addressed the colonel, who averted his eyes and searched for words with great difficulty.

"I beg your forgiveness…I do not know how this happened…I never had any suspicion. She left my wife a letter…here it is," he said, handing it to Elizabeth. "Miss Lydia says they went to Gretna Green to marry…but…"

"Marry? But how…? She is only fifteen…and how can he support a wife?" Elizabeth's astonishment continued as she took the note and read it eagerly.

Mr. Bennet waved his hand while taking a glass offered by his brother-in-law.

"I would have wagered my last penny that this could not happen. Why would he marry her? She has no money, no connections to help him…and he is ruined and burdened by debts. He will never marry her…"

"Oh, poor silly girl," Elizabeth whispered when she finished her youngest sister's joyful letter. She wiped her tears then sat by her father, crushing the paper in her hands. She glanced from one gentleman to the other as if begging for a signal of hope that did not come.

"I admit I share Mr. Bennet's fear," the colonel added. "Lieutenant Denny confessed after a long interrogation that Wickham never mentioned anything about a wedding. I went to inform your family personally, and Mr. Bennet and I came to track their route. I did trace them to Clapham but no farther. It seems they took a hackney coach from there. They were next seen on the road to London. I have reason to believe they are in Town. I must be with the regiment tomorrow night, but I am ready to do everything I can to…"

The colonel seemed to have lost all composure, and his speech was barely coherent.

"Colonel, please take a seat and have a drink. Let us all talk about this calmly. Surely, we will find a solution. It is a painful situation, indeed, but we will find a way…" Mr. Gardiner attempted to intervene while Elizabeth struggled to breathe and to fight the tears that stung her eyes.

"There is no other way but to find them and to force him to marry her," Mr. Bennet answered before requesting a glass of water. His face was red, and he spoke hastily, pacing around the room.

"I should not have allowed Lydia to go to Brighton. You were right, Lizzy, I should have listened to you. How did we not guess what kind of man Wickham was? And why would he run away with Lydia? He must know that she has nothing to tempt him. Did anyone notice his partiality to her? I know he used to favour Lizzy. How could he elope with your own sister, Lizzy? What kind of man is this? How is it that we were all so easily deceived? He laughed at us and treated us like the fools we were."

Elizabeth took her father's arm, trying to support him, while the colonel again attempted to apologise for not treating the situation as carefully as he should have.

"Sir, no one could blame you. Nobody could have imagined such a thing might occur," Mr. Bennet offered. "None of us suspected such a devious character. If it is anyone's fault, it is mine alone."

"Papa, please, you will harm yourself. We will find a way, just as my uncle said. It will be of no use to torment yourself further…"

"Who else should be tormented if not me, Lizzy? I have not been a good father; I know that. I have been too indolent, too careless, and this is the result. Sadly, there will be many others besides Lydia affected by this situation. I do not see how this can be resolved in an acceptable way. I would be content if we could find them and at least know Lydia is safe. Now I am thinking of all sorts of tragedies…"

"Papa, please…this excessive distress will not allow you to pursue any measure in the best and safest way. I do not believe there is anything you can do at this time of night. If there is something that must be done or some place to go, perhaps I could go with my uncle. You and the colonel must rest for a little while…"

Mr. Bennet removed his daughter's comforting hand from his arm.

"We cannot rest, Lizzy. How can you even suggest it? We will check every inn in London. It will take a day or two or three, but somebody must have seen them. We have not a moment to lose. And your coming with us is not even worth discussing."

"Papa…"

"Lizzy! I shall not hear a word of disobedience from either of my daughters! Enough is enough! We will go now!"

"Let us go, Brother. We will take my carriage. I will give orders that your horses and the coachman are taken care of. The fewer people involved in this story, the better. Lizzy, please inform your aunt. Tell her we will return when we have an answer."

The gentlemen left in haste, their steps sounding in Elizabeth's ears long after they departed. She kept repeating to herself that her youngest sister had eloped with Wickham and they were nowhere to be found, still hoping it was a mistake, a confusion.

Moment by moment, her mind admitted the truth as well as the justice of her father's statement. Wickham had no real affection for Lydia, just as he had none for Mary King and likely many other young ladies before. He must have been forced by his creditors to run away, and he took with him the first silly girl he found. He would likely abandon her somewhere—if only their father could find her in time.

For the present, she did not consider the effect of Lydia's actions on their family, on their future; her only fear was for the safety of her sister and of her father—whose state of turmoil was different from anything she had ever witnessed before. Their mother must have been in great suffering too; Lydia was her favourite child. And poor Jane, how did she bear all this?

And there was nothing she could do to help them—neither those at Longbourn nor those in London.

Her father said he was the only one to blame. But she felt guiltier than anyone else. She was the one who believed Mr. Wickham from the beginning; she introduced him to her family as a trustworthy friend. She spoke highly of him in front of her younger and more naïve sisters. It was her fault that Lydia considered him a charming, kind, and honourable man and fell in love with him so much that she readily agreed to elope with him.

How was it possible that none of them discovered Wickham's real character, her father had asked—because she had been blind, foolish, and hasty in judging him, and that influenced her entire family and allowed the situation to occur.

In the middle of the room, Elizabeth stared at the door with her hands trembling and tears falling down her cheeks, still holding Lydia's letter tightly.

She looked at the crumpled piece of paper as she recollected a letter she had recklessly torn because of her unreasonable anger, and words flew in front of her eyes: "the vicious propensities—the want of principle" … "his life was a life of idleness and dissipation." The words had been written for her to read and to understand, but she dismissed them—words that, if treated with proper consideration, might have disclosed Wickham's true character a long time ago and kept her sister from becoming a victim of his deceit.

Mr. Darcy had long tried to warn her. He offered her the truth, and she threw it away. She threw away her sister's peace and happiness—as well as her family's future. It was her fault, and the punishment struck her forcefully.

If only he knew, he would surely rejoice in his success. What man would not?

She moved hesitantly, as in a nightmare—one foot in front of the other—to her aunt's chamber. She briefly wondered how her aunt—barely recovered from her illness—would receive such news. But she had to share it, just as her uncle required. Perhaps Mrs. Gardiner might think of something…perhaps an idea to aid the difficult quest.

But Elizabeth knew her hopes were futile. Without an extraordinary, merciful accident of luck, finding Wickham and Lydia was a daunting task, impossible to solve. Everything seemed lost.

Chapter 3

A night and a day of cold rain mirrored the cold fear inside the hearts of Elizabeth and her family.

Colonel Forster returned to his regiment as he planned, disappointed and downhearted for being unable to help. Despite all their efforts, there was no sign of the fugitives.

Mr. Bennet would not agree to rest until the second evening of his arrival in Town. He declined meals and conversation, and his distress broke Elizabeth's heart. She felt helpless and found little comfort in her aunt's words of encouragement. She needed all her strength to keep her composure in front of her young cousins, although she would rather have locked herself in her room and cried in solitude.

After Mr. Bennet retired for the night, Elizabeth and the Gardiners gathered at the dinner table. The silence and tension were unbearable, but none of them found the will to start a conversation. By the end of the first course, Mrs. Gardiner finally inquired.

"Lizzy, did you write to Jane? They must be apprehensive not knowing what is happening."

"I did, Aunt, but sadly there was nothing I could tell her. Nothing has really happened, and I fear nothing will. If only we could find Lydia and bring her home safely…"

"Dearest, we count on you to be strong for your family. They will need you to support them. Let us hope and pray that things will end up better than we can foresee now," Mr. Gardiner added.

"I will try to be strong, Uncle, but I cannot deceive myself…" Elizabeth answered, wiping her eyes. Her aunt gently squeezed her hand in comfort.

"I will continue the search tomorrow, first thing in the morning," Mr. Gardiner assured them. "I shall not stop until I find something."

"It is such a difficult, blind effort," Mrs. Gardiner added. "If we at least had some indications to narrow the quest...if we only knew some of Wickham's preferred places or friends in London. Colonel Forster said none of his fellow officers in the militia knew much about Wickham before he joined the regiment."

"He surely did not appear from nowhere," Mr. Gardiner replied severely, growing angrier with each word. "I will track him down eventually. How dare he believe he can trifle with a young lady who is not without family or friends and get away with it? I will expose his character to the entire world, and not only will he never find a decent living, he will be removed from polite society forever."

"He does deserve all this and more," Mrs. Gardiner answered, still caressing Elizabeth, who only listened in silence, lost in her own thoughts, her eyes fixed upon the empty table.

The lady continued. "I was thinking...what if I sent an express to my relative in Lambton? He told me himself that he was born and raised at Pemberley—only five miles away from my hometown. Somebody must know something of him..."

"But, my dear, an express to Lambton and the answer from your relative will take days! We cannot afford to wait that long. It might be a good idea as a last recourse, but we must be careful how we word the questions. We do not want to spread our bad news more than necessary."

"Then I shall start writing it straight away and ask for your opinion before I send it. Will you help me, Lizzy?"

No answer came, as Elizabeth appeared far away from them, tears moistening her eyes as she bit her nails nervously.

"Mr. Darcy," she whispered, and her words startled her relatives, who exchanged worried glances. It was evident their niece was more affected and disturbed than they believed.

"Lizzy? What are you saying, my dear? Yes, Mr. Darcy is from Pemberley," Mrs. Gardiner answered tenderly, as if talking to a child.

"Mr. Darcy knows Wickham very well...he could give us some indication about where we should search. If only he would want to. Nobody knows Wickham better than Mr. Darcy...if he would only agree to help us…" she repeated then started to cry steadily and left her place at the table, moving to the window.

"My dear, you are the bravest young woman I ever met, and it pains me to see you so distressed." Mrs. Gardiner caressed her hair. "Let us not take this so tragically. I know it is agonising, but Lydia is neither the first nor the last young woman to fall in love with a gentleman and elope with him. Even the ton has such stories. And you cannot seriously believe Lydia is in danger. He would not jeopardise her safety, would he? You once thought highly of him. Why are you now so inclined to presume the worst?"

"I did once think highly of him, Aunt," Elizabeth answered through her sobs, "and that is why I feel so guilty now. I have been a blind fool, and I allowed myself to be deceived by his appearance of goodness. It has been many weeks now since I began to change my opinion of him, but sadly I did not tell anyone. His not going to Scotland but hiding in London with Lydia with no news for her family has eliminated any doubts remaining about his character. He will never marry a woman without money; Papa is correct. He could not afford it, even if he were deeply enamoured of her. What about Colonel Forster's statement? He knows very well that this elopement cannot have a positive outcome."

"But would Lydia consent to live with him on any other terms than marriage? And if she is in any real danger, would she not be able to find help?" Mrs. Gardiner continued.

"I know not what to say; perhaps, I am not doing her justice, but she is so young, and she has never been taught to think on serious subjects. She has been allowed to dispose of her time in the most idle and frivolous manner. For many months now, nothing but love, flirtation, and officers have been in her head. I am sorry to see dear Papa so pained, and I cannot put the entire blame on him. We all carry guilt for the present situation; we should have done more to discipline Lydia. And now we have to suffer the consequences."

"Lizzy darling, let us talk rationally. Tell me again: Are you confident that Mr. Darcy might know about Wickham? How can you have such information?" Mr. Gardiner inquired.

"Yes…I am certain…" she whispered, rubbing her hands. "Mr. Wickham told me that the late Mr. Darcy was his godfather and they grew up together at Pemberley. And Mr. Darcy himself confirmed his close connection between them."

"Yes, yes, Wickham told me the same when we met at Longbourn. But I was under the impression they were rather enemies than friends," Mrs. Gardiner added.

"That is true...Mr. Darcy has a poor opinion of Wickham...but he might have information to help us find him," Elizabeth continued in a low voice.

"But is Mr. Darcy even in town? Do you know his address? How can we find him? And how can we possibly apply to him with such a request? From what I know, you did not consider him a friend, Lizzy," Mrs. Gardiner spoke animatedly. Elizabeth only shook her head.

"I do not know, Aunt...I do not have an answer to either of your questions. I do not know..."

"Finding Mr. Darcy's address would not be a problem. His family is well known in Town, I imagine. And for other details, I would suggest talking to Mr. Bingley or his sisters. We already know their location since you and Jane visited them last spring," Mr. Gardiner addressed his wife. "I believe Lizzy's idea is exceedingly helpful. I will take care of it first thing in the morning. And I will talk to Mr. Darcy myself. He might not be on friendly terms with Lizzy or the family, and he might be proud and disagreeable, but if he is an honourable gentleman, he will at least give me some hints. I will approach him carefully. Yes, that is what I will do," Mr. Gardiner concluded, his expression suddenly more lighthearted, content that they had found a way to continue their search.

"Only if Mr. Darcy is in Town and he agrees to talk to you," Elizabeth whispered.

"I trust he will, my dear. I cannot wait to tell my brother Bennet. Lizzy dear, if only you had come up with this idea last night, we might have found them by now. But it is well as it is—thank God. Now let us retire. We have another hard day tomorrow," her uncle said.

It was midnight before Mr. and Mrs. Gardiner went to sleep with lighter hearts and new hope.

In the solitude of her room, Elizabeth was more restless than the rapidly falling rain. Her soul was empty and her mind tormented. She blamed herself for giving unreasonable hope to her relatives and for placing Mr. Gardiner in a most humiliating position. What would Mr. Darcy do when he discovered her uncle from Cheapside at his door, asking for help to find Wickham? Even before she rejected his marriage proposal, he probably would have refused to be involved with people in trade. She could not imagine he would behave politely after everything that happened between them.

Was there a way to inquire without disclosing the entire truth—perhaps not even mentioning Mr. Gardiner's connection to her? But would Mr. Darcy talk even for a moment with an unknown man not within his circle of acquaintances? Her heart ached thinking of her father's new disappointment.

Why was she so reckless in suggesting this solution? How could she offer the last man in the world who was likely to help them as an anchor for their hopes?

But was he even in London? Likely, not—the members of the ton usually spent the summer on their estates in the country. Perhaps it would be better if they were unable to speak to him at all. It would have been better had she not thought of Mr. Darcy at all.

And yet, for the next hours, Elizabeth thought of little else. All her wonderings, worries, and fears for her youngest sister now spun around Mr. Darcy. The more she struggled to remove him from her mind, the more he seemed to invade it.

The rain and Mr. Darcy haunted her until dawn, and in the morning she had fewer tears and less hope. They had to continue their quest by themselves. Mr. Darcy would never help them.

THE BREAKFAST TABLE NEXT MORNING WAS MORE ANIMATED THAN ELIZAbeth expected. When she finally appeared, her uncle had already informed her father about the new possibility rising from a discussion with Mr. Darcy.

Mr. Bennet, however, expressed his doubts and reservations.

"I saw that man a couple of times in Hertfordshire, and he never addressed a single word to me—not to me or any others in the neighbourhood. He only answered Sir William's direct questions, and from what I heard, his replies were far from polite. I expect he will treat such a request with indifference and disdain—that is, if we ever come close to his house."

"Brother, since both you and Lizzy seem to have a history of dislike for the gentleman, I will take the task upon myself. It is still raining, so please rest. I trust I will come with some details by the evening," Mr. Gardiner answered.

"Very well, do as you wish. We have nothing to lose anyway," Mr. Bennet agreed.

An hour later, Mr. Gardiner departed, his first destination being Bingley's residence on Grosvenor Street.

It was raining for the second day in a row, much to the disappointment of the children who missed their daily visits to the park. The siblings started their lessons with the governess, watched by their mother.

Mr. Bennet retired to the library while Elizabeth moved from one room to another, staring out of the windows and waiting for news she knew would never come. The lack of sleep and fatigue made her even more unsettled, and her mind filled again with the darkest thoughts.

Around noon, she was astounded to see her father prepared to leave.

"Papa, are you going somewhere?"

"Keep your voice low, Lizzy. I do not want your aunt to hear me. I will lose my mind if I stay here without doing anything. I must have some activity. I will hire a hackney coach for the day, and I am going to search a few other inns in the northern part of the city. Every hour counts."

Elizabeth intended to oppose him, but her father's distress was painfully obvious, as was his unusual pallor. A quarrel was useless, even more so as she could see the benefits of his plan.

"I believe it is a good idea, but I will come with you. Let me tell Aunt that we are going for a long walk and will return in a few hours."

"Lizzy, you cannot—"

"Papa, let us not argue and waste precious time. I am determined to come with you!"

Half an hour later, sheltered in a coach, Mr. Bennet and Elizabeth still argued over the propriety of a young woman being involved in such a quest.

"Papa, I am sorry to say so, but with Lydia's elopement, I see little reason to speak of propriety. What concerns me now is to find her safe and to be certain you are not exhausting yourself and putting your health in danger. Nothing else matters."

"Dearest Lizzy, I just realised last night that I cannot even afford to die because that would mean leaving all of you without protection, means, or future. I must stay strong, at least until one of you enters into a good marriage—although I doubt you could find a man of sufficient income to support a mother with four other daughters. However, I would have died of grief if you had accepted Mr. Collins. Even the comfort of family safety would not have been worth paying that price. If only Mr. Bingley would return to Netherfield. Oh, dear—do I sound like your mother?"

Elizabeth laughed nervously.

"Papa, please do not speak of death! But you must be careful neverthe-less. As for marriage, you know our chances were not very high in the past; now, there is little hope of marriage to decent gentlemen. I do not believe we should speak of Mr. Bingley's return."

She struggled to conceal her turmoil as she remembered how easy it would have been for her to save her family from distress. She did receive a marriage proposal—from a man who could afford to support the entire town of Meryton. But would he have agreed to support the Bennets? Would he have even allowed her to see her relatives again once they were married? Surely, no one could imagine Mr. Darcy inviting her mother and younger sisters to Pemberley or carrying on a polite conversation with Mrs. Phillips.

The more she thought of it, the more clear it became to her that such a marriage would have brought nothing positive to her family. That thought made her bear a little easier the guilt and regrets for not considering the con-sequences for her family of her refusal. In truth, the moment she rejected Mr. Darcy and later ripped the letter in his face, she never wondered for a moment about the effect on her parents and sisters. Did she make the big-gest mistake of her life, one she would never be able to repair?

Mr. Darcy—would Mr. Gardiner find him, talk to him? Would he say anything useful for their search?

"Lizzy, this is the first inn. I will speak with the innkeeper. Please stay here. I will return shortly."

Mr. Bennet's words startled Elizabeth and awakened her from her musings. She intended to follow him, but her father's sharp glance changed her mind. There was nothing she could do anyway; the inn's entrance was only a few steps from the carriage, so she could easily see anything that was happening.

However, Mr. Bennet returned in a few minutes with no result.

Three hours and five inns later, despair enveloped both Elizabeth and her father. Nobody had seen the couple, and nobody had even heard of a Mr. Wickham. There was nothing to be done but return to Gracechurch Street and start looking on the other side of Town the next day.

All their speculations, plans, and hopes were confounded once again. Another day had passed with only more rain, more disappointment, and more fear.

IT WAS THE THIRD DAY SINCE HE RECEIVED NEWS OF WICKHAM'S ELOPE-
ment with Miss Bennet, and Darcy's world was shattered. He had found
no rest for the last three nights, and sleep would only steal him on occasion for a few minutes. Fatigue threw him into a state of torment that kept
him frequently in the library while he endured the passing days and nights
and waited for the pain to become more bearable.

He did not join his sister and aunt for dinner, and he refused every meal
brought by his servants. He demanded that both Watts and Wilson not interrupt him; so, when insistent knocking on the door continued to bother
him, he yelled harshly:

"Go away!"

The door opened, and tentative steps were heard. He gazed at the door
and attempted to rise as his sister approached.

"Brother, how are you? You look very ill. Has anything happened? I beg
you; tell me how I can help you…"

"It is nothing, dearest. I am only busy. I apologise for not coming to see
you. Tell me how you have been these last days?"

"William, it pains me to see that you will not tell me what troubles you
so. I know it is something very grave. Have I upset you with our last argument? I would do whatever you say only to see you content. You have not
been yourself for more than a year now, and I know it is my fault…"

He gently embraced Georgiana, holding her tightly while he caressed
her hair. "My beloved sister: never, never think I am upset with you! I confess I have been preoccupied with disturbing matters lately, but it will pass
soon. I have not joined you for dinner precisely because I know I am poor
company. Now, come sit here. Would you like to have a cup of tea with me?"

"Oh yes, I would like that very much."

"Excellent, let me ring for some refreshment. Have you come alone?
Where is Aunt Amelia?"

"I have come with a maid. It is only a short distance distance, as you
know. Aunt Amelia is not very fond of this weather."

"So tell me: How have you been these last days? It is still raining—so no
walking in the park, I imagine?"

The siblings spent more than an hour together, each trying to appear
cheerful to comfort the other.

"Dearest, what would you say if we moved to Pemberley for the next months? Until spring, most likely. Would you agree? I hope Aunt Amelia will join us too. I know she is not fond of London."

Georgiana hesitated a moment. "Yes, of course. I will agree to anything you decide."

"But I really want to know your preference. That is why I am asking you," he said with a warm smile.

"I love Pemberley, Brother; you know that. I was just wondering…"

"Yes?"

"Would it be possible, do you think, that sometime in the future, I invite someone to keep me company at Pemberley?" the girl asked shyly, barely meeting her brother's gaze.

His answer also came after a brief hesitation. "Do you have someone specific in mind? Perhaps that new friend, "Miss Lizzy?""

"I confess…I intend to talk to her and tell her my name and to ask for hers. And perhaps we could begin a correspondence. I would enjoy her presence at Pemberley sometime in the future. That is…if she agrees. Aunt Amelia says we should send an invitation to her father to ask for his permission."

She was obviously struggling to search for the proper words, and Darcy forced a smile.

"Dearest, here is my promise to you: you can always invite anyone to Pemberley, and I will do everything I can to support your decision. I trust your judgment and your wisdom. I only wish to know more about any of our guests, no matter who might invite them. As you know, I only allow our closest acquaintances at Pemberley. That is why I would appreciate all the details about your new friend as soon as you have them. And I would gladly join you in writing to her father when you decide and provide her all the necessary arrangements to travel safely from her house to ours."

She watched him, her face suddenly bright, her eyes shining with tears.

"Thank you so much, Brother!"

"I would do anything to see you happy. You should always remember that. Now—would you be so kind as to play for me a little? I would really love some music."

When Georgiana finally returned to her aunt's house late in the afternoon, Darcy kept her company. He felt ashamed for the distress that his selfish behaviour had caused his sister again, so he decided to prove to her there was no reason to worry about him. He tried to have a pleasant conversation with their aunt, shared his plan to return to Pemberley, and had an early dinner with the two ladies.

Darcy was relieved when he was eventually able to retire to his own solitude and silence. His mind—lacking sleep and tormented by dark thoughts—needed rest and quiet. He entered the house and hurried directly to his apartment.

He was surprised and displeased when Watts handed him a note while helping him undress.

"Sir, a gentleman, called on you—a Mr. Gardiner, I believe. He said he had some urgent and important business to discuss with you. He wished to wait, but I told him you would likely not return this evening. I knew you would not want to be disturbed by a stranger. I asked him to leave a note."

"You did very well, Watts. Indeed, I do not want to talk to any stranger. I cannot imagine what he wanted from me, and I am surely not curious to find out."

"Very well, sir. Here is the note."

"Put it there and bring me some brandy. Then you may retire; you are not needed tonight."

"As you wish…good night, sir."

Watts left, and Darcy cast only a glance at the piece of paper. Why would a stranger write him a letter? The mere thought of reading it recalled Elizabeth: her rejection, her fury towards him, and finally her elopement with the least worthy man in the world. His memories swung between distress and anger, and he settled his emotions with a glass of brandy—then with another.

Neither his annoyance nor his sorrow vanished; only his body became languid and his senses numbed as he lay on his bed. Once again, dawn found him awake but dreaming.

And his dreams were again filled with countless images of the same sparkling eyes, smiling red lips, soft silky skin, teasing voice, and bright laughing smile—everything he desired and craved but painfully knew he would never have.

In the Gardiners' house, the adults were gathered in the dining room, sharing their common dejection. None had eaten anything since morning, and still they showed no interest in the food in front of them. The day had been disappointing, all the routes proving to be closed and useless.

Mr. Bennet said almost nothing, drinking absently from his glass while staring at the wall.

"Uncle, I am amazed that you managed to discover Mr. Darcy's residence in such a short time without any help," Elizabeth said shyly, tormented and incredulous about the astonishing news. "How can we ever repay your kindness and effort?"

"Do not even mention it, dear," Mr. Gardiner replied. "It was nothing of consequence. Even though the Bingleys are out of town for the summer and I could find no help from them, it was rather easy to find Mr. Darcy's house. My business partner has connections all around London, and he seems to know everything about everyone."

"Except for Lydia and Wickham. Nobody seems to know anything about them," Mr. Bennet said sternly.

"So, you were not able to speak to Mr. Darcy, but you left him a note?" Mrs. Gardiner inquired.

"Yes. The servant informed me that Mr. Darcy was out for dinner with his sister and was not expected to return soon. I imagine his sister has a house of her own. I wrote Mr. Darcy my name and address, and I expressed my hope that he would allow me a few moments of his time for a matter of life and death—and that I would return tomorrow at noon."

"I find it a very appropriate note," his wife approved. "I am certain Mr. Darcy cannot ignore it. I know him to be the son of two very respectable parents; surely, he cannot lack compassion. What do you think, Lizzy?"

"I…we can only hope, Aunt…if only…I pray to the Lord that my uncle will find something tomorrow."

"I will go again to talk to Mr. Darcy," Mr. Gardiner said. "It is fortunate that he is in London. I will find a way to make him speak to me for a few moments. I was tempted to wait outside his house today, but I thought it would be awkward, and it might give him the wrong impression about my behaviour."

"I doubt he will care about your behaviour, no matter how proper or improper it might be, Brother," Mr. Bennet interfered coldly. "Let us go to sleep; this conversation has no purpose and no ending. Tomorrow we will start the search again—from inn to inn, from door to door. Nobody will help us; we must accept the truth."

The gentleman walked to the door, stepping tentatively as if an unbearable burden were crushing his shoulders. He attempted to close the door behind him, but he leant against the wall as if his knees would not support him.

Elizabeth hurried to him. Mr. Gardiner offered to help his brother-in-law to his room, but Mr. Bennet asked to be left alone.

"Aunt, what is happening with Papa? Should we not call a doctor? He is unwell; I noticed it yesterday. He almost fell...he cannot be well..." Elizabeth spoke tearfully.

"Of course, we will fetch a doctor if needed. But I think my brother is only very fatigued and deeply distressed by worry—as we all are. I am sure he will be fine as soon as we find the smallest indication about the runaway couple. It will do no good if you become unwell too. And I completely disapprove of your being as unwise and incautious as your father, wandering around the most dangerous places in London, Lizzy. I will not allow that again!"

"But how can I be wise and cautious when my father falls ill and my sister is lost forever? How can you even ask this, Aunt? Do you not know how helpless I feel that I cannot do anything? That I am useless?"

Elizabeth's voice was broken by tears, and her aunt's caresses did not calm her in the slightest.

"Lizzy my dear, there is nothing more any of us can do but hope and pray for a better day tomorrow. Please sit down; I will return in no time with some herbal tea for you and your father. It will surely help you both to sleep. The dawn will find you more at peace; I promise you."

"I will go to check on Papa, Aunt. I do not need to sleep or to be at peace. I just need to be certain he is well. And I must do something more than just pray and hope. Papa was right; nobody will help us out of this. We must help ourselves," Elizabeth whispered, squeezing her fists together with determination, her face paler than ever.

By dawn, it was proven that Mrs. Gardiner could not keep her promise: Elizabeth did not sleep at all and was more disturbed than ever. The storm in her mind and heart had lasted the entire night, and it was still not settled. To the common distress of the last days was now added turmoil for the resolution she had taken.

As soon as the sun rose, she would go and see Mr. Darcy! She would go alone without informing any of her relatives and expose herself to his censure and disdain.

She would be at his mercy and would do anything needed to convince him to tell her what she needed to know. No risk, no fear, no concerns could make her change her mind; therefore, nobody would know about her plan.

It would be her secret and his—this second secret, even more painful and burdensome than the first.

The servants were barely awake when Elizabeth asked for her uncle's carriage to be prepared and left the house. She wrote a quick note to her aunt, informing her that she needed a ride to clear her mind and asking them to have breakfast without her if she happened to be late. Mrs. Gardiner would certainly be worried about her actions, but it could not be avoided.

She was aware that the timing was most improper. Besides the shock of seeing her at his door, Darcy would also be astonished and disdainful that a woman could call on him alone at that time of the day. But she had no choice—and nothing to lose.

The ride from Cheapside to the Park Lane area was long, and she needed to be there before he left his house or before he began receiving other visitors.

Her only hope was that he could find enough generosity in his heart to listen to her and to offer her some information about Wickham to direct their search—or to agree to receive her uncle later that day and provide him with the details he might refuse to give her.

The horses moved steadily, and the sound of the carriage disturbed Elizabeth's thoughts. She was not certain what to expect, but she feared the worst. *"My temper would perhaps be called resentful. My good opinion once lost is lost forever,"* he had confessed publicly one evening at Netherfield. That was his general conduct towards ordinary people. Then how would he react towards someone who had probably hurt and offended him more than anyone else? Was there something worse than "resentful"?

Another thing that troubled her was the impossibility of expressing her regrets for what had happened between them—not for refusing his marriage proposal but for the gratuitous insult she bestowed upon him and for her insensible reaction to his letter.

She understood that she was wrong soon after the event, just as she recognised weeks ago that she had misjudged Wickham's character. But now such a confession was useless, and it would surely bring even more damage to their relationship. No apologies, no explanations were possible as they would sound insincere. He would surely take them as a poor attempt to gain his favour and induce him into complying with her plea for help.

There was nothing else to do but to suffer the consequences of her own behaviour and to pay for it.

The carriage stopped in front of the house, and she instructed the coachman to wait a few houses away. She moved hesitantly towards the main door and knocked. A footman appeared, staring at her in puzzlement.

"Yes?"

She cleared her voice and struggled to articulate.

"I am here to see Mr. Darcy."

"Is the master informed of your visit?"

"No. But I trust he will agree to speak to me nevertheless."

"Does he know you?'

"Of course. Mr. Darcy has been acquainted with my family and me for more than a year."

"Very well, I will check to see whether he can receive you. I am not certain that he has even left his apartments yet."

"Thank you. I know the time is improper for a call, but it is a most urgent and grave matter that can bear no delay. I am confident Mr. Darcy will understand as soon as I explain it to him."

"I will pass your request forward," the servant finally agreed, apparently uncertain about his own decision. "May I have your name?"

"Miss Elizabeth Bennet. I will wait outside if necessary," Elizabeth said, taking a step backward.

The man hesitated only a moment.

"No need, ma'am. I am sure there is no problem if you wait here in the hall."

Elizabeth remained alone, suddenly feeling trapped, a sense of panic enveloping her as she wondered whether she should stay or run away.

She soon heard voices, and a woman of middle age with handsome features and a confident posture appeared, measuring Elizabeth with critical eyes.

"I am Mrs. Gilbert, the housekeeper. I understand you are here to see the master."

"Indeed."

"He is being informed as we speak, but I must warn you that it is very unlikely he will receive you without previous notice."

"I understand that—thank you. I will wait."

LORY LILIAN

Elizabeth's kind politeness seemed to gain the housekeeper's sympathy. "You should come inside and take a seat. May I offer you tea?"

"I thank you, no. I do not wish to interrupt your daily tasks. I will wait here as long as necessary."

Elizabeth remained alone again; she clasped her hands together to hide her increasing nervousness. So far, she had found out that he was at home and there was a slight chance she would see him eventually. That was as good news as she could hope for.

To her disbelief, only a couple of minutes later, another servant appeared and bowed to her.

"Miss Bennet, the master awaits you in the library. I will show you to him."

Her knees weakened, and her steps became unsteady. She prayed she would manage to overcome her turmoil and behave reasonably when she faced him.

The notion that he agreed so quickly to receive her was equally surprising and frightening. Was he willing to learn what she had to say and to offer his help, or had he hurried to see her just for the chance of throwing her out of his house?

The servant stopped in front of an impressive door and opened it slowly.

"Miss Elizabeth Bennet to see you, sir."

She dared to glance inside the room. The curtains were pulled shut, and she could barely see. She only observed a long desk by the window and a figure resting on the chair behind it.

His voice startled her, and cold shivers joined a sudden lump in her throat that left her speechless. The door closed, and a chill darkness held her in its grip.

Chapter 4

That morning had every sign of being an ordinary one. It arrived as many others had with only torment for Darcy's tired mind.

However, unlike other mornings, he suddenly decided to behave differently. He determined that he would put an end to the useless torment of the last months and regain control of his life. The time had come. He had been foolish too long. He could not allow himself to go on in the same manner.

He had to pay attention to his responsibilities. Too many people depended on him and too many expectations were demanded of him to afford such a failure.

Darcy moved to the library early. He instructed his servants that he not be disturbed until he rang for them. He also wrote a short note to Georgiana, informing her he would be busy the entire day so she would not worry about his absence.

He opened the curtains, then the window. It was a pleasant, though still cloudy, morning. The air smelled of freshness.

Darcy spread the pile of papers on his desk. His solicitor had sent him several letters, which he never took the trouble of answering. Also, his uncle the earl had written him twice on both business and family matters, and he had offered no response. He had neglected everyone but would do so no more.

His sister, his aunts, his cousins, his tenants—all needed his support and consideration. He was compelled to keep his mind clear, keen, and concentrated on what was important.

There was no room left for Elizabeth Bennet in his thoughts.

His disappointment in her was now complete: she responded to his love with disdain, to his passion with derision, and to his commitment with a reckless elopement with Wickham. Where was she now? Were they wedded? Would she accept staying with that man without marriage? And where would she live? What income would they have? Where would Wickham take her?

He furiously pulled the curtains closed again, pacing the room in darkness.

How could he be so weak in keeping his own resolution? How could it happen that, in less than a minute, he started thinking of her again? Would he ever be able to get past this? Beyond her? His life would be miserable as long as he was haunted by this obsession but—silly Elizabeth—hers would be the same by the side of one of the least honourable men. Wickham—the man she chose over him.

If only he could rip her out of his heart too, he would perhaps be peaceful and tranquil.

When the door to his library opened, he only shouted: "Leave!" But his valet Watts approached him bravely.

"Sir, I apologise for the intrusion. I know your orders, but I could not ignore the matter. A young lady is calling on you. She claims it is a most urgent situation. Mrs. Gilbert was uncertain of how to proceed, and I took the liberty of informing you."

Darcy glanced at his valet with an incredulous expression mixed with curiosity.

"Besides my sister and my cousin, I can hardly imagine any other young lady needing my advice on an urgent matter. This is quite peculiar. Is the young woman still here?"

"Yes, sir. She is waiting in the main hall."

"Very well, go fetch her, and we will see what she wants."

The servant had almost exited the room when Darcy called to him. "Watts, do you happen to know her name?"

"Yes, sir. Miss Bennet. Miss Elizabeth Bennet."

Darcy's shoulders seemed to crumble under the weight of the news.

How could it be? Elizabeth Bennet at his door? What could she possibly wish from him? Could it be that Wickham sent her? Surely, he would not dare do that. What if she told Wickham about his foolish marriage proposal? Was Wickham aware of his feelings for Elizabeth and now trying to gain some advantage from it? No, that would be too vile even for that scoundrel. And she—would she lower herself to take part in such a scheme?

She introduced herself as Miss Bennet—could that mean they were not married yet? They eloped several days ago—he had lost count—where had they been all that time?

Darcy heard steps and briefly thought he should open the curtains again, but he had no time before the door opened. He managed to sit in his chair, his fists pressed together to hide his nervousness. What a fool he was to be so distressed, he scolded himself while filling a glass of brandy and emptying it in one gulp.

Watts introduced the visitor, and she stepped in hesitantly.

"Miss Bennet...do come in."

The coldness in his voice sounded strange even to him. He struggled to keep his composure as he stretched to pull the curtains open. The sun's light entered through the window, and he narrowed his eyes to protect them from such brightness. Then he turned and finally, after more than four months of torment, laid his eyes on the object of his affliction.

"Miss Bennet..."

"Mr. Darcy..."

Their eyes met briefly, as neither of them had the strength to linger. He did not invite her to sit down, but she seemed not to notice. Her hands were clasped together on her reticule.

He observed the dark circles under her eyes and the sadness that had washed away her usual liveliness. She did not look happy with her present situation. Had she finally discovered Wickham's true character? He knew he should rejoice in her suffering, but his heart was heavy, and he desperately wished to comfort her. He was as weak and foolish as ever, and he realised he had to fight harder to overcome his feelings.

"May I ask what the purpose of this unexpected visit is?" he finally inquired.

"Sir, I beg your forgiveness for disturbing you...I know how surprised you must be...and please believe me that I would never have dared to bother you if the matter was not a most urgent one. I struggled about whether to come here today; it was a very difficult decision for me, one I never imagined I would make. And I am well aware you are not pleased to see me either... but I desperately need help, and you are the only one who can offer it..."

Darcy listened to her explanation, every moment increasing his turmoil. She had no restraint in telling him that she struggled to come to him against her will. Had she been sent then? She needed to stop dithering and come to the point so he could refuse her, ask her to leave, and never see her again.

"I confess I am surprised; I would imagine I am the last man in the world of whom you would ask anything. It is unwise to make a request of someone arrogant, conceited, and disdainful of the feelings of others," he replied.

The words had come out of his mouth without his mind even noticing.

Elizabeth paled even more at that harsh censure; she should have expected it, but she seemed hurt nevertheless.

"But I suspect you did not come here at this early hour to critique my character again. You told my servant it is something of great importance. What could it be? You are not harmed in any way, I hope." His voice lacked any emotion.

"Forgive me...I am not harmed...it is about something...someone... about Mr. Wickham."

He breathed deeply, waiting for her to continue. So Wickham did send her, and she dared to ask him something about that scoundrel. His fists were clenched so tightly that it hurt. How could he bear to hear anything more about this?

"I see...and what can I do for your friend Wickham? Is he still suffering because of my unfair treatment?"

His sharp voice and icy glare were almost menacing—he intended that —and she bit her lips for a moment then continued.

"We need help to find him...if you could only tell me a few things about him. My father and my uncle have been looking for him for days now. Colonel Forster helped us with the search too, but nobody knows much about his previous life before he joined the regiment. We suspect he is hiding somewhere in London, and they searched every inn...but it takes so long, and nobody knows anything about him. The situation is tragic for my family..."

His expression changed, and his eyes widened. What was she talking about? They were searching for Wickham? So he eloped with her then abandoned her?

Darcy gazed at her, astounded and lost for words, wondering how it was possible that the woman he thought to be exceptionally bright could end up in such a situation. What was he to do? What answer could he give to such a disclosure? Why was she giving him all these details?

"Miss Bennet, what is it exactly that you expect me to do?"

She started talking again, stepping forward. "Sir, I am begging you, if you could only tell me about Mr. Wickham's old habits or friends…since you have known each other for so long…where he used to stay in London… anything. I know I should not dare to ask you of all people, but we have no one left. My father has fallen ill because of this situation…I feel so guilty. I know it was my fault for trusting this man from the beginning…I have been such a fool…if only I had listened to you…or read the letter you gave me, my family would not be suffering now."

She started to sob, and he could bear no more. Pain, pity, disappointment, anger, and sorrow turned into a storm of feelings that defeated his reason and his logic. She stood there, looking younger, thinner, and weaker than usual.

His fantasy came to a close. The present image of her demolished all his past dreams, and everything he believed about her was changed forever.

This was not the brave Miss Elizabeth Bennet who walked across fields to take care of her ill sister. Her witty mind and sparkling eyes were nothing but a dream, an ideal fancy drawn by his mind.

Darcy looked at the woman who had filled his senses for a year, crying in front of him. The woman who proudly rejected him when he offered her his entire world was mourning the suffering of her family when she could have offered them a lifetime of safety and comfort. How strong her hate for him must have been and how powerful her attachment to Wickham to find herself in that situation.

And now, she was begging for his help.

He should ask her to leave and refuse any connection to her. He should not have even agreed to receive her in the first place. He had no responsibility and no desire to become involved in the Bennets' downfall. He owed her nothing.

He poured himself another glass of brandy.

"So you believe that, with a bit of information about Wickham's past, you will be able to locate him?"

He was surprised at how clear and calm his voice sounded. From her startled glance, he could see that she, too, had noticed the change.

"Yes…forgive me, I dared to tell my uncle that you might know something. My uncle came to see you yesterday, but you were not at home. He said he would return later today. Nobody knows I am here…and nobody knows about…what happened in Kent…except Jane…"

The more her torment increased, the more he regained control of his emotions. He wondered how they had found his address, but that detail was of little importance.

"What is your uncle's name?"

"Mr. Edward Gardiner..."

"Yes, I was informed. Miss Bennet...what do you hope to accomplish if you discover Wickham's whereabouts?"

"My father and my uncle will demand him to do his duty. He must be forced to marry if there is no other way."

He felt dizzy and nauseous; his head ached, and his thoughts were again spinning in his head. So she asked her father and uncle to force Wickham to marry her. Was she that desperate? He wished nothing but to put an end to this wretched conversation.

She continued her pleading, taking one step closer to him.

"Sir, I imagine that any request from me is repugnant to you, but I know you are an honourable gentleman who would not take revenge on my family in such a difficult time..."

He stepped back.

"Truly? You believe me to be an honourable man now! May I ask when your opinion of me improved so significantly? You cannot possibly think I would be fooled by such attempts at flattery."

"Sir, I only...I understand that you are still offended and angry..."

He did not take his eyes from her and stepped back even further, rage causing his fingers to tremble.

"Please refrain from presuming how I feel. My feelings are not a subject of conversation for you. And I would certainly not 'take revenge' on anyone, madam; no honourable man would do so, not even one who usually does not behave in a gentlemanlike manner."

Elizabeth lowered her eyes to the floor then looked at him again. What could she dare answer?

She lifted her chin as she gathered her courage, but her voice had no strength left.

"I can only apologise for what I said four months ago. I see that my offenses are not easy to forget, even more so as most of them were probably unfair. But I trust your honour and generosity can rise above the past...I... we would be forever grateful to you for any help...if there is anything my family or I could do to repay your efforts, we would certainly do it..."

"The offenses you inflicted mean little compared to the suffering you brought to your family, Miss Bennet. I know remorse will be your severest punishment for some time. But I expect you to have the civility of not suggesting that you *repay* my efforts. How would you propose to do that? What could you possibly offer to convince me? And would you be willing to offer *anything* I might demand of you in order to achieve your purpose?"

Her cheeks and neck became red, and she bit her lips nervously. Was she about to cry again?

"Sir, I did not mean...I am sure you would not..."

He laughed bitterly. "Have no worry, Miss Bennet. Any interest I might have had in you is long gone. I have no concern and no desire left for anything regarding you. My good opinion, once lost, is lost forever."

"Yes, I remember you saying that," Elizabeth whispered, looking around as though she was uncertain whether to sit or leave.

"Miss Bennet, it is useless and unwise to continue this conversation. It was a thoughtless decision to come here alone in the first place. I will speak to your uncle if he calls on me again. Yes, I do know more details than I would like to have about Wickham; sadly, no one knows him better than I do. That is precisely why I am so sad and disappointed to see you in this position, which easily could have been avoided if you only had the courtesy to read the letter I wrote you...but that is irrelevant. I will only say God bless you, Miss Bennet."

Elizabeth looked at him in apparent bewilderment. She covered her mouth with trembling fingers and tears fell on her cheeks. Darcy averted his eyes from her as he could not bear to witness her suffering.

"Sir, did I hear you correctly? You will talk to my uncle? I cannot believe... this is...this is so unexpected and so amazing. How can I ever thank you?"

Her face, coloured by sudden excitement, expressed all that her rushed words could not, but he did not care to watch or to listen. He could not endure either her despair or her gratitude.

"Gratitude is not necessary, Miss Bennet. You owe me nothing, as nothing of what I do is related to you personally. I would help any family that happened to fall under the evil influence of Wickham."

"Yes...I know...I do not expect any special consideration...I only...thank you. I should leave now..."

Emotion prevented her from speaking further. She walked hesitantly then suddenly leant to find support against the wall.

Darcy gazed after Elizabeth, counting her steps out and wondering why she moved so slowly. He remembered her joyfully walking through the fields of Hertfordshire or Kent, but those images seemed old and fanciful.

Then, with concern, he noticed her hesitation and hurried to her, catching her just as she fell.

He quickly carried her to the settee, brushing his fingers over her temples and forehead then taking her hands in his, squeezing them gently and calling her name. What was happening? Was she ill? Was she hurt in some way? He was tempted to send for a doctor, but Elizabeth recovered quickly. She opened her eyes and looked at him, mere inches away, then started to apologise for her weakness. He offered her a glass of water, but she refused, and neither of them moved for a few moments.

Her soft, bare fingers in his palms stirred his senses and made his skin shiver. They sat together on the settee, their hands joined and their knees touching. Her head was lowered as she tried to conceal her embarrassment; he desperately searched for the proper way to respond in that dreadful moment.

She raised her eyes to meet his, her eyelashes heavy with tears; she struggled to breathe, her tongue wiping her dry lips. Her fingers trembled so violently that he tightened his hold to stop them.

Only a few brief moments were needed before his heart defeated his will and his emotions conquered his reason.

He knew he should be angry with this woman who did him so much injustice, that he should loathe her wanton behaviour and despise her faulty character.

But all he felt was a warmth that overtook his body and his mind with an enormous desire to protect her.

His fury shifted to the man who had caused all that pain and who would —likely—harm her many times in the future. He could do little about that, but he could do something before he departed from her forever.

He slowly withdrew his hands.

"Miss Bennet, please try to calm yourself. I will talk to your uncle later today, and we will find a way. I truly do not know how this situation could find an acceptable resolution, but if there is a drop of good in all this turmoil, we will find it. And we will surely discover Wickham. Now, may I bring you something? Should I fetch someone?"

His voice was so gentle that Elizabeth's face lit. She quickly stroked her face and attempted to stand.

"Oh no, that will not be necessary. I am fine…I am more than fine…I must return home this instant. I took my uncle's carriage, and he will need it. I will send him to you right away if that is acceptable. Sir, I cannot thank you enough…please forgive me for all this trouble…"

Her restlessness increased as her face gained some colour.

"I rang for the servant; he will show you out," he said politely.

Her recovery brought them one step closer to their separation. She was as eager to leave as he was frightened to see her walking in sorrow to an unhappy future.

She started to speak animatedly, smiling through tears as she walked towards the door.

"Thank you, but I can find my way out. What comfort I will bring to my family! If we can find Lydia safe and bring her home, my prayers will be answered. Papa is desperate, and he cannot stop blaming himself for not being more careful, perhaps more strict with her. And sir, I know you never approved of my youngest sister's behaviour, and rightfully so. Her only excuse is that she is very young—not even sixteen yet. It was easy for her to fancy being in love with an officer whom we all praised and welcomed into our house. It was entirely my fault: had I been more careful, had I not been so thoughtless in believing his stories and approving his character, Lydia would surely not have been so easily convinced to elope with him… but now, thanks to your kindness, we can hope she will be found soon…"

Darcy listened to her ramblings, walking after her towards the door. Each word sounded like thunder, shattering his thoughts and preventing his mind from perceiving the meaning of Elizabeth's speech. She continued to talk about her youngest sister, Lydia, and he could not—for his life —comprehend what the youngest Bennet sister's lack of education and decorum had to do with the present situation.

The last statements turned his anxiety into a bustle of wonder and questions that he did not dare address to her. Watts entered and escorted Elizabeth out. She followed the servant after she again thanked Darcy, but he offered no reply, still incredulous at this new piece of information.

For several minutes, he remained still, supporting himself on the heavy wooden desk. His head was spinning, and his eyes stung while his heart pounded wildly.

What had happened? Was it real or was he still in the midst of a nightmare? Was it possible that he had been wrong all the time, or was he losing his mind? Who was it that eloped with Wickham? Could he have made such a foolish error? He had been such a pompous fool that he did not even ask Mr. Clayton for details. Had he himself added to his torment in the last days? If so, he thoroughly deserved it!

He recollected the entire conversation with Elizabeth word for word, and he finally reached the only possible conclusion: indeed, Lydia Bennet was the one who eloped, the one who had been deceived by the scoundrel. The Bennets had searched for the fugitives for days, and most likely Elizabeth realised he could help them, so she summoned the courage to appear at his door—exposing herself to his resentful behaviour—and to beg for help in discovering her sister.

He was equally shocked and relieved to realise she was not the one who eloped with Wickham! Not for himself—he had no doubt that any connection between Elizabeth and him was cut forever—but for her. It saddened him deeply to see her in pain and to imagine her spirit broken by Wickham; fortunately, he discovered that would not happen.

Her behaviour towards him in Kent had been horrible indeed; she had mistreated him most undeservedly. But she was not at all wanton and reckless and did not expose her family to grief and despair. How could he ever have believed she would?

Their entire conversation, based on his misconception, had been disturbing—even cruel on his part—and it was entirely his fault. What was it exactly that she said to make him so angry, rude, and insensitive?

He almost threw her out of his house; he imprisoned her in fear and despair before he finally admitted he would help her uncle. He offended her with all his rage, all his hate, and all his love! How could he be so cruel to her? And why?

A mere moment in her presence made him lose his temper, his control, and almost his mind. Again.

Was it precisely the realisation that his love was still there, alive and perhaps stronger than before? Was his outrageous behaviour a response to his own weakness?

Darcy closed the curtains again. A growing trepidation made him pace the room several times, trying to decide the best course of action.

Of one thing he was certain: no connection between Elizabeth and him would ever be renewed. Without any doubt, their paths would take them in different directions.

He must do something to cure himself of this obsession, to return to his life, his duty, and his responsibilities. He had to take care of his sister, his aunt, his fortune, and the people who depended on him—and of the Darcy inheritance. He needed to find a way to provide an heir. He had to ensure peace, tranquillity, and safety within the circle of his close family.

Elizabeth Bennet soon would be forgotten, like a dream—the sweetest and most horrible at the same time—shattered by the dawn.

But until then, it was also his duty and his responsibility to solve the present situation created by Wickham. How could he not understand this the moment he was informed about the elopement? How was it possible that he preferred to withdraw, ignoring all the problems around him, instead of considering the distress of the girl who had become Wickham's new victim? Coincidentally, it was the Bennet family, but it would have been equally grave no matter the name. This selfish neglect was only another of his many faults, and he was compelled to remedy it without delay.

During the ride back to Cheapside, Elizabeth's thoughts were confused by conflicting emotions. She found herself smiling through tears, wondering at her luck in succeeding in a task she considered hopeless from the beginning.

She could not recollect accurately how their conversation unfolded. She remembered that it was a difficult one: she felt offended and hurt at times, and he was somehow different than she remembered him. But all of that mattered little since he had agreed to help them.

Elizabeth entered her uncle's house, eager to share her good news, but she was received by her aunt's troubled countenance.

"Lizzy, where have you been? You frightened us! You were missing for hours!"

"Oh, dear aunt, if you only knew…I have excellent news to share. Where is Papa? And my uncle?"

"They are both in the library, and I must warn you that they are quite upset with your disappearance."

"I imagine, but please come with me. I think you will all forgive me when you hear what I have to say."

The two gentlemen, however, were not as eager to listen to her explanations. They expressed their displeasure and scolded Elizabeth for her behaviour. When they heard she had visited Mr. Darcy, their astonishment and disapproval only increased.

"You will soon have to admit I was correct in my decision, even if it was not proper," she insisted. "Mr. Darcy has agreed to speak to you, Uncle. If I had not gone to talk to him, he might not have received a complete stranger. Your name meant nothing to him."

"You might be right, but you should have informed us, Lizzy. I could have come with you and talked to Mr. Darcy then," said Mr. Gardiner sternly.

"But, Lizzy, you and Darcy had argued since the day you first met. How did you dare approach him with such a request? A matter so delicate could hardly be discussed, even with a close male friend," Mr. Bennet interjected.

She blushed, slightly embarrassed. "Perhaps, because I knew his poor opinion of me, I decided to proceed this way. I had nothing to lose and everything to win if I could convince him. And he agreed to offer his support quite readily, which proves that my decision was correct."

"True—all that matters now is the positive outcome of your action. I say, it is strangely kind and generous of him to offer his help. Let us not allow him time to change his mind. Shall we go, Brother Gardiner?"

"Certainly. I hope and pray that our search will end soon and we will finally reach a resolution to this unfortunate situation."

ELIZABETH STRUGGLED TO ACCOMPLISH EVEN A SMALL TASK, BUT HER APPREHENSION made her useless at anything. Mrs. Gardiner, working on her embroidery, tried to calm her, but the effort was in vain.

To the tumult of her meeting with Darcy and her stormy feelings of shame, surprise, puzzlement, disbelief, and embarrassment was added her fear for the possible result of her father and uncle's endeavour. How would their conversation with Darcy proceed? Would they find Wickham? Would a confrontation take place? Would they bring Lydia home?

By noon, the sun had dispersed the clouds, and Elizabeth welcomed her young cousins' insistence on playing in the park. After three days of rain and three sleepless nights, nothing was better than a little time outside.

Elinor and Edward's enthusiasm brought a smile to Elizabeth's lips, and the weight on her soul lightened somewhat.

As soon as they entered the park, the children started to run. Elizabeth immediately spotted the countess and Miss Anna and walked towards them. Elinor and Edward were already caressing Mist and Didi, laughing loudly.

"Miss Lizzy—what a pleasure to see you again," the countess said kindly.

"Lady Hardwick, Miss Anna—I am delighted to see you too." Elizabeth smiled, then a moment later she frowned as she remembered her present situation.

She sat on the bench, squeezing her hands together.

"We were afraid you had already left town," Miss Anna continued.

"No…not yet…but I expect we will soon…hopefully…"

"We will leave soon too. That is why my aunt and I were thinking…would you mind if…" Miss Anna seemed too nervous to express herself properly, so the countess smiled and handed Elizabeth a piece a paper.

"Miss Lizzy, it would give us great pleasure to hear from you even after we all leave London. So if you agree, here is where you can write to us—either to my estate in the North or to my townhouse. We do not have fixed plans yet, but all the letters will be directed to me."

Elizabeth could not conceal her surprise; she took the paper and looked at it with interest and no little emotion.

"I would like that very much…very much indeed," she whispered, forcing a smile to which Miss Anna responded with one of her own.

"Unfortunately, I do not think this will be possible," Elizabeth continued, and the countess looked puzzled while Miss Anna immediately lost her glee.

"Of course…as you wish," the countess concluded with obvious uneasiness.

Elizabeth could not bear to know they were disappointed in her or believed she might not want to further their acquaintance. They were too kind to deserve such a cold refusal.

She looked around carefully, except for the two playful children and the ladies' servants waiting at a distance, no one else was in their proximity. She moved a little closer and spoke hesitantly, rubbing her hands.

"There is something I must confess, something I should keep secret, but I cannot, precisely because I value your friendship so much. I am sure it will be a significant obstacle for any future connection between us, and yet I cannot conceal it from you."

"Miss Lizzy, this sounds quite frightening. Are you unwell?" the countess inquired.

"Oh no, I am quite well," Elizabeth replied in a quiet voice to avoid being overheard even by her cousins. "It is just that…my father has arrived in town since we last met in the park. He is here to solve a most delicate family matter. My youngest sister…she is not sixteen yet…she eloped a week ago…her intentions were to marry but we know this has not happened yet. My father and uncle are searching for them as we suspect they are in Town…"

Elizabeth could barely gather the courage to look at the two ladies in front of her. The countess appeared astonished, but Miss Anna's countenance was completely pale and still. She grabbed the small basket in her lap so hard that Mist meowed, frightened. The young woman petted him gently, pulling the kitten to her chest to calm him.

Elizabeth was confident she could understand her companion's reaction.

"I know anyone would be appalled by such a situation. But my sister is very young, and the man who stole her heart is an officer and a close acquaintance to our family…so she had every reason to trust him. But I also understand that nothing can justify such behaviour, and it cannot remain without consequences for our family and our name. That is why I wished to tell you the entire truth. I would never dare to put you in an uncomfortable position by being connected with me in any way. And that is why I would not dare write to you."

Elizabeth felt defeated by the distress that had threatened her mind and heart for so many days. Her strength weakened, her self-control vanished, and she only hoped not to appear a complete fool in front of the two ladies.

"Miss Lizzy, is there any way we can help you?" the countess inquired.

"No…I thank you, no…I have high hopes that my father and uncle will find them today. My greatest desire is to know my sister is safe."

"We pray that everything will come to a better resolution than can be foreseen now," the countess said. "Please keep us informed about the outcome of this situation in the next few days."

Elizabeth stared in disbelief, wondering whether she had heard correctly.

"Does your ladyship wish to meet with me again?"

"Why on earth not?" the countess replied calmly.

"I imagined that…I know very few people of your ladyship's position who would. Forgive me...I am so silly...I do not know what is wrong with me. I can hardly speak coherently."

"Miss Lizzy..." Miss Anna's gentle voice interrupted Elizabeth's stammering; the young woman continued to talk, holding the kitten tightly, her blue eyes heavy with tears. "I understand you very well, as I was in the same situation only a year ago. You see now that you also have good reason not to speak to me..."

Elizabeth's bewilderment was now complete. She could not trust her ears, and her lips did not dare say a word. Surely, she had not understood correctly. This perfect, impeccable, accomplished young woman! It was impossible to imagine her in the same situation as Lydia.

"I did not quite elope," Miss Anna continued, "but I was convinced to do so. The gentleman was also very close to my family...I have known him all my life...but as you said, nothing can justify such thoughtless behaviour. I was fortunate enough that my brother arrived unexpectedly only a day before the elopement. I could not bear the notion of betraying and abandoning him, so I confessed everything to him...which was also fortunate, as I discovered that the object of my affections was neither honest nor genuine in his claimed fondness for me. I hope your sister will not have to suffer such disappointment..."

Elizabeth and Miss Anna looked at each other for a few long moments, dark brown and light blue eyes locked together, sharing sadness and shame, silently speaking a language understood by both.

Each had put her soul into the hands of a near stranger, confessing a menace to their futures—even to their lives—and they seemed mutually to agree to share the burden as they split it in half so each could carry it more easily.

The children's joyful laughter and Didi's happy barking startled them, breaking the silence; the countess intruded briskly, attempting to ease the distress of both.

"What my niece tried to say is that such accidents may happen to anyone; even the brightest and most well-educated woman may lose her heart and sometimes even her mind to a handsome man. Miss Lizzy, this is not the first and certainly not the last case of this kind. As long as your sister is uninjured, there is no tragedy in it. If they eventually marry, all the better. If not, the world will surely not end. There will be rumours for a while, but they will soon cease. I dare say that, from this point of view, it is a good thing that your family is not a prominent one. The fewer people who know you, the quicker the gossip will die."

"I do not know what to say..." Elizabeth whispered. "Except that your courage is remarkable and your wisdom praiseworthy, Miss Anna."

"There is no need to say anything else for now." The countess smiled while her niece only thanked Elizabeth with eyes full of gratitude. "Once the situation with your sister is resolved, I would suggest we all three have a long conversation over a nice cup of tea. We would be very pleased if you could visit us one of these days. I will be delighted to receive news from you."

"I would like that very much, Lady Hardwick...very much indeed..." was all Elizabeth could answer to such a generous invitation.

When the time to separate finally came, the farewell was warmer and longer than any time before. Elizabeth's confidence grew as her heart became lighter from the sympathy shown by the countess and the trust proved by Miss Anna's startling confession. No matter how many people censured their family for Lydia's elopement, the two ladies' support was strong enough to compensate.

In their luxurious carriage, Georgiana petted her kitten and dared look at her aunt, who was caressing Didi.

"Aunt Amelia, do you blame me for my confession to Miss Lizzy? Do you believe it was a mistake?"

"I do not blame you, dearest; I was only surprised. I know you to be a private person, and I did not expect you to open your heart to someone whose complete name you do not even know."

"I cannot explain what came over me, but I saw her so sad, so ashamed, and suffering so much for her sister that I imagined how William must have felt for me. She does not know my name either, and yet she had the strength to share her story with us. I sensed she could understand me just as I understand her. Is it not strange that, when I finally found someone I could be friends with, she is going through the same ordeal that I did?"

"I understand what you mean, dearest. And yes, it is a little strange. You two seem to have much in common, although you are quite different. I admit I am curious about how all this will end, and I am now even more eager to learn further details about Miss Lizzy."

"So am I, Aunt. Perhaps it will happen tomorrow. I hope it will."

Chapter 5

As soon as Elizabeth left his house, Darcy urged Watts—his most trusted servant—to deliver a long note for Mr. Clayton, requiring information about Wickham's precise location; then he spent the next hours waiting, anxious and impatient.

He needed time to accept that the visit actually took place and even more to put aside his previous anxiety about Elizabeth's eloping with Wickham.

He awaited Mr. Gardiner's arrival with eagerness but also with concern. He could only wonder what kind of man he was. All he remembered from previous discussions in Hertfordshire was that Mr. Gardiner was in trade, lived near Cheapside, and was Mrs. Bennet and Mrs. Philips's brother. None of these circumstances sounded encouraging, and the notion of collaborating with such a man about a delicate situation was rather distracting.

Just at noon, Darcy was informed of *two* visitors, and the news made his heart skip a beat. Was it possible that she returned with her uncle?

He was surprised but relieved to see Mr. Bennet entering together with a younger gentleman.

After an awkward greeting and several apologies from the visitors, the formidable introductions were finally made. While he witnessed the gentlemen's embarrassment, Darcy realised that, during his stay at Netherfield, he had never exchanged a single word directly with Elizabeth's father, and he was as much a stranger to him as was Mr. Gardiner. How faulty had his behaviour been in Hertfordshire?

He tried to sound as amiable as possible when he eventually spoke.

"Please come in. Would you like something to drink? Some refreshments maybe?"

The visitors appeared to be uncomfortable and abashed while they hesitantly chose a place to sit.

"A drink would be fine, sir, but I beg you do not trouble yourself. We apologise for any interruption; I imagine how unpleasant all this must be for you, so we will keep it as brief as possible. Having to bear the visits of two Bennets and a relative in one day, only to discuss another Bennet, is surely not your favourite way to spend time. I must say, it is not my favourite way either," Mr. Bennet said in bitter irony. He took the offered glass of wine, then looked around and continued.

"But I must say this library is astonishing. If I had one half as wonderful as this at home, I would never leave it. In truth, I hardly leave my own library anyway, except when my own careless behaviour puts my family in such a desperate situation."

Darcy was uncertain whether he should smile or not. The resemblance between Elizabeth and her father suddenly became visible to him.

"I thank you, sir. I do pride myself on my library—as well as the one at Pemberley, which is even larger and richer in volumes than this one. It is the work of generations, and I struggle to preserve it properly. Now, would you mind explaining to me, from the very beginning, what exactly has happened?"

"Yes, of course; forgive my ramblings."

With reluctance and restraint, Mr. Bennet shared the shameful situation of his family. As he spoke, Darcy realised once again the extent of his foolishness in presuming that Elizabeth was the one who eloped. He should have known that she could not abandon her family out of some wanton inclination, and even more, he should have realised that Wickham preferred—as always—a younger woman whom he could influence and control, someone who would obey him unconditionally.

"This is why we suspect they are in town," Mr. Gardiner added when his brother-in-law ended the narration. "We apologise for disturbing you with a matter that is so intimate to our family. If you could only suggest to us where we might search for Wickham, we will not detain you a moment longer."

One of his concerns was relieved. Mr. Gardiner was nothing like his sister, neither in appearance nor in manners.

"Mr. Bennet, Mr. Gardiner, it gives me no pleasure to confess that this matter is intimately familiar to my family and me. George Wickham was my father's godson, and we spent most of my childhood together. His reckless behaviour affects me too. My parents—as well as his, I suppose—would be disappointed and pained to know the kind of man he has become."

"Yes, Lizzy told me that. It is a shame that we did not know his true character from the beginning. All of Meryton—men and women alike—were smitten with this rascal. I am sure my own wife would have eloped with him if he asked her," Mr. Bennet continued angrily.

Darcy felt Mr. Bennet's hidden reproach and was ready to offer a reply when the gentleman himself spoke further.

"I do not mean you have any responsibility in this, Mr. Darcy. It was, after all, not your duty to open the eyes of the blind. Perhaps if I had taken the time to speak to him directly instead of only mocking my daughters about the man, I would have had a word to say. Or if I had taken more trouble to censure my family when it was needed..."

"Let us not argue about the biggest share of responsibility," Darcy intervened. "Since I spoke with Miss Bennet early this morning, I did make some inquiries. There is...someone...who is very aware of Wickham's whereabouts. I thought it would be better for him to continue the quest and inform me of the result. Wickham might become scared and run away if he saw any of us."

"That is extraordinary...so you think we can hope to have an answer soon?" Mr. Gardiner could not restrain his astonishment.

"Quite. If you prefer, you may return home and rest. You must be exhausted from the efforts of your search. I will send you a note as soon as I have the details."

"Oh no, we could not possibly rest until we find something," said Mr. Bennet and then added, "However, we do not want to keep you from your business; we can easily wait in the carriage."

"That will not be necessary," Darcy replied without hesitation. "I have no other fixed engagements today. I will order more drinks and some refreshments as it might take a while. You are most welcome to choose a book while we wait," he answered with a politeness that puzzled both his visitors. He noticed it and wondered how awful his behaviour must have been in Hertfordshire if they were surprised by a mere expression of civility.

"If you do not mind, I would be grateful to take a look at this marvellous collection of books. It would certainly help keep my sanity," Mr. Bennet accepted, walking along the impressive shelves.

"Sir, we thank you again for your kindness. We were lucky to find you in Town," Mr. Gardiner addressed the master of the house.

"It is truly fortunate because next week I plan to travel to Pemberley. A few days later and I would have been gone." Then he explained amiably, "Pemberley is my estate in Derbyshire."

"We know that," Mr. Gardiner responded, slightly more animated. "My wife is quite familiar with the place. She grew up in Lambton, which I understand is only five miles from Pemberley. She has told me several times that she has never seen a more beautiful place."

Darcy's countenance softened. "Truly? What a lovely coincidence indeed. I hope to have the chance of thanking Mrs. Gardiner personally for such praise."

Both Mr. Bennet and Mr. Gardiner exchanged astounded glances at this unexpected friendliness.

"I…she would be much honoured, I am sure," Mr. Gardiner managed to articulate.

Conversation continued as slowly as expected. It was neither a happy time nor an opportunity for carefree chatting. Darcy dared not ask anything that could betray his interest in Elizabeth, and the visitors avoided anything that might displease their host.

"Is Mr. Bingley in good health?" Mr. Bennet finally inquired. "We have wondered about him."

"Yes, he is…as far as I know. I have rarely seen him lately as he is spending the summer with friends." Darcy felt uneasy speaking with Mr. Bennet about Bingley, but the gentleman seemed content with the brief information.

The uncomfortable wait came to an end at the entrance of Mr. Clayton. He approached Darcy, briefly greeting the strangers. He was offered a drink, and Darcy encouraged him to talk.

"Mr. Bennet and Mr. Gardiner share my interest in this story, so you may speak openly. Do you have Wickham's address?"

"I have, sir. He is staying in a rented room in a place near Mrs. Younge's."

"Did you approach him?"

"Not at all, sir—just as you asked me. He has paid for the room until the end of the week."

"Is my daughter with him?" Mr. Bennet inquired hastily.

Mr. Clayton answered, slightly uneasy. "There *is* a young lady with him.

I did not make inquiries about her identity, but I can do so if necessary."

"No indeed, we will go there ourselves right now. Please show us the location," Darcy replied, then hastened the other two gentlemen to follow them.

"We can all take my carriage, and you can retrieve yours later," Darcy suggested. "We must catch Wickham unguarded if we want this matter resolved today."

The two gentlemen silently followed his commands—surprised, incredulous, and hopeful. It seemed unreal that their difficult search and worry could end so easily.

There was silence inside the carriage, four men struggling to prepare themselves for a most unpleasant confrontation. More than half an hour later, they reached the small inn in the eastern part of town. Once his duty was accomplished, Mr. Clayton retired.

Darcy was the first to enter and had a private conversation with the owner. The others could only suspect what he was doing, but their trust was rewarded when, a few minutes later, he silently invited them to follow him up the stairs. On the second floor, they waited a few moments to catch their breath and control their emotions before Darcy knocked sharply.

Mr. Bennet's heart ached as he heard Lydia's voice. The door opened, and Wickham's shocked face appeared. He immediately attempted to close it again, but Darcy placed his boot forward and pushed it forcefully.

"Wickham! We meet again. What an unpleasant surprise, would you not agree?"

In Gracechurch Street, the passage of time was painfully slow.

That afternoon, Elizabeth shared with her aunt a part of her conversation with the countess and Miss Anna. Although she trusted her aunt with all her heart, Elizabeth decided not to disclose anything about Miss Anna's elopement. Still, Mrs. Gardiner was impressed and astonished by the two ladies' kind and generous reaction and expressed her eagerness to know more about them and perhaps even to meet them one day.

As time passed, they started to count every minute, watched through the window for every carriage, and wondered about the possible outcome.

After the children were prepared for sleep, time slowed even more under the complete silence. Retiring for the night was impossible to consider, so they kept each other company until midnight.

When the main door opened, they both ran towards it, and their distress turned to joy as they saw Mr. Bennet holding Lydia's arm tightly.

With equal distress and relief, Elizabeth noticed her sister seemed unharmed, but her eyes were swollen from crying while her father appeared unsteady on his feet.

Elizabeth rushed to them, embracing her sister tightly.

"My darling Lydia, I am so happy to see you! How are you, dearest? I missed you so much, and I was so worried for you! But you are safe now. Let me look at you. How are you feeling?"

"Lizzy, please take Lydia to clean herself and rest...I need to rest for a moment too," Mr. Bennet said weakly.

"Papa, are you unwell?" Elizabeth released her sister and took her father's arm, supporting him.

"I will be fine as soon as I lie down," Mr. Bennet replied as he walked towards his room. "I only need rest and silence...and a glass of wine would be most welcome..."

"Brother, where is my husband?" Mrs. Gardiner asked with deep worry as she took Lydia's hand and directed her inside.

"Do not worry; he will return soon. He remained with Mr. Darcy to talk with Wickham. You have no reason for concern—other than we are both sick from spending time with the most dishonourable man ever to join a militia. Now, Lizzy, leave me and see to Lydia."

"I will send you some food and drink, Brother," Mrs. Gardiner answered, still concerned by the brief information she received. "I will have something for Lydia too. I know she must be not only tired but also starved."

Lydia's sudden cries startled them both, and Elizabeth returned to embrace her sister.

"Oh, Lizzy, did you hear Papa? What shall I do? I feel so bad! I cannot hold my tears."

"It will pass...we will take care of you," Elizabeth said tearfully, holding her tight. "Come, we will share the same room so I can watch you. Everything will be fine, and your suffering will pass soon."

"It will never pass. I am devastated, and I feel I will die of pain and shame."

"Lydia, are you in pain? Are you hurt? Should we fetch a doctor?"

"Why should you fetch a doctor? I am in pain because my heart is broken. I hoped at least you would understand and help me."

"I will do anything to help you, dearest. And your heart will heal soon… you are very young, and you have all the time in the world to find an honourable man and to marry in a few years."

"Lizzy, you are so silly! What do you mean to marry in a few years? I will marry in a few days! I am almost married already! But Papa is so cruel and unfair! He said such horrible things about George! It must be Mr. Darcy's fault. What business had Mr. Darcy to talk to George? Why was he even there? Papa took me by force. I did not want to leave George. And even worse, he said he would not buy me a trousseau. And I do not have a proper bonnet and dress either! I cannot possibly marry this way! And where is the food Aunt promised me? Lord, I am so hungry, I could eat ten courses."

No matter how well Elizabeth believed she knew her sister, she refused to comprehend and accept Lydia's careless, insensitive speech. All her concerns, sleepless nights, and distressing hours of fear seemed now useless and even ridiculous.

"I see. We were very worried for you, Lydia. It was thoughtless to just run away. How could you not think of all the trouble you caused Colonel Forster and your family?"

"Why would you be worried? I told Harriet precisely where I was. You should be happy for me. I am the youngest one and already married."

"You are not married, Lydia, can you not see that? And you informed Mrs. Forster that you were going to Gretna Green, which obviously did not happen."

"Surely, you are not scolding me, Lizzy! You have no right to do so! I will marry soon as George solves some money problems, he said. As soon as I am married, everybody will envy me! But Papa must purchase me the trousseau I need. Nothing less would please me!"

"Here is the food you were waiting for, Lydia. Come and eat, and let us sleep. We will discuss tomorrow what pleases you or not. It is almost midnight."

"Oh, look how much food there is! I did not eat much in the last few days, but I did not need food since I had the company of my dear George. Lizzy, you know nothing about what a man's company means. I can laugh when I think that I know more about men than any of you do. Oh, and I want a glass of wine too. I discovered I really like wine!"

While Lydia became more cheerful and greedily enjoyed the tasteful meal,

Elizabeth's heart grew even heavier than in the past days. Shame and sorrow added to her distress as she realised there was nothing to be done with her youngest sister. Lydia was finally discovered and brought home safely—in this, Elizabeth's prayers had been heard. Could she dare hope and pray for anything more?

Lydia slept peacefully the entire night, but Elizabeth found little rest. She heard her uncle return long after midnight, and she left her room to talk to him, but Mr. Gardiner had hurried to his bedchamber, so she would not dare disturb him.

The following morning, however, she woke very early, prepared herself a cup of tea, and waited.

Finally, her father joined her. Mr. Bennet looked as pale and tired as he had the previous night. Elizabeth helped him sit and placed a gentle kiss on his cheek.

"Papa, you look quite unwell. Should we fetch a doctor?"

"Nonsense, Lizzy, I am well enough. Please pour me a cup of coffee then come sit by me; we must talk."

Elizabeth got coffee for her father and herself; Mr. Bennet took his with trembling hands.

"Your sister slept well, I imagine."

"She did, Papa. She is still sleeping."

"Just her usual habit…I am content to see her so well and serene, but it does pain me to witness how little understanding she has of the world. I tried to convince her to return home with us, you know. But she would not have it; she cares about no one except Wickham, and she is not even concerned about when, or if, they will eventually marry…"

"Oh, Papa, I am sorry for your distress, but I am afraid you are correct: her only preoccupation seems to be the lack of a trousseau."

"I took her from there last night because I was too ashamed to allow Mr. Darcy to hear her excitement at being 'all but married' and her request that I order the new gowns she will need as a married woman."

Elizabeth's torment increased, and she could conceal her curiosity no longer.

"Papa, how did you find them? Was Mr. Darcy with you? Did I understand you correctly? You said he remained with my uncle…to talk to Mr. Wickham?"

"Mr. Darcy found them in a small inn. It would have taken weeks for us to discover them by ourselves, but as it was, we exerted no effort except in going there. It appeared Darcy had the means and the knowledge to track Wickham—and the will to waste his time on it, which was unimaginable. I tell you, Mr. Darcy is truly the most extraordinary person. I was shocked by how different he seemed, compared to when we met in Hertfordshire. I was a bit intimidated by him to tell the truth. And, Lizzy, he has a splendid library. Did you see it? You were so smart to suggest talking to him. We could not have found them without his help unless Wickham himself had appeared voluntarily."

"I am glad my suggestion helped you. But did you have time to visit his library? So you spent some time in his house? And in what way did Mr. Darcy appear different to you?"

"In every way. He was a very polite host and quite generous in helping us. Indeed, he is obviously not a friendly man. I would wager he rarely laughs or indulges himself in easy chatter; his temper appears to be severe too. I would not want to have Darcy as an enemy. But to us, he was as helpful as a close friend would be. We never expected that."

"Papa, please be more clear. What did Wickham do when he saw you? I really need all the details," Elizabeth whispered, intrigued and increasingly nervous.

"Wickham was rather scared when he saw us, and he seemed terrified once Darcy confronted him. Of course, that did not stop the scoundrel from being a despicable excuse of a man."

"Was he? Is it so?" She could hardly keep pace with her father's story as her mind was overcome by countless, disturbing questions.

"He is such a low sort of human being, Lizzy. He showed no restraint in placing the entire blame for the elopement on Lydia. He declared he could not marry because he is unable to support a wife. He is without a commission or any means of living. Even more so, he implied that he was burdened by debts and he could take on no other commitment until he was free of them. In other words, he threatened us that, if we do not pay his debts, he will distance himself from your sister."

"Oh, Papa...is this possible? But why did Lydia say she will marry in a few days?"

"Because Lydia is silly and childish...and always hears only what she wishes to. The tragedy, Lizzy, is that we do not have a way out of this. If Lydia did not want to marry Wickham, I would readily accept any consequences, and we would all go home safely, hoping for the best. But she does —it is her only purpose in life now. If we do not let her marry him, we will be thrown into the midst of a scandal that Lydia herself will perpetuate. If we approve her marriage, we must pay Wickham's debts and then find a way for them to live. Most likely we will condemn her to a life of misery and will also obligate ourselves to a degree from which we will never recover."

"Papa, but…how can you provide them with the means of support? Neither you nor Uncle has any connections for such an endeavour. And how much money can he expect from you? How large could his debts possibly be?"

"I talked to your uncle when he returned last night, Lizzy. Wickham has already presented a list of creditors, which does not include those from Hertfordshire. I would venture to presume the total sum owed is close to several thousand pounds."

"Dear Lord, several thousand pounds?" Elizabeth rose and paced the room in great torment and needed several minutes before she managed to stop. "Papa, how could you afford to pay even half this sum? How could anyone dare to demand such a sacrifice from you?"

"Lizzy, calm down my dear. Your distress only troubles me more. I am not certain how we will fix this, but my brother Gardiner promised he will help me find a way."

"But, Papa—I know for certain that my uncle cannot spend such a sum either. And even if he could, he has children of his own, and he must take care of them."

Mr. Bennet waved his hand to stop her tirade, wiping his forehead with his handkerchief.

"My child, what concerns me even more is this: If Wickham accumulated such debts when he had a commission in the militia and no one to support, what will happen once he marries and has no income at all?"

"True, Papa…God help us, this is such a tragic situation. There is nothing we can do…"

"It is tragic indeed," said Mr. Gardiner, entering the room and greeting them briefly. He poured himself a cup of coffee then sat near his brother-in-law.

"Upon my word, I have never been as furious at another man as I was last night," Mr. Gardiner continued. "And I am still astonished that Mr. Darcy was able to control his rage. Several times, I was sure he would harm Wickham. God knows, I would not have stopped him."

Elizabeth listened with growing turmoil; the image of an angry Mr. Darcy was not entirely strange to her. Mr. Gardiner continued, gently touching her hand.

"Lizzy dear, what was in your mind that you admired that fellow so much? I always praised your wit and your wisdom, but somehow you did not use either when it came to Wickham. By the way, he had the nerve to mention to us that you and he were always good friends, and he is pleased that you will now be family as soon as his unfortunate situation is solved."

Elizabeth clasped her hands together to stop their trembling, narrowing her eyes to stem her angry tears. She was mortified by Wickham's impertinence but even more by her own folly; she lowered her gaze and sealed her lips. What could she answer? What explanation could justify her stupidity?

Finally, she murmured, "No censure is undeserved, Uncle, and I blame myself more than anyone else could. If only I could do something to remedy my wrong. But what should we do now?"

"There is nothing we can do. As I told my brother Bennet last night, Mr. Darcy instructed me to wait until we have word from him. I do not know what this means precisely, but I could not possibly contradict him. He seemed to believe he could find a reasonable outcome to the situation. Besides, I would not know how to proceed anyway. Wickham does not wish to marry as he claims he cannot support a wife. Lydia wishes nothing else but to marry, which I imagine would be the best solution for the entire family. Therefore, we must find a way to accomplish it. We just received another letter from Longbourn with my sister demanding details about the wedding. We have little choice in solving this madness, Lizzy. I shall go out to meet some of my customers and see how I can put together the payment for Wickham's debts. You must encourage your father to rest as much as he can."

"I will rest, do not worry," Mr. Bennet answered bitterly. "I have little to do anyway. I have no choice at all; we must force Wickham to marry Lydia, and that is the end of the story."

"Such a sad conclusion, so painful and tedious. He is such a dishonourable man. Poor Lydia will be so unhappy," Elizabeth whispered.

"Yes, he is. And we must beg him to marry your sister and give her a miserable life. What more can a father bear?"

"Dear Papa, please do not trouble yourself so…"

"I must—it is the truth, Lizzy. Now please do me the favour of writing to Jane and telling her something to calm your mother. I will lie down a little longer; I am in no mood for breakfast."

DARCY BREATHED DEEPLY AS HE LEFT THE INN, FURIOUS AT THE IMAGE OF Wickham's impertinent smirk. How could he put himself in the strange position of negotiating with that scoundrel? If only Lydia Bennet had the good sense not to marry him, things would be so much easier.

But surely, that would be disastrous for the entire Bennet family. The meagre chances they had to make honourable marriages would be gone forever. The scandal and its effects were impossible to avoid.

Wickham demanded that Mr. Bennet pay his debts. He had evidently lost his mind completely. How could he imagine that was even possible? He was even more stupid than he was reckless. He attempted to blackmail Mr. Bennet, forcing him to put his entire fortune at stake. Of course, Wickham had little to lose while Mr. Bennet had everything to fear. If the deal were not sealed, Miss Lydia would return home, and the entire shame would fall upon the Bennets. Nothing good would come of that situation —and they could not afford an even bigger scandal by telling the world how Wickham deceived them.

Of course, the idiot would remain without his commission, without a means of support, and with more debts to follow. But that was his usual way, and he would surely find another victim. The colonel—his cousin—furious after Wickham's attempt to elope with Georgiana, had proposed finding a way to get rid of Wickham for good. Darcy should have listened—a colonel in his majesty's army surely knew better about these things.

But for the time being, it was his duty to make amends in a situation that was mostly his fault.

Darcy was certain the Bennets and the Gardiners together could not afford to pay Wickham's debts and were even less able to ensure him a proper commission, which would cost at least five hundred pounds. Even a partial attempt would mean a pecuniary sacrifice that would jeopardise their families' futures, and it was not fair of him to allow it. The entire Darcy family should have been more rigorous in curbing Wickham's recklessness. They should have dealt more harshly with his faults and punished him accordingly before he succeeded in damaging more than one honourable family.

And when they met in Meryton, he—Darcy—should have warned Colonel Forster at once about Wickham's true character before people fell victim to his dishonourable schemes. Since that did not happen—since he was too proud and too careless of the feelings of others and of the possible outcomes of his indifference—it was now his responsibility to remedy his mistake.

And he had already found a way. He would repay Wickham's debts; besides helping Mr. Bennet, it would be gratifying to hold the power of throwing the rascal into debtors' prison at any time. Wickham would be at his mercy, and he could demand anything from him. As for the rest, it depended on Miss Lydia Bennet's final decision. Perhaps her relatives—and her older sister—might succeed in putting some reason into her head.

Again, his thoughts turned to Elizabeth.

A thought—cruel and selfish, he admitted without hesitation—troubled him. He wondered how Elizabeth felt at that moment. Did she blame herself, not only for being partial to Wickham and believing his lies but also for rejecting a marriage proposal that would have given her and her entire family a bright future? Were she Mrs. Darcy now, the scandal would mean little to the Bennets. She would have no worries—it would be her husband's duty to settle the matter. Did she feel any sort of regret? Was she suffering for her unwise decision not to read his letter?

Likely, yes, those things and many others probably tormented Elizabeth now. He knew he should be satisfied with the situation. Any man—any human being—would be. He finally had his revenge. Life itself had accomplished enough to satisfy his four months of rage.

Perhaps, this was the Fates telling him his proposal was a mistake. He imagined what the scandal would have meant for the Darcys—and the entire extended family—if Elizabeth were now Mrs. Darcy. Wickham would be his brother-in-law! Poor Georgiana would be forever troubled, Lady Catherine and likely the Matlocks would cut any connection with him, not to mention the gossips of society. Yes, it seemed Elizabeth Bennet's horrible rejection was a lucky one for him. He was such a fool to have suffered all that time. He should be relieved. Pleased. Happy.

And yet, he felt nothing but a grip in his chest and a wave of ever-growing anger against Wickham.

There was something good in that anger, though. The more he helped the Bennet family, the sooner he solved this matter. Elizabeth and her father would return to Hertfordshire, and the turmoil of knowing she was in dangerous proximity would end. Perhaps he would see her again a couple of times before then—if the situation required it. Would he? Should he?

Caught deep in thought, he entered his house, retired directly to his library, and then hurried to write several notes. He had things to take care of, which was much better than sitting in the dark and suffering in solitude. These two days were so different from the last four months that they seemed a breach in his life.

It was still related to Elizabeth; she was still at the centre of his distress but not in the same way that he feared a few days ago. She was still ever-present in his mind—in his thoughts—and close to him in her presence; therefore, he could not possibly be at peace. But he was content to have something to do—even if it meant unwillingly helping Wickham.

Chapter 6

The next day, late in the afternoon, Darcy's carriage stopped in Grace-church Street. The sun was still shining, and it was quite warm, especially inside the carriage. Darcy stared at the large, handsome house, situated across the street from a small park. The neighbourhood appeared to be animated and pleasant; he remembered how Bingley's sisters mocked the Bennets' relatives living near Cheapside. Back then, he never imagined he might visit them one day. In truth, until that moment he did not remember having visited the area before.

He was reluctant to step down. He had hesitated for hours before coming although he did have important news to share with Mr. Bennet and Mr. Gardiner. He had sent a note the previous evening, attempting to put them at ease, and now he was ready to explain all the details.

But he knew that was not reason enough to be there. He could have asked the two gentlemen to visit him. Yes, like the fool he was, against his own will and judgment, he exposed himself to ridicule once more in an attempt to catch a glimpse of her. As preposterous as such a gesture was, he could not fight it. And now, being there, he realised even more the absurdity of his behaviour.

He was prepared to leave when the door opened, and the master of the house appeared, hurried towards him, and bowed in greetings.

"Mr. Darcy! Sir, what an honour to see you here. Are you looking for us? Please do come in, sir. What an honour indeed."

Darcy replied politely to the gentleman's enthusiastic invitation. There was nothing else to do but follow him inside. The grip in his chest tightened as the door closed behind them.

"Sir, please come in. My brother Bennet will be happy to see you."

"How is Mr. Bennet? Please do not trouble yourself; I will not stay long. I only came to bring some news that I hope will please you both and to decide how you prefer to proceed with the final details."

"Mr. Darcy, you are too kind. You should not have troubled yourself to come so far. I mean—I am very glad you did. My brother has been unwell the last two days to be honest. The fatigue of the journey, the lack of sleep, and all this distress...we feared for his health. Lizzy is taking care of him every moment. Please come in."

Even before they entered the drawing room, Darcy heard Lydia's shrill voice and other voices trying to temper her. The first thing he noticed once the door opened was Elizabeth's back and the heavy curls of hair dancing on her nape as she spoke angrily with her younger sister. On a settee were Mr. Bennet and another woman—probably Mrs. Gardiner.

He readily noticed Elizabeth's astonished expression but struggled to keep his gaze away from her. Just being in the same room aroused an unsettling feeling, and it proved how wrong he had been to come.

"Mr. Darcy, what a surprise." Mr. Bennet stepped towards him. "We surely did not expect to see you in Gracechurch Street. I hope it was not too much trouble for you to come. I cannot say how sorry we are that we are wasting so much of your time on this sad affair."

"Mr. Bennet, I am pleased to see you again. You are well, I hope?"

"Reasonably, thank you."

"Sir, please allow me to introduce my wife to you," Mr. Gardiner said.

"It is an honour to meet you, Mr. Darcy. You are most welcome in our home." Mrs. Gardiner curtseyed elegantly, and Darcy could not but admire her manners.

"I am delighted to meet you, madam. Please accept my apologies for coming unannounced and at such an improper hour. I shall stay only a few minutes, but there is something urgent I must speak about with Mr. Gardiner and Mr. Bennet."

"I hope you speak of my wedding, Mr. Darcy," Lydia yelled. "Have you done something to my betrothed?"

"Lydia!" Elizabeth tried to censure the outburst. "Mind your words!"

"Leave me alone, Lizzy!"

"Mr. Darcy, shall we go to my library? May I offer you something to drink? We surely will need a strong brandy if I surmise the subject of our conversation correctly." Mr. Gardiner turned his back to his impertinent niece.

Darcy felt Elizabeth's intense glare, but he still did not turn to meet her eyes, even for an instant.

"A drink would be fine," he replied. "I intended to inquire whether Miss Lydia is still determined to marry or had changed her mind—but the answer is obvious."

"Of course, I want to marry as soon as possible," Lydia intervened again. "But Papa is so cruel, and he will not allow me to buy a trousseau! He has always been mean and unfair to me. If Mama were here, she would be on my side."

"Of course, she would! That is why we have come to this point." Mr. Bennet attempted to end the clamour. "I have nothing more to say—let us not look more ridiculous in front of Mr. Darcy."

"I shall not accept this! I am the first of my sisters to marry, and I deserve to have a lovely wedding! You must consider that my other sisters might not ever marry at all! Papa, listen to me!"

"Lydia, I shall not have such behaviour in my house!" Mr. Gardiner shouted severely.

Mr. Bennet stepped to the chair hesitantly while Elizabeth held Lydia's arm, forbidding her from moving towards their father.

"Then let me leave! I want nothing but to be with George! You are holding me against my will!"

"Miss Lydia," Darcy addressed her directly, "are you then decided on this marriage? Will you not take some time to consider it? This is a life-changing step for a young lady at such a tender age and without confidence in her future."

"We tried to convince her otherwise," Mr. Bennet said, his voice weakened. "I am aware this would put our family in a more difficult situation, but I would not trade my youngest daughter's life for the others' tranquillity. Yet, she is unmoved. We have to proceed further with this wedding although I have no hopes for her felicity or for the worthiness of her husband. But I will surely not turn this into a celebration, and I will not spend the little money I have on lace, a trousseau, or other nonsense."

"You cannot refuse me what is right! You have always been unfair to me! If Lizzy were in my position, you would have given her anything! You are a bad father to me!"

Elizabeth's cheeks burned then paled. She glanced towards Darcy, who again refused even to acknowledge her presence. Her voice trembling, she grabbed her sister's arm.

"Lydia, you forget yourself! We will go upstairs immediately!"

"I am not going anywhere until Papa accepts my request. And you, Lizzy —you are only jealous because George was your favourite once, and you are upset that he chose me instead of you!"

"Lydia!" Elizabeth cried again, her face altered by dismay and embarrassment.

"I am not listening to you, Lizzy! Papa, you shall give me the money, or I shall write to Mama immediately. You should be happy that I am the first one to marry! Everybody will envy me! You should be proud of me, but you care for nothing but your stupid books. You never do anything for us!"

The Gardiners both attempted to intervene, but Darcy's stern voice was the first to break Lydia's tirade.

"Miss Lydia, you should not address your father in such a way. I dare say he has been put through enough distress and expense. He certainly has done anything he could, perhaps more than the present situation deserves. A good daughter would think more thoroughly on the consequences of her behaviour."

"You have no right to tell me what I should do, Mr. Darcy! I do not even know why you are here! All this is your fault!" Lydia fought back with anger, louder than before. "If you had not taken from George what was rightfully his, he would not be in a difficult position now. He was left a living, and you denied it to him! You at least owe him that much."

Lydia's words fell like thunder in the room, and a deep silence covered everyone's shock. Elizabeth dared not breathe, let alone look at Darcy. Her grip on Lydia's arm tightened so much that her fingers turned blue, but Lydia seemed not to care.

Darcy's tone, although low and calm, bore a cold sharpness that froze the chamber.

"Miss Lydia, I shall not waste my time making amends to Wickham's falsehoods. I will only tell you this: if he were an honourable man, he would have received the living. But in that case, he would be a clergyman now, he never would have come to Meryton, and most certainly, he would not have eloped with a fifteen-year-old girl. These nerve-wrenching conversations and this soon-to-be wedding never would have taken place—much to my comfort and satisfaction. However, since he is such a dishonourable rascal, here we all are, experiencing these unpleasant moments and witnessing the ruin of your future."

Darcy's response was unbearably harsh, and his scathing voice made it even fiercer.

Lydia's reply came weak and hesitant. "You have no right to say such terrible things about George."

"Yes he does, Lydia," Mr. Bennet intervened. "He has the right to do and to say anything he pleases. Mr. Darcy wasted quite a lot of time helping us to find you and to convince Wickham to marry you, which the scoundrel had no intention of doing. Please understand, child, that he has no real affection for you. He would have eloped with any girl who agreed, and if she happened to have a little money, even better. He blamed *you* for the elopement! Can you not see the truth?"

"That is a lie—I shall not listen to it! I will not speak a moment longer with any of you! I will marry George within a week, and we will be very happy! If I do not see any of you ever again, so much the better!"

"Lydia! Come with me this moment! Now!" Mrs. Gardiner ran the words through her teeth while grabbing Lydia's arm. She whispered, unsuccessfully hoping not to be heard by Darcy. "Do not fight with me, young lady! I shall not hesitate to drag you out of this room if necessary and confine you to your chamber! You are no better than a spoiled child, and you will be treated accordingly."

The awful confrontation and the burgeoning tension were broken by the sound of the door opening and closing in haste behind them. The gentlemen remained still, each of them avoiding the others' eyes. Elizabeth sat down, her gaze lowered to the floor. She was trembling from distress, wondering what Darcy thought and lacking the courage to look at him.

Mr. Bennet cleared his throat.

"Mr. Darcy, I beg your forgiveness for my youngest daughter's manners. She is beyond any excuse, and I cannot blame her more than I blame myself for her behaviour. She has lost her mind to this rascal, and I can do nothing. They must marry—it seems the only solution. It saddens me deeply to know that I am responsible for her future unhappiness and cannot save her from her own folly. Of course, it is not even certain that we can convince

Wickham to marry. Since I cannot comply with his demands, perhaps it would be better just to refuse him and to be done with it. That way, I will know for sure that I ruined all my daughters' fates. Great accomplishment for a father indeed..."

Elizabeth hurried to his side and took his hand, whispering tenderly, "Papa, please do not speak so. We are fine—we will manage. Jane and I will take of everything."

"Yes, yes, Lizzy...I know you will..." Mr. Bennet said absently.

Both father and daughter raised their eyes in surprise when Darcy took a few steps forward and spoke with a warmth and friendliness they did not expect of him.

"Mr. Bennet, you should not be too harsh on yourself. Miss Lydia's age is responsible for her behaviour, surely. And when a young girl gives her heart away, sometimes her decisions are made despite the family's advice. I am confident that, no matter what the future holds for her, she will always have the comfort of your support and affection. There are times when a father can do only so much..."

Elizabeth was amazed and puzzled by Darcy's behaviour. His kindness and care for her father were unthinkable. He had shown her, beyond any doubt, that he resented their entire past and loathed even the thought of being in her company. He proved it clearly by not addressing a single word or glance to her since he arrived at her uncle's house.

However, with her relatives—and especially with her father—his manners were more than amiable. He had helped them to discover the fugitives; he appeared to have made some more inquiries on his own; now he came personally to deliver the news. And besides all this, he showed uncommon sympathy for a situation that would make most people censure the entire Bennet family. It was as if he were trying to protect Mr. Bennet, and the motives for such generosity were incomprehensible and disturbing to Elizabeth. That he despised and hated her, she could understand. But why he became so cordial to her father was a mystery she could not possibly explain or understand.

"You are too generous, sir," Mr. Bennet answered. "I am aware that the present situation is due to my past neglectful parenting. We all know that such a situation would never occur under—let us say—your supervision."

Darcy looked at the gentleman for a moment, and Elizabeth was sure his countenance had changed. To her increasing turmoil, Elizabeth sensed that he was avoiding her glances on purpose, but she could not trust either her perception or her reason concerning him. She had misjudged him and his character too completely and too often.

Eventually, she heard him reply, his tone equally friendly but somehow hesitant.

"There are people—unfortunately George Wickham is one of them —who manage to charm a young heart and deceive it, pushing her against her family's best intentions. Women older and wiser than Miss Lydia have fallen into this trap," Mr. Darcy declared with no trace of arrogance or censure in his voice.

"In this, I will not contradict you," Mr. Bennet admitted with a trace of mockery. "Even my Lizzy, whom I consider one of the brightest people of my acquaintance, was quite smitten with Wickham at one point and considered him a close friend until recently."

Elizabeth struggled to speak calmly, wondering how much embarrassment and distress she could bear in one day.

"Papa, please do not joke about this. I feel ashamed and guilty enough for my wrong first impression, but it has been many months since I ceased considering Mr. Wickham a friend."

"Forgive me, my dear, I did not mean to offend you. After all, you warned me against allowing Lydia to go to Brighton. I should have listened to you. But I never imagined Lydia could be in any danger, and God knows I could not believe Wickham to be quite so bad."

Darcy's uneasiness was now apparent to Elizabeth.

"Mr. Bennet, Mr. Gardiner, forgive me for interrupting you, but it is quite late. Could we speak privately for a few moments? I would like to discuss the steps to be taken under the present circumstances."

Yes, he did intend to escape from her presence; Elizabeth was certain of it. Or perhaps she was of so little significance to him that he just ignored her. *"My good opinion once lost, is lost forever,"* he had said, and he was now proving it. She knew she had no right to be bothered by it. Surely, she could not expect forgiveness from such a proud—and resentful, he admitted—man, who had been so deeply offended. She bit her lips to dissipate her ridiculous thoughts. Why would she be preoccupied with his behaviour towards her? She mattered not in the present situation, and she would accept even worse treatment for the reward of having her family helped and her father at peace.

"Certainly, sir, as you wish," Mr. Bennet answered. "However, I keep no secrets from Lizzy—we can speak openly before her."

"I understand; still, I would rather keep this conversation among gentlemen," Darcy replied decidedly.

Neither Mr. Bennet nor Mr. Gardiner had any other opposition. The host took the lead towards the library, and the door closed behind them.

THE NEXT HOUR WAS A TORMENT FOR ELIZABETH. SHE ARGUED WITH LYDIA for a while under the strict supervision of Mrs. Gardiner. Lydia's anger was directed at all of them—equally—and she was impossible to convince by any reasonable argument.

Exhausted and afraid she might be tempted to say something painful against her own sister, Elizabeth abandoned the fight and retired to her chamber.

The silence and solitude offered her nothing than more distress. She wondered again and again at the fact that Darcy decided to come to her uncle's house, exposing them both to a disturbing new meeting. He left her with no doubt that he loathed her presence as he purposely ignored her. And when the opportunity arose, he insisted on her being removed from their company.

But the more uncivil his manners were to her, the kinder he acted towards her family—especially her father.

A sharp, painful thought invaded and tormented her mind while her heart raced unsteadily: How different would everything have been if she had accepted his marriage proposal? How would his kindness towards her father have been expressed? Would such an incident have even occurred? Surely, Wickham's character would have been exposed to her entire family —perhaps to all of Meryton. No honourable young lady would have fallen victim to his charms. If only...

But which was more difficult to bear: the threat of having her sister's happiness ruined and her family's future jeopardised, or the prospect of being forever trapped in a marriage with Mr. Darcy?

Her turmoil was impossible to temper, so Elizabeth left her room and went downstairs, impatiently looking for a sign of the gentlemen. Slowly, she stepped towards the library, and after glancing around to be sure she was not seen, she leant her ear against the heavy door. To her distress, she heard arguing and recognised her father's voice:

"Mr. Darcy, this is not to be borne! We cannot possibly accept this. It is unthinkable."

Then Darcy's reply.

"Sir, I assure you that I have no intention of debating this matter or abandoning my intentions. We may stay here and argue until morning, but my decision is made. I only wished to inform you."

Again, her father and uncle opposed him stoutly, and Mr. Darcy answered something unintelligible. Elizabeth's heart nearly stopped for an instant then started beating so loudly that she was afraid they might hear it from inside the library. What could possibly be the reason for their argument? What did Darcy intend to do that her father opposed so strongly? Could it be something related to her? Was that the basis for his refusing her presence at their discussion? Oh, surely not—it was completely unreasonable to imagine such a thing. She was a simpleton to imagine that she might be significant to him. And why was she even thinking of that? Obviously, Lydia was not the only silly one in their family.

But still, why were the gentlemen debating so heatedly?

Elizabeth startled when Mrs. Gardiner appeared unexpectedly and pulled her quite unceremoniously into the drawing room.

"Lizzy, have you lost your mind? What are you doing? Spying at doors? What if Mr. Darcy had caught you? Could we possibly make a worse impression and prove more lack of decorum to the gentleman? Upon my word, I wonder that he did not run from our house an hour ago! The man must be a saint to bear such offenses."

Mrs. Gardiner was angrier than Elizabeth had seen her in a long while —perhaps ever.

"Please forgive me, Aunt; I was just curious. I apologise for all the distress we caused you…"

Mrs. Gardiner interrupted her with a gesture.

"Lizzy dearest, I do not want to put any blame on you, but…I must say I was quite shocked to see Mr. Darcy in my house, and I am embarrassed by everything that happened. I still cannot believe that he agreed to assist your father and uncle. No other gentleman of Mr. Darcy's stature would allow himself to be involved in such a sordid story. Did I ever mention to you that I grew up in a small town only five miles from Pemberley?

Pemberley is Mr. Darcy's estate, and his family is one of the most prestigious and admired in Derbyshire. I never dreamt to see the master of Pemberley visiting us. He tried to help Lydia, and she repaid him by offending him horribly. Not to mention your previous unfavourable account of Mr. Darcy, Lizzy. You described him to us as if he were in possession of all the faults and wrongs in the world. And now you are spying on him? Is this how we show our gratitude?"

Elizabeth swallowed the sudden lump in her throat, unable to reply. She had never considered that her aunt could be so affected for reasons of her own. She recollected Mrs. Gardiner speaking of her childhood in Derbyshire —even remembered Mrs. Gardiner chatting with Wickham at Longbourn about this—but until that moment she had not given it much attention.

Mrs. Gardiner—usually calm and self-confident—was nervous and troubled about Mr. Darcy's mere presence in her house. What would she think or do, knowing that Elizabeth had rejected his marriage proposal with the greatest lack of civility? That was a secret Elizabeth was doomed to carry forever.

And the question returned, even more disturbing and repeated by Mrs. Gardiner herself: Why would he put everything aside to help them? What did he have to gain from all this? And what was he fighting about with her father?

There was no time for further discussion as the gentlemen entered, and they barely had time to rise and curtsey.

Elizabeth searched their expressions with unconcealed interest. All three of them were obviously troubled, her father more than the others. Mr. Bennet was pale, and his eyes had lost any spark; he said nothing and avoided Elizabeth's inquiring eyes.

"I shall leave you now; please wait for a note from me tomorrow," Darcy addressed the gentlemen with a warm friendliness that contradicted any previous disagreement.

Mr. Bennet shook hands with the guest, and Elizabeth witnessed her father bowing to Darcy with an expression of deep emotion that she had never seen before.

"Sir, I cannot express my gratitude, and I will never—"

"Mr. Bennet, I confess I am in a great hurry as I am quite hungry, and I am sure you must be too," Darcy hastily interrupted him in an apparently cheerful mood, which shockingly clashed with Mr. Bennet's. "I will wait for you both tomorrow at noon. I wish you all a lovely evening."

He greeted the ladies, looking only at Mrs. Gardiner, then left. A profound silence fell behind him, two pairs of eyes staring at the other two with complete incomprehension and uneasy curiosity.

A SENSE OF RELIEF ENVELOPED DARCY WHEN HE EVENTUALLY FOUND HIMself in the solitude of his carriage. He was exhausted from his argument with Elizabeth's father and also from his efforts to avoid Elizabeth. He struggled to keep his eyes from her, to not address a single world to her, and to demand she be left out of their discussion. He went to the Gardiners' to see her, to be in her proximity—probably for the last time—and then he denied himself that gratification. However, all his senses were desperately aware of her presence. Even when they were in the library, fighting over the payment of Wickham's debts, his thoughts were only of her.

Now everything was settled. Wickham's debts were in his hands, and hopefully, a commission would soon be available for that scoundrel in the North. The expenses were less significant than the satisfaction of being able to control Wickham.

He would marry poor, silly Lydia Bennet; Darcy himself secured them a special license. That was a mistake he could not avoid. Mr. Bennet was not fortunate enough to prevent the marriage as Darcy had done in Georgiana's case. It was painful for Darcy to observe Elizabeth's father struggle to reach a haven in a stormy situation that could have no positive resolution.

Darcy was reluctant to confess to Mr. Bennet his intention to take Wickham's debts upon himself. He suspected the gentleman would reject it; therefore, he only shared his decision after everything was done and could not be changed. Both gentlemen's opposition was as strong as he expected, and they argued longer and more strongly than the subject deserved. Finally, Darcy had his way. In exchange, he asked the gentlemen to promise him their secrecy about the matter

He did not want Elizabeth to know the true extent of his involvement. He did not want to create a wrong impression or to be subjected to expressions of gratitude from her. But he could not ask Mr. Bennet to keep the details from his favourite daughter—not without raising her suspicions. So the only solution was to require that the details of their affair be restricted to the three gentlemen.

Of course, Wickham knew too, and there would always be the danger of disclosure from such an untrustworthy man. But surely, he had no reason to make himself even more of a fool in front of Elizabeth. If he ever revealed that secret, he would do it more from stupidity than intention. But would Elizabeth agree to speak to Wickham on private matters again after everything that had occurred? She did mention earlier that it had been months since she ceased considering Wickham a friend. Was it possible that she guessed some of his true character on her own? Mr. Bennet also declared that Elizabeth had insisted that he forbid Lydia to go to Brighton. Had she changed her feelings even though she did not read his letter?

Darcy shook away his thoughts and turned his attention outside. He must learn to banish any concerns regarding Elizabeth. He had to force himself to dismiss her from his mind. And from his heart. He had to conquer his weakness. He had now accomplished an important duty and helped her family out of a dangerous situation. He had proved to her that his resentment was not so strong as to make him happy about her tragedy. He had shown more courtesy than anyone could expect from him. The past was now closed, and in his future, there was no place for even the memory of Elizabeth Bennet.

Chapter 7

The moment Mr. Darcy closed the door, Elizabeth immediately questioned her father and uncle. The gentlemen indicated the ladies should follow them to the seclusion of the library; inside, Mr. Bennet refilled his glass of wine and sat heavily in an armchair.

Mr. Gardiner took the lead in the conversation. "It seems that Mr. Wickham has come to his senses and they will marry in three days. Mr. Darcy generously took upon himself the unpleasant task of negotiating with the man. Wickham only demanded the part of her inheritance that rightfully belongs to Lydia—to which your father readily agreed. Fortunately, Mr. Wickham was unexpectedly offered a commission in a new regiment in Newcastle. They will leave the second day following the wedding. Mr. Darcy was also kind enough to procure a special license for them, so everything is done."

"Truly? So everything is settled? So easily? But how is that possible? And what about his debts?" Elizabeth inquired in disbelief, staring at her father and uncle. Both gentlemen avoided her gaze, turning their attention to their glasses.

Mr. Gardiner continued. "It seems the debts are not as large as we feared. Everything has been resolved."

"Indeed," Mr. Bennet repeated in a low voice. "Everything has been resolved, with less trouble on our part than we imagined. Now, Lizzy, enough of talking. Please write to Jane to calm the cries at Longbourn. Then take Lydia and purchase one new dress and one nightgown for her, and I want to hear nothing more of this. We will leave for Longbourn immediately after the wedding. I would leave sooner, but I cannot trust Wickham to wed until I see it with my own eyes. Now excuse me, I intend to rest for the remainder of the day."

"And I must attend to duties I have neglected recently. I expect to return home no sooner than dinner," Mr. Gardiner said, kissing his wife's hand.

The two ladies were astonished by the gentlemen's obvious reluctance to volunteer any details, but neither dared insist further. Elizabeth, however, hurried to her father's side and held his arm as she walked with him to his chamber.

"Papa, are you well? May I help you with anything?"

"Only with what I asked you, my child."

"Very well…and…please forgive my indiscretion but…how was your conversation with Mr. Darcy? I understand that he helped procure the special license. And Mr. Wickham's unexpected commission—surely, it came precisely when it was needed. Was Mr. Darcy involved in that too? Does he expect any compensation for his assistance?"

It felt uncomfortable to bother him further, but she was troubled by the recollection of the heated argument she heard in the library and the fears and speculations they roused in her mind.

Mr. Bennet stopped and turned to her. "Lizzy dearest, the kindness and generosity showed by Mr. Darcy towards our family are so extraordinary that we will never be able to repay him. And he did not allow us even to express our gratitude. So all we can do is keep him in our hearts and prayers; we will likely never see him again."

Mr. Bennet entered his room and shut the door decidedly while his words stirred a turmoil that left Elizabeth trembling. She stepped hesitantly down the hall as countless new questions spun in her head and made her dizzy.

THE FOLLOWING EVENING, DUE TO LYDIA'S INSISTENCE AND AGAINST THE opposition of everyone else, Mrs. Gardiner invited Wickham to dinner. Since the wedding was scheduled in two days, it was likely that no other opportunity would arise. The little chance of happiness Lydia could expect depended mostly on the proper, supportive relationship she—and her future husband—would have with her family.

Mr. Bennet had spent most of his time in solitude—either in his chamber or in the library, eager to leave Town as soon as possible. The idea of a dinner with the man who had started all the mess raised a strong—although brief—resistance from him just before the meal.

Elizabeth diligently carried out her role as an elder sister, keeping Lydia company both at home and on their visits to various dressmakers. She attempted to make Lydia see the danger of an uncertain future and to diminish her loud and reckless enthusiasm.

By the time dinner began, Elizabeth's patience had faded, and the appearance of the soon-to-be groom—with a broad, easy smile on his face—ruined her mood completely. She struggled to keep her composure and calm her father's vexation while barely touching her food.

Lydia and Wickham, however, indulged their appetites, praised every course, and expressed their excitement for the wedding and the journey north.

"Oh, I cannot wait to visit Mama on our way to Newcastle. I am sure all my sisters will envy me—I know you do too, Lizzy. What a joke that I am the youngest and yet the first one married."

Mr. Bennet did not respond, exchanging an angry glare with Elizabeth.

"You have little time for visits since you start your new commission within a fortnight," Mr. Gardiner said.

"True. I look forward to beginning a new life, which I have every reason to hope will be very successful," Wickham replied confidently.

Mr. Bennet rolled his eyes. "I am sure you have. And why would you not, considering all the success you have achieved thus far."

Mrs. Gardiner intervened to avoid conflict. "It is good for a new family to have the chance of a new beginning and to build a future together. I am sure you will both take this opportunity very seriously."

"As I said—just as they both did before," Mr. Bennet concluded sarcastically.

The evening passed awkwardly. To Elizabeth's disbelief, Wickham showed no apparent sign of remorse, nor did he attempt a single word of apology.

After dinner, Mr. Bennet retired unceremoniously to the library while Mr. Wickham declared he would remain with the ladies—to his intended's loudly expressed joy.

Mr. Gardiner moved between the library and the drawing room, sharing his company.

Elizabeth took her cup of tea to the settee, unwilling to participate in the conversation. A few minutes later—to her complete amazement—Wickham brought his glass of wine and took a seat next to her.

"Miss Bennet...I am glad that we have a moment to talk. I have been looking forward to it the entire evening. You are well, I hope?"

"I am, sir—as well as can be expected. As for 'talk,' considering the distress we must endure, I wonder that we can carry on a decent conversation at all," she replied coldly, hoping to put an end to the discussion.

However, he continued. "I understand that the present situation was a surprising development for your entire family. I also imagine that your personal feelings might be uneasy...and I confess I feel somehow guilty; I am tempted to blame myself for it."

She narrowed her eyes, breathing deeply to keep her composure. "Mr. Wickham, you may allow yourself to feel entirely guilty. Who else is to blame? Certainly not a young, silly girl of fifteen who fantasised about being in love with a gentleman more than ten years her senior! Surely, we had higher expectations of decorum from a gentleman and an officer in his late twenties than in a girl who is barely more than a child," she responded, struggling to keep her voice low. She observed her uncle and aunt glancing at them while Lydia continued to rave about balls and the officers in the new regiment.

"Your point might be valid if presented in that way," Wickham answered, his surprise apparent. "I understand your vexation—"

"As for my personal feelings, they are just as they should be on discovering that someone, whom we believed to be a friend, has betrayed our confidence and contrived a plan that might ruin our family forever! I, too, cannot but feel guilty for the premature trust and hasty good opinion I bestowed upon you most unwisely."

He turned pale for a moment, but a smirk quickly returned to his face. "I see...it pains me that your opinion has changed so severely. I understand it is hard to believe, but even the best of men may fall sometimes for the sake of their hearts. This is a fault that I am ready to accept."

"Mr. Wickham, please do not take me for a fool once again. Had I the smallest suspicion that you bear any affection for my poor sister, I would be more than willing to welcome you to our family. But we both know that you left your regiment for dishonourable reasons, and you took with you the first silly girl who agreed to be your victim. You only consented to marry her because your pecuniary demands were satisfied."

Wickham coloured slightly and emptied his glass in a single gulp.

"Well, I...things are not always as they seem, but you seem determined to think ill of me. I sense it might be the influence of someone whose main concern has always been to harm me. I never imagined that Darcy was a friend of yours or that he might become involved in a matter that only concerns your family. It looks like there have been many surprising developments lately…"

Elizabeth's anger united with her embarrassment. "Mr Darcy in no way is a friend of ours—quite the contrary! He became involved in this matter because I sought out and begged for his help in tracing you and finding my sister. He was as reluctant and displeased to offer his assistance as I was appalled and ashamed to apply to him. Thank God, his help was useful after all. We are grateful to him, and my family will be diligent in showing him deserved gratitude."

This time, her words had the desired effect. Wickham was left speechless, and he rose to leave; suddenly, he changed his mind and sat again, replying through gritted teeth. "If I had known that your family was willing to support my situation, I would have behaved differently, but I was left with few choices. And if I had been given what was rightfully mine from my godfather—"

Elizabeth had had enough. "Mr. Wickham! Surely, you would not dare to insist on the story you related to me when we first met! Not without explaining to me why you hurried to malign the name of your godfather's son all over Hertfordshire the moment Mr. Darcy left the neighbourhood. I am not aware of the details of your dealings, but it has been many weeks since I began to suspect that Mr. Darcy's refusal to grant you the promised living must have had very sound reasons."

She paused to regain her composure then continued, straightening her shoulders. "Since I am trying to maintain some appearance of decorum, I shall cease this conversation immediately. You should return to your intended now and show her a bit of attention. I am quite tired, and I shall retire immediately. Good night."

Elizabeth said good night to her uncle and aunt and then left the room, hurrying to the library. She spent another hour with her father—he reading, she lost in her thoughts and remorse—before she went to her room. There were only two nights left before they would leave London. If only she could rest a little, she would want for nothing else.

"CAN YOU IMAGINE THAT TODAY IS MY LAST DAY AS MISS LYDIA BENNET? Dear Lord, how strange it sounds," Lydia said the next morning while eating her breakfast. "And you, Lizzy, will leave with Papa tomorrow, but George and I will spend our wedding night in London. Oh, how romantic! I cannot wait to come to Longbourn as Mrs. Wickham! I will be much more important than Jane, being the only married sister. Lizzy, you should all come to visit me. I am sure to procure perfectly good husbands for you too."

"Thank you, Lydia, but I am not particularly fond of either your method or the type of husbands you procure."

"Lord, Lizzy, you have become so boring! I am glad I will be so far away. I shall have as much fun as I can without having to listen to your lectures."

"I hope you will be happy, Lydia. Now—I will take Elinor and Edward to play in the park. Would you like to join us?"

"God no! What a strange notion to go and play in the park with the children. No soon-to-be bride would do that. I will sleep a little more; a married woman does not have much time to rest."

Elizabeth uneasily admitted to herself that she was relieved by Lydia's refusal. She hoped to meet Miss Anna and the countess again—and she was embarrassed to compare Lydia's careless joy with the sadness and despair in Miss Anna's voice as she confessed her own past indiscretion. As much as she loved Lydia, Elizabeth could not deny that she felt ashamed of her youngest sister's manners and thoughtlessness.

With the tumult of Lydia's situation, Elizabeth had little time for anything else, but now she hoped her mysterious friends had not left town and would have a chance to talk again. There was no time for the countess's invitation to call or for tea, but a pleasant conversation would suffice. She did have the note with the countess's address, but she wondered whether she would dare write without having a clear understanding with either the lady or Miss Anna.

As she entered the park, Elizabeth's curiosity was resolved when she noticed the two ladies waiting on their usual bench. The children immediately ran to greet them cheerfully and hurried to play with Didi, who rewarded them with joyful jumps and barks.

Elizabeth curtseyed. "What a pleasure to see you! I was afraid you might have left town before I had the chance to say a proper goodbye. We return home tomorrow."

"Miss Lizzy—do come and sit with us. We are happy to see you too. You must write us your address. We wondered how we could ever find you if we did not meet again," said the countess.

"Oh, so you are leaving?" Miss Anna inquired shyly. "Is everything well with your family? With your sister? I hope you do not mind my asking."

"I thank you for your concern. My sister will marry tomorrow. Yes, everything is as good as can be expected."

"I am glad to hear that. We will leave too," Miss Anna continued. "I am content that we have this chance to say our proper farewells. I have been delighted with our meetings and conversations."

"As have I. It has been an honour and a joy to spend time with you," Elizabeth replied.

"It is a pity, though, that we never had time for that tea. But perhaps other opportunities will arise," the countess added.

"Your ladyship is very kind."

"Well, Miss Lizzy, if you wish to write us, we would be very pleased. Do you still have the address I gave you? You may send the letters there, and they will be directed to me wherever I may be since our schedule for the next months is not yet fixed."

Elizabeth glanced from one lady to another. "I would like that very much...very much indeed...I was wondering if—"

Her voiced was silenced, and her eyes widened in astonishment when an angry voice shouted, "Georgiana, Aunt Amelia, what on Earth are you doing here! Miss Bennet, how dare you approach my sister behind my back! What mischievous scheme is this?"

In disbelief, Elizabeth saw Darcy's face, discomposed by fury, his eyes darkened and narrowed in rage.

"Mr. Darcy, I—" She attempted to summon a shred of calm.

"William!" Miss Anna cried with apparent surprise. "What are you doing here? And what do you mean? Why are you upset?"

"What I mean, Georgiana, is that you have no business being in this part of Town nor to meet with certain persons without informing me. Of course, I am upset. How were you convinced to keep this a secret from me? I did not expect that from you," he continued, his voice low but as sharp as a razor.

"William, I do not understand your harsh words and certainly not your voice. This is the park we have visited for several weeks now. And this is our friend, Miss Lizzy," the young lady answered in a trembling voice, her blue eyes moist with tears, while Elizabeth glanced from one to the other in astonishment.

"Nephew, for heaven's sake, you are making a spectacle of yourself—and us!" the countess replied harshly. "Have you taken leave of your senses? Do you and Miss Lizzy know each other? If so, a gentlemanlike greeting would be appropriate; any other conversation should be delayed for a more private place and time."

Darcy looked at Elizabeth for only an instant, then averted his eyes and cleared his voice.

"You are right, of course. We shall leave now—please allow me to escort you to the carriage. Good day, Miss Bennet."

He took both ladies' arms and gently but decidedly walked them towards the carriage. Miss Anna turned her head, and her gaze met Lizzy's for a moment, but she was too far to read any apparent feelings. Elizabeth remained in the middle of the park, silent and still, struggling to comprehend this piece of news that disturbed her mind once again.

Surely, it was not possible. Surely, it could not be true that the only persons she befriended and admired in all of London—and met in a small park near Cheapside—happened to be Mr. Darcy's sister and aunt. Certainly, the Fates could not be so cruel as to laugh at her once again. Miss Anna was Georgiana Darcy? But how? Why did she conceal her name? And what was she doing so far from home?

And he—Mr. Darcy—what did he imagine? He must have thought they had some sort of conspiracy! He asked her how she dared approach his sister behind his back. What was he thinking? Did he truly accuse her of a mischievous scheme?

Elinor and Edward hurried to her, asking why Didi, Miss Anna, and the countess had left so soon, but she had no answer—either for the children or herself. She tried to calm them and held their little hands while they returned to the house, praying that the terrible pain in her head allowed her to arrive safely.

INSIDE THE CARRIAGE, DARCY FOUND IT DIFFICULT TO BREATHE FROM SURprise and anger. He had journeyed there to deliver to Mr. Bennet the final papers for the wedding and for Wickham's commission; he planned to stay only a few minutes. He knew the Bennets were to leave Town the next day, and the certainty of never seeing Elizabeth again was both alleviating and frightening. But at least his torment would be at an end.

A short distance from his destination, he was astounded to observe his aunt's carriage. He glanced around and finally saw Georgiana and the countess in a small, unfashionable park, talking to another woman. He walked towards them and noticed Didi playing with some children who looked familiar to him—and then he froze. He did not recollect precisely why he was so furious and severe, nor why he offended—in public—both Elizabeth and Georgiana. But he harshly removed his sister from her company as quickly as possible.

The carriage rode steadily; the tension inside was so heavy that it made the air difficult to breathe. Georgiana kept her gaze out the window, her eyes narrowed as if she were struggling to focus and fight back tears.

"For how long had you been seeing Miss Bennet?" Darcy inquired coldly.

"For as long as you very well know since, as you prefer, we constantly kept you informed," the countess answered sharply. "The length of our acquaintance with Miss Lizzy—or Miss Bennet as you called her—matters less than your manners, which distressed three ladies. I can hardly remember when I have ever felt so uncomfortable. I was unaware that we must have your approval for every step we take in order to avoid your making a sudden appearance and offending everyone nearby."

Georgiana's eyes moistened with tears, but she continued to stare outside. She clasped her trembling hands together, still silent.

"I apologise for any offense I might have given you, Aunt. But you must understand how I felt when I discovered your strange friendship with someone well acquainted with me, whose identity was kept hidden. I do not expect to approve every step but certainly the most important ones since I am responsible for you both," Darcy concluded.

"But is this young woman a stranger or not? Would you be so kind as to enlighten me? How do you come to know her?" the countess insisted severely.

"She is the daughter of a country gentleman who owns an estate a few miles from the one Bingley rented in Hertfordshire. I met the family last year when I spent a couple of months at Netherfield," he answered hastily.

"And?" the countess continued. "What exactly are your objections at present?"

"I found it wrong that Georgiana chose to conceal her identity and to visit parts of London we barely knew existed, befriending people completely unknown to all of us. But I said nothing, only to discover that she has built a close friendship with someone I have known before and of whom I cannot approve. This is what happens when one is not careful in dealing with strangers."

"I am sorry that you are upset, Brother," Georgiana whispered. "I was wrong indeed; I am as poor a judge of people's character as I was in the past —forgive me, please. But you should not have addressed Miss Lizzy as you did, even more so since you happen to know her. Surely, you cannot believe she knew my identity any more than I knew hers. I was the one who went there; I was the one who introduced myself as 'Miss Anna.'"

"Georgiana, I can see you do not agree with me. But you must know I want only your well-being. There is nothing I would not give you, nothing I would not do to assure your happiness. I allowed you this liberty, but we must all admit it was not the wisest thing to do."

Georgiana finally faced her brother, holding his gaze. "But, William, I still do not understand what I have done that is so wrong. I just made a new acquaintance whose company I enjoyed, and by coincidence, she proved to be someone of whom you disapprove. Is Miss Lizzy—Miss Bennet—a dangerous criminal who threatens our family? Have I put us in danger by spending time with her in the park?"

The question took Darcy by surprise, as well as the tone—half sharpness, half pain. He cleared his throat, glared at his aunt, then looked at his sister again.

"Dearest, we are not talking about a dangerous criminal, nor did you put the family in danger…but it could have happened, so you must be cautious in the future. You easily became friendly with someone whose situation in life is far below yours, who concealed her true identity from you. People tend to take advantage of your generous heart."

The carriage stopped in front of the countess's house, and Georgiana hurried to open the door. Before she exited, she turned to her brother.

"I see that you refuse to understand my words and insist on placing the blame where it does not belong. You must not worry—that friendship has ended for good. It is fortunate that you discovered the truth in time and restrained me once again from being foolish. I shall never again do anything before asking your opinion," she said then ran inside the house, tears falling down her cheeks.

"Georgiana!" he called in vain.

The countess followed her niece and then turned briefly to Darcy.

"You are being irrational, Nephew. You need to rest and put your thoughts in order. We shall not have a formal dinner tonight, so we do not expect any company. Have a good day."

Darcy was left in the middle of the street, uncertain of what to do and wondering how it could have occurred. Elizabeth Bennet was the ruin of his life; she continued to destroy his peace of mind and heart every time he thought he might escape her forever.

He walked towards his house, his head down, staring at his own feet. The light, the warmth of the shining sun, and the sound of others' voices felt like painful burdens weighting his shoulders and slowing his progress towards the refuge of his dark library.

How was it possible that he allowed this to happen? He should have known that something was wrong the first moment that Georgiana's tales disturbed him and the description of "Miss Lizzy" sounded familiar to him. He had been oblivious to Elizabeth's presence in town for the last two months. He only became aware of that fact when she visited him, asking for his help. But he should have checked. He should have known and done something.

The sorrow in his sister's eyes was unbearable. She seemed deeply hurt, in such pain that he wondered what precisely he had told her that did so much damage to her gentle soul. Only a few days ago, his sister was voluble, full of life, and excited at the prospect of developing this newly gained friendship. Everything was gone now—just as Georgiana said.

And Elizabeth's expression the moment she observed him in the park —her pallor, the dark shadows around her eyes, her obvious turmoil the moment he took Georgiana away—did she know who Georgiana was? Was it possible that she suspected the connection and purposely encouraged it? Could he assume she was so unworthy of trust?

Elizabeth had little consideration and certainly no regard for him. She had told him as much. Her apology when she was in need, her pleading and frequently expressed gratitude, meant nothing. If not for her fear regarding her family, she would have treated him with the same disdain and mistrust as she did before. He knew he could not rely on a single word from her.

What about Georgiana? What kind of interest could Elizabeth have in her if she indeed guessed her identity? Surely, she must have known that he would never allow a close friendship between them. Did she hope Georgiana could help with the elopement of Lydia? No—that could not have been the case; Georgiana seemed attached to Miss Lizzy for almost two months while Wickham eloped less than a week ago.

Perhaps Elizabeth did not know who Georgiana was but guessed she must have been a rich heiress—perhaps an heiress of the countess—and hoped for better connections in town to help her and her sister find proper husbands? Yes—that must have been the case. Perhaps she finally understood the opportunity she had lost by refusing him and feared that neither she nor Jane would ever marry. Perhaps back in April, her hate and disdain for him forbade her to think of the consequences of her gesture, and the idea of marrying him was worse than the concern about remaining unmarried. How much she must have hated him...

He paced the room, filled his glass, sat in the chair, then rose again. What if she had accepted him? What if, due to her concern for her family, she had agreed to be his wife? How would his life have been—loving her with all his heart while she cringed every time he touched her, kissed her, or embraced her?

Shivers as cold as ice ran down his spine. Every thought of her, any speculation, only brought him more turmoil. Even worse, she somehow managed to torment Georgiana too. Every time she touched his life in any way, there was only pain. And it seemed it would never end.

He helped her family to overcome a most difficult situation because that was what his duty demanded from him. He considered Wickham to be his responsibility, and he could not leave it on the unsteady shoulders of Mr. Bennet—who was nothing but an innocent victim. He saved the situation and expected nothing in return.

But he should have done it without any interaction with her family—or at least with her.

Being in her company changed him completely; his manners, his character, his mind, and his heart always betrayed him when she was involved. He had no control over his rage and resentment. His mind was full of anger against her while his heart—his foolish heart—only felt tenderness.

He knew that only too well, and yet he was too weak to stay away. The best proof of this was his repeated visits to the Gardiners' house although he could have avoided it. He only hoped for a glimpse of her.

He saved her sister—and in exchange, she hurt his.

Georgiana was always restrained, careful, and even fearful with strangers —just as he was. How was it possible that, of all the women he ever met who had raised his interest, only Elizabeth made him completely lose his mind without even trying? How was it possible that so many accomplished young women tried to befriend Georgiana without success while Elizabeth won her attachment so easily?

What kind of power did Elizabeth Bennet have over them?

Chapter 8

Minutes passed as slowly as hours for Darcy while he walked wildly around his library. He felt restless, angry, and culpable for his improper reaction—without knowing how to remedy it.

He realised that he forgot to hand the papers to Mr. Bennet and considered sending his servant with them but postponed that decision.

Eventually, he decided he must speak to his sister again and give her a fuller explanation. He knew that Georgiana's torment would increase over time, and the damage caused by her distress would be more difficult to palliate later.

He needed only minutes to reach his aunt's house and was not surprised when the servant informed him that neither the countess nor Miss Darcy was available for visits. After some insistence, he was finally invited to Georgiana's apartment and was not surprised to find both of them there.

Darcy attempted a smile as he asked for their permission to sit. He took a chair and placed it close to Georgiana's settee.

"My dearest, I come to apologise and to explain the reason for my displeasure. I realise I was wrong to react as I did, but you must understand my surprise to discover the identity of the friend you have been speaking about for weeks."

Georgiana gave him a look shadowed with pain.

"I was as surprised as you were—and most certainly Miss Lizzy was too. I was quite prepared to tell her my real name before you appeared. You accused her of mischievous schemes when you well knew that *I* was the one who did not reveal my identity. You offended her while she was only kind and friendly to me."

"I admit I might have been hasty and unfair, but things appeared to lead to that conclusion."

"What things? You found me talking with a young lady in a public park. That was all. And you suddenly became so angry…"

"For a moment, I suspected you both knew each other's real identities and entered into a friendship that you hid from me."

"But why would I do that? I know I gave you reason to distrust me, but why would I keep secret a friendship with someone acquainted with you? What would I—or Miss Lizzy—have to gain? I know that, for years, many ladies have attempted to befriend me with the purpose of drawing your attention. Is it not possible that I have a friend who enjoys my company without knowing I am your sister? Is there nothing valuable about me beyond the fact of being your sister?"

Georgiana lost the battle with her tears, and his heart ached to witness her sadness. He gently embraced her and felt her resistance in his arms; then she finally rested her head on his shoulder, sobbing.

"My dear, you are more valuable to me than anyone else I know; you must never doubt that. It is my privilege to have you as my sister. And I am sure Miss Bennet—and anyone else—would be fortunate to have you as a friend. But there are other things to consider. Even if Miss Bennet was as genuine as you were in this newly found friendship, several other circumstances are against it."

"Would you be so kind to reveal those circumstances to me? Do you trust my judgment enough for such a favour, or should I not be allowed to decide for myself?"

"Georgiana, please do not speak so. It is…first, there is little chance that you and Miss Bennet could actually meet again in the future. She has no business in the North, and she is rarely in town. As for us, it is unlikely that we will visit Hertfordshire, especially since Bingley has no plans to return to Netherfield."

"Your familiarity with Miss Bennet's business and Mr. Bingley's plans is quite amazing. Have you seen him lately?" the countess intervened in a mocking tone.

"Aunt, please…let us not digress from the subject," Darcy replied.

Lady Hardwick threw him a sharp glance. "Certainly. Heaven forbid that we digress from the path you drew! And speaking of paths, I can foresee many opportunities for us to trespass in Hertfordshire if it comes to that. I may even be tempted to purchase a small estate in the area."

Georgiana's eyes widened in surprise; then a smile twisted her lips as she slowly regained her composure.

But Darcy frowned. "Dear Aunt, we must approach this subject seriously."

"Then do be serious, Nephew. Do not treat Georgiana like a child and me like an old fool. Tell us once and for all why you behaved so strangely with regard to this Miss Bennet. Why do you despise her, and why do you want to cut all connections between her and your sister? Do not come back with silly arguments about her abode! If that were the only inducement for friendship, we would all display a card with our residence tied around our necks so we could decide, whenever we meet new people, whom we should befriend or not!"

Lady Hardwick sipped a little more port while she rolled her eyes in displeasure.

"I do not despise Miss Bennet...in fact, I understand why you enjoy her company. She is witty and well read and pleasant...and yet, I have reasons of my own to disapprove of your connection with her. I would rather have her as far as possible from us, and I strongly believe that she would prefer to be nowhere near me as well. Since we met in Hertfordshire, Miss Bennet and I have not been the best of friends—quite the contrary."

"Brother, now I am even more puzzled. Your opinion of Miss Bennet seems to be a positive one. I remember now that you even mentioned her in one of your letters from Hertfordshire. But you seem decided against her and say you are not friends. Is she to blame for that?"

He hesitated a moment. "If we were to measure it, I would bear the greatest share of the blame. Perhaps, if my manners were less cold and my behaviour more amiable, things might have been different."

"I will not insist upon this, but I confess I still do not hear anything against my friendship with Miss Lizzy...Miss Bennet...except for your past misunderstandings with her. But all this discussion is in vain; I suspect she would not want to hear anything about me now. I wonder what she thought about my dishonest behaviour and my attempt to conceal my identity. She is entitled to suspect me of a mischievous scheme or of losing my mind. If I could at least explain to her...I feel so bad for ending our acquaintance with her. Can we not talk to her one more time or send her a letter?"

"We can if you insist, but…"

He hesitated, wondering whether he should tell his sister the disturbing news.

"Georgiana, there is another reason that, at present, makes my opposition even stronger." He took her hands in his and attempted a smile. "Since you insist on my being honest, I will do as you ask. My dear, the Bennet family is going through a difficult time now. The youngest of the Miss Bennets has left her family, and she eloped a week ago."

"William, I know that…Miss Lizzy told us a few days ago. We met her in the park, and she looked devastated…and as we inquired, she confessed the tragedy and expressed her concern—for us! She insisted we should not speak to her again in order not to be affected by association with such a dishonourable situation."

Darcy looked at his sister in amazement. He tried to guess when that had happened while Georgiana continued, again overwhelmed by emotion. "Can you imagine anyone more generous? In the middle of such suffering, she was more preoccupied with our well-being. Surely, you cannot hold this happenstance against her."

"I will say, I was quite impressed," the countess interjected. "Even more, I offered her my help, but she politely refused. I gave her my address, but she assured me she would not disturb us, and she did not. Now please explain to us, Darcy: How can this be a fault in her character, a reason for you to oppose her friendship with your sister?"

The two pairs of eyes searching his face inquiringly—together with his own surprise and distress—delayed his answer; then the words came hesitantly.

"I did not know you were familiar with the elopement. And no, I do not hold that against Miss Bennet. But, my dear, do you know with whom her sister eloped?"

"I do not; at that time, I did not even know her full name, nor did she know ours. She said the man was an officer—shame on him! Why would the name be of any consequence?"

"Because it is George Wickham, dearest," he whispered, and Georgiana's face lost its colour as her eyes widened in disbelief. She blinked repeatedly several times, her lips trembling.

"George Wickham? But how can that be? She said he was an officer. Did she deceive us? Why would she conceal the truth from us? George Wickham knows Miss Bennet's sister? How can this be? How?"

She was obviously fighting her tears, and Darcy kissed her hands tenderly.

"Miss Bennet did not mention the name because she did not know who you were, and she could not imagine Wickham held any importance for you. Besides, in such situations, people wish to keep the details as secret as possible."

"That is true...but how did George meet the Bennets? He is not an officer, is he? Did he deceive them?"

"He joined the militia last autumn...and his regiment was settled in Meryton, only a few miles from Mr. Bennet's estate. Then the regiment encamped at Brighton for the summer, and the youngest Miss Bennet was invited by the colonel's wife to join them. The rest—"

"The rest is the same: the same habit, the same scenery, only a different silly girl..."

Darcy's heart broke at his sister's distress. All her past suffering seemed to be reborn, and it was not difficult to see that she was on the edge of tears.

"Did they marry?" Georgiana asked, and Darcy exchanged a worried glance with their aunt.

"They will...tomorrow. I am sorry to say that Wickham is as dishonourable and cowardly as ever. He had no intention of marrying that poor, silly girl. She is enamoured of him, but he has no affection for her. He hid from the Bennet family, and it was difficult to find them."

"How...how do you know all this?"

"Mr. Gardiner—Mr. Bennet's brother—called on me. He asked me for any details that might help them discover the couple. I confess I helped them. We...they barely convinced Wickham to accomplish his duty and only after they paid his debts. He is a horrible man, dearest. You must not suffer for him."

Darcy caressed the girl's hair, embracing her. He kissed her temples while she whispered, "I do not suffer for him, William, but for my own foolishness. I was so close to being in that girl's place. When I remember all the pain I caused you..."

"Georgiana, please remember that nothing pains me if I know you are well. You are the most important person in the world to me. Please do not forget that, my dear. You must promise me."

"I promise..."

Several moments of silence followed while the siblings embraced and the countess enjoyed her port, elegantly bringing a handkerchief to her eyes.

"So, this is what you were doing in that part of town? Visiting Miss Bennet's family?" Georgiana asked.

"Yes."

"I see...William, there is something else I must share with you. When Miss Lizzy told us about the elopement, she was so devastated and frightened for her sister that I tried to calm her, so I confessed to her that I was once close to eloping myself. I did not mention George Wickham's name either, but I wanted her to know that I understood her sorrow. I hope you will not be upset with me," Georgiana spoke hesitantly.

Darcy could not conceal his bewilderment. "That is quite a surprise. I would not expect you to share a secret with someone you barely knew—a secret you insisted on keeping private even from the closest family. But since that is what you decided, I have no reason or right to be upset. Besides, I am quite confident that we should not fear Miss Bennet's discretion."

He saw that his sister was surprised by his calm reaction. Considering his offensive statements towards Elizabeth, Georgiana expected him to be furious about her confession. Of course, she would never know that he was the first to confess that dark, painful secret to Elizabeth in a letter she refused to read.

When Darcy looked at it from Georgiana's point of view, the entire situation with Elizabeth looked completely different. The two of them had grown unexpectedly close and had found the strength to trust and confess to each other their most painful secrets. Georgiana felt that Elizabeth liked her for herself—not for being a Darcy—and he knew only too well what she meant. He also knew how completely right Georgiana was: Elizabeth liked her precisely because she was unaware of her identity. His suspicions were not just wrong but quite ridiculous.

His uneasiness increased as he scolded himself for his faulty actions and words. All his fury, resentment, and reproaches seemed unjustified and simply malicious when he spoke of Elizabeth in her absence. He only tried to point out her wrongs and to compensate for his still-powerful attraction towards her.

And Georgiana's question remained unanswered: How could he object to his sister's befriending Elizabeth Bennet—unless he was afraid of falling under her spell again?

He had saddened his sister for only one reason: his own weakness and lack of control.

He looked at Georgiana's distressed expression once again then gently caressed her hair.

"My dear, if everything I told you has not changed your mind, you may write a short letter to Miss Bennet. Since I must speak to Mr. Bennet tonight, I will deliver it to her."

Surprise brightened Georgiana's face; she stared at her brother in disbelief, then embraced him in haste, and hurried to the desk in search of pen and paper.

Darcy felt his aunt's insistent gaze upon him, but neither of them spoke.

Two hours later, Darcy's carriage was traveling back to Gracechurch Street. In his right pocket, he carried a piece of paper bearing Georgiana's elegant writing—the second time he would give Elizabeth a letter to clarify a distressing misunderstanding. And while he counted the minutes until he would see her, he wondered what he could say to explain this latest example of his ungentlemanlike behaviour before they separated forever.

ELIZABETH STRUGGLED TO MAINTAIN A CALM APPEARANCE IN THE PRESENCE of her relatives. She briefly informed her father, uncle, and aunt of the astonishing coincidence that her new acquaintance was Mr. Darcy's sister. She felt uncomfortable speaking of it, but she had to make certain that, if Mr. Darcy returned to hold her responsible for some imagined fault, her relatives would not be taken by surprise.

Mr. Bennet declared that he was expecting Mr. Darcy and began to worry about whether the gentleman would return.

For Elizabeth, every moment increased her turmoil. She was desperate to discover the reason Miss Darcy kept her identity secret and travelled halfway across town to spend time in a small, unfashionable park. What did she tell her brother that made him so astonished and angry on seeing them?

As for the gentleman in question, Elizabeth was intrigued, offended, and equally angry. He had been impolite, rude, and unjust, and she felt incapable of reproaching him for anything directly since they were so much in his debt. Her only relief was the knowledge that each of them would leave for separate destinations the next day and put the entire matter behind them.

In the evening, when Mr. Bennet and Mr. Gardiner were at the edge of their patience and trying to decide whether they should go to Mr. Darcy themselves, the gentleman finally arrived.

He apologised for the delay, offered a brief explanation while he handed the papers to his hosts, and cast a glance towards Elizabeth. Both turned slightly pale then coloured, avoiding looking at each other for more than an instant.

Relieved, both elder gentlemen hurried to invite Mr. Darcy for a drink while Mrs. Gardiner extended an invitation for dinner.

Darcy accepted the drink, thanked Mrs. Gardiner, and expressed his hope that another opportunity for dinner might arise in the future; then —to everyone's puzzlement—he asked permission for a private conversation with Elizabeth.

"I have a message from my sister—for Miss Bennet—and I would rather deliver it personally if there is no inconvenience for you."

The others glanced at each other, Elizabeth blushed slightly, and then Mr. Bennet answered, "Of course, sir."

"Would the drawing room be acceptable?" Mrs. Gardiner inquired, and at Darcy's approving nod, she invited them in and closed the door behind them.

Silence fell heavily upon them both. Since Elizabeth's anguished visit to Darcy House, this was the first time they were alone—the first time that they were forced to look at each other or to speak to each other.

Elizabeth unconsciously straightened her shoulders and clenched her fists to gain her courage, expecting a confrontation.

"Miss Bennet, I believe you know the subject of this private conversation," he began.

"I imagine you wish to talk about my acquaintance with Miss Anna... forgive me...Miss Darcy. It is obvious and understandable that you are displeased with the situation. But I cannot accept your implied accusations that—"

"I am displeased as well as shocked," he interrupted her. "I never imagined you might be the 'Miss Lizzy' my sister spoke of. Georgiana is a very private person, and she has few friends outside the family."

"And Mr. Bingley's sisters, I imagine." The moment she spoke, Elizabeth regretted her reply.

"Miss Bennet, this is not a time for trifling and certainly not at my sister's expense."

"Sir, I apologise, that was not my intention. I was only trying to...it does not even matter. You seem determined to misunderstand everything I say."

"I did misunderstand both your words and your behaviour in the past, but I trust I ceased doing that four months ago."

"Quite the contrary, sir. You are not—"

"This discussion is not about me or you but about Georgiana. My sister's well-being and happiness are all that matter to me. I know she grew quite fond of you, and my aunt gave you her address—which is also astonishing. They planned to even have a correspondence with you! I must know what your intentions are as it is my duty to protect them both."

"What do you suspect my intentions are, sir? You instantly accused me of mischievous schemes, so your opinion must be already fixed."

"I admit that, under the astonishment of the discovery, I thought you intentionally approached my sister because you feared you might not convince me to assist your family in discovering your sister and attempted to gain some advantage through Georgiana. I was confident that you had discovered her hidden identity while concealing your own or you had convinced her to keep your relationship hidden from me—that you betrayed her genuine friendship for ulterior motives." Darcy stopped and stared at her, cold and severe.

Elizabeth replied, hoping her voice expressed ample determination. "Sir, I cannot accept such an unfair accusation. You must allow me to tell you the truth, which is far from what you imagine. I must speak my mind."

"That will not be necessary, Miss Bennet. I fought against my first impression, and I talked to my sister and my aunt, so I already know the entire truth. She told me about your confession to her regarding the elopement and hers to you. I do not approve of it, but I cannot hold it against you. I understand that you were a comforting companion to my sister when she needed it, so I am here to admit my wrongs to you and to apologise for my manners when we met in the park. I know only too well how it feels to bear unfair accusations without being given a chance to defend oneself."

His glare was as sharp as a blade, and Elizabeth paled. Then her strength evaded her, and she needed to sit in the nearest chair. She could not take her eyes from his dark gaze and found nothing to answer.

It was Darcy who averted his eyes first.

"My sister wrote you a letter. She was worried about your opinion of her and wished the opportunity to explain the motives for her behaviour."

He handed her the letter, and Elizabeth took it with trembling fingers, careful not to touch his. He withdrew his hand hastily as if the proximity of her hand might burn him.

"Please tell Miss Anna—Miss Darcy—that I thank her for her concern; I do not question her reasons. I am only grateful that I had the pleasure of her company all these weeks. I…" The words became heavier as the weight of emotions—from her past with him and her present interactions with his sister—overwhelmed her.

"Miss Bennet," he called her, and the sudden warmth in his voice was astonishing enough to turn her gaze back to him. "Anything you wish to say to my sister you should put in a letter. I cannot stay longer to take it myself, but you can have it delivered either to my aunt's address or to mine. In either case, Georgiana will receive it without delay."

Elizabeth's last remnants of composure vanished. She stared at him, dumbfounded, wondering whether she had understood his words correctly. Did he just give his consent for a correspondence between her and Miss Darcy? What could this possibly mean?

"Since I know you leave Town tomorrow and it is unlikely that we shall meet again in the future, I wish you all the best and every happiness, Miss Bennet."

He bowed and left the room in such haste that Elizabeth barely had time to follow him with the tear-shadowed eyes she could no longer conceal.

She expected a confrontation, she expected him to be unreasonably angry, and she expected him to offend and accuse her. She was prepared to fight with him, and she was ready to stand up for herself, to defend her opinions and her behaviour against his cruel reproaches.

Instead, he was calm—although not entirely composed. He was sympathetic and fair though his resentment was still apparent. He obviously neither forgot—nor forgave—their quarrel at the Parsonage. Any conciliation he made regarding the situation with Georgiana was only a sign of affection towards his sister.

He still held a grudge towards her—he said as much with few words. And yet, he granted her family the gift of peace and tranquillity.

Everything he had done since they met in London was owing to his duty and character. His favours were done not because of her but regardless of her.

And as she stared at the closed door, Elizabeth suddenly realised how much that thought troubled her and how saddened she was by the revelation that she would never see him again.

Mrs. Gardiner entered, but Elizabeth, deep in thought, did not notice. She startled when she felt a gentle hand on her shoulder.

"Lizzy, are you well?"

"Yes, yes, Aunt, I am fine…Mr. Darcy brought me a letter from his sister. I was about to read it."

"Then I shall leave you alone. When you are ready, please join us for dinner."

Elizabeth heard few of her aunt's words. She opened the letter eagerly, careful not to tear it. The recollection of a torn letter came to her mind, but she banished it and began to read.

Dear Miss Lizzy,

I hope you do not mind my addressing you this way, but it is the name of a friend whose company has been a comfort to me at a rather difficult time.

I have not enough time—nor paper and ink—to explain the reasons for not disclosing my identity to you nor to apologise for the distress you went through because of my brother's intervention. I beg you to forgive him. He is the kindest and most generous man, and he would never harm anyone intentionally, but he was surprised to see us together, and because he wishes to protect me, he always fears the worst. I pray that, by the time you read this, he will have already spoken to you and settled things properly.

It might be difficult to believe under the present circumstance, but I was determined to reveal the entire truth to you a few days ago, and only the unexpected events with your family prevented me from doing so. My decision to spend time in a park far away my residence and to conceal my true name was due only to my wish for some peace where nobody knew me. I did not expect that I would meet someone who would become dear to my heart and who could be hurt by my actions.

I know you will leave Town tomorrow, and I wish you a pleasant journey and all the best to your family. If someday you find the strength to forgive me, I would dearly love to hear from you again.

Sincerely,
Georgiana Darcy.

Elizabeth smiled as she wiped her tears, amazed by the young woman's modesty, kindness, and genuine affection. Even more, she had a strange sensation that she could feel the sorrow and loneliness in Georgiana Darcy's heart, hidden behind her written words. Elizabeth recollected Miss Bingley's flamboyant praise of Miss Darcy, and she could easily imagine that the behaviour of other women—in their quest for Mr. Darcy's wealth—was the same. No wonder the girl wished to be as far from her house as possible.

She was also impressed that Miss Darcy's first concern seemed to be to justify her brother's behaviour. There was no doubt that the affection between the siblings was strong and mutual.

What had happened within this family? What could induce Mr. Darcy to be such a peculiar sort of man, so different from one moment to the next? Why was Miss Darcy so timid and so apparently lonely although she had the love and support of her brother and aunt?

Surely, a great influence was the loss of both parents at an early age. Georgiana must have been only a child when her mother passed away. Elizabeth thought of the happy sounds and loving madness in her own house and shivered as she imagined how she would feel without her family.

She moved to the library, sat at her uncle's desk, and quickly began to write.

Dear Miss Anna,

Your letter was a wonderful surprise, and I cannot thank you enough for your considerate gesture.

I would not wish you to waste time, paper, or pen giving explanations that no one has the right to demand.

Your company—your friendship—has been one of the most beautiful experiences of my life, and I feel grateful for it. I have rarely met anyone whom I liked and admired as much, and I pray that the future will bring me another opportunity to benefit from your company. Until then, any sign from you would be most welcomed and greatly appreciated.

Please have no concern for Mr. Darcy's reaction. I have long known of his deep affection for you, and I can easily understand his wish to protect you —so no offense was taken.

I shall keep both you and Lady Hardwick in my thoughts and prayers.

Yours,
Lizzy Bennet

ELIZABETH'S LAST DAY IN TOWN STARTED WITH A RESTLESS NIGHT, CON-tinued with Lydia's wedding, and by noon found her and Mr. Bennet in the carriage travelling towards Hertfordshire.

Neither of them talked much; recent days had exhausted them. For both, the reasons for distress carried the same names: Lydia, Wickham, and Mr. Darcy. But their reasons were not similar. Father and daughter had things to conceal, and their lifetime of trust in each other was now broken, burdened by secrets.

In the evening, they arrived at Longbourn, and they were received with cries, tears, joy, and countless questions. Mr. Bennet informed his wife that her favourite daughter would visit them in two days on her way to the North and declared he did not wish to be present for that event. Then he asked for his dinner to be served in his library, where he immediately retired.

Elizabeth was not equally fortunate. She had dinner with her mother and sisters and offered them detailed information about the Gardiners, Lydia's new gown, and the wedding. Later, when she finally entered the solitude of her room, she hurried to bed, hoping for nothing more than to catch a few hours of desperately needed rest.

However, Jane soon entered and sat near Elizabeth, asking why she was so pale and how her time had been in London.

"Oh, Jane…if you only knew…I missed talking to you so much. I trust nobody in the world as I do you. Stay with me; I have so many things to tell you."

The two sisters cuddled together in the bed, just as they used to when they were little, and Elizabeth freed her mind and her soul with the confession that had burdened her for so many days.

Later in the night while Jane struggled to comprehend everything she had learnt, Elizabeth finally fell asleep, warmed by her sister's presence. Just before her dreams overtook her, she wondered whether there was anyone who offered the same warmth and comfort to Mr. and Miss Darcy so they could rest in serenity.

Chapter 9

Darcy hoped his peace of mind would return once Elizabeth left Town, but three days later, he discovered how wrong he was.

The lack of rest—of his mind and body—left its traces on his face. It was even worse than before their meeting because her closeness brought back feelings that he hoped were long gone.

Preparation for their departure to Pemberley within a week was the only diversion from thoughts of Elizabeth. Since he planned to remain in Derbyshire for a longer time, he needed to complete his business in London. Therefore, he barely left his house at all; he made and received no calls except with solicitors.

Elizabeth's departure affected Georgiana too.

After receiving Elizabeth's letter, his sister was now calmer, more at peace—that was apparent both in her expression and in her playing and singing. But she lost all interest in the outside world—and more than once, they found her with the curtains closed as if she were trying to keep the sun out too.

One day, Darcy had tea with his aunt at Lady Hardwick's house. As usual, Georgiana was practicing diligently in the music room.

"I look forward to Pemberley," Darcy said.

"I am sure Georgiana will feel better there," her ladyship replied.

"I look forward to riding with her through the Pemberley woods again," he admitted, neither of them daring to voice the true reason for their concern.

"Yes, she has been an excellent rider even from her infancy. You taught her well. You taught her well in everything, Nephew. She has grown up to be a remarkable young woman. You should be proud of yourself."

"I am proud of her, Aunt. But her character was without flaws from the beginning; I deserve no praise for that."

"Of course you do. There are many young ladies in her position—even older than her—with the benefit of both parents, who are far less accomplished than Georgiana."

"Accomplishment is a relative term," he said, recollecting a conversation with Elizabeth at Netherfield. "I am content to know Georgiana is happy."

"Happiness is a relative term too," the countess answered. "Both you and Georgiana wish to see each other happy, but are you seeking your own happiness, Nephew?"

He smiled. "Not particularly. If happiness is interested in finding me, it will."

"But you must help it a bit, my dear boy. You should allow the sun and the world to see more of you. Look around for someone who can capture your heart and excite your mind—someone worth fighting for, someone who will break the routine of your life into pieces, only to put it back together in a happier shape. Someone to complete you."

A sharp pain pierced his heart at every word, and he answered more bitterly than he would have liked.

"You, my dear aunt, are a true romantic. I doubt that what you just described exists anywhere but in novels or poetry. I, for one, am perfectly content to return to Pemberley and escape the dusty heat of London in the summer."

"Pemberley is wonderful but a little too silent…too sad. It would benefit from more joy, more laughter, more balls, more liveliness."

Darcy cast a glance at his aunt. "I do not remember many balls or much laughter at Pemberley. And I surely do not miss them."

"Oh, but they were there, at least when your father and I were children. Anne—your mother, God rest her soul—was fond of quiet and solitude. She was neither strong nor animated, and George did everything he could to fulfil her wishes."

"That I remember. My parents had a happy marriage, as short as it was," Darcy concluded. Lady Hardwick sipped some tea without responding as he expected.

"Did they not?" he insisted, and her ladyship offered a smile.

"They had a good marriage—one of the best among our acquaintance.

Your father knew his duty, and he dedicated his life to his family."

Darcy watched his aunt intently. It was the first time that he had such a conversation with her, and he did not miss the shades in her statement.

"Is there any difference between a good marriage and a happy one?" he asked, and Lady Hardwick's lips twisted in a smile.

"Oh yes, there is. My first marriage was a *good* one. Both Thomas—God rest him—and I were content to follow our families' arrangements, and we slowly grew fond of each other. My second marriage with my beloved Frederick was a *happy* one."

He frowned as his aunt's face brightened in blissful recollection.

"The difference is in the spark, in the pure joy of being close to your loved one, in the quivering of your skin, in the restlessness and yearning for each other's nearness. And so many other things that an aunt cannot share with her nephew," she said with a laugh while Darcy felt his cheeks warming.

He needed no details. He understood his aunt's meaning perfectly. He had already felt and suffered for every sensation described by Lady Hardwick. Yes, he did know what happiness looked like, and for a short while, he believed it had found him. But it stormed into his life and then refused to stay. Perhaps he was not meant to be happy.

Later that day in the silence of his library, Darcy recollected the conversation with his aunt. He had always imagined his parents having a happy marriage, but now that Lady Hardwick voiced it aloud, doubts began to trouble him. The countess suggested that his father's devotion to his mother was from duty more than love, and Darcy realised he had no reason to either confirm or deny it.

Both he and Georgiana had been blessed with their parent's affection, care, and kindness. They had the happiest childhood one could desire. As for George Darcy and Lady Anne, they were always solicitous, courteous, and attentive to each other. He had never heard them address a single harsh word to each other nor contradict each other on any subject—nor did his father ever refuse his mother anything.

Darcy suddenly recollected teasing jokes from past family parties that implied Lady Anne was the one who chose George Darcy as her future husband during her second year out, and she was not to be deterred from her decision. Lady Catherine—Lady Anne's sister—often claimed that, once a Fitzwilliam woman wished for something, it would always be hers.

He took it as a joke; it was unthinkable that Lady Anne—the living image of beauty, fragility, gentleness, and perfect manners—could impose her will on anyone.

While Darcy had loved his mother deeply, he had always been closer to his father and proud to be George Darcy's son. He could not remember a single flaw in his father's behaviour and character. Was it possible that his father never knew true happiness in his too-short life?

From that day on, Darcy's torment grew, adding to his present distress a concern for his family's past. He was tempted to ask for more details, but he feared it would be a disrespectful intrusion into his parents' life, so he controlled his curiosity and ceased any inquiries. But he still wondered —countless times—whether Pemberley was indeed too silent and too sad.

FOUR DAYS BEFORE THEIR DEPARTURE, DARCY'S CONCERNS FOR GEORGIANA increased. She was less animated, less voluble, and less inclined towards company. Although she was as polite as usual with her brother and aunt, her only interests seemed to be Mist, Didi, and her piano.

In a desperate measure, Darcy proposed that they pay a brief call on the Gardiners to make their farewells; he hoped the presence of the children and a visit to her favourite park might help her mood.

His plan had moderate success. The Gardiners were surprised yet happy to receive them. The introductions were slightly awkward, but the children showed no restraint in embracing Georgiana and asking about her pets. Mrs. Gardiner spoke about Derbyshire and Lambton, and Georgiana allowed herself to be engaged in the conversation.

When they left, though, she became rather quiet again and answered Darcy's questions only briefly, expressing her favourable opinion about the Gardiners.

Once they were at home, a surprise appearance changed their daily schedule. In the drawing room, Bingley was waiting for them while he enjoyed a glass of brandy. To Darcy's disbelief, Georgiana seemed delighted to receive their friend.

"I just arrived in Town, and I hurried to call on you. And you are leaving for Pemberley, I understand? I thought you had cancelled the trip since it is so late and the Season will soon start."

"We are happy to see you, Bingley. Come—let us sit. No, we did not cancel our journey, quite the contrary. We plan to remain at Pemberley at least until next spring."

"Yes, we are not fond of the Season; in this, William and I are very much alike." Georgiana smiled.

"Oh, do not let him influence you! He is a real ogre and a solitary one. Once you are out, I promise to take you to all the parties and balls in Town." Bingley laughed, gently kissing the young girl's hand.

Georgiana blushed. "I will use your metaphor and confess that I am a solitary ogre since I completely share my brother's feelings on the subject. Now please tell us more of you and your sisters. They are in good health, I hope?"

"Yes, they are; they just arrived home with me. But I did not tell them I was visiting you, or they would have been here by now too. I have disturbed you without warning, and that is enough for one day. Oh, and no man in his right mind would compare you to an ogre, but with Darcy, it is a different story," Bingley said, well humoured.

"It is always comforting to know you have a loyal friend who appreciates you fairly," Darcy responded with mocking severity.

Drinks and refreshments were served, and the group was happily completed by the arrival of Lady Hardwick. Her ladyship greeted their guest with warm politeness. The countess had been partial to Charles Bingley since the day she first met him but less so his sisters; therefore, she did not inquire after them.

Darcy was exceedingly content to see his friend in better spirits than when he left town and Georgiana so at ease in talking to him.

"So you have spent these last two months in Oxfordshire?" Lady Hardwick started the conversation.

"Yes, Mr. Hurst's cousin—Edmund Spencer—invited us all for the summer, but I returned earlier."

"I know the Spencers; the estate is lovely, I assume."

"It is, your ladyship, and quite large."

"Better than the one you rented in Hertfordshire?" the countess asked, and Bingley paled, glancing at Darcy.

"No...not at all...Netherfield is a fairly good property. It must be even more pleasant in the summer. I rented it last September, so I would not know."

"How is that possible? You are a landlord now. You should take care of your estate. Just ask Darcy—he takes care of his own and two of mine. I am sure he would be happy to provide you with boring business advice," Lady Hardwick said teasingly.

Bingley coloured, and Darcy observed his uneasiness. He attempted to intervene in the conversation that Lady Hardwick—without realising—had directed towards a sensitive subject that still appeared to affect Bingley.

"Yes...well, I am not quite a landlord. I do not think I will keep it...I am considering giving it up..." Bingley mumbled.

"Really? Are you displeased with the estate? Or with the neighbourhood?"

"No...quite the contrary...I left Netherfield last November, and I have not returned since. My sister suggested I should give it up...and Darcy supported that suggestion."

It was Darcy's turn to lose a bit of composure as both ladies looked at him. The countess turned to Bingley again.

"Forgive me, my dear, I do not mean to intrude. You seem unwilling to speak of it. I imagine you were truly disappointed in it since you abandoned it after only two months."

"Yes, I was very excited...it is a beautiful estate...and the house...the neighbourhood is quite lovely too. I had a most pleasant time there. Probably the most pleasant I can remember..." Bingley's pained voice and gloomy countenance were evident to his companions.

The countess smiled. "Well, well...my dear boy, do I sense a matter of the heart? What else could induce you to leave so quickly a place you seem to be so fond of?"

Bingley stared at her ladyship, his eyes and mouth open in astonishment. Georgiana blushed at her aunt's daring and rather improper questions.

Darcy stepped forward. "Aunt Amelia, I suggest we change the subject. Bingley is clearly uncomfortable, and I would be too in his place."

"I am sure Bingley knows I inquire only because I am fond of him and wish him nothing but the best. And I know a thing or two about matters of the heart myself."

"I do not doubt that," the gentleman replied. "I am fond of your ladyship too, and I have always been honoured and touched by your affection. It is just rather painful to speak of it."

"It must be serious since your usual, charming smile has faded and your liveliness has all but disappeared. Only suffering from love can bring such changes in a young man like you."

"Aunt, please. This is not a proper conversation for any of us," Darcy intervened again more severely. But Bingley took a seat closer to her ladyship.

"I cannot deceive your ladyship. It was indeed a serious matter of the heart. I was quite charmed by a beautiful young lady I met in Hertfordshire, but unfortunately, she did not return my affection."

Georgiana covered her mouth with her hand to conceal her surprise, and Lady Hardwick touched Bingley's arm.

"I am very sorry for your disappointment, but I am even sorrier for the young lady herself, and I am certain she will soon regret it. I have rarely seen a young man with so many good qualities: kindness, amiability, honour, a good fortune, and handsome features. Any young woman would be happy to be your wife."

"Your ladyship is very generous," Bingley replied sadly. "But I do hope she will not come to regret it or to suffer for any reason. She is truly wonderful, and I cannot hold any grudge against her. I wish her nothing but happiness."

"And there is the proof of your admirable character, young man. I only hope you will find another lady to steal your kind, generous heart," the countess responded.

"I doubt that will happen soon," Bingley answered.

"It will happen; you must trust me on this. As for the present, I know suffering is painful and seems endless, but it is much better to discover another's true feelings earlier rather than later."

"That is true. Besides, there were some objections against her family too. So perhaps it was for the best that I left," Bingley added, glancing at Darcy again.

"Charles, may I offer you another drink?" the host intervened to change the subject, but Lady Hardwick would not have it.

"Objections? Of what kind? And who objected?"

"All sorts of objections—mostly related to her mother and sisters' lack of decorum. I did not mind it, but my sisters, and even Darcy, were quite opposed to them."

"I see...so your sisters and Darcy had objections..." The countess turned to her nephew. "I would like a glass of port, please, if your offer includes me too." While Darcy hurried to obey, she continued.

"May I inquire: What was her family's situation? I presume her dowry was not a substantial one?"

"Her father owns an estate close to Netherfield. And I imagine her dowry was not significant, but I never gave it any thought. Her character and her beauty were beyond any other considerations."

Lady Hardwick did not restrain her wonder. "I must admit that I am curious. Why would such a young lady reject your admiration and affection? Did she give you any reason?"

Bingley appeared surprised by the question. "She did not…I did not…I never confessed to her…I cannot say she rejected my affection. But I am certain she was aware of my feelings, and for a while, I had no doubt of hers."

"Forgive my curiosity. If you prefer, we can change the subject of our conversation as Darcy has repeatedly suggested. But I cannot help being puzzled. If you did not confess your feelings, then was she ever confident of your affection? Did you only presume the lack of hers? Then, you left Netherfield and have been suffering all these months without even being sure of the truth?"

"Aunt, such situations are difficult to judge from afar and dangerous even to attempt for anyone who is not acquainted with the entire matter. I shall not allow this visit to turn into a distressing one for my friend," Darcy interfered with a severity that admitted no opposition as he offered a glass to each of them.

The countess rolled her eyes in disapproval but took the offered drink. Bingley, however, seemed to ignore Darcy; his pallor increased, and he stared at Lady Hardwick, completely dazzled for a few moments.

Then he whispered, "It is not possible…I never…I believed…indeed, you are correct, your ladyship. That is precisely what I did."

He finally took the offered brandy, and as everyone drank, an awkward silence filled the chamber.

Georgiana spoke up shyly, clearing her throat and attempting to dissipate the difficult moment.

"I just met someone who is also from Hertfordshire—someone you might know quite well, sir. My brother told me she also lived in the neighbourhood of Netherfield. Do you remember a Miss Bennet?"

Bingley dropped his glass and stared at Georgiana, appearing to be lost in disbelief.

"Jane was in town?" he whispered.

Darcy rang for a servant to clean the shards and struggled to keep his countenance during the unpardonable circumstance born of his aunt's stubbornness. He quickly turned to his friend.

"No—it was Miss Elizabeth Bennet. But she returned to Longbourn a few days ago," he replied seriously.

"Oh…" Bingley hurried to pour another drink for himself.

"Miss Bennet is Miss Elizabeth's sister?" Georgiana inquired, puzzled by the turn of events.

"Yes," Darcy and Bingley replied together, and the latter continued, resuming his seat.

"Was Miss Elizabeth in good health? Was she alone in town? I know she was very fond of Jane…Miss Bennet…and they were rarely separated."

"Yes…from what I learned, Miss Elizabeth was in Town to offer support to her uncle and aunt. She took care of her young cousins; that is how I met her…in the park. It was a happy coincidence."

Bingley seemed to struggle to understand Georgiana's answer.

"I see…I am sorry I did not return. Miss Elizabeth is a most pleasant young lady. And very handsome…I always admired her. I would have enjoyed seeing her again."

"I liked Miss Elizabeth very much indeed," Georgiana admitted. "I am glad you approve of her."

"I most certainly do. Who would not? Did I mention she is very smart? Jane—I mean Miss Bennet—used to say Miss Elizabeth was smarter than many gentlemen. She surely is smarter than I am; I give her that. And she is also very affectionate and caring. Do you know she walked more than three miles from Longbourn to Netherfield to take care of her sister who had fallen ill?"

Bingley's mumbled recollections troubled Darcy as much as they amused Georgiana and the countess. It was not difficult for the ladies to guess that, behind the many praises for Miss Elizabeth, the recipient of Bingley's interest was still Miss Jane Bennet—whose name was only mentioned in haste.

"We can easily recognise the Miss Elizabeth we know in your description," the countess said. "Darcy was rather reluctant to give us any details about her."

"Aunt —" Darcy attempted to intervene.

"I am not surprised to hear that," Bingley answered. "Darcy has never approved of the Bennet family, and I cannot blame him for that. Their manners are not always what propriety or decorum require. But the two eldest Miss Bennets are beyond reproach."

"I never said otherwise," Darcy admitted. "Bingley, since is quite late, would you like to join us for dinner?"

"Thank you, but I cannot. Miss Darcy, Lady Hardwick, it was such a pleasure to see you today, and I hope to meet you again before your departure."

Farewells were taken, but a moment before Bingley left, the countess called to him.

"Mr. Bingley, I was just thinking…since our journey to the North will take us close to Hertfordshire, it would be a lovely opportunity for us to visit the estate that you so praised and perhaps to stay a day or two there. Such a pity that you gave up on it and will not be there to receive us," Lady Hardwick said.

Her words left Bingley dumbfounded in the middle of the large hall while Darcy threw a glare filled with reproach towards his aunt. Her ladyship elegantly turned her back, took her niece's arm, and walked towards the dining room.

The two gentlemen stared at each other in silence for a moment before Bingley stepped hesitantly towards his carriage.

DURING DINNER, DARCY WAS MOSTLY SILENT. HE DISAPPROVED OF HIS aunt's inquisitive approach to his friend and her tactless conversation on a subject that obviously made Bingley anxious.

But the countess looked quite pleased with herself, and Georgiana was no different. His sister was clearly pleased that the conversation with Bingley confirmed her positive opinion of Elizabeth. Darcy alone was determined to avoid any reference to the Bennets—and especially to *her*.

"Miss Jane Bennet must be a remarkable beauty," Georgiana said suddenly.

"Yes, she is," Darcy agreed.

"Is she as spirited as Miss Elizabeth?" the countess asked.

"Not at all."

"Do you disapprove more of her or of Miss Elizabeth?" the countess continued.

Darcy struggled to remain calm. "I believe we already discussed this. I beg you not to open the subject again."

"Forgive me for being exceedingly curious. However, while I understand your consideration that a friendship with someone below her situation in life would be inappropriate for Georgiana, I cannot comprehend for the life of me why you believe that a gentleman's daughter, exceptionally beautiful and impeccably mannered, is unfit for a young man whose fortune was made in trade. Just as I find it hard to accept that Miss Bennet's family is objectionable for their behaviour since Bingley's sisters are so far from perfection themselves. Not to mention some of your own relatives."

Georgiana chuckled and quickly swallowed some fresh water. Darcy frowned as the countess continued.

"Bingley is a good man but not very self-confident. He looks up to you with so much admiration that he would never doubt anything you say, nor would he dare question the truth of your opinions or make decisions against your advice. When one has such a loyal friend, it is wise to refrain from making judgements that might affect such a friend's life to the point where he could lose his chance for happiness."

Darcy met his aunt's gaze and held it for a moment, hesitating to give an answer. Her eyebrows rose in challenge.

"Would you not agree, Nephew?"

"Your ladyship is more often right than not," he replied, forcing a smile.

The evening ended with another lovely performance from Georgiana. Elizabeth Bennet's name was not mentioned again, but Darcy felt it was still in everybody's thoughts.

Chapter 10

At noon two days later, after a morning spent with his solicitors, Darcy received a note from Bingley, asking to join him at the club. He was first tempted to invite Bingley to his house but abandoned the thought. If Bingley wanted to meet at either of their homes, he would have suggested it. He probably wished a private meeting to avoid any interference from their families

However, the moment he entered the carriage, he regretted his acceptance: the weather was unbearably warm, and inside the carriage, the air was impossible to breathe.

The club appeared mostly empty, and Bingley awaited him in obvious impatience at a secluded table.

"Thank you for coming. There is something important I must speak to you about. It is hot outside, is it not? London is not a proper place to be in summer."

"Bingley, you look ill. What is the matter?"

"Nothing is the matter; I mean—I had a bad night. Several bad nights actually."

They enjoyed a glass of brandy then Bingley continued.

"Have you read the newspapers recently? I made a shocking discovery. Can you imagine that the youngest Miss Bennet—Lydia—wedded Mr. Wickham a few days ago?"

"Yes, I know."

"It was quite unexpected, was it not? I remembered him having an inclination towards Miss Elizabeth; of course, she was too smart to enter into such an imprudent marriage. But her younger sister? How will they live? I doubt Mr. Bennet has much to offer as a dowry."

"Bingley, did you bring me here to speak of Wickham? I must be honest with you: if I had known, I never would have left my house in such impossible weather."

"No, not at all. I want to ask you...I am considering returning to Hertfordshire. To open Netherfield again. What do you think?" Bingley's voice and eyes showed his resolution about the plan and his anxiety to hear his elder friend's opinion.

Darcy was not surprised by the news after Bingley's conversation with Lady Hardwick. More than eight months had passed since Bingley left Netherfield, and he still seemed as troubled as he was in the first days. Any incentive was enough to encourage him to return. But still—he seemed to expect Darcy's approval.

He swallowed more brandy, choosing his words carefully. "Charles, I think you should be confident in your own decisions. If you want to open Netherfield, you should go to it."

Bingley's eyes widened in surprise. "Truly? But last November you said it would be better for me to give up any connections with Hertfordshire!"

"I know what I said. At that time, I was certain that I was acting for your benefit. I hope you believe that I was convinced my points were valid and that your happiness could not possibly lie in Hertfordshire. I still cannot say beyond any doubt whether I was right or wrong. But what I have learnt in these past months is that I am in no position to give you advice on such personal matters."

"So you agree with my plan? I should like to know I have your approval."

Darcy concealed his uneasiness behind a tentative smile.

"I do not deserve such consideration from you. There is something more that I have to confess, and I am afraid it will upset you—and rightfully so."

"What are you saying, Darcy? I could never be upset with you."

Their glasses were refilled, and Bingley watched him with curiosity. Darcy finally met his gaze.

"In the winter, Miss Bennet—Jane Bennet—was in town for three months. She stayed with her uncle and aunt in Gracechurch Street. I did not meet her personally, but your sisters told me that she visited them and they returned the call. I purposely concealed this fact from you, and I have no excuse for it. My interference in your affairs was absurd and impertinent."

Bingley's face coloured as he frowned. He seemed to struggle to understand what he heard, blinking and swallowing as he stared at his companion.

"You are telling me she was in town all that time and came to my house, and I was not informed?"

"Yes…I cannot do anything but apologise again and hope for your forgiveness."

"You concealed such extraordinary news from me although you knew how important it was? If you were convinced of her indifference, why would you keep her from me?"

Bingley's voice rose in anger, and the few club members in attendance glanced at them. He breathed deeply, gulped his brandy, and glared sharply at Darcy.

"I never would have expected such a betrayal from you. You are not the honourable man I thought you were, and I will never forgive you. What excuse do you have for your outrageous behaviour?"

"None. It was only a preposterous presumption that I knew what was best for you. I do not deserve your forgiveness."

Bingley asked for more drinks, and as their glasses were filled again, he glared steadily at his friend.

"What if Jane Bennet's feelings were not what you led me to believe? What if she suffered at my departure? What if she felt only half of the pain I had to bear? How will you ever compensate for her sorrow since you did not care for mine?"

Darcy's fingers clenched his glass, but he found no reply.

Bingley took another sip of brandy and inquired further. "Why are you telling me all this now?"

"My confession was long overdue. I could not allow you to return to Netherfield without knowing the entire truth. And I still have something to add. As you know, I met Miss Elizabeth in Kent last April. I have reason to believe that her opinion is the reverse of mine regarding her sister's feelings for you. And Mr. Bennet—to whom I talked a few days ago—inquired after you in quite a friendly manner."

Bingley's countenance expressed complete disbelief. "You think I have reason to hope for a fair reception?"

"I do. But please allow me another moment—there is something more that I must tell you since you will surely hear about it upon your return to Hertfordshire."

"Is there more? Have you done anything else to hurt Miss Bennet? Perhaps together with my sisters?"

The words sounded spiteful, but Darcy could not blame his younger friend.

"It is about Wickham. As you guessed, his marriage was not a regular one. He left his regiment because of his creditors…he had debts of a thousand pounds. He convinced Lydia to elope with him, and he agreed to marry her only after his debts were paid and a new commission purchased for him."

Bingley forgot to breathe. He brushed his fingers through his hair and asked for coffee.

"I must give up brandy if I want to keep track of all this news," he declared. "How on earth do you know all this?"

"Wickham hid in London, and Mr. Bennet searched for them for days. Miss Bennet—Elizabeth, I mean—asked me for help."

"You helped the Bennets to track Wickham?" Bingley asked.

"Yes—is that so astonishing? Do you not believe me capable of a charitable gesture?"

"It is astonishing—not that you offered your assistance but the entire story. If only I had been in London…I cannot imagine how much Jane must have suffered. If I could have done something to help them too…"

"There was nothing more you could have done. It was fortunate that I knew the scoundrel's den very well. It was no effort at all—except to restrain myself from strangling him. I only inform you now because you will surely hear the rumours, and Miss Bennet herself might still be distressed about her sister's marriage."

"I thank you—it was a very considerate gesture. I must leave now. This meeting has proved to be most shocking. I did not expect such a disclosure. I must think more on it…"

"Bingley, I apologise again. I hope you know how much I value your friendship and how fond I am of you, although this cannot compensate for my wrongs to you."

Bingley gave him another stern look.

"I will leave for Netherfield in a few days, and I will try to renew my acquaintance with the Bennets. I expect you to visit me on your way to Pemberley."

Darcy averted his eyes. "I cannot promise that. My plans are not fixed yet. It depends on many things. Besides, Georgiana and my aunt…"

"From what they told me, they are anxious to see Netherfield. I shall not insist further, but you should remember that I await your visit."

The short ride from the club to his house was filled with heat and distress. Darcy was relieved by his confession to Bingley. He regretted the pain caused to his friend—by both his past actions and the present disclosure. But it had to be done, and it was for the best.

Bingley was angry and disappointed, but at least he was prepared for what to expect on his return to Netherfield. And it proved to Darcy once more how wrong he had been in thinking Bingley's feelings only a mere infatuation. Perhaps Bingley had been in love many times *before* but not *after* Miss Jane Bennet. His heart seemed to belong only to her. Whether Miss Bennet's feelings were similar to Bingley's, whether their connection would be bonded by a wedding, and whether their marriage would be a happy one or not, only God could know for sure, and only the future would prove it. He—Darcy—had no right and no business to interfere ever again.

The carriage stopped at his destination, and Darcy quickly emerged. He was immediately hit by a wave of heat and hurried inside, but at the door, Watts was waiting for him.

"Sir, you are expected at Lady Hardwick's house immediately. The countess is ill; the doctor was fetched and is already there."

Darcy was momentarily paralysed with astonishment, and he needed all his strength to move. His steps—as hasty as possible—seemed painfully slow, and it felt like hours before he arrived there.

In the main hall were three servants and the housekeeper, who tried to give them orders to which nobody listened. At Darcy's entrance, silence fell upon them.

"Where is my aunt?" he cried. "What happened?"

"Lady Hardwick fell in the music room...she was with Miss Darcy. We could not wake her for a long time. The doctor is with her now...he said to wait here..."

He considered going to her ladyship's apartment but hesitated.

"My sister is with Lady Hardwick?" he inquired.

"No, sir, only the doctor and her maid are with the mistress. Miss Darcy must be in her apartment. I am not sure, but there is no other place she can be," the housekeeper replied hesitantly.

That answer increased Darcy's uneasiness. He thought Georgiana might have returned home, but he banished that thought; surely, she would not abandon their aunt. He hastened upstairs and knocked on his sister's door, but no answer came. Carefully, he pushed open the door and entered the small hall. Not a single sound could be heard, and he thought she had fallen asleep. He opened the door to her bedchamber and entered, looking towards the bed. Georgiana sat in the middle of it, her arms closed around her knees gathered at her chest. He called her, but she did not appear to hear him. He sat by her, gently calling her name.

"Dearest, what are you doing here? Are you hurt?"

She remained silent, and he stroked her hair.

"My dear, tell me what is wrong?"

"How is Aunt Amelia?" she murmured.

"The doctor is with her—we will have to wait. I am sure she will be fine. We just have to see what the doctor advises us. We will take care of her."

"It happened the same with our mother...she fell down while I played the piano...and she never woke up again," she whispered with the incoherence of a troubled child.

Darcy was speechless. He embraced her tightly, wondering how he could possibly comfort her. He remembered something that was lost in the recesses of his memory: after a long illness, when everybody hoped she was recovering, Lady Anne died one day as she listened to her daughter playing the piano. Georgiana was six.

He kissed his sister's hands. "My dearest, I am sorry that I was not with you back then. But I am here now. I will ring for some tea, and we will wait together. Let us hope and pray."

With great effort, Darcy managed to bring her to a reasonable state, but her fingers still trembled so badly that she could not hold the cup.

Minutes passed painfully slowly; finally, Dr. Miller finished his examination and offered a calm answer to their anxious inquiries.

"Her ladyship's state is as good as can be expected at her age. The fainting fit was mostly due to this uncommon heat; she has suffered such weaknesses several times in the past."

"Has she? I was not aware of it," Darcy replied.

"Well, she is surely not the kind of lady to alert people to any discomfort. I recommend she avoid going out in the sun. If she wishes to take a stroll, early in the morning or after sunset would be the proper times. And she should rest as must as possible—any useless effort should be avoided."

"Yes, of course," Darcy answered as Georgiana asked permission to see her.

"Of course, her ladyship is already inquiring after Miss Darcy. She can do whatever she pleases if she gives proper consideration to my advice. I shall come to see her again tomorrow."

While Georgiana hurried to her aunt, Darcy showed the doctor to his carriage. He inquired again whether there were other things to be cautious about, and the doctor assured him he had no reason for extensive worry.

"We have plans to leave for Pemberley soon. Should we postpone them?"

"Mr. Darcy, if your plans are not urgent, my advice would be to avoid travelling in such hot weather. However, as I said, I have no reason to believe her ladyship's life would be in danger—only her comfort. But a long journey in such extreme warmth might be difficult for anyone."

"Very well, Dr. Miller, we will do as you recommend. There is nothing so urgent as to be worth even the smallest danger. We shall expect your visit again tomorrow."

The doctor's words put some of Darcy's concerns to rest, but others remained to trouble him. He was in the position of changing his plans again, and he needed to make adjustments, but he did not hesitate a single moment. His aunt's well-being was not to be disregarded.

His worry for Georgiana tightened his chest, and he was at a loss as to what would be the best course of action. She possessed a kind of sensibility that often disturbed her tranquillity. Her own reactions were obviously harming her, and he was helpless to know how to assist her. Her balance —her peace—had been so deeply shaken during the last year that her recovery appeared to be laborious and grievous.

Pensive, he went to his aunt's apartment, asking permission to see her. Lady Hardwick was in her bed, impeccably arranged as always, and Didi, lying at her feet, watched her carefully. Darcy kissed the countess's hand.

"Your ladyship looks better than most people even when she is unwell," he complimented her. "It seems we worried for nothing."

"Oh, you flatterer…come and sit here. I was telling this sweet girl that you were silly to worry over nothing. I am as fine as ever. This heat is horrible. Who has ever seen such weather in London? For Heaven's sake, it reminds me of India!"

"I have never been to India, so I shall take your word for it," Darcy answered, glancing at Georgiana, whose face had lost none of its earlier pallor. "And speaking of travelling, we will delay our journey to Pemberley for a few weeks. September will surely be a much better month for spending three days on the road."

"Dear nephew, please do not change your plans for me," the countess said.

"Aunt, it is already decided. Now, did I mention that I met Bingley today at the club? He gave me some news that I believe will cheer you both. He has decided to open Netherfield again, and he will leave for Hertfordshire within a few days."

He did not miss Georgiana's mirth or Lady Hardwick's pleased grin.

"Well, I have always admired young men who decide to remedy their wrongs. I dare say he will not be bothered by the warm weather. But then again, he is three times younger than I am."

"Your ladyship is three times stronger than most of us," Darcy replied. "Now, Georgiana and I will let you rest, and we will return to see you in the evening."

During the following two days, Darcy divided his time equally between the two houses. When he had a moment of calm, his mind wandered towards Hertfordshire, wondering what Elizabeth was doing, but he never allowed that disturbing thought to last more than an instant.

He received a report that Wickham had arrived at his new regiment and taken over his new commission; he knew there were few reasons for joy though. Wickham was incapable of keeping any honourable profession for long, and he feared he had not heard the last of it. The same day, a letter also arrived from Mr. Gardiner, informing him about the newly wedded couple's arrival at their destination and containing almost a page with expressions of gratitude, which Darcy quickly gave up reading.

On an impulse, he sent a reply to Mr. Gardiner, inviting him for a drink. Besides his interest in hearing more news of Elizabeth—which Darcy barely admitted to himself—he recognised that he truly enjoyed Mr. Gardiner's —as well as Mr. Bennet's—company, particularly as he had missed male companionship in the last months.

Before dinner, however, he was bothered by the unexpected arrival of Miss Caroline Bingley. At the announcement, he first worried that something had happened to Charles to justify such an improper visit. However, he was quickly proved wrong.

"Mr. Darcy, you must help me stop a disaster; you are our only hope as Charles refuses to listen to us and is determined to bring ruin to our family."

"Miss Bingley! What a surprise."

"Sir, Charles has decided to return to Netherfield tomorrow. As sly as he is, he only informed us today. It is easy to guess what his intentions are. I thought he had abandoned that madness, but I fear he wishes to pursue Jane Bennet again!"

"This seems like Bingley's personal business; it has nothing to do with me."

"But, sir, you know only too well that any connection with the Bennets would be a tragedy. You agreed that such an alliance would mean my brother's misfortune and misery. You must do something. Charles will undoubtedly listen to you."

"May I offer you something to drink?"

"To drink? No indeed—I have not a moment to lose. I have come to ask that you accompany me and talk some sense into Charles."

Darcy poured himself a glass of wine.

"I apologise if my previous injudicious interference led you to believe that I have any intention of repeating it. Sharing my unwarranted opinion on a matter that only concerned Bingley was a mistake that I will struggle to avoid in the future. Bingley is an honourable man who evidently knows his mind and his heart well enough to make the right decisions."

Caroline Bingley grimaced in astonishment.

"What do you mean, sir? Surely, you are joking; this cannot be!"

"Miss Bingley, it is not my intention to be disrespectful, but if there is nothing else I can help you with, I must go to my aunt's house. Please convey to Bingley my wishes for a safe and easy journey. Now—may I show you to your carriage? I am in quite a hurry."

A still dumbstruck Caroline Bingley was elegantly escorted out by a decided Darcy who helped her into her carriage and sent her away before she could form any further insistence or opposition.

As the carriage started to move, Darcy meditated that he had just made the first step to remedy one of his many faults: that ridiculous alliance with Bingley's sisters against his friend's wishes.

A Man with Faults

ALMOST A FORTNIGHT HAD PASSED SINCE ELIZABETH RETURNED HOME. The newly wedded Wickhams visited Longbourn briefly on their way to his new regiment, but the meeting went as expected: great excitement from Lydia, Kitty, and Mrs. Bennet, indifference from Mr. Bennet, and reserved politeness from Elizabeth, Jane, and Mary. As for the people of Meryton, whether their congratulations and good wishes were genuine or not was difficult to say.

The joy of reunion with her mother and sisters, the relief of knowing Lydia's situation was resolved somewhat satisfactorily, and the comfort of having Jane's company made that time a happy one for Elizabeth. She told her eldest sister everything that had happened in London, including her upsetting visit to Mr. Darcy's house—a scene that had Jane in tears. And not without distress, the two sisters discussed the unfairness of the unanimous prejudice against Mr. Darcy and the injustice of the general appreciation for Mr. Wickham; neither hesitated to assume the largest part of guilt for their mistake.

Mr. Bennet's admiration for Mr. Darcy made him mention the latter's name frequently, but Mrs. Bennet could only remember his refusal to dance with Lizzy, his pride, and his arrogant manners. She refused to believe that Mr. Wickham would not have married Lydia of his own will.

Elizabeth resumed her habit of taking long strolls, sheltered from the warmth under the shade of the trees.

Her thoughts often returned to London—to her relatives, to Georgiana and Lady Hardwick, and not rarely, to Darcy. She found herself thinking of him more than she did after she returned from Kent—and in a different way. Besides her gratitude towards him, she tried to find answers to questions about his behaviour, explanations for the gestures she never would have expected from him, and speculations about his future intentions. Small things would bring back recollections of him, and with no little distress, she realised he was vividly and constantly present in her mind. She hoped it would pass the moment her life returned to its usual rhythm, but she feared things would never be the same. Elizabeth was content to see that at least Jane looked more serene and less grieved than she had been a couple of months before. Even Mrs. Bennet spoke less about Mr. Bingley—apparently resigned to their betrayal by the master of Netherfield.

Elizabeth's relative peace was disturbed one day on receipt of two letters:

one from Georgiana—which Elizabeth opened with joy and excitement —and the other from Mrs. Gardiner, part of their regular correspondence. She first opened her aunt's note and was astonished to read—among the usual information about the family—that Mr. Gardiner had been invited to have a drink with Mr. Darcy one day. What could be the meaning of this? Once Lydia's marriage was accomplished, was Mr. Darcy still desirous of her uncle's presence? Was he still seeking the company of someone who was in trade and lived near Cheapside? Surely, he could not have any interest in extending their acquaintance. Was it possible that Mr. Darcy's interest in Mr. Gardiner was amiable and genuine?

Elizabeth took the letter from Miss Darcy with equal eagerness and anxiety. While reading, she found that the Darcys had not left Town yet and would remain for another couple of weeks because the countess had difficulty bearing the warm weather. Georgiana had written purposely to inform her about the family's plans, and Elizabeth wondered whether Mr. Darcy had any knowledge of it. Had he given his consent for a regular correspondence? Should she write Georgiana in return?

She scolded herself for her childish reaction. Had she lost her reason? Why would she set her mind upon Mr. Darcy and judge even the smallest happenstance from his perspective?

Elizabeth shared her doubts with Jane, who listened to her with calm but could offer no clear opinion or answer to Elizabeth's inquiries.

The following day, however, it was Jane's turn to suffer the turmoil of a most unexpected report—shared by Mrs. Bennet and loud enough to be heard from Meryton.

"Oh, my dear Mr. Bennet—you cannot guess what I heard! Girls, where are you? Jane, Lizzy—come here! I understand that the housekeeper at Netherfield has received orders to prepare for the arrival of her master. Mr. Bingley is coming to shoot here in the country for a few weeks. What do you think?"

Elizabeth cast a glance at Jane, who turned completely pale; she had no time to speak a single word as Mrs. Bennet continued.

"Well, I for one do not care much about it. He is nothing to us, and I am sure I never want to see him again. But he may come if he wishes; it is his estate after all."

None of the girls spoke much on the subject and Mr. Bennet even less. As she watched her sister carefully, Elizabeth could not stop wondering about the sudden return of Mr. Bingley and Mr. Darcy's possible connection to it. He knew the former had been away from London, and most likely, he had returned in the middle of the summer. Had he spoken with Mr. Darcy? Elizabeth wavered as to the greater probability of Mr. Bingley's coming there with his friend's permission or being bold enough to come without it. Whether he was still partial to Jane or not, Elizabeth did not even dare consider.

"Mr. Bennet, you will visit him as soon as he arrives," Mrs. Bennet instructed her husband.

He barely lifted his eyes from his book. "I shall do no such a thing; it cost me a lot of time and effort to visit him last autumn as you promised me he would marry one of our girls. Did he? Not at all. Just look at Mr. Wickham—he married one of my daughters without my taking the trouble of even greeting him or speaking to him. I think I like my present son-in-law better than my ex-future to-be one," Mr. Bennet responded with sharp mockery to Mrs. Bennet's complete distress.

When the noise finally ended and they were alone, Jane said, "Lizzy, I know I appeared distressed, but do not imagine it is from any silly cause. I do assure you that the news does not affect me with either pleasure or pain."

"I am glad to hear that, dearest," Elizabeth replied, her voice even less convincing than Jane's was.

Elizabeth could easily perceive that her sister's spirits were affected by the surprising news. She was more disturbed and less calm than ever before. And with each passing hour, Jane's distress seemed to increase.

The next day, a soft breeze cooled the summer weather, and while the rest of the family retired for an afternoon's rest, Elizabeth took Jane for a walk. Arm in arm, they enjoyed the fresh air, sharing thoughts and concerns, when the sound of a horse startled them. They barely had time to turn around before seeing Mr. Bingley pull harshly on the reins of his horse, which halted inches from them.

He dismounted and stepped hesitantly, his eyes searching them, while Jane tightened her grip on Elizabeth's arm and began to breathe strangely.

"Miss Bennet, Miss Elizabeth! What a surprise to meet you here! A very pleasant one, I assure you. I did not expect to see you so soon," he mumbled while Elizabeth smiled, put her hand on Jane's to comfort her, and curtseyed to the gentleman.

"Mr. Bingley, we are happy to see you too. We heard of your arrival, so it was not quite a surprise, but we did not expect to see you on your horse just now."

"Well, I lacked the patience to stay in the carriage for so long in such warm weather. My sisters are in the carriage...they will arrive in an hour or so...excuse me, are you in good health? Your sisters, your parents?"

He spoke to Elizabeth, but he tried to steal a glimpse at Jane, whose colour changed from moment to moment. Elizabeth smiled again, her doubts about both the gentleman and the lady suddenly disappearing.

"Well, I am not a rider, so I cannot understand that, but since you have arrived earlier, perhaps you would like some drinks and refreshments? The journey from London is a short but not an easy one."

Bingley's face brightened, and he could not conceal a large grin.

"Thank you; you are very considerate. I would like that very much, but I do not want to intrude. I would not want to bother your parents or sisters..."

"They will all be happy to see you again, I assure you," Elizabeth replied. Jane only nodded, her cheeks and neck flushed, her eyes meeting Bingley's only for an instant.

The gentleman's face soon matched Jane's.

"Please allow me to accompany you on your way home. This is indeed a most pleasant surprise."

Bingley's arrival turned Longbourn into a cacophony of voices and cries, which were unsuccessfully suppressed. Mrs. Bennet was beyond herself with excitement while Mr. Bennet took the trouble to leave his library and greet the gentleman.

Drinks and refreshments were served, and when everybody eventually reached a state of relative calm, Mrs. Bennet inquired:

"Sir, may I ask why you have been away for so long and what fortunate occurrence finally brought you back? You were very much missed, and it was a pity to see Netherfield abandoned."

He appeared embarrassed, and he was saved by the glass of wine from which he gulped greedily.

"I thank you, madam, you are very kind. I also missed all my friends from Hertfordshire. It was a hasty decision to resign from Netherfield last winter—one that I intend to remedy."

"I am glad to hear that," Mrs. Bennet answered with unconcealed contentment. "Have you been in Town all this time?"

"Not at all; in fact, I was rarely in London this year. I was quite surprised to discover that Miss Bennet, Miss Elizabeth, and Mr. Bennet were in Town during the last months, and I deeply regret that I was unaware of their visits. My friend Darcy just gave me the news a few days ago when we discussed my return to Hertfordshire."

Elizabeth and Jane both paled, although for different reasons. Mr. Bingley's confession was enough to put an end to one's distress and to increase the other's. And to allow no doubt or speculation, he concluded:

"During Mr. Bennet and Miss Elizabeth's stay, I was unfortunately in Oxfordshire, but with regard to Miss Bennet's visit last winter, although I was at home, I was not informed until recently."

"We are glad that you returned, sir; that is all that matters," Jane finally spoke, blushing most becomingly and melting Bingley's heart.

"I am very glad too…very glad indeed…oh, and Miss Elizabeth, I forgot to mention: Miss Darcy and Lady Hardwick spoke very highly of you. They might even stop and visit us on their way to Pemberley. I hope Darcy will comply with their wishes. I insisted that he do so."

"Truly? I would like to see Miss Darcy and Lady Hardwick very much. I believe everything depends on Mr. Darcy's will, as always," Elizabeth attempted to joke.

"True—Darcy likes to always have his way," Bingley said lightly, relaxed and pleased with the progress of his visit. "It is fortunate that he is so clever that he is rarely wrong, and generous to admit it when he is. I hope he will come to visit; after all, he encouraged me to pursue my decision to return to Netherfield. I did not need his approval, but I was happy to have it nevertheless."

"I look forward to seeing Mr. Darcy again; in truth, I have rarely met such a remarkable gentleman," Mr. Bennet added.

Mrs. Bennet expressed her point of view decidedly. "But you must admit that his manners could benefit from a little softening, and his dancing habits at balls need much improvement."

Her daughters blushed in embarrassment, Mr. Bennet rolled his eyes in exasperation, and Bingley laughed in approval.

The conversation soon became a friendly exchange, and Mr. Bingley became more animated with each glass of wine, so nobody noticed that

Elizabeth was becoming more silent with every passing minute.

MR. BINGLEY'S RETURN WAS THE TALK OF MERYTON, AND MRS. PHILIPS declared people were wagering about the length of his stay in the neighbourhood. It was said he planned to shoot for no longer than three weeks, but then the arrival of the rest of the family would not have been justified.

Neither Caroline Bingley nor the Hursts were much seen in the area. They spent all their time at Netherfield, to such a degree that some wondered whether they were truly there.

Mr. Bingley visited Longbourn regularly—Miss Bingley and Mrs. Hurst only once, for half an hour. They also issued an invitation to the eldest Bennet sisters, and Elizabeth suspected they had done it at the special request of their brother.

It was not difficult to observe that their arrogance and disdain towards the Bennets had not diminished in the slightest. Fortunately, Jane had grown wise enough to recognise their true character. As the superior sisters barely interacted at all with the rest of the Bennets, no offense was taken.

More significant to Jane was that the sisters' rudeness was greatly compensated for by the gentleman's amiability. Mr. Bingley's preference for Jane Bennet was soon a matter of universal knowledge, and although more restrained and elegantly concealed, the lady's affection was no longer a mystery.

Therefore, at the beginning of September, Mr. Bingley invited Miss Bennet and Miss Elizabeth for a short walk in the Longbourn gardens. Elizabeth found great interest in the study of some particular flowers, so her pace slowed considerably—to the satisfaction of Mrs. Bennet who was watching through the window.

A few minutes later, Jane and Mr. Bingley's flushed and glowing faces left little doubt about the outcome of their private conversation, and Elizabeth could only embrace both of them and wish them all the happiness in the world.

That day, after a brief conversation with Mr. Bennet, Mr. Bingley finally became engaged to Miss Jane Bennet almost a year after his first arrival in Hertfordshire, a bit of news that travelled to Meryton with the speed of light. Once again, the peace of the little town was stirred by an event that occurred in the Bennet family.

Mr. Bingley remained at Longbourn for dinner, and the excitement entertained them all until much later than usual. Elizabeth had to suffer another sleepless night, this time in listening to her sister's effusions of joy.

"Dearest Lizzy, how can I bear so much happiness? This cannot be—I do not deserve it. Oh, Lizzy, can you imagine? Only a month ago we were so devastated for poor Lydia…and I was certain I should never see him again. And now I am so blessed, so fortunate. He has loved me all this time, Lizzy. I will be Mrs. Bingley before Christmas. Is this real? I am afraid I am dreaming and will wake up soon. Lizzy, is he not the most handsome man? And the kindest. And his smile is so lovely…"

Jane rambled until long after midnight, and Elizabeth watched her mostly silently, her heart filled with love and excitement for her sister's well-deserved felicity. She briefly thought that she had not heard her sister speak so much and so incoherently all together in her entire life, but then again, she had never seen Jane so happy before either.

When she finally lay in her bed, her senses remained alert. Sleep was kept away by the recollections of another marriage proposal—the one addressed to her that brought so much turmoil and pain. It still hurt after more than five months and probably would never cease its torment.

Chapter 11

In London, September brought milder weather and the return of the ton, as well the start of preparations for the Season. The streets, the shops, and even the clubs became increasingly more crowded.

The countess's health seemed to be as good as ever, much to Darcy's satisfaction. He completed the arrangements for their journey north and was eager finally to begin it.

But there was another reason for his eagerness, one that he hardly admitted even to himself. The journey to Pemberley meant a short stop at Netherfield—and the chance to see Elizabeth Bennet one more time.

Although he "forced" himself to be happy when she left, and to feel relieved to have the protection of a great distance between them, his true feelings were quite different, and he struggled with them every night and every day when he had a moment of solitude.

He hoped that the meeting, which would surely trouble his life again, would be useful and comforting for Georgiana. She was still reluctant to leave the house and to confront the busy streets and noisy parks. The only people she was interested in were her aunt and her brother.

Therefore, she often declared she would be happy to meet Miss Lizzy again but appeared reserved at the idea of being introduced to so many new people. And Darcy saw his error once again: he had spoken so unflatteringly about the Bennet family when he first saw Georgiana with Elizabeth that it was no wonder she was reluctant to make their acquaintance.

Darcy spoke to his sister one afternoon while they were both reading in the library. "Dearest, I have good news. The Matlocks have returned to Town, and they are very anxious to see us. Lady Matlock invited us for dinner the day after tomorrow—perfect timing before we leave for Pemberley." Georgiana's interest was indicated only by a timid smile.

"I have missed uncle and aunt very much. And our cousins too. Is Richard still with his regiment?"

"I did not ask, but I will write Lady Matlock immediately."

"Would you please ask her who will attend the dinner party?" she pleaded shyly.

"My dear, I suspect it will be a family dinner since they have just returned home. So most likely, our uncle and aunt, Henry and his wife Eleanor, and hopefully Richard and the three of us if Lady Hardwick agrees to join us."

"Oh, I just realised that Cousin Eleanor has the same name as little Eleanor Gardiner." Georgiana smiled.

"Indeed. If you wish, we can pay another short visit to the Gardiners too."

"Perhaps...if we have time. We will leave for Pemberley in less than a week, you said. Now would you mind if I go to Aunt Amelia's house? I shall take a maid with me, and I would rather sleep there overnight to keep her company."

"As you prefer, dearest. But I will take you there; I feel more at peace that way."

"I thank you, William, but you must not worry about me. I am perfectly well."

He smiled and kissed her hand. She was not well, and he was worried.

Their curiosity about Richard Fitzwilliam was satisfied the same afternoon when the colonel unceremoniously barged into Darcy's house, greeting his cousin enthusiastically.

"I just arrived home, but I could not delay coming to see you. How have you been all these months? What news do you have? And how is Georgiana?"

"We are well enough. Let me pour you a drink. Are you hungry? I have quite a lot of news to share if you ask me."

"Really? Well, what are you waiting for? No, I am not hungry; our cook stuffed us with five incredible dishes. A glass of brandy would be perfect —or two. Share your news, and afterwards I will go to see the ladies."

Since Colonel Fitzwilliam was Georgiana's second guardian and Darcy's closest lifetime friend, there were few mysteries between them. Despite the differences in their natures, they had always trusted and supported each other.

Except for Lady Hardwick, Richard was the only one who knew all the details of his dealings with Wickham, about the scoundrel's plans to elope with Georgiana, and about his sister's painful "accident" that threatened her life.

The only secret Darcy did not—and would not—disclose to his cousin was the marriage proposal he made to Elizabeth in Kent. That was a memory to remain hidden in his heart and his mind and to torment his present and his future.

Not surprisingly, though, the moment Richard Fitzwilliam met Elizabeth, he had felt there was a strange connection between her and Darcy. Due to Darcy's strange manners towards the lady and her peculiar reaction to him, the colonel was confident the relationship between them was an uncommon one, but in what way he could not guess. However, he continued to tease Darcy about it whenever he had the chance, amused to see his cousin uncomfortable about the subject.

With their glasses filled, the two cousins began to talk. Since they had last met at the beginning of the summer, there were many stories to unfold.

An hour later, the colonel filled his glass for the third time.

"So that miscreant is now married to the youngest Bennet sister?"

"Sadly, yes."

"And how did you discover this event?" the colonel inquired.

"Clayton informed me first. But the details were related to me—you will not believe it—by Miss Elizabeth Bennet. She happened to be in Town, and they were desperate to discover the fugitives, so she came to my door, pleading for me to help her father and uncle."

"Miss Elizabeth Bennet...what a lovely young lady. I remember her saying more than once that the two of you were not friends, so I imagine it was difficult for her to apply to your generosity."

"More than you think. I was very surprised; I did not expect to see her," Darcy admitted. "But since I had Clayton watching Wickham, there was no difficulty on my part to discover him."

"But your involvement was much more than that. I am surprised Miss Bennet's father and uncle accepted your participation."

"They did not. We argued and fought to exhaustion—more than I could bear and more than Wickham deserved—but I left them no choice. I did everything that was my duty to resolve the situation to my own satisfaction."

"How did you manage to purchase the new commission for him after he evaded the militia?"

"Through General ——."

"Ah yes, I should have realised. Yet another honourable living provided for Wickham that he will waste."

"Most likely; I am sorry I have no reason to contradict you," Darcy replied.

The colonel turned angrier. "That idiot has tormented you and Georgiana too much in the last years. He broke your peace and put that sweet girl in danger more than once. Why on earth was I always away and never able to deal with him personally? I would surely have been more *convincing* than you."

"Perhaps. You are not a colonel for nothing," Darcy tried to mock him, but his cousin remained severe.

"And may I ask what the total sum was to ensure this wedding?"

Darcy cast a glance at his cousin and refilled his glass. "Around ten thousand pounds."

The colonel did not even blink. "I suspected as much."

"But you must swear your secrecy, Cousin. Except for Mr. Bennet and Mr. Gardiner, nobody knows the extent of my involvement, and it is my wish that it remain so. It is likely that Miss Elizabeth and Mrs. Gardiner suspect I made the purchase of the new commission possible since neither of the gentlemen had the connections for such an arrangement. But the financial details are private."

"As you wish," Colonel Fitzwilliam agreed. "But it would have cost you twenty times less to get rid of Wickham forever."

Darcy let out a bitter laugh. "Considering how much I have already wasted on the scoundrel, even having him murdered is not sufficient."

"I have to say I am puzzled: Why did you take such a burden upon yourself? The Bennets are not family—not even friends from what you told me. Why would you spend a fortune to save their reputation?"

Darcy knew his countenance had changed. He had addressed that question to himself many times, and he was not confident he had given himself an honest answer. But he repeated it to his cousin nevertheless.

"It was my fault and, therefore, my duty to remedy the situation. Starting with my beloved father, we all hold our share of blame in Wickham's misdeeds. We either excused or attempted to hide his behaviour and character. And I am more at fault than anyone. The moment I saw him in Meryton, I should have spoken with Colonel Forster and given him information about

Wickham's true inclinations. That at least would have warned him and induced him to supervise the rascal more closely."

Colonel Fitzwilliam's eyebrow rose in challenge. "That is nonsense. You have done more than anyone else has and, certainly, more than he deserved. You cannot live your life following Wickham and warning everyone about his character nor continue to pay his debts."

"I shall do that no longer. General —— knows Wickham's past, and he will be cautious with him. Besides, I own all his debts. I can throw him into debtors' prison whenever I please for my own amusement."

The colonel grinned. "Well, I would surely do that and then laugh at him, but you will not."

"Do not be so certain; I lack amusements lately," Darcy replied.

"Well, you have not been very amusing in the last months, I grant you that. I am content to see your mood slightly improved since I last saw you. I know too well that this time has been difficult for you, and I regret not being able to help you more."

"You helped me enough in that I know I can count on your support and advice. I have missed our conversations," Darcy declared.

"I imagine you found few gentlemen to spend time with in London during the summer. Conversely, I was only among gentlemen in my regiment. Neither of the options is ideal, I assure you. I need to see more lovely faces."

Darcy laughed. "Yes, London was quite deprived during the summer, although I was pleased to meet Mr. Bennet and his brother-in-law, Mr. Gardiner. Despite the unfortunate circumstances, I confess I found them enjoyable companions."

"Really? I have never heard you speak of Mr. Bennet before."

"I know. I wasted my time in Hertfordshire, despising the people I met rather than attempting to understand them. I could have spent entertaining moments talking of books with Mr. Bennet rather than listening to the nonsense spouted by Bingley's sisters and Hurst. My fault and my loss."

"I would like to meet these gentlemen sometime. By the way, is Miss Elizabeth Bennet still in Town? I would like to renew acquaintance with her too. Hers is one of the lovely faces I would enjoy anytime."

"No, she is not. They left the day of the wedding. As for Mr. Gardiner, I might invite him to have a drink with us one day."

"I would like that. What about Bingley? Is he around?"

"He returned to London, then he left…he decided to open Nether-field again."

"Did he? Well, well, quite a lot of news, indeed," the colonel said.

Darcy forced a smile. "I have another bit of news, or better said, an extraordinary coincidence. Georgiana and Aunt Amelia made a surprising acquaintance in the park—someone she quickly came to like and considers a friend."

"Georgiana made a new acquaintance in the park?" the colonel asked incredulously.

"Yes—without either knowing the true identity of the other. It was a genuine bonding between her…and Miss Elizabeth Bennet. They called each other 'Miss Anna' and 'Miss Lizzy.'"

"What on earth are you talking about, Darcy? Miss Elizabeth? But you said she was not in town anymore. We must have had too much brandy," the colonel concluded.

"Forgive me; let me try to be more clear because the story is quite astonishing…"

For another quarter hour, Darcy related to the colonel the final piece of news. He did not conceal his worry as he spoke of his sister's peculiar preference for choosing a park far from home and keeping her name hidden. He also confessed his improper reaction and the pain he caused his sister, as well as his eventual approval of correspondence between Georgiana and Elizabeth.

"Bingley invited us to visit him at Netherfield on our way to Pemberley, and both Georgiana and Aunt Amelia are delighted with the prospect of meeting Miss Bennet again," Darcy concluded. "What is your opinion of all this?"

The colonel appeared disconcerted. "I am astonished…very strange coincidence indeed. I am not surprised that Georgiana liked Miss Elizabeth Bennet. She is everything lovely and bright, and her manners are pleasing. Such a friendship would benefit Georgiana, I believe. I am still trying to understand why you would first oppose—what you held against Miss Elizabeth."

"There were many considerations, but I set everything aside and decided to allow Georgiana to do as she wishes."

"I fully support your decision. My only concern would have been related to Wickham. But since Georgiana knows of the wedding and is not troubled by it, I am willing not to give it more consideration than the man is worth."

"I was concerned about Wickham too, but now I worry about other things. I do not know what to do, Richard. Georgiana is more restrained every day. She hardly leaves the house. She refuses to go outside or to meet people. She declares she missed you and your parents but is reluctant to join you for dinner tomorrow evening. She agrees with anything I say and seems only to have interest in her pianoforte. I am not capable of understanding what troubles her, and I fear I cannot be as good a brother as she deserves."

"Darcy, all I can do is to take half your burden on my shoulders and offer you any help you might need. I do not understand Georgiana although I love her with all my heart. But I do know, beyond any doubt, that you are the best brother one could hope for, and you will surely find a way to alleviate her distress."

"You are too generous with me, Cousin. Now let us go to the ladies. They will be thrilled to see you. You have always been a ladies' favourite." Darcy attempted a joke to dissipate the tension of their previous conversation.

"I shall take that as a compliment although I am not certain it was meant that way," the colonel answered in mock seriousness.

As Darcy hoped, Georgiana was indeed happy to see her cousin and rewarded his visit with a large, joyful smile while he responded with an affectionate embrace.

They spoke for half an hour, and Georgiana even laughed a couple of times.

However, at the colonel's invitation, she declined to take a walk with him, but she promised they would have dinner together at the Matlocks in two days.

DARCY SPENT THE NEXT MORNING IN THE LIBRARY AS WAS HIS HABIT. IT was too early for breakfast, but he was already on his second cup of coffee.

To his contentment, preparations for travel were complete: luggage packed, horses and carriages prepared. Their journey was scheduled to begin in three days, and he decided not to allow anything to interfere with his plans.

On one of the remaining days, Darcy intended to pay another call to the Gardiners, together with Georgiana. The second day was dedicated to dinner with their relatives, and the last day was meant for rest.

The prospect of moving to Pemberley suddenly became the solution to all the problems they had faced lately. Pemberley meant peace, calm, and shelter. It meant home. He had been away too long and was eager to return. Nothing would delay them any longer.

His thoughts were interrupted by a knock on the door, and a servant entered before Darcy was able to dismiss him.

"Sir, I apologise for disturbing you, but an express has just arrived."

"An express? At this hour? From where?"

"From Hertfordshire," the servant answered, handing him the paper.

Darcy easily recognised Bingley's handwriting. Concerned about the nature of the urgency, he opened the letter eagerly and read, a smile growing with each word.

Darcy,

Today I proposed to Miss Bennet, and she accepted me. Mr. Bennet gave us his blessing, and we will marry in four weeks, the first Thursday after Michaelmas. Yes, so soon. I feel like the Heavens embraced me and God put his hand on my shoulder.

My sisters are upset and angry, and I hear only that I ruined our family name. But I could not care less. Jane's smile gives me strength and patience.

I am only sorry that I have nobody to drink with to celebrate my bliss.

If your plans are not yet fixed, I would like nothing better than for you to come to Netherfield a few days before my wedding and be at my side when I wed Jane. If you cannot, I will understand—I do not wish to interfere with your schedule. But I hope to see you soon nevertheless.

C. Bingley

Darcy read the erratic writing twice while his stomach tightened with excitement. Yes, it was an urgent matter indeed, one that his generous friend could not refrain from sharing with him.

As he read the news for the third time, two thoughts spun in Darcy's head. The first: How would he ever deserve Bingley's forgiveness for almost destroying his felicity? And second: Would he ever be granted just a small portion of such bliss?

Bingley deserved to be happy just as he deserved people around him to share his happiness, to support him, and to encourage him at the beginning of his new life. Bingley wanted his friend to be by his side, and he deserved to have his wish granted.

Darcy had asked for the express messenger to wait, so he quickly took a pen and answered.

Bingley,

I congratulate you and Miss Bennet for such wonderful and well-deserved news.

I have no plans that cannot be changed to be at your side on such an important day. I am sending you this letter immediately so you know you can count on my presence. I shall inform you further about the specific date of our arrival at Netherfield once I discuss the travel details with Georgiana and Lady Hardwick.

Have trust that I am drinking a glass of brandy to your bliss.

F. Darcy.

He sealed the paper, handed it to the messenger, then filled a glass and emptied it with one gulp, just as he promised.

When the time for breakfast arrived, Darcy went to the countess's house, wearing a smile on his face. He imagined Bingley's merriment and his attempt to hide from his sisters, Mrs. Bennet's excitement, and Mr. Bennet, surely in his library, hiding from the din.

What was Elizabeth doing? She was certainly relieved that he had failed to ruin her sister's happiness. But he had been close to doing so, and now he could admit that her accusations were correct.

His smile was soon washed away by another thought that only increased his sense of guilt. What if Bingley had not visited them that day? What if his aunt had not questioned Bingley and given him her honest opinion? What if the countess had not given Bingley the idea to return to Netherfield and try to win Miss Bennet's affection? Would he have confessed the entire truth to his friend before it was too late? Would he have struggled to remedy his mistake, or was it only fate that repaired his wrongs?

Had he done anything right in the last couple of years? Was there anyone around him that he had not hurt with his proud and inconsiderate manners? Since his own sister preferred to live away from him, did anyone truly enjoy his company?

He tried to regain his lost smile when he entered the countess's house and to appear cheerful when he greeted his aunt and sister.

"Good morning, Brother. Please take a seat by me. Have you eaten?"

"Dearest, I bring news. I just received an express from Bingley this morning. He has proposed to Miss Bennet, and they are to be married after Michaelmas."

Georgiana's eyes brightened with joy. "That is wonderful indeed. Mr. Bingley must be so happy. And Miss Bennet too. I am sure Miss Lizzy is also exceedingly delighted. There must be such joy in their family."

Lady Hardwick laughed. "I have always admired a decided young man, but I did not hope for such a sudden resolution when we last spoke. Miss Bennet must be less indifferent towards him than he feared."

"Are you pleased with the news, Brother?" Georgiana inquired. "I know you had objections to the Bennet family."

"Yes, I am very pleased as long as Bingley is content with his choice. It is not for me to raise objections if they do not bother Bingley."

Lady Hardwick laughed again. "If Miss Bennet is as beautiful as I was told, any objections to her family are of no consequence. When one marries for love, few things matter except the spouse. After all, nobody shares their marriage bed with the in-laws."

Darcy cast a reproachful glance at his aunt while Georgiana blushed with embarrassment. The countess patted the girl's hand.

"Forgive me, my darling, it is not a proper subject for a young girl, but I know my point to be correct, as I discovered myself."

"Dear Aunt, I agree with you; it is not a proper subject for a young girl," Darcy answered in earnest. "But there is something else we must discuss. Bingley mentioned that he would like for us to attend his wedding."

"That would be lovely," the countess said.

"Yes, I already sent my acceptance. But I must know your opinion because we need to change our plans again and to postpone our departure for another fortnight. We should be at Netherfield no sooner than four days before the wedding. I expect both Netherfield and Longbourn will be rather crowded with the Hursts, Caroline Bingley, and the Gardiners. What do you think?"

As he spoke, he watched Georgiana carefully. Distress shadowed her eyes, and she hesitated to answer him. She glanced at her aunt then back at her brother.

"What do you think we should do, William?"

He kissed her hand and answered as gently as possible. "I think we cannot refuse Bingley. We can stay a couple of weeks more in Town. We can have dinner with our relatives a few times—perhaps attend the opera one evening —then leave for Hertfordshire a day before Michaelmas, stay at Netherfield until the wedding, and depart for Pemberley after the wedding breakfast."

"It seems an excellent plan," the countess agreed.

"How many sisters does Miss Bennet have?" Georgiana continued her inquiry.

"There must be altogether four sisters remaining at Longbourn," Darcy replied.

"And what are they like?"

"I do not know them well enough to say. I remember Miss Mary Bennet plays the piano. Of Miss Kitty I hardly recollect anything, but I believe she is close to your age."

"My dear girl, it should be enough that you know Miss Elizabeth, and you will have me and your brother with you. I am confident that you will enjoy your time there," the countess added.

"I believe so," Georgiana agreed reluctantly.

"Besides, Netherfield is large; you may have privacy whenever you wish," Darcy concluded. "Shall we do this for Bingley?"

"Yes...of course. Oh, I wonder what Caroline and Louisa have to say about this marriage."

"We do not know, but I am confident it will be amusing to discover," Lady Hardwick replied. "Oh, the fun we will have at Netherfield."

The more diverted the countess acted, the more hesitant Georgiana became. Darcy kissed his sister's hand again to comfort and reassure her, wondering how he would bear four days in Hertfordshire only three miles from Elizabeth. Why was he exposing himself to such torture?

Chapter 12

Since the engagement, Longbourn had become the centre of the neighbourhood. Mrs. Philips and Lady Lucas called almost daily on Mrs. Bennet; the courses for the wedding breakfast were discussed, agreed to, and changed just as frequently. Mary was at her mother's disposal, writing down every decision to avoid missing anything important. Letters to Mrs. Gardiner were written with details for purchasing Jane's trousseau.

The betrothed couple bore everything bravely. As long as they could be together, take a stroll in the garden, or simply gaze at each other, their blissful serenity remained untouched.

Bingley was a regular guest for dinner at Longbourn, unlike his sisters who never visited the family after the engagement was announced. Bingley struggled every day to find a reason for his sisters' rudeness; therefore; either Miss Bingley or Mrs. Hurst appeared to be ill every day while the other was attending her.

One evening, as Mrs. Bennet described the degree of her nerves' wretchedness, the soon-to-be groom said happily, "Darcy just sent me a note that he will come for the wedding with Miss Darcy and their great aunt, the countess. They will stay at Netherfield a few days. I look forward to seeing them."

Elizabeth startled and felt her face colour while she tried to remain calm and sip her tea. She cast a glance at Jane, who responded with a sympathetic look. Both knew of Darcy's plan to stop at Netherfield on the way to Pemberley, but his residing in the neighbourhood several days was as distressing for one as it was pleasant for the other.

Mrs. Bennet dropped her fork. "Mr. Darcy will come for the wedding? And a countess? Here? Mr. Bingley, do you want me to die in anguish? I hoped you would have more consideration for my poor nerves, considering I am the mother of your future mistress of Netherfield!"

Bingley dared not move or even breathe.

"I apologise, ma'am...I did not imagine that...have I done something wrong? Are you displeased with their arrival?"

"Displeased? I am indeed! How could you inform me only now? A countess in my house? And the most demanding and pretentious of all men! Now I have to change the entire menu! We must have at least ten courses! What am I going to do? Mary, fetch your notebook and read to me what we have so far! Oh, dear Lord, I must go speak to Hill at once."

"Mrs. Bennet, would you be so kind as to allow us to finish our dinner before you drive our cook completely out of her mind?" Mr. Bennet pleaded. "You have three more weeks to torment yourself and us. I see no reason for such haste."

"Mr. Bennet, you are mocking me although I am only struggling to honour our family name. How could you possibly be so insensitive?"

"I praise your efforts and struggles, Mrs. Bennet, rest assured of that. However, I can safely assure you that, unless they are not allowed to eat from now until then, neither Mr. Darcy nor any countess would be capable of handling ten courses for breakfast, even a wedding breakfast."

"Oh, Mr. Bennet, you do not know anything about weddings or countesses. You must keep in mind that it could be our only chance to make an excellent impression, as it is likely none of our other girls will marry so well."

"Mama!" cried all four of them, some in embarrassment, some in disagreement, and some in frustration.

"I must talk to Hill; I cannot bear this by myself. Mr. Bingley, do tell me, is there anything else I should know before it ruins the entire wedding?"

Bingley turned pale at the prospect. "No...not from me...nothing else...I apologise..."

Mrs. Bennet dismissed Bingley with a wave of her hand, and he gazed around silently, still wondering what he had done wrong. Fortunately, he met Jane's tender eyes and her sweet, enchanting smile and forgot about the incident the next instant.

A day before Michaelmas, Lady Hardwick's carriage travelled steadily towards Hertfordshire. Inside were Darcy, the countess, and Georgiana. Behind them, Darcy's carriages followed, filled with their personal belongings as well as the ladies' maids and the master's valet. Two other carriages took the direct road to Pemberley.

"I say, Lady Matlock is correct. Everybody is returning to Town for the Season; only we are leaving. There must be something wrong with us Darcys," Lady Hardwick declared. Didi was resting on her lap, and Mist was within his basket held tightly by Georgiana.

"I am glad we will finally see Netherfield. I wonder whether they know we are to arrive today," Georgiana said absentmindedly.

"I would hope so," Darcy replied. "I gave Bingley all the details."

The countess laughed. "A man marrying for love in a few days surely does not care about his friends' travel plans. But we can be certain he is at home."

"I am worried we might disturb them...I would not want to intrude," Georgiana continued. "I wonder whether Mr. and Mrs. Gardiner have arrived at Longbourn. I truly like Mrs. Gardiner."

"As do I," Darcy agreed.

"And I look forward to making their acquaintance," Lady Hardwick said. "I have heard so many positive things about them, Georgiana, that I might be jealous that you like them better than me. "I have argued with your aunt Fitzwilliam for the privilege of spending time with you. In a family filled with insensitive men, you are our sunshine."

"Dear Aunt, you are too kind, and so is Aunt Matlock. I am happy we delayed our departure from town so that I could spend more time with them."

The countess caressed the girl's hair. "And they were delighted to enjoy your company, as we all are. You must know how much joy you bring us with your sweetness, your gentleness, your generous nature. We all love you so much, Georgiana."

"And I love you," she whispered. "I wish nothing more than to be worthy of my name, of my family, and to deserve your affection. I cannot bear to know that I disappointed my relatives. Especially you and William," she ended, her voice trembling with grief.

The countess was overwhelmed with tenderness and embraced the girl, kissing her forehead.

"Oh, my sweet thing, let me kiss you. I love you too, dearest. You two are my children and heirs. Everything I have will be yours one day."

Georgiana turned pale, and her eyes became heavy with tears.

"Dear Aunt, please do not ever speak of this. I do not wish to hear the word 'heir' again! I want to think I will have you with me forever."

"And so you shall, dear girl. Now, how did we come to talk of distressing things when we are going to a household that prepares for a wedding? Oh, and speaking of distress, let us gather our strength for meeting Louisa and Caroline."

Georgiana smiled through her tears. "I cannot speak other than kindly about them. They have always been nice to me, but I know that is partially due to their admiration for William."

"I have reason to suspect Miss Bingley's admiration for me has diminished," Darcy responded mockingly in a poor and unsuccessful attempt to amuse his sister.

They were only a half hour from their destination, and their eagerness, as well as their fatigue, increased.

"William, which comes first on our journey? Longbourn or Netherfield?" Georgiana asked a few minutes later.

"First Meryton, then Longbourn, and Netherfield is the last. Would you like to stop for a time in Meryton?"

The girl seemed to panic. "No! But perhaps we might happen to see Miss Elizabeth…"

Darcy's loving gaze rested on his sister—too shy to make new acquaintances, now suddenly excited to meet someone she considered a close friend.

To his usual concern was added the fear that his sister might suffer another disappointment.

It would be understandable that Elizabeth Bennet, reunited with her family and caught up in the middle of the happiest event, might not be equally enthusiastic about seeing Georgiana again. For his sister, that would be another blow to her fragile self-confidence.

He turned to his companions, trying lighten his tone. "Would you ladies mind if I make the last part of the journey by horse? Watts can lead you in my absence. Thus, I will arrive a little sooner and discover Bingley's precise whereabouts so that we can determine our schedule. I will wait for you on the road; you cannot possibly miss me."

They were surprised, but they accepted his proposal without hesitation. Therefore, a few minutes later Darcy was galloping ahead, defying the warmth of the noonday sun. He passed Meryton, briefly recollecting his first arrival in the area, which began the most painful year of his life. There was no trace of officers, and there were few people on the streets, but curiosity turned several eyes towards him, and he responded with a brief nod.

With each minute—each step—that brought him closer to Longbourn, the turmoil inside him increased, and he reluctantly admitted that concern for his sister was only a part of the inducement for his haste. He hoped —and dreaded—to see Elizabeth before the others. He wished to see her expression the moment she laid eyes on him. Was she expecting them? Surely, Bingley had informed the Bennets of their arrival, so she could not be surprised. But would he ever know what she truly felt, or would her behaviour be tempered by gratitude? Even were she not aware of the extent of his involvement in the Wickham affair, he expected her to be thankful for his assistance. So she would likely be polite, perhaps silent, not daring to contradict him, welcoming him even if her true inclination was to avoid him.

Of course, he should not give consideration to such thoughts. As long as she was kind to Georgiana, nothing else should matter to him. If he could only command his mind and his heart to obey his demands…

Unconsciously, he pulled on the reins as Longbourn appeared around a bend in the road. The path was sheltered from the sun by old trees, and a soft breeze cooled his flushed face.

He dismounted, allowing his horse to take a few steps, and briefly considered entering the house to ask Mr. Bennet for some water for his stallion. Of course, a moment later he was ashamed of himself for concocting such a ridiculous scheme.

He gazed at the house with its open windows and looked for someone in the yard.

"Mr. Darcy! You are already here!"

He startled to hear the voice that he craved and feared. He turned slowly to confront the image of his dreams and his nightmares in front of him, her eyes widened in surprise, her cheeks crimson, and her hair loosened at the back of her bonnet.

He bowed as he struggled to suppress the tremor of his tone.

"Miss Bennet…"

At Netherfield, Mrs. Hurst and Miss Bingley showed considerably less interest than usual in the Darcys' expected visit. With the possibility of their brother's ever marrying Miss Darcy completely ruined and

Mr. Darcy's presence considerably reduced, any hope for a bond between the families was lost forever. Consequently, the presence of the severe and aloof gentleman, his sister, and his aunt became more a burden than a joy.

Mr. Hurst expressed his hope that Darcy would be in a mood to hunt and play cards. In the two ladies, he had no interest at all.

Bingley, however, was impatient to see his friend and anxious for his estate to make a good impression with Lady Hardwick. Therefore, their rooms were impeccably arranged, and fresh meat, fish, and fruits were purchased along with special demands of the cook.

But Mr. Bingley spent little time at Netherfield. He usually had his breakfast then called on his betrothed, spent the day with her, returned home to change his clothes, and joined the Bennets for dinner.

Longbourn was overwhelmed with a cacophony from the moment the Darcys and the countess's visit was announced. Mrs. Bennet spread the news all around Meryton, taking it as a compliment and proof of consideration for her beautiful daughter. And her success was not insignificant since Mrs. Philips and Lady Lucas called several times to ask for details.

Mr. Bennet appeared oddly preoccupied with Mr. Darcy's visit too. He rearranged some of the shelves in the library, refilled his reserve of wine and brandy, and often mentioned his admiration for the named gentleman. When the family was alone, he instructed his wife and youngest daughter to watch their manners, to treat Mr. Darcy with due consideration, and to "mention Wickham only if the man happens to die unexpectedly."

"Oh, Mr. Bennet, you are joking of course. Surely, we do not need your ungenerous censure! When have we ever not treated Mr. Darcy with consideration? He never visited Longbourn, so we barely spoke to him. It was he who was rude and refused to dance with Lizzy," Mrs. Bennet responded.

Jane was—as always—the peacemaker and the centre of calm in the house, although her own excitement and nervousness often coloured her face and moistened her eyes.

As for Elizabeth, she could not describe her state of mind and heart as other than agitated. She knew not what she felt, but she admitted she had never been as nervous. Whether the cause was related to her sister or to other persons, she could not—would not—dare examine too closely.

That she was happy with the prospect of seeing Miss Darcy and Lady Hardwick again, Elizabeth had no doubt. But how she felt regarding Mr.

Darcy's return was still uncertain.

Her opinion of him had changed a great deal since April and had also changed since she knocked on his door in London. Then she was relieved —although slightly regretful—at the notion of never seeing him again. And now, they would meet one more time on the same ground where their acquaintance began but in completely different circumstances. Could this be the real *last time*? Would there ever truly be a last time since his best friend would now be her brother-in-law and his sister maintained a correspondence with her? Did he understand as well as she that they might be thrown into each other's path in the future?

"Lizzy, would you come for a walk with Charles and me? Mama says she has no use for us inside," Jane whispered.

"Of course." Elizabeth smiled at her blushing sister. She had assumed the role of a chaperone for the two betrotheds, but that, fortunately, would end in five days.

They walked in the small grove near the gate, crossed the path, and continued beyond. Soon, Elizabeth found herself preoccupied with her surroundings while Jane and Bingley walked well ahead, barely visible from behind the trees. Her sister's happiness was so great that it passed from Jane's soul to fill Elizabeth's too. Life had been good to them.

In the silence of the autumn day, the sound of hoof-beats raised her curiosity, and she turned towards the road to observe the newcomer. She needed less than a heartbeat to recognise Darcy as he halted, dismounted, and seemed to walk slowly towards the house. He was only a few steps away, and if in the past she had avoided his presence many times on her strolls, now he was the guest eagerly awaited by her father and her future brother. She hurried to him and called his name, trying to sound composed and polite when she greeted him. Her eyes were instantly drawn towards his hair, which had been disturbed by the wind, the neckcloth loosened to cool his skin, the dark gaze, and the familiar severe countenance. His right hand —ungloved—held the reins, and for a moment, her eyes lingered on his long, powerful fingers. She felt her cheeks burning and finally glanced at him, just in time to see his proper bow.

"We did not expect to see you…I mean, we did but not today. Mr. Bingley informed us of your arrival," she mumbled, blushing even more from embarrassment for her incoherent speech. It was not surprising, though, considering that their earlier private conversations had turned into arguments and turmoil. Their history was not a good precedent for a calm and pleasant conversation.

Darcy continued with a slight uneasiness. "I am sorry to hear that. I did send Bingley all the details of our travels. I do not want to intrude—"

"Oh no, you are not intruding, I assure you. My father will be happy to see you…and Mr. Bingley…I believe he forgot to tell us the specific date of your arrival, but you are welcome nevertheless."

"Thank you. Is your family in good health?" he inquired, unable to keep his eyes from her.

"Yes…they are in excellent health. We are very happy," she said. Then she lowered her voice, took a step forward, and locked her eyes with his. "And I must take this opportunity to thank you for that, Mr. Darcy. I am aware that your kindness had a great influence on my family's tranquillity and my sister's present felicity."

He interrupted her with a determination that was close to severity. "Miss Bennet's felicity is entirely due to Bingley's decision to pursue his happiness despite some ungenerous past advice and interference. I have no merit in it —quite the contrary. As for any other past events, let us forget about them and hope things will improve for the better."

A little smile twisted his lips, and she stared, mesmerized, at the dimples that appeared on his cheeks. She had not seen him smile since that dreadful day at the Parsonage.

"Have Mr. and Mrs. Gardiner arrived? I know they planned to come a few days before the wedding."

"No, not yet. We expect them tomorrow," she said, again astonished by his friendly tone as he mentioned her uncle and aunt.

"I see…and is Mr. Bennet at home?"

"Yes, he is. Would you like to come in? Forgive me; I am a very poor host. Papa will be very pleased to see you."

"I look forward to seeing him again too. Do you happen to know where Bingley is?"

"Mr. Bingley? Yes, of course…he is here…somewhere…"

She looked around as Darcy kept his eyes on her face. Her obvious uneasiness, tentative smiles, and friendly voice enhanced her charms—and his distress. There, on her own ground, she was much as she used to be a year before when she had captured his heart. And his self-control, composure, and even his reason were again in danger of betraying him. He had just arrived and talked to her only a few minutes, and he already dreaded the moment he would leave without knowing when or whether he would see her again.

Still gazing at Elizabeth, Darcy heard the sound of a carriage then Georgiana's voice calling timidly. He briefly wondered how they had arrived so soon after he did, but his attention was drawn to Elizabeth's countenance. She was momentarily bewildered, then her expression brightened, and joy glittered in her eyes as she stepped cheerily towards the carriage.

If he previously had concerns about Elizabeth's true feelings for Georgiana, all were gone in an instant. What he observed on Elizabeth's face was pure delight on seeing his sister, and that could only come from sincere affection.

"Miss Anna, what a wonderful surprise! Forgive me, Miss Darcy…and Lady Hardwick! Welcome to Longbourn. This is quite amazing…"

To Darcy's utter surprise, Georgiana jumped down and stretched her hands towards Elizabeth.

"Miss Lizzy, I am so happy to see you again!"

They held hands and looks for a moment, then Elizabeth laughed and impetuously embraced Georgiana, whispering, "Oh, what joy to see you again!"

The young woman was momentarily abashed by the friendly gesture; then she hesitantly put her arms around Elizabeth, returning the hug. Watching her in contentment, Darcy tried to remember whether he had ever seen Georgiana embraced by anyone except their closest relatives.

"Darcy, you are finally here! Miss Darcy, Lady Hardwick!" Bingley shouted his joyous greetings from afar as he rushed towards them, holding Jane's hand tightly.

He bowed to the ladies and shook his friend's hand. "Welcome! I can hardly believe you are all three here! Such a wonderful surprise!" Bingley continued.

"We decided to stop at Longbourn on our way to Netherfield because we suspected we would find you here," Darcy said then bent his head towards Jane.

"Miss Bennet—it is a great pleasure to see you again. Please allow me to convey my most sincere congratulations for your upcoming wedding. I believe no one could make my friend happier, and it will be an honour to stand by his side during his oaths to you."

"You are very kind, Mr. Darcy. We are delighted to have you here. No moment would be happy for Charles without your presence," Jane replied warmly, offering her hand to Darcy, who kissed it politely. Everyone in attendance understood that the small exchange meant much more than a mere polite greeting.

"Miss Darcy, Lady Hardwick, please allow me to introduce my betrothed to you," Bingley said proudly.

Georgiana curtseyed elegantly, and the countess smiled.

"Miss Bennet, you are even more beautiful than I was told," Lady Hardwick said.

"It is an honour and a pleasure to meet you both," Jane responded, her large smile proving the sincerity of her words. "Would you like to come inside for a few minutes? Perhaps for some refreshments and drinks? You must be exhausted from the road."

"Or would you rather go to Netherfield and settle yourself first?" Bingley offered.

"It is your decision, ladies," Darcy addressed his companions. Georgiana hesitated a moment then glanced at her aunt.

"Well, the last part of the journey is always the most difficult, so tea would be most welcome," Lady Hardwick finally voiced her acceptance.

Her response was met cheerfully by the Bennet sisters, and the group walked towards Longbourn's main gate while Bingley directed the other two carriages towards Netherfield.

"We must hurry to inform the others of your arrival," Bingley announced, hastening his steps and still holding Jane's hand.

Elizabeth took Georgiana's arm while Darcy, pleased with the friendly and protective gesture, offered his support to Lady Hardwick.

"I am very happy to see you," Elizabeth repeated to Georgiana.

"And so am I," the girl answered.

"Was the journey tiresome?"

"No, not at all. It is always a pleasure to travel with my brother and my aunt. And it is a short distance compared to the journey to Pemberley. We will need three days on the road."

"Yes, I imagined as much...but I am sure the beauty of Pemberley is worth the effort."

"Indeed it is. But you have a lovely place here too. Oh, and Miss Bennet is so beautiful and so lovely! My brother said she was."

"Thank you, Miss Darcy. And yes, Jane is very beautiful, but she also has the most generous heart and most admirable character. I am sure you will get along very well while you stay at Netherfield. The moment we met in London, you reminded me of her. I believe that is why I grew attached to you so quickly."

"Oh, you are very kind; I do not deserve the comparison. But it is admirable the way you speak of your sister. I confess, I would like to have a sister too…"

"Well, you will have the chance to experience that since I have four, and I will gladly share them with you." Elizabeth laughed.

Darcy and Lady Hardwick looked at each other, then at the two young women walking in front of them, arm in arm. Their amazement was great; within minutes, Georgiana was chatting in a lively manner with Elizabeth, completely changed by the presence of her new friend.

Neither their care, their love, their concern, nor their support had done as much for the girl's spirits as had the reunion with Elizabeth Bennet, and Darcy could not decide whether he should be content or concerned, witnessing once more the influence of Elizabeth Bennet over the life of a Darcy.

As they approached the door, all four stopped at the despair-filled voice resounding through the open windows.

"Mr. Bingley, what do you mean Mr. Darcy is here? Now?! With the countess?!"

"Yes, Mrs. Bennet. And with Miss Darcy," Bingley answered candidly.

"And with Miss Darcy? But…but…but…surely, they cannot come in… why did I not know sooner? Look at this house…this is a mess…and I have nothing prepared except cold meat and some cheese and some soup and some fruits. And some biscuits…and neither of us is dressed properly to receive such guests. And Lizzy! She must look really wild! Oh, dear Lord, this will be the death of me…"

Bingley attempted to calm his future mother-in-law. "Mrs. Bennet, I beg you not to trouble yourself. You do not have to offer them anything. We are prepared at Netherfield, and they will only stay for a few minutes to greet you."

From outside, Lady Hardwick laughed behind her hand as she could anticipate the answer to such an unwise statement.

"Not offer anything?" Mrs. Bennet cried. "Let them leave my house without any hospitality? Mr. Bingley, I have not been so offended in a long while!"

"But ma'am…"

"Do not say another word, sir! If Jane were already married, she would now be in danger of becoming a widow!"

Both Darcy and the countess tried to suppress their laughter while Jane's voice sounded upset and appalled.

"Mama, how can you even say such a monstrous thing? Please calm yourself. We will prepare a tray of refreshments and some drinks in a moment. You may go and change if you wish. I will take care of our guests."

"Go and change? How could I be so disrespectful to our guests? I am not going anywhere!"

"Mrs. Bennet, enough of this before we all look ridiculous to our guests," the master of the house declared sternly. "I am sure you will be a dutiful hostess as always. I am going to welcome Mr. Darcy now, and I trust we will find enough food and drinks to entertain our guests. Nobody has ever left Longbourn either starved or thirsty."

Elizabeth coloured with embarrassment, and Georgiana became disconcerted, but Darcy and the countess could barely hide their amusement.

The door finally opened and they stepped in, greeted enthusiastically by Mr. Bennet, whose arm was tightly held by his wife.

Behind them, Bingley wore a huge grin, Miss Bennet an enchanting smile, and Kitty and Mary confused expressions.

Darcy bowed politely and attempted to warm his countenance as he considered he had never visited Longbourn before.

"Mr. Bennet, Mrs. Bennet, I am delighted to see you again. We apologise for disturbing you with our impromptu arrival."

"Nonsense, nonsense," Mr. Bennet said. "We are happy to see you. Do come in."

Chapter 13

Thank you, sir. May I introduce my aunt, Lady Hardwick, and my sister, Miss Georgiana Darcy?"

Introductions were performed, and everybody took a seat. Lady Hardwick was invited to choose first and selected a comfortable armchair by the window. Georgiana appeared suddenly uncomfortable with all the new people around her, and she chose a settee close to her aunt while Elisabeth occupied the place next to her.

Refreshments and drinks were offered; despite Mrs. Bennet's earlier complaints, the dishes were rich and tasteful. However, the only one to show no restraint in her appreciation was the countess. The others were too distracted, too nervous, or too curious for an appetite.

"Mrs. Bennet, this is a lovely room—perfectly fitted for a family gathering," the countess said.

"Thank you, your ladyship. We enjoy spending time here. Unfortunately, it is not as large as we would like for receiving guests. I hope you are comfortable."

"Very much so. And I have to compliment the efficiency of your household. I know how difficult it is to entertain a large number of guests who just happen upon you. And the cold meat is cooked to perfection."

Mrs. Bennet was on the edge of her seat. "Your ladyship is very kind. I always resolve to have at least three courses ready for unexpected situations."

"Very wise indeed. And the cheese—did you select it yourself?"

"Your ladyship guessed correctly. I am always careful to choose the ingredients personally, especially the cheese and the fruits."

Lady Hardwick generously continued to compliment Mrs. Bennet, whose despair slowly evaporated. Kitty and Mary dared not speak, staring from the countess to Miss Darcy. Towards Mr. Darcy, neither had the courage even to glance.

"Mr. Darcy, Mr. Bingley, would you join me in the library for a drink?" Mr. Bennet proposed.

The former looked at his sister, who still seemed uneasy. Elizabeth whispered something to her, and a smile appeared on Georgiana's face, which convinced him instantly that she was fine.

"Yes, I would like that very much," he answered.

Bingley was still reluctant to leave his betrothed, so Mr. Bennet had to call him twice, much to the others' amusement.

The moment he stepped into the library, a sense of peace and comfort enveloped Darcy. It was a small chamber, perhaps a quarter the size of his library, but the richness of the books and arrangement of the room expressed a deep love of reading. He immediately recollected an evening at Netherfield when Elizabeth preferred reading to playing cards, much to the puzzlement of Hurst. Now he had no doubt from whence she inherited that passion. He startled as Mr. Bennet spoke, guessing his thoughts.

"This is my favourite place in the house; most of the time nobody else enters except Lizzy," their host said, offering each a drink.

"I can imagine why," Darcy answered. "Not why nobody else enters here, but why this would be your favourite place. This library is perfectly arranged for enjoying an excellent book in solitude. And I spotted several exquisite editions."

"I am glad you noticed, sir. I am quite proud of them. Of course, it cannot compare to your library..."

"The *love* of books has no degree of comparison, Mr. Bennet. Would you not agree?"

"Yes, I would, Mr. Darcy."

Darcy's time with Mr. Bennet was highly engaging, and he discovered many appealing aspects to the gentleman he had once ignored or criticised.

He thought often of Georgiana and hoped she was not overwhelmed by the Bennets' exuberance. He also feared that Mrs. Bennet would mention Wickham at some point and worried about whether his sister could bear such a stressful subject. Therefore, half an hour later, he apologised to Mr. Bennet and moved to take a quick look into the drawing room. Through the open door, he heard a profusion of voices and observed Georgiana listening attentively to something related by Mrs. Bennet, smiling while the others around her were laughing. The only one who noticed his presence and even held his glance for a moment was Elizabeth. She gave him a re-assuring nod, and he thanked her with a slight bend of his head then returned to the library more at peace.

ELIZABETH WAS SURPRISED AT HOW WELL THE VISIT WAS PROGRESSING. Lady Hardwick showed remarkable generosity towards her mother, complimenting her every time an opportunity arose. Her ladyship also involved Jane in conversation and even addressed specific questions to Kitty and Mary, who slowly gathered their courage enough to answer.

The former "Miss Anna" remained silent and apparently struggled in such a large company. But she gradually became comfortable as time passed and even expressed her opinion from time to time. The new acquaintances appreciated her sincere smile and the interest she showed in every subject. Even the less perceptive of them understood that Miss Darcy was not only shy but kind and not at all proud.

The discussions moved from wedding arrangements to the wedding break-fast and from travelling to the North to the Gardiners' anticipated arrival.

Mrs. Bennet prided herself on her eldest daughter's beauty and declared she would certainly be the loveliest bride Meryton had ever seen.

"I confess I am so relieved that one of my daughters is marrying at home. We were quite disappointed when my youngest—Lydia—married last month In London, and none of our friends saw her. But thank God, she came to visit us. She is such a joyful girl; she has always been the heart of any party. And her husband—Mr. Wickham—is the most handsome officer I have ever seen. Everyone in Meryton was enamoured of him, but he preferred Lydia, which was no surprise as there was nobody as lovely as her."

Elizabeth observed Georgiana's sudden pallor and Lady Hardwick's discomfort. Jane flushed while Kitty and Mary chose to remain silent.

The countess again led the conversation forward safely. "I am confident that Miss Bennet will be one of the most beautiful brides in all of Hertfordshire. In truth, I have been in the midst of the London Season for more than forty years now and have rarely met a young lady with such a flawless figure and impeccable manners as Miss Bennet. Mr. Bingley is a very fortunate man."

Jane Bennet forgot to breathe from such an extraordinary compliment while Mrs. Bennet was on the edge of fainting.

"Lady Hardwick, thank you," Jane whispered.

"Your ladyship is right as always. I am the most fortunate man in the world," Bingley intervened animatedly as the gentlemen returned to the drawing room, still holding their glasses of brandy. He quickly moved to his betrothed, who was now completely crimson.

The countess laughed. "And you deserve to be, young man. I have only seen you together briefly, but I am confident you are ideally suited to each other."

Elizabeth felt pride and joy bursting in her heart, and she could not avoid glancing at Darcy. His eyes held hers only for a moment, but it was enough for her to observe there was no disdain, disapproval, or displeasure in his dark look. Any objections Mr. Darcy might have had against his friend's union with her sister seemed to have vanished.

"Oh, I am so happy you came to visit us," Mrs. Bennet declared. "Your ladyship is the kindest and most generous peer that ever existed, and so is Miss Darcy. I must say, neither of you resembles Mr. Darcy in any way."

All eyes widened in disbelief at such an offense, and silence fell upon the room momentarily. Elizabeth felt her entire body freeze in embarrassment. Georgiana's hands began to tremble.

Mrs. Bennet, perfectly serene, glanced at her husband by pure chance, and only when she observed his angry face did she realise she might have said something wrong; she hurried to remedy her mistake.

"Oh, but Mr. Darcy is very tall and handsome and worth twice as much as Mr. Bingley, so his manners are not quite repulsive. It is just that he is not an amiable sort of man."

"Mrs. Bennet!" her husband yelled. "Mr. Darcy, I beg to apologise to you; I am sure Mrs. Bennet's words, however vexatious they might sound, were meant another way. My wife surely did not intend any offense. We are all grateful to you and honoured to have you in our house."

"I certainly did not mean any offense, I was only saying...I do not..." Mrs. Bennet looked at each of her guests, desperately realising that she had somehow managed to spoil their good mood in mere seconds. She tried to apologise, but her nerves took her breath away and left her speechless.

To everyone's complete shock, Darcy stepped forward and smiled at his hosts, speaking gently. "Mrs. Bennet was spot on with her observations. It is fortunate that my sister resembles my aunt rather than me. Where I would contradict you, ma'am, is that I am certainly not twice as worthy as Bingley."

Darcy's mocking statement and his smiling face left the Bennets even more puzzled and Georgiana still distressed by the offense given to her brother.

Without thinking, Elizabeth intervened in a desperate attempt to dissipate the tense moment. "But you are certainly tall and handsome, sir. On this, everybody agreed the moment you arrived in Meryton."

Darcy's jaw dropped in astonishment as he stared at a flushed Elizabeth. Georgiana and the Bennet sisters chuckled, and Lady Hardwick hid her laughter behind a napkin.

Mrs. Bennet sensed an opportunity to make further amends. "Indeed, sir, when you first entered the assembly room, your features and your stature were universally admired. If only you had not offended Lizzy and refused to dance with her, nobody would have held anything against you. We all wagered that she would never dance with you ever again, but we were proved wrong after all."

Silence again fell like a thunderclap over the party, and nobody dared to speak; not even their breathing could be heard.

Suddenly, Lady Hardwick started to laugh as the others watched in bewilderment. "Mrs. Bennet, I have to say this is the most entertaining visit I have had in years. Tasty refreshments and diverting conversation all at the same time—one can rarely find such enjoyment even at St. James's."

The countess's statement normally would have diverted Mr. Bennet. However, at that moment he could not decide whether he should be amused at his wife or angry with her. His most important guest and primary concern, Darcy, looked uncomfortable; he was certainly not the sort of gentleman to laugh at his own expense. That was reason enough for Mr. Bennet's worry to overcome his mirth.

In truth, Darcy was more distressed by Elizabeth's mocking compliment than by Mrs. Bennet's remarks. He stared at her but had no luck in catching her eye again. And, while he realised he was being ridiculous, he could not help wondering whether the statement reflected her true feelings.

Slowly, the conversation returned to safer ground. Mr. Bingley invited Mr. Bennet to hunt with them as soon as Mr. Gardiner arrived.

"I am sure my brother Gardiner will be very pleased with the invitation," Mr. Bennet said; then he addressed Darcy. "Also, I would ask for the favour of your joining us for dinner at least one evening if there is no inconvenience."

The guest exchanged quick looks with his sister and aunt before answering. "It would be our pleasure."

"Would tomorrow evening be acceptable?" Mrs. Bennet quickly asked.

"Perfect," Darcy replied.

"If you gentlemen plan to hunt tomorrow, I would be happy to show Miss Darcy and Lady Hardwick the neighbourhood," Elizabeth said.

"A short carriage ride would be nice, but I am certain I will spend quite a lot of time resting since we have a long journey ahead of us," the countess declared.

"And we could also go riding sometime, could we not?" Georgiana asked animatedly.

"Of course." Elizabeth smiled. "Jane is a skilled rider, and she will keep you company. I will be content to follow you on foot as long as I can then wait for your return."

At Georgiana's silent question, she continued. "Sadly, I am no horsewoman; better said, I have not ridden since I was very young and have no plan to do so. I confess I am rather afraid of horses."

Miss Darcy showed genuine surprise and said with the innocence of a child, "You are afraid of horses? I would not imagine you were afraid of anything, Miss Lizzy."

Elizabeth responded with mock seriousness. "I am sorry to disappoint you, Miss Anna—Miss Darcy—but you must accept me either on foot or by carriage."

"Oh no, you do not disappoint me; I was just surprised. I am sorry I insisted on riding…we will manage without it."

Elizabeth laughed and took Georgiana's hands in hers. "If we are to spend more time together, I must warn you about my bad habit of teasing those around me. You must not take me seriously too often. Jane may testify to this."

"It is true, Miss Darcy," Jane replied. "As for her riding skills, we will try to make her change her opinion once I move to Netherfield. She must visit me daily, and she cannot always walk, so she has no other choice. And you are right, Miss Darcy; Lizzy is the most courageous person I know."

"I believe it. And I pray that you will succeed in convincing her to ride. There is nothing more enjoyable. My brother taught me when I was very young. If we had more time, I would ask William to teach Miss Elizabeth. He is an excellent teacher in everything," Georgiana continued without noticing the sudden blush that her words brought to both Darcy and Elizabeth.

Bingley added, bringing a chair close to his betrothed, "Darcy might be an excellent teacher, but he is stern, sometimes impatient, and always frightening. You must take my word on that; he was my tutor on several occasions when we were at university."

Darcy glanced around until his eyes finally met Elizabeth's. He noticed a sparkle of laughter behind the long lashes, and with an impulse stronger than his will, he let his guard down and replied mockingly:

"A teacher can excel only as much as the pupil allows."

Bingley laughed wholeheartedly. "On that, I cannot argue with you. It might be the reason you were successful with Miss Darcy and less so with me."

The tension was gone, and cheerfulness and good humour returned.

Darcy watched his sister and aunt obviously enjoying their time in a rather small and crowded room, surrounded by a din of voices that never occurred in their home. They stayed for more than two hours, and neither of them appeared willing to leave for the more comfortable Netherfield.

It was the first time he had been at Longbourn, and it felt more comfortable than the houses of some old acquaintances. He felt well. At peace. Comfortable. Feelings he rarely experienced at the same time.

The Bennets did not behave differently than before, but his judgment and response to them had changed.

Yes, Mrs. Bennet's manners were questionable, but on closer look, they reminded him of those of another aunt—Lady Catherine de Bourgh. Mr. Bennet might have treated his family rather too casually, but so did his uncle—Lord Matlock—who was only fortunate in having two sons instead of five daughters.

How was it possible that he treated these people with such unfair disdain and accused them of all the wrongs in the world? And why had he amended his judgment so drastically? Might it have been because he had recently felt the pain of groundless accusations, that he had been awakened to the unfairness of his previous opinions? Or that his lasting affection for Elizabeth made him more indulgent towards her family? Or perhaps it was just due to his effort to know them better, acknowledging their qualities together with their faults.

LATE IN THE AFTERNOON, THE GUESTS RESUMED THEIR TRAVEL AFTER A friendly farewell and the promise to meet again the following day.

When they arrived at Netherfield, Bingley dismounted in a hurry to welcome them ceremoniously into his house.

Miss Bingley and the Hursts appeared, and salutations were exchanged.

"Miss Bingley, Mrs. Hurst, Mr. Hurst, how nice to see you again," the countess said. "What a lovely home your brother has. Mr. Bingley, I congratulate you for it."

"We are honoured to have you here, your ladyship," Caroline answered. "Please come in; we have been waiting for you for hours." Not a word was said about their stop at Longbourn as if Mr. Bingley's sisters pretended it had not happened.

"Did you have a pleasant journey, I hope?" Caroline continued.

"Quite," the countess replied. "Fortunately, it was rather short."

In the drawing room, they took comfortable seats and then looked at each other in awkward silence.

"Georgiana, we are happy to see you again," Mrs. Hurst finally said.

"Thank you; I am very pleased to see you too."

"Have you been in Town all summer? Alone?" Miss Bingley went further with the inquiries.

"Yes...and no, not alone. With my brother and my aunt."

"London is horrible in the summertime," Mr. Hurst added.

"Still, it has some particular charms if one knows how to discover them," the countess intervened. "But I agree that summer is better spent on a lovely estate when the heat becomes unbearable. And speaking of that, Netherfield looks charming, Mr. Bingley."

"It is pleasant enough, but Charles could have chosen better," Mrs. Hurst answered sharply, and it was no mystery to anyone that she referred to more than just the estate.

"No, indeed," Bingley responded decidedly. "Renting Netherfield was the best decision of my life. Now, would you allow me to show you to your rooms? You must be tired."

"We will have dinner in about two hours—is that acceptable?" Caroline asked.

The countess expressed her approval. "Perfectly, thank you. We will have time to rest until then."

Bingley led them personally, inviting each of them to their own room. As they were about to enter, the countess addressed Darcy, wearing a broad grin.

"Nephew, I look forward to hearing more about the circumstances of your refusal to dance with Miss Elizabeth, as well as those when you did dance. Would you be so kind as to indulge me, or should I ask Mrs. Bennet about the details tomorrow?"

Georgiana chuckled, and Darcy looked momentarily perplexed. Bingley answered with a mischievous smile on his lips.

"I can also provide those stories to your ladyship at length as I was present on both occasions."

"Really? Well, I always knew you were a thoughtful young man," Lady Hardwick joked.

"Bingley, I begin to suspect that you invited me to Netherfield to use me for your own amusement," Darcy replied with mock severity.

"No, indeed; but if the opportunity arises, I cannot waste it, my friend. For years, I dared not smile in your presence, let alone tease you. It is time for revenge now that I am about to marry—would you not agree?"

"I must think carefully about this: What does one's marriage have to do with being cruel to his guests?" Darcy answered.

"I stand ready to compensate for it with a glass of brandy if you wish," Bingley offered.

"And I will join you and have a glass of port while I listen to your stories," Lady Hardwick concluded; then both she and Georgiana entered their rooms.

Darcy entered his room, followed by Bingley. Once they were inside, his host's voice suddenly changed, as well as his countenance.

"Darcy, I must thank you."

"What on earth for?"

"For coming to Netherfield as I requested. Our last meeting in Town was mostly an argument, and I did not restrain myself from casting a lot of blame on you for my leaving Jane. Now I know that my weakness and indecisiveness are more to be condemned than your interference."

"Bingley, you are too generous, as always. You must know that we came to Netherfield not only because you asked me but also because it gives us real pleasure. We were looking forward to seeing you again. It is I who must thank you for forgiving me so readily and placing our friendship above your justified anger."

"I am sure you know how valuable your friendship is to me."

"As yours is to me."

"I am also grateful for the patience you showed with the Bennet family. I remember your having many objections against them, and not all of those were undeserved. So I imagine it was not easy for you to spend such a long while in their company. I admit that Mrs. Bennet's manners and comments are not always proper. I apologise if you felt offended, but as Mr. Bennet said, she rarely intends harm."

"Well, my earlier objections to the Bennets might have been warranted, but they were surely uncalled for, and I hope I have grown wise enough to understand that. As for our visit today, I assure you I found it quite pleasant. Challenging, but pleasant."

"Truly? I am relieved to hear that. I confess I feared that my marriage to Jane would ruin our friendship. I believed you would wish to keep as much distance as possible from the Bennets, especially considering their present connection to Wickham. And as much as I love Jane, my heart was heavy at the thought of losing my best friend."

"Bingley, I would be a fool unworthy of your loyalty if I gave up our long friendship so easily. I admit, however, that I shall do everything in my power to keep Wickham as far from Georgiana and me as possible. I would not have come to your wedding if Wickham were here. But it still would not have affected our friendship, which I trust will last for many years."

"Good...excellent...well, I will leave you now. I believe you are already familiar with this room. Shall I see you in two hours? I am very glad that you came—very glad indeed."

"So am I, Bingley, never doubt that," Darcy said in complete honesty.

"Oh, and...Darcy, you are indeed an excellent teacher. One of the best I ever had. Also, you must not worry; I will never reveal any story about you, not even to your aunt," Bingley said seriously.

"I never worry about your loyalty, my friend." Darcy patted Bingley's shoulder then continued less grave but equally earnest. "I believe you are wise not to tell stories about me, or I could share a few, too, when we are next in Miss Bennet's company."

Bingley's mouth and eyes opened in bewilderment and mistrust; Darcy laughed to ensure that his friend knew he was only joking, and Bingley breathed in relief.

"I say, Darcy, people are often anxious around you when you are haughty and aloof, but when you tease and mock them, you are truly frightening."

Their light-hearted exchange was both diverting and consoling. It was proof that Bingley had gone past their disagreement and forgiven Darcy's interference, and it ensured their friendship would continue. Darcy was astonished once more by Bingley's generous heart and kind nature.

Once alone, he looked around, and his chest clenched. He was more than familiar with the room. It was the same one he used last year, the one that hosted his turmoil and struggles, the one from which he attempted to escape his obsession with Elizabeth. And he had failed. Now he returned, and his obsession was still alive—as was his discontent.

DINNER TOOK PLACE AT THE EXACT HOUR WITH PERFECT ARRANGEMENTS and five tasteful courses.

The conversation, however, was scarce; no subject seemed to raise anyone's interest for more than a few minutes.

"I hope you found your rooms to your liking," Caroline addressed Georgiana and Lady Hardwick.

"Having had the pleasure of spending some time at Pemberley, we know Netherfield cannot compare to it nor with your ladyship's estate, I am sure," Louisa added. "But we hope you are comfortable enough."

"Very much so; your care is appreciated," the countess answered.

"My room is excellent too. I could not ask for a better one," Georgiana responded. "And Caroline, I want to thank you for taking care of Mist and Didi before our arrival."

"Oh, it was nothing, truly. We have enough servants here to accomplish any domestic tasks. However, I could not but wonder why Charles delayed you for so long. It was hardly acceptable." She glared reproachfully.

"Mr. Bingley is not to be blamed; it was our decision to stop at Longbourn. I especially insisted on doing so," Georgiana declared daringly.

Both sisters looked puzzled.

"Why would you insist on that?" Caroline asked.

"I wished to see Miss Elizabeth."

"Eliza Bennet? What for?"

"She is my friend, and I missed her," Georgiana replied with serenity, and Caroline's fork froze in the air.

"Your friend? How can that be?"

"I met Miss Bennet in London a couple of months ago, and we became friends," Georgiana continued.

"That is unheard of. Forgive me, but I find it hard to believe. You and Eliza Bennet? How could you be friends?"

"I cannot understand why you are so surprised, Miss Bingley," the countess intervened.

"Why? Because the Bennet family is surely not one to be connected with the Darcys or with your ladyship."

"I am surprised to hear that. We visited them today, and we had a pleasant time. And Miss Elizabeth is a spirited and lovely young woman. Both Georgiana and I like her very much."

A grimace twisted Caroline's handsome features. "This is quite astonishing; I have known Eliza Bennet for almost a year now, and I see few things to be admired in her. She has neither beauty nor manners, and her impertinence is very unbecoming."

"Caroline, you are unfair as usual," Bingley interrupted, but his sister continued, much to Georgiana's embarrassment and discomfort.

"There was a time when Mr. Darcy shared the same opinion, but it seems things have changed lately. There must be a new trend in Town to befriend people from low-class families."

Lady Hardwick's eyebrow rose in obvious displeasure, and she frowned while answering sharply, "Well, the definition of 'low-class' has changed lately too. I have great affection for Bingley, and I believe he is an excellent and valuable friend to my nephew; however, only a few years ago, it would have been unacceptable for a gentleman to be friends with or to marry someone whose fortune was made in trade. I am rather pleased that times have changed, are you not, Miss Bingley?"

Caroline and Louisa were frozen in silence at such severe censure.

"I for one am very content, Lady Hardwick" Bingley answered. "Not long ago, we never would have been admitted to Pemberley, nor could we have imagined having a countess at our dinner table. And I could not have hoped to marry a gentleman's daughter of perfect beauty."

At such a conclusion, nobody had much else to add. Offenses had been given and received in a manner mean enough to ruin the general mood.

Caroline and Louisa abandoned any attempt at conversation, and Mr.

Hurst's suggestion of playing cards was rejected. As the guests were rather tired, the evening ended, much to everybody's relief.

But few of Netherfield's inhabitants found sleep easily—and Darcy less than anyone.

To him, that half day spent at Longbourn brought a revelation that settled his long-lasting struggles. He might have been angry, resentful, disappointed, and pained after Elizabeth's harsh refusal, but his love for her had never vanished. He knew it the moment he laid eyes on her again in the grove and her mere smile burst into joy in his heart. His love had changed; the passion and impetuosity that made him propose that day at the Parsonage had been crushed by his reason and hidden deeper within his soul. But it was always there—she was always there—safely tucked away in his heart.

He dared not consider that Elizabeth might ever reciprocate his affection. That path was closed to him. Her behaviour towards him became less embarrassed, a bit more composed, and friendlier, but he would never be mistaken about her again. It was not affection but politeness, gratitude, amiability. It was enough though—much better than he could have imagined a few months ago. Since fate decided to bind them through their friends and family, it was a relief to know they could bear to be in the same room.

The struggle in his mind and the turmoil in his heart would never be known to her, and he would gradually learn to live with it.

Chapter 14

Dinner conversation at Longbourn that night was entirely about the visit Mrs. Bennet chose to take as a compliment paid by the illustrious guests to Jane and personally to her. She even sent a note to her sister Mrs. Philips, informing her that Mr. Darcy, his sister, and his aunt —a countess—had called on them just as they arrived from London and spent about three hours at Longbourn, complimenting her food and the efficiency of her staff. Others in the family wrote to no one.

Elizabeth had been pleased to see Lady Hardwick and especially Miss Darcy again as if they were part of her family. As for Mr. Darcy—his presence, his manners, and his behaviour were equally surprising and, therefore, distressing. She had known for some time that he would come to Hertfordshire, and she thought she had reconciled herself to the idea. But she was proved wrong from the moment she met him in the grove until he left Longbourn. And when he was gone, she found herself trying to remember his words, his gestures, and his gazes, and she wondered whether there was something else hidden behind them.

Although his manners were amiable, her distress in his company was more intense than in the past. The visible change in him was certainly not due to her—she was well aware of that—but to his relationship with her father as well as to the presence of his sister and aunt. So she tried to guess his true opinion of her, hoping the passage of time had softened his anger and resentment.

Even though she had come to recognise better qualities in him, she did not regret refusing his marriage proposal or censuring his manner in addressing it. At that moment—given the information she had and his pride in being responsible for separating Jane and Bingley—she felt her answer was the only choice. But sorrow for her unjust offenses and her reckless gesture of destroying the letter grew stronger, along with her self-reproach. She still hoped that someday they would be able to have a sincere, unbiased discussion and clear up everything so she could ease the weight she had carried for many months.

Elizabeth found sleep long after midnight, and she was startled by the sound of rain against the window. Autumn had demanded its due, and she worried that the weather might affect their plans for the next days and Jane's eagerly awaited wedding day.

Her night was restless, but by morning, the rain stopped and the smell of fresh air was intoxicating. The family did not gather for breakfast. Mr. Bennet requested coffee and cold meat in his library, and Mrs. Bennet kept to her room until late, declaring she needed to rest in order to gather her strength for supervising dinner. The sisters ate very little; then Mary turned to her study, Jane to the packing of her luggage for the upcoming move to Netherfield, and Kitty to complaints of boredom from one sister to the other.

Elizabeth chose to take her usual morning walk before anybody needed her help in any way.

Darcy woke abruptly to the sound of wind. The window was wide open, and it was still dark, but no star lit in the sky.

He shivered as the breeze cooled the sweat on his skin. Half asleep, he brushed his fingers through his hair and looked for water to ease his thirst.

He had barely slept a whole hour, and his mind was foggy. Then he realised it was not the wind that woke him but rather a dream filled with Elizabeth's image. He did not remember the details, but he imagined himself holding Elizabeth tightly in his arms, her body brushing against his, her soft lips yielding to his kisses, and her skin shivering under his touch. His senses were alive to her scent, her warmth, her softness, and her whispers.

Ashamed of his own weakness, he stood in front of the window and allowed the chilling breeze to calm his fevered body. He then filled a glass with water, emptied it in one gulp, wet his hands, and wiped his face. Finally, he lay back in bed, hoping for the dawn. Eventually, he fell asleep with the window wide open in an attempt to calm the heat inside him.

Two hours later, sunlight, voices in the back yard, and a strange headache woke him again. He was neither more rested nor calmer—but at least the rain had stopped.

Darcy hurried downstairs and was pleased to see Georgiana and Lady Hardwick gathered around the table, chatting with Bingley. The other two ladies, however, barely answered his greetings and then kept a grim silence that proved the previous evening's arguments were not forgotten.

"Darcy, welcome! Did you sleep well? What would you like to eat? Come, take a seat." Bingley's enthusiasm, though well meant, increased Darcy's headache.

"I will only have coffee. What were you discussing if I may ask?"

"We were speaking of our plans for today. I usually go to Longbourn immediately after breakfast, but now I cannot abandon you, so I shall settle my schedule according to your wishes."

"The Bennet family is waiting for the Gardiners today, so I imagine they will be very busy," Darcy replied. "So I am not certain we should disturb them until dinnertime."

"I agree with Mr. Darcy," Caroline finally spoke. "These days we purposely try to avoid Longbourn as it is quite disorderly there—much more than we can bear."

"I believe this happens to any family when a wedding is planned," Lady Hardwick said. "But it is understandable that not everybody is comfortable with it."

"I fear my sisters are generally not comfortable with anything related to the Bennets," Bingley declared.

"Charles, let us not discuss our family affairs in the presence of our guests," Louisa insisted.

"We will not; however, some things are obvious." Bingley addressed his sisters sternly. "We will have dinner at Longbourn tonight. From your statement, I take it you do not want to join us.

"I am sure there will be more people than the Longbourn dining room can accommodate," Caroline answered.

"Then it is best that you stay home," Bingley concluded. "As for now, Miss Darcy, would you not like to take a ride around Netherfield? Perhaps visit Miss Elizabeth briefly? I am sure she will be happy to see you, and I will be delighted to keep you company."

Georgiana's face brightened. "Yes, I would like that very much. I mean

—if my brother and my aunt approve."

Darcy hesitated a moment, long enough for the countess to reply.

"My dear, I would rather stay in my room and rest a little longer. But I promise to be ready in time for dinner. Until then, I will stay with Didi and Mist."

"Are you well, Aunt?" Darcy inquired with concern.

"Yes, I am very well, my dear; do not worry about me. Just arrange your plans so you can enjoy your time here as much as possible."

Darcy watched his aunt carefully; she appeared to be well indeed. Then he looked at his sister and Bingley.

"Very well—let us do as you two want. We can take a ride around the estate, call at Longbourn briefly, and then return home and prepare for dinner."

"I will change my clothes for riding immediately," Georgiana said enthusiastically and rushed to her room.

Shortly thereafter, the three of them left on their horses, and Lady Hardwick walked back to her chamber. Caroline and Louisa watched through the window, speculating about the strange relationship between Eliza Bennet and Georgiana Darcy, whom they had tried for years to befriend. Mr. Hurst offered no opinion.

The riders were led by Bingley, who directed them towards the main path to Longbourn. Darcy observed, smiled to himself, and said nothing.

"It is still cloudy, but the weather is very pleasant. I love the smell of the trees after a rain," Bingley said.

"It still might rain again," Darcy added.

"Maybe later, but the clouds have dissipated for now. And we will reach Longbourn very soon. Miss Darcy, if you look to your right, there is a lovely view of Netherfield. Of course, it is nothing compared to Pemberley."

"It is very lovely, Mr. Bingley. The colours of autumn are beautiful."

"It has been one year since we first came to Netherfield. Do you remember, Darcy?"

"I do remember."

"It has been a long year, has it not? So agonising…I cannot believe how perfectly well everything has turned out."

"Indeed…" Georgiana whispered, staring absently in front of her. Suddenly, she spurred her horse, then reined it in after a short distance, and dismounted to Darcy and Bingley's puzzlement.

"Miss Lizzy!" she called, and only then did the gentlemen observe Elizabeth walking through the trees.

"Miss Darcy! Oh, and the two gentlemen. Good morning!" Elizabeth greeted them with spirit.

"Are you walking alone in the wood?" Georgiana asked with apparent surprise.

"Yes, I do so quite often. It is my preferred spot when I wish to take a stroll. I am as familiar with these paths as I am with my own room," she said with a smile.

Both gentlemen dismounted and bowed to Elizabeth. Darcy immediately added the reins of his sister's horse to his own.

"What a happy coincidence to meet you here," Bingley said.

"Not really." Elizabeth's smile was slightly nervous as she felt Darcy's gaze upon her. "I am here almost daily if the weather is reasonable. So anyone who might pass by here would meet me."

"It is fortunate that we did," Georgiana answered. "We intended to come and see you a little bit later…only for a moment…we know you are waiting for Mr. and Mrs. Gardiner today, so I imagine you are busy. We did not want to disturb you."

"Your presence is never a disturbance, Miss Darcy. We are happy to have you at Longbourn whenever you wish. And Lady Hardwick? Her ladyship is well, I hope?"

"Yes she is. She is not fond of cloudy days, and she was still a little tired, so she preferred to rest. Didi and Mist are happy to keep her company."

"I hope your visit to Longbourn was not too trying. We are a rather *animated* family, and it can easily become tiresome for those not accustomed to our ways."

"Not at all. We had a lovely time yesterday, I assure you," Georgiana declared.

"I am glad to hear that. So, do you have fixed plans for this morning?" Elizabeth addressed Georgiana.

"Not really; we are taking a ride in the neighbourhood so I can see more of the country. I have really enjoyed it so far."

"So…since we are here and you do not have any fixed engagements, would you like to see Oakham Mount?" Elizabeth offered. "We might not have time for such a trip in the next few days because it is a long walk from home, but from here it is only another half hour. And the view is spectacular."

"Oh yes! Yes, I would like that very much," Georgiana answered. She looked at her brother for his consent, which was delayed.

"How will we reach it?" Darcy inquired.

"We will walk. Or I can walk, and you may ride. Whatever is more convenient for you." Elizabeth barely concealed a laugh as she imagined how appalled Mr. Darcy must be at the suggestion of walking all that distance.

During the conversation, Bingley became restless; he looked around, moved from one side of the group to the other, and finally said, "Forgive me, would you mind if I decline? Miss Bennet knows the surroundings much better than I do anyway. I should go to Longbourn and see whether I can be of help. Yesterday I left rather early and…would you mind? I am sorry I must leave you…"

Bingley's struggle to divide the time between his friends and his betrothed amused his companions, and Darcy took pity on him.

"Have no concern about us, Bingley; we will manage well enough. I will take care of the ladies and see you again later."

Elizabeth was tempted to tell Darcy he might go with Bingley. Surely, she could accompany Georgiana on a path she had taken all her life without a guardian at their back. She would clearly have been more at ease without him; he seemed tense and uncomfortable, and that affected her own mood.

But she dared not say a word. If a day before he seemed to bear her mother's offensive remarks rather well, she would not take the risk of upsetting him by suggesting his presence was not welcome.

"Very well, we will trust you in this, Miss Bennet. Let us walk," Darcy concluded, following the ladies and leading the horses.

As Elizabeth indicated, they needed about half an hour by foot. It was a moderately difficult path, enhanced by a hint of dark autumn redness in the trees and shrubs and a fresh breeze bearing the scent of rain.

When they arrived at the uppermost point, Elizabeth invited them to admire the valley, and Miss Darcy gasped in delight.

"This view is beautiful indeed—one of the best I have seen. I am happy you suggested we come here, Miss Lizzy."

"I am delighted you like it, Miss Darcy, and I hope it was worth the effort; I know it is not an easy walk. Other than Jane, none of my sisters has made it this far on foot. And Jane only did so because she is too sweet to refuse me."

"Yes, I can imagine she would do that. Miss Bennet is truly a most generous person," Darcy replied, and Elizabeth started to laugh.

"I am sure Mr. Darcy decided to join us for the same reasons," she whispered to Georgiana.

"I confess I did. Except for the 'sweet' part, which is as far from an accurate description of me as possible," Darcy responded, and Elizabeth turned to him, bewildered by his mockery.

"I hope you are not exhausted by the exercise, sir," she dared tease him back.

"Oh, I am sure he is not. William is very strong," Georgiana said with so much admiration and respect that Elizabeth could barely conceal her laughter.

Darcy observed her amusement and briefly held her gaze. "The view is truly worth the effort, Miss Bennet. It is also the first time I have seen it."

"I am glad you enjoy it, sir."

"I most certainly do. I wonder what else I missed seeing when I was last in Hertfordshire." His voice was serious, and Elizabeth wondered about the true meaning of his words. She saw him stare somewhere towards the valley, appearing lost in thought.

"William, you should have asked for recommendations of places to visit from Miss Lizzy while you stayed at Netherfield. Neither Mr. Bingley nor his sisters seem fond of spending time outdoors," Georgiana said. He turned to her, and Elizabeth was amused to see the siblings' eyes glowing with mirth for a reason of their own.

"You are right, dearest. I shall keep that in mind for the future. Now if you do not mind, I would suggest we return. Look at the sky—there are signs that it will probably rain again soon. By horse, we could reach Longbourn in a few minutes, but on foot, we will need at least an hour."

"That might be true; we should hurry back then," Elizabeth admitted.

Darcy, still holding the reins, walked behind the two ladies who were now stepping arm in arm, supporting each other. He knew Georgiana was not used to walking long distances, but she was obviously making an effort to indulge Elizabeth. He was pleased to see his sister at ease and open in Elizabeth's presence. Their obvious bond threatened his contentment with a fear. The more Georgiana became attached to Elizabeth and the more she enjoyed her time in Hertfordshire, the more she would suffer when they left. And it was no different for him; he was well aware of that. As long as he made himself believe he hated her, despised her, and blamed her for the torment of the last months, the easier it would have been to break any connection with her. But as his opinion slowly changed, her manners towards him softened, and fate bonded him to her through Georgiana and Bingley, his situation became more difficult and painful.

His thoughts were disturbed by Elizabeth's voice unexpectedly calling to him. "Mr. Darcy, I understand and take your censure to heart. I admit it is my fault for not being able to ride that it will take such a long time to return to Longbourn. And if rain comes before we arrive, I will immediately bear the guilt."

She was half-serious, half joking, and he wondered whether she knew how deeply her smiles and teasing cut his soul. He still remembered those soft lips bowed by smiles in his previous night's dreams, and he did not trust himself to endure her amused look.

But he managed to reply with composure, "I was certain you would, Miss Bennet. As my sister said, it is strange that such a determined young lady does not excel in an activity that many people enjoy. I am sure that even the horses that now follow us steadily are puzzled that we humans are not using them properly."

Elizabeth stopped to look at him, and their eyes finally met for an instant, then she started to laugh wholeheartedly. She turned to Georgiana —who was equally amused—and whispered: "Does your brother happen to speak to animals too?"

"I am not certain, Miss Bennet, but he well might," Georgiana replied, still uncertain whether the teasing between her brother and the Bennet family was diverting or offensive to him.

"Despite your tendency to argue with me every time an opportunity arises, I hope you will admit that this time I am right, Miss Bennet. And when you start to ride, you will surely discover that it cannot replace the pleasure of walking but could be a faster and equally delightful choice."

"I am willing to admit that, sir; I am just doubtful whether I want to experience it anytime soon. Oh, and I hope my tendency to argue with you has somewhat diminished recently."

Again, they exchanged glances while Miss Darcy gave them a sideways look, somewhat amazed since she had never before heard a lady speak to her brother in such a forthright manner.

A few minutes later, Longbourn appeared in their sight just as the rain started. Large drops fell slowly along with a chilly wind.

"Georgiana, take your horse and ride to Longbourn. I will accompany Miss Bennet on foot," Darcy said as he quickly sorted the reins.

"But, William—I would rather remain with you. I cannot leave by myself," the girl argued.

Darcy put his hands on her shoulders. "Dearest, please listen to me. I would also like you to take my horse. There is no point in all of us getting soaked. Ask Bingley to put the horses under shelter, and stay warm inside. We will follow you in no time."

The girl glanced from her brother to Elizabeth, her eyes tearful from distress. She was unwilling to abandon them and ready to fight her brother on that. Elizabeth stepped forward.

"Miss Darcy, I fully agree with your brother. Please do as he asks. Besides, you would do me a great favour by reaching Longbourn sooner. My parents will surely be worried about me if they have no news."

"That is not fair, Miss Lizzy—you only wish to trick me into listening to William. You both treat me as if I were a child," Georgiana replied with obvious displeasure.

"Not at all, Miss Darcy. I would have done the same with my own sisters. I am already distressed for exposing you to this weather; I beg you do not make me feel worse," Elizabeth pleaded.

"Very well…but I shall ask Mr. Bingley to send a carriage for you," Georgiana agreed reluctantly.

"You may do that, dearest, if you do not see us coming by then. Now hurry." Darcy helped his sister into the saddle and tied the reins of his horse, and Georgiana departed in haste.

He then turned to Elizabeth as the rain increased steadily.

"Come, Miss Bennet; we must hurry. Please take my arm."

"Sir, I am so sorry that I put you in this unpleasant situation. You should have left with Miss Darcy; I assure you I do not mind. I am well accustomed to walking this distance, including through rain or snow."

"I am sure you are, Miss Bennet, as I am equally sure you cannot seriously believe that I would run and hide from the rain and leave you here alone. As I said, you should take my arm so we can move as quickly as possible."

Elizabeth saw the rightness of his suggestion, so she reluctantly took his arm. She held it with the same reserve that she would hold something harmful. She marvelled at the feelings aroused inside her and felt herself shiver as she tried to keep pace with his long strides.

"You are cold; it is good we only have a short distance remaining," he said. "Would you take my coat? Although I am afraid it is so wet that it would do more harm than good."

"No…thank you…" She knew her cheeks were burning and felt grateful that he could not see her face. He had noticed her quivering but fortunately misunderstood the reason. How could he suppose something that was a puzzle even to herself?

The hold of her hand on his arm tightened. She was walking arm in arm with a man who, until a few months ago, she hated—the man she considered responsible for her sister's suffering and believed to be unfair, cruel, and disrespectful even to his dead father's wish. The man whose marriage proposal she violently rejected.

"Look, we are already home," Elizabeth said, her voice trembling. "It was much faster than usual."

"True. And it would surely have been even faster by horseback," he responded in earnest.

She glanced at his profile. "Will you never cease teasing me about my lack of riding skill? It is quite ungenerous of you," she replied and then blushed as her voice sounded more flirtatious than she intended. Her uneasiness increased when, after a brief hesitation, he answered in the same manner.

"I apologise for any inconvenience, but I am not certain whether I will ever stop. Since you have few faults I can make sport of, I must preserve the one I found."

She chuckled. "That answer is abominable, sir, and as I said—quite ungenerous!"

The conversation struggled to be light, but both were aware of the lack of composure in their voices. The attempted mockery tried—with little success to dissipate the tension and discomfort of being alone and in such an intimate situation. They were soaking wet, her hand tightly gripping his arm, and their bodies touching at times during the hasty walk.

"Again—I apologise, Miss Bennet. But my remark was true and serious. We easily could have ridden together on my horse and it would have taken only a couple of minutes to arrive. However, I did not dare suggest a solution that would have been equally improper and uncomfortable for you. I imagine you would rather freeze in the rain than accept such a proposal from me."

This time Elizabeth turned towards him, astonished and distressed by his statement and by its hidden implications. He stopped too, and their eyes locked. The entrance to Longbourn was only steps away, and she withdrew her hand from his arm. She licked her lips that, despite the raindrops falling on her face, suddenly felt dry.

"You believed me unreasonable to refuse a sensible suggestion for our mutual comfort, and yet you chose to join me in a situation that was solely my fault. Why would you do that?"

He frowned, and his gaze deepened while her breathing became unsteady. Then a smile lifted the corner of his lips and narrowed his eyes.

"Because I am a complete fool. But one with rather gentlemanlike behaviour—at least most of the time. Now, let us enter; we have spent enough time in the rain."

THEY WERE MET IN THE YARD BY BINGLEY AND JANE; GEORGIANA WAS behind them, covered with a large, dry towel and looking at them with worry.

"Oh, thank God you arrived so quickly; I had asked for the carriage to be prepared," Bingley said.

"Lizzy, let us go upstairs at once," Jane said decidedly. "Miss Darcy, would you join us, please? You should both get out of those wet gowns immediately."

As the three ladies left, Bingley turned to his friend. "Come—you must change your clothes too. I can offer you a robe and a glass of brandy from Mr. Bennet. I have sent a servant to Netherfield to procure dry clothes for you and Georgiana; he should return shortly."

"Thank you, my friend; that was thoughtful of you," Darcy answered, following Bingley while his eyes gazed after Elizabeth.

"Yes, well…in fact the carriage was Miss Darcy's idea, and sending John to Netherfield was Jane's," Bingley mumbled, happy to at least offer his friend a glass of brandy.

Upstairs in the bedroom, a blanket of wet clothes appeared on the floor with an eruption of voices.

Under Jane's strict supervision, both Georgiana and Elizabeth were quickly dried and cleaned.

Elizabeth tried to calm her sister. "Jane, we are fine—do not worry."

"I see you are fine, Lizzy, but I would like to know you will continue to be so in a few days and not catch a bad cold. So please keep the towel on your hair a little longer; you are still wet," Jane replied then turned to Georgiana.

"Miss Darcy, for the moment, you will take one of Lizzy's dresses. And please allow me to loosen your hair; it must be dried too."

"Of course, Miss Bennet; thank you for your care," Georgiana answered meekly, glancing at Elizabeth, who could barely withhold her laughter. Jane had suddenly turned into a severe mistress who accepted no contradiction, but Elizabeth knew too well that it was due to her sister's affection and care for their well-being.

A knock on the door introduced Kitty and Mary bringing tea. First, Elizabeth and Georgiana were offered large hot cups and asked to sit close to the fireplace. Then the other three sisters took a seat and a cup of tea, and everybody finally managed to be calm.

"Miss Darcy, you are an amazing rider. As fast as lightning," Kitty said admiringly.

"Thank you." Georgiana smiled, red cheeked from the compliment and the hot tea. "But I confess it was more my concern for Miss Lizzy and my brother than my riding skills that induced me to ride so fast."

"Oh, you should not worry for Lizzy," Mary said. "She does that all the time. Once she was caught in snow and returned home half frozen."

Elizabeth laughed. "Thank you, dear Mary. Please say something else to embarrass me in front of Miss Darcy."

"But it is true, Lizzy. None of us can keep pace with you, not even when we walk to Meryton!" Kitty added.

Georgiana turned to Elizabeth. "Mr. Bingley told us you walked three miles from Longbourn to Netherfield to take care of Miss Bennet. My aunt and I found that to be an admirable gesture."

"Yes, I did, but it was nothing. I would walk much further for any of my sisters," Elizabeth said smiling.

"I imagined as much." Miss Darcy returned the smile then turned to the others. "Miss Lizzy was incredibly courageous saving my little kitten. She actually climbed a dangerous tree and took Mist down before he could run off or hurt himself. Mist is my cat."

"Yes, I can imagine Lizzy doing that," Jane agreed.

Elizabeth waved her hand in disapproval. "Miss Darcy is too kind; it was nothing. But you know—Mist is a very rare breed of cat. He is actually blue. I have never seen one as beautiful."

"He is? A blue cat?" Kitty asked incredulously.

"Yes, Miss Kitty. He is a sort of greyish-blue," Georgiana said. "My aunt purchased it for me."

The conversation continued in the same manner, increasingly animated, five young women enjoying each other's company. Elizabeth was amazed that Miss Darcy seemed comfortable among her sisters. She easily adapted to Kitty and Mary, and her younger sisters quickly recognised Miss Darcy's superior education. They heard her speak of music, theatre, and books—and Miss Darcy appeared more willing to talk than Elizabeth had ever seen her before.

Dry clothes from Netherfield finally arrived. The maid handed over the package then announced that Mrs. Bennet and the gentlemen awaited them in the drawing room where refreshments were prepared.

The others left, and Elizabeth helped Georgiana change while their conversation continued.

"I really liked the trip, Miss Lizzy. Thank you for suggesting it. And although the rain interfered with our plans, it was a lovely opportunity to spend more time with your sisters. They are all so nice and friendly."

"We were happy with your company too, Miss Darcy. I can safely say that you charmed my entire family. And…I hope you do not mind my asking, but…would you mind calling me by my given name? Elizabeth—or Lizzy as my family does," Elizabeth asked, watching carefully for Georgiana's reaction. The girl's eyes showed her immediate approval.

"I would like that very much…and please call me Georgiana. I would like that very much indeed."

"Very well, Georgiana. That is lovely indeed—as long as Mr. Darcy does not mind," Elizabeth added.

Georgiana looked puzzled. "Why would he mind? I am sure he would not, Miss Lizzy—forgive me, Lizzy—I know my brother seems severe, and I know you two have had disagreements in the past…and he was upset and unfair when we met in London…but he was only worried for me. I have… it was a difficult year, and it was entirely my fault that I gave him reason for concern. But he is indeed the best man and the best brother. Everybody who knows him shares the same opinion."

The girl's voice trembled as her anxiety increased. When her eyes moistened with tears she obviously struggled to overcome, Elizabeth held her hands.

"Georgiana, any past disagreements I might have had with Mr. Darcy are long gone. I know he is doing everything for your benefit; anyone who sees you together can testify to this. Now—shall we join the others? They must be expecting us."

"Yes, of course," Georgiana whispered. "Lizzy, I am very happy that we have come to Hertfordshire—very happy indeed. I will be sorry to leave."

"As will I, dear Georgiana," Elizabeth answered, holding the girl's arm gently.

The moment they entered the drawing room, they were met by Mrs. Bennet.

"Lizzy, I have always known that you favoured your father over me, but I never imagined you had so little consideration for my nerves. Where on earth did you get the strange habit of wandering outdoors, child? And you took your guests with you and kept them in the rain? How could you do that? What if somebody was harmed just before Jane's wedding?"

Elizabeth glanced at Darcy in embarrassment, but he seemed to be occupied with his drink.

"Mama, it was unfortunate that it began to rain. The walk to Oakham Mount is usually a pleasant one, and both Mr. and Miss Darcy enjoyed it."

"Of course, they said they enjoyed it. What else could they say? Upon my word, Lizzy, if the king himself should happen to come to Longbourn, I am sure you would take him for a walk—preferably in the rain to be certain he fell ill afterward," Mrs. Bennet concluded angrily.

Darcy choked and spilled his drink, then glanced at Elizabeth who was watching him with cheerful eyes. He could not remember when he was so amused. And the image of his sister—smiling at Elizabeth's side and appearing perfectly at ease—lifted his mood even more.

Laughter filled the room, but Mrs. Bennet remained solemn. Elizabeth decided to make peace, and she embraced her mother.

"I apologise for the distress I caused you, Mama. And I promise that, if His Majesty ever comes to Longbourn, I will allow you to set the schedule."

Chapter 15

After noon, the Gardiners arrived, and the reunion was a pleasant one. After two visits to Gracechurch Street, Georgiana was already at ease with their family; greetings were friendly, and the children did not hesitate to embrace her and ask about Didi and Mist.

Soon after, Bingley and the Darcys left for Netherfield to change and to retrieve the countess. Lady Hardwick waited for them impatiently; she had learnt of the incident with the rain, so she was anxious to know all about it.

"I am sorry to hear you had bad luck, but you honestly should not have left the house in such weather," Louisa said.

"I hope you are not leaving again; it is raining very badly and will likely continue all night," Caroline added.

"The Bennets expect us for dinner," Bingley answered, appalled at the suggestion he disappoint his intended. "But you are still welcome if you want to join us. Mrs. Bennet insisted on my telling you that."

"We appreciate the invitation, but as I said, it would be too crowded. And the weather is totally inappropriate for a late night visit," Caroline replied.

"As you wish, but I hope the rain stops soon so we can hunt tomorrow. And I cannot even imagine that it will rain on my wedding day," Bingley concluded.

"Louisa, Caroline, will you not come with us tomorrow if the weather has improved? We plan to take a longer trip with the carriage to see all of Netherfield, Meryton, and its surroundings."

"Dear Georgiana, you are very kind, but I have already seen the neighbourhood more than once. And Netherfield is not as large as Pemberley —there is not much to see," Caroline answered.

"But I am sure we will have a lovely day nevertheless," the girl said. "You are more than welcome if you change your mind."

"I thank you, but that is unlikely."

"My sisters were not curious to see much of the Pemberley estate either," Bingley remarked. "But it is good you have Jane and Miss Elizabeth to keep you company."

"Oh yes, today we walked with Lizzy all the way to Oakham Mount and back to Longbourn," Georgiana replied enthusiastically, and all eyes were drawn to her.

"Georgiana, I had not imagined you were on such familiar terms with Eliza Bennet." Caroline clearly expressed her surprise as much as her displeasure.

"Lizzy and I are friends. May I ask why you disapprove of her?" Georgiana's daring inquiry was another surprise, and Caroline glanced at her sister then back to Miss Darcy.

"Yes, I would very much like to know the same," Bingley said. "From the very beginning of our acquaintance you have done little but criticise the family, Miss Elizabeth more than the rest."

Darcy took his glass and moved towards the window. He knew too well the answer to that question, and he remembered the day he told Caroline about his admiration for Elizabeth's fine eyes.

"I did no such thing," Caroline argued. "I am only being honest. You cannot accuse me of being as blind as you are, Brother."

"Young ladies—especially those in want of a husband—often disapprove of each other," Lady Hardwick said with obvious amusement. "However, I find it hard to believe that Miss Bingley and Miss Elizabeth could share an interest in the same gentleman, so there must be other reasons for their misunderstanding. However, with Bingley marrying the eldest sister, you must find a way to improve your acquaintance. It would be quite inelegant to maintain a conflict within the family."

"Your ladyship is right of course. When Jane becomes the mistress of this house, I expect Miss Elizabeth and the other sisters to be here quite often. So everyone who stays in this house must treat them with the proper consideration," Bingley added.

"Yes, well, I doubt any of the Miss Bennets is accustomed to what 'proper' means," Caroline murmured while she poured herself a cup of tea.

Darcy observed that his sister was already distressed by a conversation that had become offensive towards her friend. Caroline's manners were as unkind as ever, and he wondered how Bingley would manage to keep her under control once he brought his wife home.

"Miss Bingley, Mrs. Hurst, when will you return to Town?" he asked.

"We are not certain," Louisa answered. "We have not yet fixed our plans."

"London was lively when we left. Most of the families of my acquaintance have already begun their preparations for the Season," he continued.

"Quite. Would you mind my asking how it happened that you left London precisely when everybody else returned?" Caroline replied.

"We had long decided to move to Pemberley for a few months, and the Season is never an incentive for me to change my plans."

"Yes, Darcy is rarely interested in the Season. And since I am to be married in two days, I will not be either," Bingley said.

"But perhaps the future Mrs. Bingley will be." Lady Hardwick smiled. "And you might enjoy showing off the exquisite beauty of your wife."

Bingley's eyes brightened. "Indeed, your ladyship gives me an excellent idea. I will ask Jane what her preference is."

"You must consider you have to renew Jane's entire wardrobe too. None of the Bennet sisters' gowns looks appropriate for London," Caroline murmured.

"I would gladly do that; in fact, I would gladly do anything for Jane," Bingley declared, and Darcy smiled at his friend's enthusiasm.

He intervened to provide help and support. "Besides, a woman as beautiful as Miss Jane Bennet does not need special gowns to draw people's admiration."

"True! I am glad you share my opinion, Darcy."

"I have every reason to, Bingley. To her beauty, Miss Bennet also adds a gentle kindness and warm manners that are becoming in any accomplished young lady."

"Yes, yes, Jane is a sweet girl, nobody denies that," Caroline interjected once more. "However, if we are to consider your own description, Mr. Darcy, you must admit that Eliza Bennet is deficient in all the virtues you just mentioned. Her features are far from perfect, her complexion tanned lately, and her manners are far from being described as gentle, kind, and warm."

Darcy swallowed some brandy then replied with apparent composure. "Miss Elizabeth Bennet possesses unique attributes that enhance her charms and are rarely seen in other young ladies."

Georgiana and Lady Hardwick smiled in approval, but Caroline seemed unable to abandon a fight that was clearly lost.

"And may I ask what attributes those might be, Mr. Darcy? Perhaps her sharp glances and impolite comments? Her ability to walk long distances?"

Darcy lost his patience, and his respect for his friend was insufficient to stop him from replying, "Yes, Miss Bingley, all those and many others but especially her fine eyes. Now that we have clarified this subject, I must beg you to excuse me; it is time to change for dinner. Georgiana, Lady Hardwick, may I show you to your rooms?"

An hour later, the three of them, together with Bingley, were in the carriage heading for Longbourn. It was still raining slightly, but the wind had stopped.

Darcy felt uncomfortable for allowing himself to be drawn into Caroline's impertinent argument. It was like the previous year; her mischievousness towards Elizabeth had not diminished in the slightest.

He regretted that he had to be harsh to his friend's sister, but he could not allow her to continue saying offensive things that might hurt his own. After all, it was not Georgiana's fault that Caroline felt ridiculously jealous of Elizabeth and unreasonably angry with the entire Bennet family.

Bingley addressed the issue. "I apologise for my sisters' impoliteness. I am sorry they placed you in the middle of such uncomfortable arguments."

"It is I who should apologise, Bingley. I am your guest, and I should not have quarrelled with your sister."

Lady Hardwick intervened. "Dear Bingley, there is no need for you to apologize to us, but you must do something with your sisters. Miss Bingley is especially rude every time she speaks of your future in-laws. And it is likely they will continue to behave the same when the new Mrs. Bingley comes to live in your house. You cannot allow it. You must realise that your future wife will have to adjust to a new life, new duties, and new expectations. She does not deserve to bear the distress of having her parents and sisters insulted by her new sisters-in-law."

"I will not permit that! Nothing will upset Jane; of that, you must be certain."

"I am glad to hear that, young man. And still—your sisters are staying in your house but refuse to visit your betrothed's family or to have dinner with them. Nor do they refrain from insulting the Bennets in every possible manner. What will happen in two days at the wedding? And how will you force them to change their behaviour?"

Bingley's discomfort was obvious; he looked from one to another, struggling for an answer.

"They are never offensive towards Jane. It seems Caroline is mostly turned against Miss Elizabeth. She is so unreasonable that I usually ignore her..."

"They might not be offensive towards Miss Bennet, but they are obviously patronising to her; I could easily observe that myself. Forgive me for insisting, but I do so for your own good. As their brother, you have affection and tolerance towards your sisters; it is only natural. But from now on, you must think with the perspective of a husband."

Bingley's uneasiness showed clearly on his face. "Your ladyship's advice is valued. I am grateful for it. I shall do that. I am happy you came to visit me, and I already regret that you have to leave so soon. You will be missed."

Lardy Hardwick laughed. "My dear boy, in two days you will surely not think of anyone but your wife, and you will hardly miss anyone once you have her company."

Bingley's face coloured, and he laughed nervously. "Yes, I imagine so... however, I shall miss your company. Darcy and Georgiana have been as close as my family in recent years. It will be hard not to see them for Lord knows how long."

"And so you have been to us, Bingley," Darcy answered. "We are not certain when we will return, but you must know that you and your family are always welcome at Pemberley—for Christmas, before or after Christmas—whenever you want. Please do not hesitate to come."

"Oh yes, that would be so lovely," Georgiana agreed.

"Well, I might just do that. No matter how fond I am of the Bennet family or of my own, I might need a little calm. Thank you, Darcy. I am certain Jane will be very pleased to hear of the invitation."

Their arrival at Longbourn was now a friendly routine. Elizabeth and Jane were the first to greet them; then the Gardiners were introduced to Lady Hardwick.

The Bennet sisters quickly claimed Georgiana and offered her a seat between Elizabeth and Jane, with Bingley and Darcy opposite them. Lady Hardwick was placed to the right of Mr. Bennet.

A MAN WITH FAULTS

As Caroline Bingley implied, the room was rather crowded and the table a bit too small for such a large gathering; however, it inconvenienced no one. Conversation began immediately and developed easily, especially as Darcy mentioned to his aunt that Mrs. Gardiner grew up in Lambton.

From their position at the dinner table, Elizabeth and Darcy could easily look at each other—and both struggled to do so but rarely. Forcing himself not to lay eyes on Elizabeth, Darcy paid close attention to his sister, who was only inches from her. Georgiana often mixed joy with uneasiness, smiles with shyness, and blushes with pallor; it seemed every subject of discussion aroused different feelings. And each time, she seemed to turn to Elizabeth for comfort. They whispered to each other all the time and called each other by their given names, and every small gesture reflected the strength of their bond.

It was established that the next afternoon the gentlemen would hunt and the ladies would take a carriage ride around the neighbourhood. Mrs. Gardiner declined politely, as she would be busy helping Mrs. Bennet finish preparations for the wedding. For the rest of them, it was decided they would take two carriages, carry baskets with food and drink, and spend several lovely hours outside if the weather permitted.

After dinner, drinks were served for the whole company in the drawing room, and pleasant conversation continued.

"Would you ladies delight us with some music?" Bingley asked.

Mary immediately rushed to the piano and started to perform dutifully. Her playing was correct but nothing more. She was listened to with proper attention and applauded when she finished.

A bit of silence followed, then Bingley spoke again. "Miss Darcy, would you play for us a little too? I have not had the pleasure of enjoying your talent for almost a year."

The girl startled, glancing in discomfort from her aunt to her brother then to Elizabeth.

Elizabeth smiled to dissipate her friend's restraint. "Or I could play, but I must warn you not to have any expectations. Or we could play together so your talent will compensate for my clumsiness."

"I am sure you are not clumsy," Georgiana said shyly.

"I can assure you Miss Elizabeth is not since I have had the pleasure of hearing her previously," Darcy intervened from the corner of the room, drawing both pairs of eyes to him. He remained composed, enjoying his brandy with the other gentlemen.

"Mr. Darcy is too kind to me—unusually so," Elizabeth whispered to Georgiana. "Trust me; I am being truthful about my skills. Would you save me by playing if I turn the pages for you?"

"Very well, it shall be as you say." Georgiana was not oblivious to her friend's little scheme.

They sat at the piano, and Georgiana began to play. At first, the idea of having so many eyes on her made her nervous, and she bit her lips in discomfort, but soon the music enveloped her, and her entire being seemed one with the piano, whose sounds were magical under her touch. Elizabeth turned the pages, shivering as the lovely music captivated her body and mind. She lifted her eyes towards Darcy without restraint, uneasiness, or distress—only wonder and admiration for the extraordinary talent she had the chance to witness so closely. His returned gaze was filled with pride and brotherly love as well as gratitude for the care shown to his sister.

When Georgiana finished her performance, a deep silence fell upon the room. Nobody spoke for several long moments until finally, Mrs. Bennet burst out, "Miss Darcy, that was just perfect! Just perfect! I never heard anyone play so beautifully. I cannot wait to tell my sister Phillips and Lady Lucas tomorrow."

The others immediately joined in expressing their admiration, and Georgiana was overwhelmed by so much praise.

"Miss Darcy, I will never dare to play again, having heard your interpretation," Mary said humbly when the compliments finally ceased.

Georgiana turned to her with surprise and obvious concern. "Oh, please do not say that, Miss Mary. Your technique is excellent. It is obvious that you practice diligently."

"I do, Miss Darcy, but my playing is completely different from yours. I only now realise how poor my skills are."

"Mary, you are too harsh on yourself," Elizabeth intervened, but her sister seemed to ignore everything except the object of her admiration.

"Miss Mary, your skills are excellent; please believe me. Would you sit near me?" Mary hurried to take a chair, and then Georgiana brushed her fingers over the piano keys.

"I love to practice too, but sometimes I prefer to forget about the technique and allow the music to lead me without thinking of anything else."

"I do not understand your meaning, Miss Darcy. Will you not show me?"

"With pleasure. Or even better, let us try together if you do not mind."

"It would be my greatest pleasure!" Mary said with delight. "Lizzy has played with me in four hands several times, but neither of us is proficient."

"Here it is: a sonata by Mozart. I will turn the pages for you," Elizabeth said, caught up in the two girls' excitement.

They started to play together, Mary following the keys rigidly, careful of her fingering. The music drew the others' attention, but the two performers soon ignored everything around them. From time to time, Georgiana whispered some indications to Mary, who seemed to follow her lead more easily with every page.

The minutes of pure delight were offered to their companions who stared at the piano in disbelief. Mrs. Bennet and Kitty appeared completely mesmerised while Mr. Bennet's countenance showed pride in the daughter he used to mostly ignore.

When the impromptu recital ended, it was rewarded with a long round of applause; tears moistened Mary's eyes then dripped down her cheeks.

"Oh, my dear child, how talented you are!" Mrs. Bennet cried. "I never knew until now, but that is only because I have too much to handle by myself. You inherited it from me; I am sure of that. Oh, that was truly beautiful."

"Thank you, Mama, but it was Miss Darcy's help entirely," Mary answered, pleased to be her mother's momentary favourite. She gracefully received everyone's congratulations, overwhelmed by a wave of attention she had never felt before.

The rest of the evening passed cheerfully, and at midnight, the party came to an end. Mrs. Bennet declared she could not remember when she had last stayed so long at a dinner party and claimed that it could well be called a private ball although nobody danced.

Warm farewells were exchanged, and the four guests returned to Netherfield. The rain had stopped, and the sky was lit by stars and a bright moon.

"What a lovely evening," the countess declared.

"Indeed," Darcy agreed. "I must say I had a pleasant time. Mr. Bennet and Mr. Gardiner are excellent companions, and we had the benefit of exquisite music. We have you to thank for that, dear Georgiana. I was very proud of you."

The girl blushed. "I certainly do not deserve such praise. It was my pleasure to play with Miss Mary. I never played with anyone except my teacher, you know."

"I imagined as much. It was beautiful—everybody agreed."

Lady Hardwick patted the girl's hand. "Well, my dear, it is good that you have so much enjoyable company from girls your own age. There will only be silence and solitude once we arrive at Pemberley. I am afraid I cannot compete with four charming young ladies to entertain you. You will now be bored alone with us. We must plan some parties and perhaps invite some of my nieces and nephews to visit us."

Georgiana appeared more panicked than pleased. "Oh, please do not do that, Aunt. I very much enjoy being with you and with William. You must not bring anyone to entertain me."

"I was joking, my dear. But I cannot stop wondering: How is it possible that you are so restrained, so reluctant to meet other people and yet so at ease with the Bennet girls whom you just met two days ago? I am just curious to understand if you would kindly tell us," the countess asked gently.

Georgiana hesitated, looked at her three companions in the carriage, and said, "Because they are honest with me. They do not just pretend to like me. And Lizzy became my friend before she knew who I was."

Her answer came as a surprise to the others. Her words, but even more the tone and the slight tremble in her voice worried Darcy exceedingly. He decided not to continue the conversation at that time, but his concern increased when Georgiana said nothing more and only stared outside into the darkness.

Once they arrived at Netherfield, each retired to their own room, overcome by fatigue. Darcy glanced at his sister often, pained to see her earlier cheerfulness lost.

He wished to approach her, to speak to her privately, but he did not dare at that late hour and decided to leave it for the next day. However, as they stopped in front of their own doors, Georgiana seemed hesitant to enter; her shoulders and head were lowered as if she were burdened.

Darcy's decision was made. "Dearest, may I come in to speak to you a moment?"

She appeared surprised but nodded in agreement. Inside, they sat, and Darcy carefully searched for the right words.

"My dear, please tell me what troubles you. You said you had a lovely time, and I noticed the same, but I can see now that you are unwell. Has anything upset you?"

Her eyes were still fixed on the floor, and she rubbed her hands together. Finally, she spoke, but her voice sounded fearful.

"William, I would like to invite Lizzy to Pemberley."

She finally looked at him, so he could not avoid her gaze. Cold shivers ran down Darcy's spine, and ice seemed to pierce his chest.

Invite Elizabeth to Pemberley? So close to him? Now, when he had decided to leave Pemberley precisely to escape her? Surely, that was unthinkable. It was not even worth discussing. He could not allow it to happen.

"When?" was all he could ask.

"Now...tomorrow. Perhaps, if she accepts, then she might come with us now. I asked you a few weeks ago in London, and you said I am allowed to invite a friend to Pemberley."

"Of course you are allowed, dearest, but I am not sure this would be wise."

"Wise? Why not?

He felt weak and ashamed of himself for deceiving his sister—for putting his own distress ahead of Georgiana's peace and comfort.

"William, I have had such a lovely time these last few days. It has been so relaxing and amusing. Everybody has been so kind to me...I cannot imagine being alone again. Do you know Miss Bennet brushed and dried my hair today? Nobody has done that since I was small except for my maid. I do not think I can bear silence and solitude again. And I cannot bear to have people visit just to entertain me. Can I not have a companion who truly cares for me?"

"Georgiana, I must disagree with you—there are many people among our relatives and acquaintances who genuinely care for you. Some of them are even close to your age. I do not know why you feel differently."

She lowered her head again and whispered, "I am sorry...I apologise..."

"Please do not apologise for what you feel. It is just...I wish I could understand you better. And about Miss Elizabeth, you must keep in mind that the sister she loves the most will be newly wed. She will want to be close to the future Mrs. Bingley. She also might be opposed to being away from her family. She might not want to leave Longbourn again so soon."

"I know, but I can ask her, can I not? She might agree to come with us now, or perhaps when Mr. and Mrs. Bingley come to visit us for Christmas, Lizzy may join them. I will be happy if I know at least that I will see her again soon, even if I have to wait three more months. I just wish to be certain you do not disapprove."

"I am not certain…we had planned to go to Pemberley alone. I did not believe you would be bored with my company before we arrived."

"Oh, please do not say that—it is unfair. There is nobody whose company I enjoy more, but you are a gentleman, you have your own business, and you…I cannot ask you to understand me. I often do not dare to speak to you."

"Dearest, please do not cry! Tell me what I can do for you to feel better. What do you mean that you do not dare to speak to me?"

"It is nothing…forgive me…I should not have said anything. But I thought you would approve. I noticed you and Lizzy are familiar with each other…and you are quite friendly with all the Bennets…you do not seem to have anything against them. Then why do you seem so displeased with my suggestion?"

"I am just worried. I know you have grown very fond of Miss Elizabeth in a short while and I would not want you to be disappointed…"

Georgiana's blue eyes danced with tears, and the sadness was so poignant on her face that he could bear it no longer. He could not continue to deceive his own sister or continue to disguise his own fear of suffering.

He breathed deeply and took her hands in his. "You may ask her, but I beg you to keep in mind that she might have very good reasons to refuse you. I do not wish you to be disappointed."

The girl's face brightened in a moment, and she embraced him tightly.

"Oh, thank you so much, Brother! Thank you! I will ask her tomorrow during our picnic. I will be careful, I promise. And I will tell Aunt Amelia in the morning. I can imagine how surprised she will be. Thank you!"

Georgiana's animated voice still sounded in Darcy's ears when he returned to the solitude of his own room. The more he thought of the girl's pained words, the more he could understand the torment behind them. She was only a child when their mother passed away, and long before that, Lady Anne's illness was the reason for concern, calm, silence, and solitude at Pemberley. Georgiana was never loud, never disobedient, and never did other than what was expected of her. She spent several hours every day with her mother, who kept to her bed most of the time. She learnt to read and play the piano at an early age so she could entertain her mother. They shared a special bond that painfully broke the day Lady Anne fell to the floor while listening to her daughter play for her. Since then, Georgiana had been mostly alone at Pemberley with numerous servants, a pained father, and a brother who saw her only during his holidays—but without friends, without other children her own age, without laughter, without joy.

Yes, Lady Hardwick had been right. There had been too much silence, too much sadness, and too much loneliness at Pemberley, at least for Georgiana.

The night passed slowly because Darcy could not sleep. He knew this was another night ruined for him. He would not be able to sleep again—not then and not for a long while. Whether Elizabeth accepted or refused Georgiana's invitation, his rest would be disturbed, although for different reasons. What could he do to be certain that his sister would not suffer? How could he take all the distress on himself and offer Georgiana the peace she needed.

He opened the window wide as he felt he lacked fresh air. Only three miles away lay the reason for his torment and struggles, the one who either kept him awake or troubled his dreams.

He suddenly knew what he had to do: tomorrow very early, he would find a way to talk to her before Georgiana could. It was the only way to be certain of the desired outcome.

Chapter 16

Darcy left his bed at dawn. Eagerness, combined with worry, had made the night dreadful. He could do little but hope that his endeavour would improve the day.

At the stables, the servants jumped to their feet when they saw him. He dismissed them and prepared the stallion himself. It was still early, and he needed something to do. The previous day, Elizabeth had mentioned that she often walked in the morning, and he hoped he would be lucky enough to find her.

The weather appeared fine. It was rather cold, frost covered the ground, and the leaves were tattered by late autumn winds.

He rode at a steady pace, noticing every detail around him. His mind was surprisingly alert after a complete lack of sleep the previous night—and several others before.

The rhythm of his heart suddenly changed; he sensed Elizabeth before he actually saw her. She apparently recognised him too, and she stopped as he dismounted and bowed to her. Her eyes betrayed surprise and also a trace of distress. Her cheeks were crimson, and a few locks of hair had escaped her bonnet.

"Mr. Darcy! You are truly a startling presence here at such an early hour. Are you alone? I hope all is well at Netherfield."

"Good morning, Miss Bennet. Yes, everything is perfectly fine; the family is still sleeping. May I walk with you a while?"

"Of course," Elizabeth answered, not at all composed. She recollected the strange days at Rosings when he would suddenly appear in her path and keep her company in an awkward silence.

Now, however, he seemed decided to speak. "And at Longbourn? Is everything well, I hope?"

"Yes—well and agitated," she said with a laugh. "You can imagine that, with two days until the wedding, none of us is tranquil. Except for Papa, who mostly stays in the library. And Jane; as always, she behaves more reasonably than any of us, although I know very well that her heart is not at ease. My aunt Mrs. Philips asked Jane why she is so indifferent. Of course, she is not—quite the contrary. But she has an apparent serenity that often makes people overlook her true feelings."

Her uneasiness made Elizabeth even more voluble than usual, and only when she finished her explanation did she realize she might have said something unwise. He immediately noticed her words.

"Yes, I remember. That is one of the mistakes for which I will never forgive myself. I hastily presumed that Miss Bennet had no true affection for my friend, and I did not hesitate to tell him as much."

"Sir, I honestly did not intend to bring up painful memories. Let us be thankful for the way things turned out and forget the difficulties on the road to happiness. Your present behaviour clearly shows your affection for Mr. Bingley, and a mistake made with the purpose of helping your friend, even starting from a wrong premise, is easier to forgive."

"You are too generous…"

"Not at all, as you well know. But Jane and Mr. Bingley are, and their present felicity spreads joy all around them."

"Indeed, we all have felt the positive influence of their presence. But I wonder whether you and Miss Bennet know that Bingley's departure last autumn was my fault. I was the one who insisted on convincing him of Miss Bennet's indifference. The worst of it is that, because of my arrogance, I was certain it was the correct assumption."

Both looked straight ahead.

"I imagined as much…and…I remember reading a few lines in your letter. It was the beginning that made me so angry…"

She felt his burning gaze on her face.

"This is the first time I am pleased you did not read further. Indeed, in my conceit, I did not hesitate to confess my entire involvement. The revelation of the truth might have been honourable, but the tone was pretentious."

"I cannot be pleased, regardless. I have blamed myself every day for my thoughtless reaction, and I will continue to do so," she admitted.

Both their voices trembled now, and she wondered with fear how they had come to such dreadful memories. She decided to put an end to a subject that was too agonising for both.

"You should know that Mr. Bingley confessed to Jane and me the true circumstances of his return. He told us that he left Netherfield not because he did not love Jane but because he feared she did not return his affection. Then he related his conversation with Lady Hardwick and her advice that convinced him to pursue his desires."

"Bingley is a better friend than I deserve."

Elizabeth stole a glance at his preoccupied countenance, and for an instant, their eyes met.

"I shall not even deny that as Jane is a much better sister than I deserve." She tried to sound half in jest and then continued in a lighter tone.

"Sir, we are grateful for your and Lady Hardwick's presence at the wedding. All of Meryton knows of Miss Bingley and Mrs. Hurst's disapproval of this marriage. Your attendance will be immense compensation for their rudeness and a sign that Jane is welcome among her husband's illustrious friends."

He turned to her in surprise. "I admit I did not think of that when I decided to come. I only considered my happiness in standing by my friend on this important day in his life. But I am content to be of help to Miss Bennet, although I doubt she needs it."

He paused, and again Elizabeth glanced at him, surprised to notice his lips lifted into a smile. He spoke again with a trace of laughter in his voice. "Yesterday, Miss Bingley made some rude remarks regarding the upcoming wedding that angered my aunt. Lady Hardwick answered that a few years ago someone with a fortune made in trade would not have been admitted to Pemberley and never could have hoped to marry the daughter of a gentleman. Bingley eagerly agreed, but you may well imagine the reaction of Miss Bingley and Mrs. Hurst."

Elizabeth was motionless in disbelief then started to laugh behind her hand. "Oh, dear Lord! I am so sorry I was not there to witness it. But I can picture it in my mind, and I will remember it every time their behaviour bothers me. Thank you for telling me, sir."

"You are welcome," he answered.

A few moments of silence followed, then he suddenly stopped, and Elizabeth did the same. Her uneasiness at being alone in his presence was not gone, but it was calmed by a sense of happiness that warmed her inside. She admitted that she enjoyed being with him and talking to him on such friendly terms, and she searched for another topic, wondering how long he would remain in her company. However, he was the first to speak again.

"Miss Bennet, I confess I came out early with the hope of finding you and having a few minutes of private talk on a delicate subject."

His statement took Elizabeth by surprise, and her uneasiness turned to distress.

"Yes, of course...I hope there is nothing grave, sir. I am a bit worried now," she attempted to joke.

"It is a matter of great importance for my sister and even for me. I know I must speak to your father to obtain his approval, but I wanted to know your opinion before going any further."

Elizabeth's heart seemed to stop beating, and her knees became unsteady; her mind could form no reply. They were having such a lovely walk and a pleasant, honest conversation—even shared painful memories and clarified their misunderstandings. And now—what could he possibly mean? What "delicate" matter needed her father's approval? Surely, he would not consider proposing again! He could not still intend to marry her! Or could he? What if he were to propose? How could she answer such a question after everything that had passed between them? After he saved her family's honour? After he corrected his wrongs with Bingley? After she and Georgiana had become close friends? Would she dare refuse him again? Did she really want to refuse him again?

Panic overwhelmed her, and she dared not look at him, so she remained silent as she feared her voice would tremble.

"Miss Bennet...you know only too well that my sister has become quite attached to you. Therefore, it might not come as a great surprise that she wishes to invite you to Pemberley."

Elizabeth's knees weakened, and she blinked several times. She finally lifted her eyes to his. She blushed, and shame overcame any other feelings as she mocked her own foolishness, scolding her ridiculous presumptions. How could she imagine he would ever propose again? What sort of simpleton was she?

He had come solely to tell her that Georgiana intended to invite her to Pemberley. Was that all?

Darcy continued, "Such a situation would surely be unbearable for both of us. Living together in the same house—even one as large as Pemberley —is unthinkable for two people who have been involved in such tumultuous circumstances. Our past cannot be easily forgotten or forgiven."

Yes, she knew that to be true, and yet she foolishly imagined circumstances had changed. They had not. He neither forgot nor forgave. His behaviour had improved, his manners towards her had softened, and his judgment of her family had become more lenient, but his feelings for her were no kinder, no less resentful. He had accepted her friendship with Georgiana and agreed to their maintaining a correspondence, as long as that did not involve her presence anywhere near him. He had agreed to spend time at Longbourn only to humour his friend Bingley, but he obviously was anxious to leave as soon as possible. That she imagined he might propose to her again was utterly ludicrous.

"That is true. Am I correct in assuming then that you mean to insist that I reject Georgiana's invitation?" she barely managed to reply. His face darkened even more, and he averted his eyes, glancing around.

"Quite the contrary, Miss Bennet. I came to beg you to accept the invitation. I understand this might come as a burden to you; you have only recently returned to your family, and you will surely not want to leave them again soon. And I realise it is selfish of me to insist but...my sister had a very upsetting year. She bore much distress and pain, and your friendship seems the only thing that comforts her..."

Her astonishment was beyond expression. Their eyes met again, and he continued, his discomfort obviously increasing. He looked as she had seen him only once before. She felt her lips trembling and bit them as she struggled to understand the implication of their conversation.

"I am well aware that the past year was a trying one for you too, Miss Bennet. I am not insensitive to the challenges you had to overcome in the last months...and I declare myself responsible for most of them. It was my fault that things did not occur as smoothly as they could have...with Bingley and Miss Bennet...and it was also my fault that Wickham was not exposed earlier and prevented from deceiving those around him. But my sister cannot be blamed for any of this..."

"Sir, you need not mention that. You must know by now that I am delighted and honoured by Georgiana's friendship. She has become as dear to me as my own sisters."

"I have no remaining doubt about that. I have observed you both closely these last few days, and I am convinced that she has found in you the friend she always desired. And I thank you for that."

He paused as though deciding whether he should speak further. Eventually, he continued. "I have never seen my sister as lively as she is with you. Neither I, nor my aunt, nor our other relatives seem to comfort her as you do. And she seems more at ease with your sisters than she has ever been with her cousins. She mentioned to me that Miss Bennet brushed her hair yesterday. Can you imagine that? She can have anything she wants in the world, but she was impressed by Miss Bennet's kind yet simple gesture."

"Dear Lord, I never thought…I mean…it was so normal that we did not even notice it. We treated her just as we are used to do among our friends. It was we who were impressed by her kindness to Mary—extraordinary indeed."

"Yes, is it not strange that we all wish for what we cannot have?" he whispered.

She dared not answer such a question, just as she knew not how to reconcile her affection for Georgiana with her own fear and restraint about being at Pemberley with him.

"An invitation to spend time with Georgiana at Pemberley seems a lovely dream. However, there are things I must consider…we both must consider…"

"Yes…"

"I confess I am surprised. Do you happen to know when she would expect me at Pemberley if I accept the invitation—and for how long?"

"I believe she hoped you could travel with us. But I warned her that, even if you accepted, you might not want to leave your family so soon. Of this, you should not worry. Whenever it is convenient for you, I shall arrange for you to travel in safety and comfort. There is also a chance that Bingley and his future wife might visit us shortly. I hope they will. So whatever is convenient for you would be fine. Once you and Georgiana decide, I will make it happen."

"Very well, sir. I appreciate that you informed me prior to my meeting with Georgiana. It gives me a little time to consider all the implications. I will think on it for the next few hours."

"Thank you. And you must not worry about my presence being disagreeable to you. I give you my word that I shall not bother you more than absolutely necessary. I intend to concentrate on my own business, and you will rarely see me at all, except probably at breakfast and dinner."

"Mr. Darcy, surely there is no need for you to hide in your own house! I would not dare demand such a thing."

"Miss Bennet, I would make any sacrifice to see my sister at peace, happy, maybe laughing more," he said with a sadness that touched her heart.

"Yes, I understand. I will return home now. I shall see all of you later, I imagine?"

"May I keep you company to Longbourn?"

"That will not be necessary, sir. Good day."

Their separation was abrupt and left both of them in turmoil, although seen from afar, the meeting went reasonably well.

Elizabeth could not forgive herself for the ridiculous assumption that a new proposal would follow, and she was angry to finally admit feeling disappointment. She could not have been further from the truth. He made it clear—several times—that he was making decisions for the benefit of his sister, even against his own will. He did not say—but implied—that being under the same roof with her would be a burden.

But if he loathed being in her proximity, why did he insist on the visit? Was Georgiana's distress so deep, so dangerous that it needed to be addressed right away? For such private, restrained people as the two siblings were, the hidden part of their suffering likely was greater than what was exposed to the world.

She rushed home, searched for Jane, and went with her to their room. She needed advice, comfort, and support to make a difficult decision, so she told her sister everything about the unusual meeting—except her unreasonable presumption and the disappointment that followed.

Darcy's distress was no less. He remained in doubt that he had done the right thing in speaking to Elizabeth without informing Georgiana, but he was at least content that the result of his endeavour was positive as it allowed them both to clarify their opinions.

But he was as uncertain of Elizabeth's decision as he was earlier. She was concerned about Georgiana and willing to help her, but she was as reluctant as he expected at the idea of their living in the same house. He understood as much from her unsaid words. The thought of having her so close, seeing her every day, and breathing the same air, was for him exhilarating and dreadful at the same time—even more so as that part of their conversation was truly satisfying to him. There were hints that her opinion of him had improved. She was apparently more ready to forgive some of his past faults, and she confirmed that she did read a part of his letter. Remembering its first words, he began to understand her angry reaction to them.

Once again, it seemed his lack of care in the manner of writing it had persuaded her not to read it. Would he ever be able to remedy his earlier wrongs?

Soon after breakfast, Longbourn was overflowing again; five gentlemen—including a strangely animated Mr. Hurst—went off on their hunting party. The ladies divided themselves between two carriages: Elizabeth, Georgiana, Mary, and Kitty together with two large baskets of food and drink in the first; Jane, Mrs. Gardiner, and Lady Hardwick in the second. Since Didi was joining his mistress, the Gardiner children were invited into the same carriage.

An hour of pleasant travel delighted the ladies. Finally, they stopped at Oakham Mount, and the Bennet sisters spread two blankets on the grass, inviting everyone to enjoy the splendid view and the tasty refreshments. The weather favoured them, as the sun was warm enough to make the early October day a pleasant one.

Lady Hardwick asked Jane how she was feeling in her last two days as Miss Bennet, and Jane blushed with equal pleasure and embarrassment. The conversation continued in the same friendly manner; however, the more voluble the others were, the more silent Georgiana became.

"Are you comfortable? Is everything all right?" Elizabeth whispered to her.

"Oh, yes—everything is wonderful." A short pause followed then the girl continued. "Lizzy, would you like to take a stroll with me? There is something I would like to talk to you about privately if you do not mind."

"Yes, of course." Elizabeth smiled, trying to sound composed.

They walked arm in arm, followed by the others' curious glances until they took a curve in the path and were sheltered from any witnesses.

Georgiana made obvious efforts to gather her courage; her discomfort was so great that Elizabeth could not bear it any longer.

"My dear, what do you wish to tell me? I hope you know you do not have to measure your words for me."

"I do know that, but it is not easy to accomplish. My heart is wide open to you, but my mind needs time to learn to speak freely," Georgiana said with a smile that contradicted the seriousness of her words. "I have never behaved with anyone as I do with you, Lizzy, as I never had a friend like you. It was very fortunate that I met you in London; I am glad we came to Hertfordshire."

Elizabeth smiled and took Georgiana's hands to share the girl's distress. "You are so sweet that you will make me cry soon. Meeting you was to my benefit, I assure you. And you cannot possibly be happier than I am with your visit. Everyone in my family has grown attached to you, and I truly consider you as close as my sisters."

"Yes, I do feel that. You have all been so kind to me...I hope to see your family again soon...I will miss you dearly. That is why..." Georgiana stopped and looked at Elizabeth; her discomfort was apparent, and she seemed to struggle with her words.

"I was wondering...Lizzy, would you like to come to Pemberley? With me? Or at least to visit me? I will be honoured if you accept. You are the only friend I ever invited...only if you wish to...I mean, if you do not mind..."

Georgiana looked so abashed that Elizabeth embraced her tightly.

"Georgiana, are you inviting me to Pemberley? That is such a generous gesture!"

"Do you think so? I am so glad! If you knew how long I have struggled with it!"

"Truly? Why would you struggle? From everything I have heard about Pemberley, anyone would be thrilled to visit. My aunt has never ceased speaking of her admiration for the estate."

"Oh, but Mrs. Gardiner should come to visit us too! William has already invited Mr. Bingley and Miss Bennet—oh, I mean Mrs. Bingley. Perhaps they could bring all your family. That would be so lovely!"

Within minutes, with Elizabeth's support, Georgiana succeeded in stepping over her concerns and changing her discomfort to excitement. Elizabeth's heart melted for the girl who had such genuine modesty and kindness. Georgiana was the type of person who gave gifts and then felt grateful when they were accepted.

"My dear, we should calm a little before you issue invitations to my entire family," Elizabeth said with a laugh. "Let us take this step by step. But

I thank you and Mr. Darcy for offering Jane such a lovely opportunity. I believe they will surely need an escape far from Hertfordshire once they are married. Living too close to his family and hers might prove to be challenging for them."

"Yes, I know what you mean," Georgiana answered timidly.

"So would you please tell me what you have in mind? When do you wish me to come to Pemberley?"

"Oh—whenever you want! I confess I was hoping that you might come with us...the day after tomorrow. But William said you might prefer to spend more time with your family...and I do not want to intrude. Whenever you wish to..."

"Very well, my dear. I will speak to my family and let you know later tonight at dinner. Would that be acceptable?"

"Yes, very much so. Thank you."

Elizabeth expected that Georgiana would completely relax once the issue of the invitation was clarified. Instead, she continued to walk—not towards their party but in the opposite direction. It was obvious that she was still troubled, and Elizabeth preferred to wait instead of inquiring. Finally, she spoke.

"Lizzy, as happy as I am at the prospect of having your company at Pemberley, there is something I must confess to you, although it might make you change your opinion of me. I was tempted not to tell you anything until you arrived at Pemberley, but it would not have been fair. I cannot keep any secrets from you. You have the right to know the entire truth before you make the decision to spend several months with me."

"My dear, you are frightening me now; it cannot be so serious. And in any case, be assured that anything you wish to tell me will not change my opinion of you."

"It is very serious. Do you remember when I confessed to you that I almost eloped a year ago?" she asked timidly, her voice barely audible.

"Yes..."

"I did not mention that it happened in Ramsgate where I was staying with my companion at that time, Mrs. Younge. But there is something else of much more consequence that I did not say. At the time, it seemed of little importance since I did not know who you were and I could not imagine there might be any connection, but now it cannot be concealed. I spoke with my brother about it the moment I discovered your true identity and your sister's delicate situation. Lizzy, the man with whom I was tempted to elope…was George Wickham."

The revelation came as such a blow that Elizabeth almost lost her balance. Georgiana's voice—although shy and tender—was like thunder in Elizabeth's ears. She looked at Georgiana in complete disbelief, both of them struggling to breathe. The girl was pale and tearful, and Elizabeth held her hands in hers, incapable of saying anything. The dramatic confession changed everything for the worse, and she wondered about the dreadful torment Georgiana had endured. How was it possible that the girl still insisted on being her friend, although she knew about Wickham's elopement with Lydia? How could she take the risk of visiting Longbourn to see her in the family of the woman who was now Wickham's wife and take the chance of hearing discussions about the man who betrayed her? She braved all this because of their friendship, because of Georgiana's affection for her. How could she ever repay Georgiana's loyalty? And how could she ever forgive herself for granting her trust and admiration to a man so horrible, so low, so dishonourable?

"My dear Georgiana," she whispered, embracing the girl tightly.

"I can see you are shocked Lizzy. Forgive me for disturbing you…I have told no one until now. Except my cousin Richard, who is my guardian, and my aunt Amelia, nobody else knows of this. Now you have every reason to condemn me. I was so blind that I allowed myself to be so easily deceived."

"Condemn you? Not at all! But I am shocked—I never would have imagined it. I know Wickham was your father's godson; he told me as much. How dare he betray the memory of his godfather so cruelly?"

They resumed their walk arm in arm, Georgiana revealing a deep torment in her voice.

"I was such a fool, Lizzy. For months, I struggled to understand his character, and at first, I thought his affection for me was stronger than the respect he owed my father. I believed that he intended to cherish my father's memory by sharing a happy life with me."

She paused to gather her strength as sadness choked her voice.

"What a simpleton I was. He was so handsome that I should have known he would not marry someone like me for sincere reasons. He wished for nothing but the monetary gain that would come with my dowry. And if I had any doubt left about his complete lack of affection for me, I had the final proof when I found that he seduced another girl of my age only a year later, using the same scheme."

"His intentions were not sincere because he is the lowest sort of man, and his outward appearance has little to do with that."

"I know now that he is worthless…but it is so sad, Lizzy. That he deceived me is of little importance, but I am thinking of my father who treated him so kindly. He even paid for George's school, you know. He would be so disappointed…"

"Oh, my dear…I cannot tell you how pained I am for your sorrow and how angry I am at Wickham! And at myself because I allowed myself to be deceived by his lies much easier than you did. I only knew him a few days, and impressed by his appearance of goodness and amiability, I granted him my trust and my friendship—for which I am deeply ashamed. You knew Wickham all your life; your father showed him affection, and you were accustomed to his presence in your parents' house for so long that it was only natural you grew affectionate and trustful towards him. And it is even more astonishing that you found the strength not to follow the plan to the end. Few women in your position would have had the same courage and determination."

Elizabeth's speech turned angrier with every word. Her own frustration, shame, and fury came to intensify her sadness for the torment Georgiana had to suffer and for Lydia's misfortune.

"Lizzy, I do not deserve such praise. It was only by chance that my brother came to visit me a day before the elopement. I could not keep the secret from him, as I could not bear to disappoint him. I confessed everything to him, and he wrote to George. I know not what my brother said, but I never saw George again."

"Mr. Darcy must have been so upset…" Elizabeth whispered to herself, but Georgiana heard her.

"He was indeed. What I regret the most is the pain and distress I caused my brother. He did everything for me, and I was such a disappointment. I will never be able to remedy this."

"Georgiana, I have known Mr. Darcy for over a year now, and we have had frequent disagreements. Many of them—I only now realise—were due to my trust in Mr. Wickham and his malicious stories about your brother.

But one thing I came to know from the beginning of our acquaintance: Mr. Darcy's affection for you. He always spoke of you with such tenderness and admiration that anyone could see the strength of his love for you. Surely, you cannot doubt that."

"I do not. I know he does everything for my happiness even when he disapproves of my behaviour. He was displeased with my decision to find refuge in unfamiliar parks and conceal my true name, but he allowed me to do as I pleased. Do you wish to know why I did that?"

Elizabeth held her arm tighter. "Only if you wish to tell me, my dear. I confess I am grateful that I met you, aside from the reasons that brought you near Gracechurch Street."

"Yes, it was the best thing to come from this. You were the only person who wished to be my friend without wanting anything from me."

"My dear, I am sure there are many others who care for you as much as I do. Why would you feel otherwise?"

"I cannot say. It might appear strange to you but…I just could not bear to meet people I know in Hyde Park. I felt like everyone knew what I did, and every glance seemed to carry with it reproach and disdain. And any time I met one of our acquaintances, they would ask about William. I am so tired of being only my brother's sister. I would readily give my life for William, but I wished that, just once, someone would like me for myself. I know I sound unreasonable and foolish…and probably my words make no sense to you, but I feel so much better talking to you. I am so grateful that you listen to my ramblings…"

Elizabeth's thoughts were a tumult then grew into a storm that overwhelmed her. She found little to say as her heart ached for Georgiana. Slowly, the girl's soul opened to her enough that she could see inside it, and the depth of the suffering and torment of a young person who seemed to have everything frightened her. Her own concerns, her own doubts, mattered little. There was nothing to discuss and no decision to delay. She could not —she would not—forsake the girl who valued their friendship so much.

"And *I* am grateful that you trust me enough to share your ramblings with me, my dearest friend. Now we should return to the others; we will have plenty of time to talk on our journey to Pemberley and in the next few months there."

Georgiana's eyes glimmered, and then tears fell over her pale cheeks.

"You are coming with me to Pemberley? The day after tomorrow," she whispered incredulously.

"I most certainly am." Elizabeth attempted to smile.

"Oh, Lizzy, I am so happy...so very happy...but you said you were not certain. Did you change your mind because of everything I told you?"

Elizabeth breathed deeply, took the girl's hands in hers again, and looked deeply into her eyes as she answered. "Yes! I do not wish to deceive you, so I shall not offer useless explanations. I am grateful for your confession. It helped me understand that now I must—and I wish to—be by your side. At Pemberley."

Chapter 17

When Elizabeth and Georgiana returned to the party, Elinor and Edward ran to them, followed by Didi.

"Lizzy, Miss Anna, where have you been?" asked Elinor. "We were afraid you were lost in the woods!"

"That is so wrong! Lizzy would never get lost," Edward stated with great pride.

"Thank you for your trust, Edward. We only took a short walk, Elly." Elizabeth caressed the children's hair.

"Look, Lizzy, we became even more friends with Didi. Oh—and Lady Hardwick said we can see Mist. Can we, Miss Anna?"

"Of course, you can," Georgiana answered warmly. "I will bring him tomorrow."

The children's enthusiasm was added to the questions coming from Mary and Kitty. Jane and Lady Hardwick remained silent, watching Elizabeth and Georgiana with equal concern and curiosity. Elizabeth smiled at her, trying to show there was no reason for worry.

They returned to Longbourn after another hour. Mrs. Bennet awaited them eagerly, scolding Jane for staying so long outside, as she was in danger of tanning her face precisely two days before the wedding. The countess declared that a trace of redness would only add to the bride's beauty, and that calmed some of Mrs. Bennet's nerves. Shortly after, the gentlemen appeared, and it was agreed that dinner would be hosted at Longbourn, but the next evening—the one prior to the wedding—each family would dine on their own.

Elizabeth exchanged only a few glances with Darcy; she also noticed his repeated looks towards his sister, so it was no surprise when he walked to the corner of the room where Elizabeth and Georgiana were having tea. It was so crowded that, although no intimacy was possible, nobody could pay attention to every conversation.

"Did you have a pleasant time?" he asked, wearing a light countenance. Elizabeth smiled, trying to conceal the cold shivers that suddenly ran down her spine.

"Yes, very pleasant," Georgiana answered, keeping her voice low. "Lizzy agreed to come with me to Pemberley right away! I am so happy!"

He looked at Elizabeth, and their eyes met for a moment. She felt her cheeks warming, and she was sure she saw a trace of colour on his face too.

"I am glad you came to an agreement so quickly."

"We did because Lizzy is very kind to me. I doubt she had any plans to travel again so soon, but she was too generous to refuse me," Georgiana said. "I am very grateful to her."

"Truth be told, I accepted mostly to annoy Miss Bingley," Elizabeth replied with such seriousness that Georgiana looked at her in disbelief. When she realised the jest, she chuckled, sharing her amusement with her brother.

"I am sure you will succeed," Darcy replied to Elizabeth, his eyes full of mirth.

She felt uneasy again, so she laughed. "Your confidence is comforting, Mr. Darcy."

"It is my goal to offer my sister and her friend the comfort they desire," he answered, half in jest. "Miss Bennet, you should know that Bingley also confirmed his visit to Pemberley for Christmas. It is still uncertain whether he will come only with his future wife or also with his extended family."

His stern—and obviously disapproving—expression did not escape his companions.

"Mr. Gardiner is reluctant to take a long trip with the children in the winter—which is perfectly understandable. Therefore, I trust I will have the pleasure of fishing with him in the summer," Darcy continued, much to Elizabeth's astonishment. Did he truly invite to Pemberley her uncle from Gracechurch Street and her aunt who grew up in Lambton? Their eyes met again briefly, then he looked towards the other side of the room and said, "Mr. Bennet can hardly be convinced to travel for less than the promise of a large library."

"Yes, I can readily testify to that; it is kind of you to ask him though, Mr. Darcy." She tried to hide her discomposure with a light tone.

"It was my pleasure, I assure you," he concluded.

This new proof of friendliness and generosity towards her family was as unexpected as it was puzzling. He had done everything that was his duty. He helped them when it was needed. He encouraged and supported his friend in marrying Jane. Nobody would dare ask more from him. And yet, his amiable gestures did not cease and even exceeded expectations. Did he feel guilty for taking his friend away last winter? Or did he feel obliged to repay her acceptance of Georgiana's invitation with more favours? She did not comprehend his behaviour or the reasons behind it, no matter how much she struggled. Would she ever come to understand Mr. Darcy's behaviour? Should she even attempt to—or better, learn not to allow herself to be distressed by anything related to him? But would such a goal not be ridiculous since they would soon inhabit the same house?

Darcy found little else to say after the brief exchange with Elizabeth, so he returned to Mr. Bennet, who invited him to the library.

Elizabeth did not announce her decision about Pemberley to her family, except for Jane. She planned to speak to her father first and only afterwards to share the information with the others.

For another half hour, the gentlemen amused themselves with drinks and talk, and the ladies discussed the schedule for the next two days, a subject that made Jane blush frequently. This time, the visit was not long. The activities of the day had been pleasant but tiring. Lady Hardwick confessed her desire to rest; therefore, the guests returned to Netherfield.

DARCY HAD FELT RESTLESS EVER SINCE HE MET ELIZABETH IN THE WOOD that morning. The certainty that she would come to Pemberley with him was rather more distressing than pleasant for him. To have something—someone—that he desired be so close to him without even having the right to dream of it—of her—was dreadful. Once Elizabeth was under his care as his sister's friend, he would not allow himself to look at her, speak to her, or even think of her in a manner that might make her feel uncomfortable. As soon as she arrived at Pemberley, she would become his responsibility as much as Georgiana was. Once again, his mind would have to struggle against his heart.

While the countess retired to her room immediately, Georgiana asked her brother for a few private moments, which were happily granted.

"William, there is something I must tell you. I confessed to Lizzy that George Wickham was the man with whom I intended to elope. I believed she should know the entire truth before she decided to come to Pemberley with me. I hope you do not disapprove."

He struggled to remain composed. "As long as you feel comfortable in doing so, there is nothing to disapprove. It is your secret, dearest."

"Thank you, dear brother. I cannot tell you how grateful I am for your kindness and support. And I am so relieved to see you do not oppose my friendship with Lizzy any longer! I noticed that her company is not unpleasant to you either."

He felt suddenly uneasy. Did his young sister also observe his preference for Elizabeth? Was his behaviour towards her so obvious?

"Miss Bennet is bright and spirited, and she possesses many accomplishments that are praiseworthy in a woman. She lacks the artificial manners, forced smiles, and insincere amiability that are often seen in young ladies. She excels in her love for reading and possesses a wide knowledge, genuine manners, and self-confidence that are, sadly, rarely traits of women who pretend to have a good education. Therefore, yes, I do enjoy her company," he admitted, attempting to sound perfectly indifferent.

Georgiana smiled. "That is such an accurate description of Lizzy! Aunt Amelia described her with almost the same words! And she said Lizzy has a beauty that is unusually striking because it does not follow classic lines."

"True," he answered seriously, troubled by a sudden warmth inside.

"William, you must help me teach Lizzy to ride when we arrive home! I am sure she would like it—and what better way to see the entire park than on horseback?"

He grinned. "Let us not frighten Miss Bennet with such torture—at least not before we reach our destination. Otherwise, she might escape before we are halfway there."

Georgiana let out a small laugh. "You are right, of course. I love so much seeing you smile, Brother," she concluded, kissing his cheek then hurrying to her room where Mist was already calling for her.

Darcy remained still for a moment, meditating on the conversation. He was surprised that Georgiana had made such a painful confession to

Elizabeth but also relieved. He thought it was better for her to know since they would spend so many months together. Besides, it was something he had already disclosed to her in April—and she refused to acknowledge. He wondered whether she would dare confront him about this information; it was unlikely since she could not possibly feel she had the right to demand of him any details he preferred to keep secret.

AT LONGBOURN, ELIZABETH TOOK THE FIRST OPPORTUNITY TO SPEAK TO her father alone. She related to him the invitation she received from Georgiana and her decision to leave with her.

"Papa, forgive me for not asking your permission first, but I truly believe Georgiana needs me. And since Jane's happiness is now complete and she will be close enough to take care of you, I trust my absence will not be a problem for our family."

"Lizzy, is Mr. Darcy aware of this?"

"Of course, he is. He also asked me to accept as he declared my company would be beneficial for his sister."

Mr. Bennet appeared surprised. "And how do you feel about it, Lizzy? Would you not find it difficult to live so close to Mr. Darcy? I know you two were never on friendly terms, which I confess I found puzzling after I came to know his true worthiness."

Her cheeks burned. "I confess I thought of that, Papa, and I expect to be uneasy at times. But I have grown very attached to Georgiana, whom I believe to be one of the most remarkable young ladies I could possibly know. And Lady Hardwick's company also honours me. However, Mr. Darcy is a true gentleman. He declared I will be treated as part of the family, and I have no reason to doubt him."

"Very well, my dear. I agree with you, but I wished to be certain that your heart is light about this journey. I will dearly miss you, Lizzy, but I confess that I would insist on your accepting anything Mr. Darcy requested from us. My gratitude to that gentleman is so deep that I could not possibly refuse him anything. And even more, as much as we might try to give Mr. Darcy, we will never be able to repay his generosity to us. Please keep that in mind and overlook any flaws in his behaviour if you happen to notice them. He might be a complicated man, but he is a very kind one—much better than most of us; you have no reason to dislike him."

"I know that, Papa. I agree that without him we never would have found Wickham until God knows when…and I feel he also had a positive influence on Mr. Bingley's return, although he denies it. You must not worry; I have long ceased to dislike Mr. Darcy."

"Excellent," Mr. Bennet said, turning his back to her. Elizabeth was certain he had wiped a few tears from his eyes.

"Besides," Mr. Bennet continued in a different tone, "he might be a little out of his mind. He invited all of us to Pemberley! I was afraid he might extend the invitation to Mrs. Philips and Lady Lucas, but thank God, he stopped before doing that."

Elizabeth laughed wholeheartedly, her eyes tearful too, then almost choked when her father concluded.

"Upon my word, if I did not know better, I would say Mr. Darcy is enamoured of one of my daughters, and he is trying to impress her. Since he did not like you enough to even dance with you, it might be either Mary or Kitty. Although, on second thought, he did dance with you at Netherfield, so who knows. Oh come, Lizzy, do not be missish; I only make sport of you. I said, 'if I did not know better.' No one could ever suspect Mr. Darcy of behaving foolishly out of passion. Now let us go and tell your mother that you are leaving for Pemberley. But let me have a glass of brandy first."

By dinner, Elizabeth still was not at ease with her father's teasing remark. Usually amused by his mockery, this time she felt uncomfortable. She recalled that Mr. Darcy *did* do rash things out of love: he had proposed to her and borne the most inconsiderate refusal. And at Pemberley, they would have to face each other every day.

Strangely, Mrs. Bennet's reaction on hearing the news of her visit to Pemberley was not as loud as Elizabeth expected. It might have been that she was preoccupied with the wedding in two days, but Elizabeth's mother declared her approval to the plan and only expressed her hope that Elizabeth would meet gentlemen of consequence in Derbyshire. Kitty and Mary, on the other hand, were excited and wondered whether they might be allowed to come for Lizzy when she returned and have the chance to take a peek at Pemberley.

Jane's distress was apparent and profound. She did not oppose Elizabeth's decision, but the prospect of her sister's being gone again was painful.

"My dear, I am certain you will have little time to think of me," Elizabeth said with a laugh. "Mr. Bingley will make sure of that."

"Lizzy!" Jane's cheeks and neck seemed on fire. "Do not speak of such things."

"What things do you mean, future Mrs. Bingley? I only talked about companionship. Do you have something else in mind?"

"Oh, Lizzy, you are so mean to me." Jane smiled in embarrassment. "On second thought, it might be good for you to leave; I will be happy for a break from your teasing."

"But not a long one, as I understand I will see you again at Christmas. Dearest Jane, how strange fate is, would you not agree? Who would think only a couple of months ago that you would marry your Mr. Bingley and I would journey to Pemberley?"

"True! But Lizzy, how will you bear to be in Mr. Darcy's presence every day? How difficult it must be for you! And for him...I am sorry that we misjudged him so completely. Poor man, to constantly see the woman he loved and who rejected him so harshly—can you imagine how much he must love his sister to do that?"

"Yes...I have thought of this a hundred times since we first discussed the possibility. I hope we manage it somehow for Georgiana's sake. Jane, my heart aches for this dear girl. Her diffidence is so intense that you can feel it. She seems to wish for little else but my company, and despite any other considerations, I cannot refuse her."

"I agree, Lizzy. I am sure that a few months with you will benefit her. Your liveliness is contagious."

"You mean my impertinence, I am sure," Elizabeth said with a smirk. "Now, help me choose what I should put in my luggage. What kind of gowns should I wear at Pemberley? Although it probably matters very little since I expect to have no foreign company."

The sisters spent the next few hours together, each distressed by the prospect of soon losing the other's company and unwilling to voice her concerns in order not to upset the other. As much as she loved and trusted her eldest sister, Elizabeth chose not to tell her about Wickham's attempt to elope with Georgiana. It was such a painful secret that she felt heavy-hearted at the thought of sharing it, even with the person who was dearest to her.

Before dinner, the family was gathered in the drawing room when the Netherfield party arrived. With surprise and concern, they observed that the two expected ladies—the favourites of all—were missing.

"Mr. Bingley, Mr. Darcy, where are Miss Darcy and Lady Hardwick? Are they unwell?" Mrs. Bennet cried, her nerves obviously affected.

"I must convey to you their apologies, Mrs. Bennet," Darcy answered. "My aunt was a little tired, and she preferred not to leave her room tonight. My sister chose to stay with her although she was looking forward to another lovely dinner at Longbourn."

"Oh yes, yes, the countess should rest if she is tired of course. Well, I was quite opposed to the idea of a trip to the woods, but nobody ever listens to me. And here is another proof that I am always right," Mrs. Bennet concluded. "Now let us sit as dinner is ready. So, Mr. Darcy, you will take Lizzy to Pemberley. I understand your estate is very large—just please do not let her wander in the fields too much."

"I assure you, ma'am, that we will take excellent care of Miss Elizabeth. She will be treated in the same way as my sister."

"How lovely! It is such a pleasant change to see you so kind and friendly, sir! I must say, your aloofness and haughtiness were quite unbecoming!"

"Mama!" cried Jane.

"Well, you must agree that Mr. Darcy looks more handsome lately," Mrs. Bennet ended the subject decidedly. Elizabeth and Jane were flustered, and Mr. Bennet angry and embarrassed. Darcy wisely remained silent and avoided a debate about his handsomeness.

Dinner went well, just as it should among family and close friends. Afterwards, Mary was asked to play, and to everyone's astonishment, she was reluctant to accept. When she began, it was apparent that her playing had changed slightly. A touch of feeling was added to her usual technique, which improved the performance significantly and brought Mary more compliments than she had received in years.

Elizabeth found a moment when Darcy was alone and approached him.

"I hope Lady Hardwick is not unwell because of our picnic. I would be unhappy to know I contributed to her discomfort."

"My aunt might be tired from the trip, but I am sure she found it valuable. Both she and Georgiana told me they had a lovely time," he answered.

"Thank you for telling me that. I hope to see them both tomorrow. Georgiana is not unwell, I trust. I dearly miss her."

"You have no reason to worry, although it is very kind of you to do so. She is well and happy since you agreed to join her on the journey to Pemberley."

"I am glad. Mr. Darcy, I...there is something that..." she whispered, looking around as she searched for words.

He felt her discomfort and decided not to prolong it. "Miss Bennet, Georgiana told me about her confession to you."

Their eyes met, and he noticed the shadows in hers.

"Sir, I found it so extraordinary... if I had known before...but I understand why you did not trust me with such a painful secret."

He looked at her again, this time longer and more intently, then answered with a voice even softer than hers. "I did trust you. Strangely enough, even though I was angry and full of resentment and blamed you for accusing me unfairly, my faith in you was steady. All the details were in the letter. I hope you will not blame me for a reluctance to offer you the same information again. I dared not betray my sister's deepest secret a second time...and yet, in the end, she did it herself."

Elizabeth blinked a few times to stem the burning in her eyes and breathed deeply to gather her courage.

"It never crossed my mind that...if I had only known. So when you first came to Hertfordshire, it was only a few months after..."

"Two months. Georgiana preferred to remain in Town with her new companion, Mrs. Annesley. She was also the one who insisted I should accompany Bingley."

"And Mr. Wickham...he knew himself guilty of such scheming, and yet he had the audacity to speak such slander of you? Such a horrible excuse for a man..."

"It was his habit to do so, even more so when he found—" He stopped and sipped some wine.

Elizabeth lowered her eyes and paled. "When he found somebody silly enough to fall for his stories and to believe them without further inquiries..." she whispered.

"Let us speak of this no more. All has passed now," he replied forcefully. "I admit I am content that Georgiana found the strength to share the story with you—as I was relieved to discover that she was not as affected by the news of his marrying your sister as I feared. I hope she will soon heal completely; your presence surely will help. Now, please excuse me; I shall go speak to your father."

He departed before she had time to reply, but what else could she have said? Everything appeared differently after that day. A pained brother, unsure of how to comfort his sister, came to a new place where everybody demanded certain behaviour from him, and he struggled to adapt to a completely unknown neighbourhood. And his worst enemy tainted his name while any response would disclose dreadful family secrets. And she—Elizabeth Bennet—the chief of all fools, allowed herself to be trapped in the dishonourable game.

"Lizzy, are you well? What happened?" Jane asked as she took hold of her arm. From across the room, Mrs. Gardiner was watching with apparent concern.

"No, I am not, Jane, but it is nothing but well-deserved self-reproach. It will pass one day. Now, let us talk to Aunt Gardiner. Is there anything else you must prepare for the wedding?"

"Nothing, Lizzy, so you have no reason to change the subject and refuse to tell me what troubles you."

"Dear Jane, if I wanted to be dramatic, I would say that I am troubled by the past and the future. Therefore, let us concentrate on the present and have another cup of tea," Elizabeth joked, caressing her sister's arm.

ANOTHER FULL, UNEXPECTED, AND AGONISING DAY ENDED LATER THAT evening. Longbourn fell into silence and darkness long after midnight, but most of its inhabitants did not fall asleep until much later. For the Bennet family, it was one day nearer the moment they would cease to worry for the future, and the excitement was not a good inducement to rest.

For Jane, it was one day closer to the end of her life as Miss Bennet and the beginning of complete happiness, and for Elizabeth—the day that changed her peaceful life at Longbourn in more ways than she could number.

Both sisters were painfully aware that they had only two more nights to share the room that had sheltered their entire life: joy and sadness, laughter and tears, hopes and fears. In two days' time, everything would be different, and each hoped and prayed for the other's happiness.

AT NETHERFIELD, DARCY AND BINGLEY REMAINED IN THE LIBRARY, TALKing and drinking until dawn. Bingley's joy and excitement were joined by anxiety and fear that he might not be a good enough husband for Jane.

After several glasses of brandy, he even expressed his concerns about how he would dare to show his passion to such a perfectly beautiful and proper woman—and Darcy needed patience, tact, and carefully chosen words to calm him and ensure him of the happiest outcome. Fatigue and brandy finally overcame them at dawn, and they fell into a deep, dreamless sleep until around ten o'clock that morning.

Their last day at Netherfield began early for the guests. The countess woke in a good mood and hearty appetite, much to Georgiana's joy, but the entire family gathered in the dining room rather late.

Breakfast was rich, tasteful, and short for Bingley, who hurried to call at Longbourn on the pretext of an urgent matter. The others remained to enjoy their meal in comfort.

"Georgiana, is it true that Eliza Bennet will join you at Pemberley?" Caroline inquired. "Charles told us as much, but I suspect he was careless as usual and misunderstood the situation."

"Mr. Bingley is correct. I invited Lizzy to keep me company for a few months, and I am very happy that she accepted."

"So what are you saying? Will she be your companion? Did Mr. Darcy hire her?"

"Not at all," Darcy intervened. "As my sister just explained, Miss Bennet will be her guest."

"But I do not understand. Why her? Why did you not invite someone who has been your friend for years and is always interested in your well-being?" Caroline insisted irritably.

"That is how I felt," Georgiana answered. "But I thank you for your concern, Caroline."

"I am afraid I do not understand. I sense it is a caprice that you will come to regret. I wonder that Mr. Darcy, as an older brother, does not censure certain inclinations that might harm you. A friend who is unfit, improperly educated, and has questionable connections cannot be proper company for a young heiress."

The countess cleared her throat. "Miss Bingley, do you still not understand that insulting Miss Elizabeth will do you no good? Such a tendency to attack another young lady in her absence is unbecoming. It might be the reason few gentlemen are courting you despite the fact that you are smart, handsome, and have a good dowry."

Caroline Bingley paled and remained still and silent.

Lady Hardwick continued. "You do realise that, starting tomorrow, Mrs. Bingley will be the new mistress of this house and can decide anything she wishes, do you not? It might come as a shock to you, but even your presence here depends on the good will of the future Mrs. Bingley."

"If your ladyship believes Charles might do anything against us, I strongly contradict you," Louisa replied.

Lady Hardwick smiled mischievously. "My dear, when a man enters into a marriage of love for such a beautiful woman, it is more than probable that he would do anything to please her. And since you take every opportunity to offend the members of her family, the solution seems clear to me. I have seen a number of young, newly wedded men abandon their sisters for far less. As I said, you will be at the mercy of Miss Bennet. If I were you, I would show extreme prudence in upsetting her. She is indeed the sweetest and kindest person I have seen lately, but one cannot be certain of the ways in which a young wife might change."

Caroline choked and spat her food while Louisa burned her lips with the hot tea.

"I wonder that we came to be the enemy in this situation," Louisa said sharply. "Last year, Mr. Darcy would not have allowed Eliza Bennet to be anywhere near his sister, and now she suddenly has become everyone's favourite—against us, who have been your friends for years."

Darcy intervened with polite severity. "Mrs. Hurst, you must know that you are among our best friends, and we do appreciate our close acquaintance. But we cannot be blind to things that are improper and unfair, either in your case or in mine. All three of us know that our ungenerous interference almost ruined Bingley's happiness, for no other reason than our own selfishness. I am struggling to remedy my mistake, not so much for Miss Bennet, whom I have barely started to know, but for the man I proudly call my friend. I strongly believe that anyone who cares for Charles should do the same."

"Excuse me; I have lost my appetite. I shall retire to my room," Caroline said and hurried upstairs, followed by her sister.

"I am so sorry that Caroline and Louisa are upset," Georgiana whispered. "I do not understand why they harbour ill will towards Lizzy and Miss Bennet."

"Do not worry; just ignore them, and they will get over it soon," Mr.

Hurst replied seriously. "Upon my word, what a waste of time. Should we not go hunting again?"

"I would rather search for Bingley," Darcy answered. "And I wish to speak further with Mr. Bennet and Mr. Gardiner as tomorrow we will have little time for conversation."

"I will come with you. I promised the children they could play with Mist today," Georgiana said.

"And I will go back to my room; a few more hours of rest will better prepare me for the journey tomorrow," the countess added.

"Then I will have some brandy and take a nap," Mr. Hurst decided. "As I said, arguments are a terrible waste of time."

The last day of the Darcy siblings' visit in Hertfordshire was spent mostly at Longbourn. The gentlemen stayed almost exclusively in the library to discuss books, plans for the future, and business. Darcy offered Mr. Bennet advice on the management of Longbourn and gave Mr. Gardiner several suggestions to improve his affairs. Bingley entered and left frequently, undecided about where he preferred to be.

The ladies split their time between the drawing room and the music room with Georgiana and Mary playing enthusiastically and Kitty turning pages for them.

Elizabeth and Jane were both heavy-hearted. Every time they sat beside each other, they held hands and shared comforting smiles. Jane's beautiful face changed from blushes to pallor every moment, flustered by her betrothed's presence and the sweet anticipation of their wedding and saddened by her beloved sister's departure.

Elizabeth fought her own silly feelings: every time she looked around at her family, a lump in her throat and an icy hole in her stomach brought her close to tears. However, the image of a smiling Georgiana and a happy, radiant Jane was proof enough that she had made the correct decision. After all, the months would pass quickly; there were already twelve since Mr. Bingley first arrived at Netherfield and six since her visit to Kent. Surely, the next few could not be any worse.

MISS JANE BENNET'S WEDDING TO MR. CHARLES BINGLEY TOOK PLACE ON a sunny and joyous morning in the presence of their extended families, more than four and twenty others, a countess, and Mr. Darcy and his sister. It was an occasion for talk and speculation, especially as the news of Elizabeth's invitation to Pemberley was now generally known. Suddenly, the Bennets were the envy of Meryton, and Mrs. Bennet was declared the most fortunate of mothers.

The wedding breakfast was hosted at Longbourn, and it was admittedly the richest that had been seen in the neighbourhood in quite a while. Lady Hardwick said several times—loud enough to be heard—that she had rarely tasted such appetising fare.

The newly wedded couple was barely apart as they mingled with the guests. Mr. Bingley held his wife's arm, touched her hand, lost himself in her eyes, and shivered at her exquisite beauty so many times that the others soon stopped noticing.

Around noon, the Darcy party, along with Elizabeth, made their goodbyes with warmth, sorrow, tears, and whispered promises to write regularly. Mr. Bennet struggled to hide his regret as he embraced his favourite daughter while Mrs. Bennet instructed her to be careful and behave properly in case she met some worthy, handsome gentlemen.

Elizabeth exchanged hugs and kisses with her sisters, her uncle and aunt, and her little cousins then turned to Jane, whose eyes were heavy with sadness when they embraced.

"Lizzy, I will miss you so much…"

"No, you will not, dearest. You will be so busy being happy with your husband that you will barely remember me. But when you finally do, please write me a long and detailed letter."

"Not even Charles will take your place in my heart, my dearest."

"I know that, my sweet Jane. But please do not be sad; I want to see you smile. Your happiness is more important to me than my own."

It was slightly cloudy when the party of three carriages finally moved forward. Elizabeth looked through the window and waved towards her family, who were gazing after them and waving back. Mr. Bennet wiped his eyes discreetly and returned to the house with his wife. Mr. Bingley placed his arm around the shoulders of Mrs. Bingley, who leant her head against him. Elizabeth smiled and withdrew her head inside the carriage. She had no doubt of Jane's complete felicity.

Chapter 18

"Dear Lizzy, I am sorry that I am taking you away from your family," Georgiana whispered. "I was so selfish…" They sat beside each other with the countess and Darcy on the opposite bench, facing them.

Elizabeth took Georgiana's hands in hers. "There is no one less selfish than you, my dear. Jane alone might equal your generosity. I shall not deny that I am a little sad, but that happens every time I leave Longbourn. Do not worry; my spirits will rise again soon," she attempted to joke.

"Your sister and Bingley seem a perfect match," Lady Hardwick said. "They will be happy together."

"I hope so—they have every reason to be."

"Now, Miss Bennet, I believe it is your turn to think of an advantageous marriage with a handsome gentleman," the countess added. "Do you have anyone in mind?"

Elizabeth blushed and struggled to keep her eyes from Darcy. She observed him turn his head towards the window.

Georgiana hurried to take Elizabeth's side. "Aunt Amelia, you should not ask such a thing."

"I apologise if I offended you, Miss Lizzy. You must know I am quite at leisure in expressing my thoughts, so let me know if I make you uncomfortable. I surely do not mean to offend you."

"It is quite all right; I am not so easily offended." She laughed nervously. "But for now, I can only think of the time I will spend with Georgiana. She promised me I will have many things to do at Pemberley."

"Yes, you will," Georgiana answered.

"First thing, I must visit the library. My father demanded from me a detailed description, including a sketch if possible." The ladies laughed, and Darcy concealed a smile and continued to stare out the window.

"My brother is in charge of the library, but I am sure he will be happy to show it to you."

"Indeed," he replied briefly.

"I never doubted Mr. Darcy's kindness," Elizabeth said, and he stole a glance at her.

"Miss Bennet, I wish to assure you in all sincerity that you are welcome to consider Pemberley your home. You may do anything you please, whenever you like."

"Thank you, sir. That is good to know—a little intimidating, but good to know."

"Pemberley might look intimidating but only until you become accustomed to its beauties, Miss Bennet."

Conversation continued for several hours. It was awkward at times with Darcy rarely speaking and Elizabeth feeling uneasy more than once, but the warm friendliness of the two ladies compensated for any discomfort.

"In few minutes, we will arrive at Nott Inn where we spend the night," Darcy informed them, then he addressed Elizabeth. "We usually stop there when we travel between London and Pemberley. Mr. Nott owns the place, and he is a diligent and reliable master. He is also careful about the honour of the guests he accepts. I have never had reason to complain about the accommodations."

"Very well," was all she had to say, meeting his eyes.

The countess added, "I confess I am rather tired. A good sleep is all I need, and an excellent dinner of course. I hope Nott's wife cooks as well as usual."

When the carriages stopped, Darcy was the first to exit. At the inn door were a man and woman of middle age who immediately bowed to welcome him.

"Mr. Darcy, we are so honoured to see you again, sir."

"I am pleased to see you too, Nott," Darcy answered.

From inside, a loud chorus of voices suddenly drew their attention, and Darcy frowned. He looked at the owner reproachfully, who shrugged his shoulders, obviously embarrassed.

"Sir, I apologise for the noise; there is a party waiting for you."

"Excuse me? What kind of joke is this?"

Elizabeth looked at the entire scene with curiosity. She was convinced it was a mistake and noticed Darcy's puzzlement and irritation. He seemed close to losing his patience.

The inn's door opened, and Elizabeth's eyes widened in disbelief as she saw Colonel Fitzwilliam appear, followed by two other gentlemen of his age and two young ladies.

"Oh dear," Georgiana whispered.

"This is a surprise indeed," Lady Hardwick commented with amusement.

Outside, the colonel hurried to Darcy, who shook his hand reluctantly.

"Richard, what on earth are you doing here?"

"Waiting for you of course! I am travelling north on some regiment business, and these people are bound for Livingston's estate in Birmingham. Since I knew your plans, I thought we should travel together."

Elizabeth saw another gentleman—younger and more handsome than the colonel—bow to Darcy while holding a young woman's arm. "In fact, my cousin Lady Emmeline insisted, to be perfectly honest. You know she always had a preference for you."

Darcy still looked displeased. "Mowbray, please avoid jokes that might make the ladies uncomfortable. Lady Emmeline, I am pleased to see you."

"As am I, Mr. Darcy. You are so rarely seen in London that one must chase you across the country to meet you," Lady Emmeline said with a charming smile.

Still in the carriage, Elizabeth turned to her companions. "Who are they? Do you know them?"

"Of course," Lady Hardwick answered. "They are Lady Emmeline Pemberton and her sister, Lady Livingston, with her husband. Both are my second husband's nieces. And that handsome young man is Lord Mowbray, their cousin. Such a nice young man—smart, pleasant, and amiable. And the last one—"

"Oh, I know Colonel Fitzwilliam. We met in Kent last spring."

Outside, the conversation continued, equally animated.

"We arrived earlier today, and we occupied almost the entire inn. We already ordered dinner—it should be ready soon," Lord Livingstone said.

"So, Darcy, how is Bingley? I heard he married an exceptional beauty. That rascal—how is it possible that he was so fortunate?" inquired Lord Mowbray.

"Bingley is very well," Darcy replied. "And yes, his wife is an exceptional beauty. Now let me—"

"But where are dear Georgiana and Lady Hardwick?" the colonel asked, approaching the carriage. He opened the door widely, greeting the ladies with a broad smile before surprise made him take a step backwards.

"Miss Bennet? Is it possible? What a wonderful surprise! This I did not expect."

"Colonel, I am so happy to see you." Elizabeth smiled, genuinely glad to see the colonel again. He was a gentleman she always admired, and his company was a pure pleasure.

"I invited Lizzy to stay at Pemberley with me," Georgiana explained as the colonel kissed her hand and helped them all from the carriage.

"Really?"

"Yes, she is my best friend," she continued.

"I am very pleased to hear that, my dear. Anyone would be honoured by Miss Bennet's friendship."

"You are too kind, sir." Elizabeth blushed.

"Not at all; I am only honest." He gently took Lady Hardwick's arm and helped her stretch her legs while her nieces and nephews embraced her warmly.

"So nice to see you all here! What a joy indeed—I really missed you," the countess said. "Now, let me introduce to you one of the most charming and accomplished young ladies I have ever met. This is Miss Elizabeth Bennet. Her sister Jane is the beautiful woman who married Mr. Bingley this morning."

Elizabeth's cheeks coloured slightly at such praise, and she curtseyed to the guests, who responded with warm politeness.

"Having the pleasure of meeting Miss Bennet last spring in Kent and being in her company for more than a fortnight, I can testify to Lady Hardwick's description," the colonel added.

Lord Mowbray bowed to her, and a large smile lit his face and his green eyes.

"Miss Bennet—I am delighted to make your acquaintance."

"Likewise, sir. And please do not believe everything you just heard; most of the praise is undeserved, I assure you."

"I would never dare distrust my aunt's words. She has always been right as long as I can remember. But the colonel must indeed be trusted only in moderation," the earl replied teasingly.

"It is rather late; we should settle into our rooms and then prepare for dinner," Darcy interjected.

"You are right of course," the colonel said and offered one arm to Elizabeth and the other to Georgiana. Lord Mowbray hurried to help his aunt, and Lady Emmeline took Darcy's arm without an invitation.

Elizabeth turned her head, and her eyes met Darcy's then held for a moment. His countenance was still dark, and he was the only one silent and thoughtful amid an uproar of cheerful voices and laughter. Lady Emmeline asked him something, and he leant his head down to her. Elizabeth averted her eyes, a sudden grip tightening her chest.

It appeared the road to Pemberley would be completely different than she expected.

THE DARCY PARTY WAS HELPED WITH THEIR ACCOMMODATIONS BY MR. Nott, the owner of the inn, and his wife.

"Sir, Colonel Fitzwilliam asked me to prepare a larger table for dinner; he said you would join their party. Is that convenient for you? Should I change your previous dining arrangements?" the innkeeper inquired uneasily.

"Oh, of course, a large dinner will be lovely," the countess interjected.

"Yes, we are fine with that," Darcy agreed.

"Very well, sir. Now please allow me to show you the accommodations."

The countess was the first to occupy her room on the second floor—a large one with several windows—clean and comfortable. Darcy glanced inside briefly to be certain all was as expected then closed the door and turned to his sister and Elizabeth.

Mr. Nott began to rub his hands and shift his weight from one leg to the other, exchanging worried glances with his wife.

"Mr. Darcy, we are currently facing another difficult problem, and I cannot apologise enough for it. I have prepared the three rooms that are your favourites, but I can see you will need four. The inn is full, and I only have one room left, but I am afraid it would not be suitable for the other young lady in your party," the innkeeper said with apparent distress.

Darcy frowned. "What do you mean?" he inquired, then he realised it was his fault that he did not think of writing ahead to engage an extra room for Elizabeth.

"It is a room situated on the top floor, half as large as the ones I saved for you with only a small bed and one small window. We already have several other guests, and the colonel's party took the last remaining chambers. We did not expect them so soon and…"

Darcy looked at Elizabeth; she was smiling with perfect calmness.

"Sir, any room will do for tonight," she answered. "Please do not trouble yourself about that. As long as I have clean sheets and some water to refresh myself, I will certainly be fine."

"Oh, but Lizzy can sleep with me," Georgiana hurried to reply, excited at the mere idea.

The innkeeper panicked again. "But, Miss Darcy, the bed in your room might not be large enough for two people."

But Darcy interrupted. "Mr. Nott, Miss Bennet will take my place, and I will settle in the one on the top floor. We do not need to speak about it further."

His answer was so peremptory that no opposition was made. The ladies were each shown into their chambers—close to each other—while Darcy walked on with Mr. Nott.

He finally entered his room and looked around: it was clean and furnished with all the necessities but small indeed and rather dark because of the one small window. But it was enough for one night, during which he knew too well that he probably would not sleep. He threw his coat on the bed and removed his neckcloth then paced a few times.

The unexpected meeting with his cousin and old acquaintances should be pleasant, and he understood their good intentions in surprising him, but he felt rather irritated without knowing why. Perhaps he was just not fond of surprises.

The colonel came through the open door. "I suspect you are not as pleased to see us as I had hoped."

"I am always glad to see you, Richard. But you know I carefully plan my journeys to Pemberley when I travel with Georgiana, precisely to avoid the unexpected. Surprises are not my favourite thing, but I do appreciate your effort to change your plans for me, and I am glad to spend a couple of hours with you. However, we shall not be deterred from our schedule. We must be home the day after tomorrow."

"I understand that. And the truth is, we only left London one day earlier than we should have—mostly due to Emmeline's insistence. You should at least pretend to be more pleased to see her."

"I would rather not joke about that subject any more. As you know,

Georgiana is uncomfortable with your jests. And we are not yet so familiar with Miss Bennet as to ignore propriety with such references."

"I could wager that Miss Bennet can easily handle any kind of joke, but I do see your point about Georgiana."

"I am sure Miss Bennet can handle a joke. My meaning is that she is with us as my sister's guest, and it is my duty to make sure she is in the sort of circumstances her father would approve."

"I cannot argue with that. So, would you tell me how it happens that Miss Bennet is in your company? I know you mentioned nothing of the kind when we last met in London."

"Georgiana had a lovely time in Hertfordshire, and she enjoyed herself exceedingly in the company of the Bennets. I have never seen her so at ease as she was there. She felt as if she was part of the family; in truth, even Mrs. Bennet treated her the same as her daughters—with some improprieties, but there was genuine affection. As a consequence, Georgiana dreaded the idea of being alone again at Pemberley without any company her own age. Therefore, she invited Miss Bennet to join her, and she kindly accepted. I doubt she intended to leave her family so soon, but she understood Georgiana needed her company."

"Very nice of her. Well, I am glad to see Miss Bennet again. I confess I have thought of her several times since we left Kent. I have rarely admired a young lady so much. If I were not forced to marry someone with a significant dowry, I would have thought of her more often."

A grin rested on the colonel's face, but Darcy remained serious.

"This is not a subject for jest. Besides, we both know that you often admire many young ladies—dowry or not."

"True—but as I said, not as much as I admired Miss Bennet. I just admitted that."

"Richard, you are at an age when you should be more earnest in narrowing your admiration towards a single lady and finding yourself a wife."

"Do you not think it strange that you of all men give me such advice? Do not speak of finding wives unless you are prepared to debate the subject. It should be much easier for you since you have complete freedom to choose as you like. And yet, you seem uninterested in doing so."

"There is another more important subject to consider," Darcy said, avoiding the colonel's discussion. "As Georgiana's second guardian, you need to know that she confessed Wickham's attempted elopement to Miss Bennet."

Surprise darkened the colonel's expression. "That is extraordinary. I know how frightened she was at the notion of her secret's being discovered. She seems to have great faith in her new friend."

"Yes. And after I carefully observed Miss Bennet's behaviour towards her, I believe Georgiana's trust is well deserved."

"That is comforting. I know how worried you are for her, and I was apprehensive that I could not help you more."

"I hope things will improve now. I also invited Bingley and his wife to Pemberley for Christmas. I would not object if the other Miss Bennets joined them."

"So—should I assume that your opinion of the Bennets has improved?"

"I believe I realised that the Bennets' faults are neither more nor greater than any of ours. And since they showed Georgiana and me nothing but kindness, their less-than-perfect manners mean little."

"Wise approach. So, will you come downstairs for dinner? We have an entire half of the dining room for our use."

"Of course we will come, and we will be pleased to spend the evening together. But tomorrow we will have an early breakfast and depart immediately afterward."

"Fair enough. We will see whether our party is as rigorous as yours so we can travel together. If not, we will each travel at our own time. So do tell me, is Bingley happy?"

A broad smile spread on Darcy's face. "Exceedingly, as you can easily imagine. I spent two nights listening to his worries about his worthiness and his struggles with how to make his wife the happiest woman in the entire country. I trust he will succeed."

"Is the present Mrs. Bingley the woman from whom you tried to separate Bingley last year?" the colonel asked hesitantly. It was a delicate subject that had not been addressed between them since last winter.

The answer came equally tentative. "Yes. It was one of the worst decisions I ever made, based on what I considered to be my honest and accurate evaluation. It almost cost Bingley the chance to marry a beautiful, kind, and caring woman whom he loves and who returns his affection."

"Well, fortunately, it was corrected, so you should cease blaming yourself so much. At least you remedied some of your errors with your help of ten thousand pounds to the Bennets."

"Richard! We shall never speak of that again."

"As you wish. But coming to the present, may I say that Miss Bennet is just as charming as I remembered her? Perhaps less voluble, but that might be from fatigue."

Darcy offered no reply, so the colonel continued. "And I am quite confident that Mowbray is also smitten with Miss Bennet."

"You talk nonsense now. Mowbray saw Miss Bennet for three minutes and exchanged a few words with her. Let us remain serious and not talk of Miss Bennet in a manner that would be equally improper and useless. I shall see you at dinner in an hour."

The severity of his answer surprised even himself, and he did not miss the colonel's puzzlement as he left the room. The mere mention of anyone's admiring Elizabeth was a reason for affliction that he could scarcely overcome.

The colonel's mockery continued to trouble Darcy more than he wished. He knew it to be silly, but it stirred his distress and destroyed his appetite. He knew his cousin had been attracted to Elizabeth from the day he met her, but he hoped that infatuation was gone. The jealousy he felt at times in Kent was reborn, as well as his guilt for being selfish. It was not impossible that Elizabeth might be suited to Richard. Their manners were similar, and their easiness with each other was obvious. There was no doubt that they enjoyed each other's company. Did it mean something more to Elizabeth? Could she be happy with his cousin, the only barrier being his lack of financial stability? What about Mowbray? He was equally easy mannered, amiable, and handsome, and his position and wealth gave him complete liberty in action and marriage. Would Elizabeth be impressed by him? And could he already be interested in her? It was not impossible, of course, as he remembered being enchanted with Elizabeth the moment he observed the sparkle in her eyes.

His breathing suddenly became unsteady. The thought of Elizabeth within his family—bonded to one of his relatives, so close to him yet lost forever—cut him inside like a knife. He struggled to calm himself as his torment was ridiculous, based on an entirely impossible premise. He hoped and prayed it was impossible. But it was out of his control; he could only wait and see what fate had prepared for them.

The first thing Elizabeth did was to remove her bonnet, gloves, and reticule and knock on Georgiana's door. At the shy invitation, she entered and found her friend staring out the window. As their eyes met, the girl smiled.

"How are you, dearest? Are you well?" Elizabeth inquired.

"Yes, very well. I was just a little surprised by the surprise," she attempted to joke.

"Yes, we all were. But they seem to be nice people. Lady Hardwick was pleased to see them."

"I imagine she was. But I confess both Lady Emmeline and Lord Mowbray make me...a little uneasy."

Mist was searching the room curiously, and Elizabeth took him into her arms, petting him.

"Have you known them for long?"

"Oh yes, since I was very young. Emmeline is...she was always kind to me...but I feel she is more interested in William than she is in me. Which is understandable of course..."

Elizabeth laughed and caressed her hair. "You should not be too harsh. It is a tendency of many women to do anything to gain the attention of a young, desirable gentleman with a good fortune."

"Yes, I know. I am glad you do not do the same, Lizzy."

"Well, my dear, I might well do so if the right gentleman should appear, so do not be too hasty to praise me."

Georgiana laughed. "I cannot believe that until I see it. Lizzy, how is it you always help me relax and turn my distress to amusement?"

"I believe it is a skill I gained living with three sisters who frequently argued and at least one of whom was always upset. Now, dearest, may I help you with anything before dinner?"

"No, I thank you. You were so kind to come and talk to me. We should wait for William. He will come to fetch us when it is time to go downstairs."

"Very well," Elizabeth replied and suddenly flushed without knowing why.

Once inside her room, Elizabeth lay across the bed for a moment, thinking of her conversation with Georgiana. Yes, Lady Emmeline seemed quite interested in Darcy, and she did not attempt to conceal it. She possessed a self-confidence that left others no choice but to obey her. She took Darcy's arm with a determination that admitted no objection. Not that he would attempt to object. He did not appear pleased to see the newly arrived group, but he rarely showed his inner opinions. And she could hardly claim any proficiency in guessing those feelings.

Elizabeth walked around her room restlessly, troubled by a strange feeling. She could not escape the thought that this was the room Darcy should have occupied—that he had occupied in the past. This was the bed where he used to sleep. Those considerations made her cheeks burn and her skin quiver as with a chill. She knew she was being ridiculous, and she felt ashamed of herself. And yet, her eyes turned repeatedly towards the pillows. There were four of them on a single bed. Did he prefer more pillows to keep his head higher while he slept? She had the same preference. How strange was that?

She refreshed her face then looked in the small mirror hanging on the wall. Her hair needed some adjustment. Lady Emmeline and her sister looked impeccable, even after hours spent in a carriage. Of course, that was laughable; why should she care about other people? She should be careful with her own appearance—nothing more, nothing less.

After tightening her pins and arranging a few rebellious locks, she sat in a chair by the window, observing the room more closely.

Though Georgiana's bed was not large enough for two persons to sleep comfortably, this one seemed to be. He always took the same room, the innkeeper said. Had he ever shared it?

"Oh, this is ridiculous!" she cried to herself. She cooled her flushed face again with water, then opened the window widely, and looked outside. It was already darkening; the sky seemed cloudy, and the wind had started to blow. She wanted to take a stroll before dinner but resisted the temptation. She was in a completely strange location, surrounded by people she did not know, so she had to refrain from any unwise gestures.

Chapter 19

The minutes passed unbearably slowly until she finally heard a knock on the door. She opened it and met Darcy's gaze but held it only for a moment. She was afraid that, had he looked into her eyes any longer, he would be able to guess her improper and self-reproachful musings.

In the dining room, the tables prepared for their party were evident through their careful placement, separated from the rest by a curtain as if it were a theatre box. Elizabeth smiled as she considered the generosity of Mr. Darcy, which surely made him the innkeeper's favourite customer.

A few other travellers, who watched them with curiosity, occupied tables in the opposite corner and greeted them silently from afar.

No other guests were at the table. Darcy invited his companions to choose their places while he went to inquire about the colonel. The countess sat at the head of the table, ensuring herself enough space to move comfortably. Georgiana took a chair near her, and Elizabeth the one on her friend's left. By the time Darcy returned, a din of voices announced the arrival of the others. and Georgiana turned to her brother.

"William, will you not sit by Lizzy? It would be nice if we were all on this side of the table."

He hesitated a moment and looked at Elizabeth. She attempted a faint smile. "Please do, sir," she said, and he nodded in agreement then took the last free chair next to Elizabeth.

The countess spoke up. "My late husband—God rest his soul—was a good man but never understood the concept of being on time. It is a family trait, no doubt of that. I shall wait a few more minutes and then will ask for the first course."

She did not have to accomplish her threat, as her relatives arrived. The countess demanded her nieces take the seats on her right, and they obeyed. Lord Livingston sat next to his wife, followed by the colonel, who was facing Darcy. Lord Mowbray placed himself at the foot of the table, opposite the countess and between the two cousins.

The first dish was immediately served with great diligence.

"Georgiana, how have you been lately?" Lady Emmeline asked. "We barely saw you at all during the last year."

"I am very well, thank you," she said with a timid smile.

"Miss Bennet, how long do you plan to stay at Pemberley?" Lord Mowbray inquired. Elizabeth was surprised by the direct question, and she turned to him.

"We have no fixed plans, sir. As long as Georgiana wants me, I imagine." She smiled.

"Oh, if it were up to me, I would say at least a year," Georgiana replied.

"So how does it happen that you left town precisely when the Season started? I know you are the heart of the parties," Lady Hardwick addressed her relatives.

"My family organised a large gathering," Lord Livingston explained. "We will stay until the end of this month then return to Town."

"So we do have plenty of time to enjoy the Season," Lady Emmeline added. "And you, Mr. Darcy? When will we have the pleasure of seeing you again?"

"We will remain at Pemberley at least until next April."

"I surely would not make the journey back in wintertime," Lady Hardwick declared.

"Will you stay at your estate too, Aunt?" Lady Livingston continued.

"I will most certainly. At least a fortnight. I hope to convince Georgiana and Miss Bennet to join me."

"I hope Miss Bennet will not be bored in the North for such a long time." Lord Mowbray turned his attention to her.

"I am sure I will not." Her answer was brief but decided.

"You may count on my company every time I happen to be in the North," the colonel assured her, and she rewarded her with a friendly smile.

"Your presence will always be welcome, sir."

A short pause in the conversation followed as the main dish was given due attention.

246

For both Elizabeth and Darcy, their closeness at the table soon became a source of distress. Every move made them touch one way or another. Their arms, their shoulders, even their legs brushed against each other several times briefly—as searing as a flame.

Elizabeth felt disturbed all the while and kept her attention on everyone at the table except him; Darcy struggled to engage in conversation with their companions on the other side of the table. However, the more indifference they showed to each other, the more intense, the more tormenting each touch was felt. And, if their determination to ignore each other appeared to be mutual, neither made any attempt to increase the distance between them as though they unconsciously enjoyed prolonging their turmoil.

"Miss Bennet, have you ever travelled a long distance from your home before?" Lady Emmeline started the conversation again.

Regardless of her lack of composure, Elizabeth succeeded in gathering herself. "'Distance' is a relative term, would you not agree? But no, I have not been in the North before. I usually travel to see my aunt and uncle in London—rarely farther."

"And are you often in London?" Lord Mowbray continued.

"'Often' is also a relative term." She smiled, slightly nervous as she felt Darcy's gaze on her face. "I would say at least four—five times a year."

"And do you attend any parties or balls? I imagine some of your stays in town are related to the Season," the earl insisted.

Lady Emmeline interfered with a critical air. "Surely, the Season cannot be as important for Miss Bennet as it is for us. Not just anybody who might happen to be in London is allowed to attend the balls and parties where you are invited."

"I am sure Miss Bennet employs her time in London much better," Darcy replied sharply, stealing a look at Elizabeth from the corner of his eye. "It is my understanding that she prefers to attend theatre plays or operas rather than useless parties."

"I never schedule my visits based on the Season," Elizabeth answered politely. "I go when I miss my relatives. For instance, this summer I spent two months in Town."

"Truly? Had I known, I would have called on you for sure," the colonel stated.

"I would have liked that very much, but perhaps next time," Elizabeth replied.

"May I ask how your sister met Mr. Bingley?" Lady Livingston interject-ed. "We were all surprised when we heard he married in such haste."

"They had known each other for more than a year from Mr. Bingley's first arriving in Hertfordshire. He leased an estate a few miles from ours, and their mutual affection grew and deepened slowly. A lucky coincidence for both of them, I would say. But their marriage was not at all a hasty one," Elizabeth answered, struggling to keep her composure.

"Indeed. But then again, I imagine it is difficult for a young woman who lives in the country to find a worthy husband in any way than by luck," Lady Emmeline declared.

"Knowing Bingley as well as I do, I must say he was the lucky one to find a woman perfectly suited for him," Darcy intervened in earnest. "Mrs. Bingley is not just an exceptional beauty, but she possesses impeccable man-ners, genuine kindness, and a generous character—all rare qualities that are not often found in one person. Such a marriage, based on the deepest love and mutual understanding, is what any man desires. Of course, the vast majority of us are not fortunate enough to succeed in our quest, and we are forced to settle for less."

"I already envy Bingley, just hearing Darcy's statement," Lord Mowbray responded seriously.

"And so you should," Darcy added then sipped some wine from his glass, sensing Elizabeth's glance and the slight movements on his right. He was thankful that he had the chance to clarify things to someone who, most certainly, would pass the words to other acquaintances in London. Mrs. Bingley did not deserve to be subjected to intrusive questions and gossip.

Lady Emmeline renewed her inquiries a few minutes later. "Are there other estates for rent in the neighbourhood? Perhaps you would have the same luck as your sister."

Elizabeth's patience slowly left her as she started to feel that she was in a conversation with Caroline Bingley.

"I dare not hope to have my sister's luck. Jane is an extraordinary person in every possible way, and she deserves complete happiness."

"But even a less extraordinary woman must be in search of a husband," Lady Emmeline continued.

"I assure you I am not. But may I ask: What is the reason for your interest regarding my future marital prospects?" Elizabeth's voice became sharper.

"I believe this subject is improper," Darcy intervened. "And Miss Bennet surely does not have to answer your inquiries."

"Of course…I was just curious…it does not happen every day that a complete stranger is invited to live at Pemberley with you. As far as I know, that has never happened before, not even with those of us who have known you and Georgiana for a lifetime."

"Forgive me; dinner was excellent, but I am rather tired. If you will excuse me, I would rather retire to my room." Elizabeth quickly ended a conversation that had become unpleasant. "Georgiana, will you join me?" she addressed the girl who appeared pale and troubled.

"Yes…yes of course…I am very tired too…"

"I will accompany you. Aunt Amelia, will you stay longer?" Darcy asked.

"Yes, dear—only for a little while. This young man here will help me to my room." She indicated Lord Mowbray.

The three of them walked towards their chambers, moving in a deep, embarrassed silence.

When they reached Georgiana's room, Darcy spoke. "Miss Bennet, I am sorry you had to bear the lack of politeness of our acquaintance. Lady Emmeline's manners were more than unprincipled."

"Sir, you have nothing for which to apologise. It was kind of you to leave your friends, but it is truly not necessary. I will stay a while with Georgiana and then go to sleep. All is well."

"Very well…as you wish. Then I shall go to my room too. It has been a rather tiring evening."

He kissed his sister's temple, then bowed to Elizabeth, and walked up the stairs to the next floor, their gazes following him.

When they were alone, Georgiana turned a sad face to her friend. "Lizzy, would you like to come in for a few minutes?"

"Of course, dearest. How are you feeling? I noticed dinner was not very pleasant for you."

"It was pleasant enough, but I felt so bad for the way Emmeline spoke to you. She is so rude sometimes. Oh, silly me, I left my shawl downstairs. I hope Mrs. Nott will hold it until tomorrow."

"Oh, do not worry. I will fetch it."

"Lizzy, please stay. I will get it myself. Lizzy—"

Elizabeth was halfway down the stairs, eager to end the incident and the entire evening. She was irritated, but Darcy's concern and Georgiana's distress dissipated her own discomfort. She congratulated herself on leaving rather than continuing the argument with Lady Emmeline. It was so ridiculous that it was not worth the effort.

Once back in the dining room, she stopped suddenly behind the now-open curtains as she heard the countess's angry voice.

"Emmeline, what on earth is wrong with you, young lady? How dare you be rude to Miss Bennet? Have you completely lost your mind?"

"Aunt Amelia, surely you cannot blame me for a few questions! That is how we always talk among ourselves. But of course, Miss Bennet is not one of us, or else she would have known how to answer instead of dashing away to hide in her room. Or perhaps she is not as witty as Colonel Fitzwilliam led us to believe."

"You are such a silly, arrogant girl! You are just like another whom I scolded a few days ago in Hertfordshire. Which is why neither of you has found a husband yet!"

"Aunt Amelia, what are you saying? You cannot possibly—"

"Hush girl! No 'Aunt Amelia'! I care for you dearly, so I must warn you not to make a complete fool of yourself in public! Miss Bennet did not run to hide; she simply accompanied Georgiana, who was obviously affected by your tasteless jests. And I am sure Miss Bennet struggled not to answer you as you deserved. If she had, you would be the one complaining about being offended; I have no doubt. As for her wit, you are my niece, and I love you, but I truly believe she is smarter than you, better read, and far more knowledgeable."

"You are unfair," Lady Emmeline replied. "I do not deserve such a lack of appreciation or such harsh censure!"

"Then behave accordingly! Your father spent a fortune on your education; you should prove he did not waste it. It might as well have been thrown out the window! Earlier today, I spoke proudly to Miss Bennet about our family connection, and now you make me ashamed to be your aunt! How will I face her tomorrow morning?"

"I still do not believe I have done anything wrong! I only asked a few innocent questions."

"Innocent questions? Do not consider me oblivious to your intentions. You are determined to gain Darcy's attention, and you would do anything for it. But you took the wrong path. He not only disliked your appearance here, but he returned to his room to escape your offensive behaviour towards his guest."

Elizabeth was startled by Mrs. Nott, who touched her arm gently. "Miss? May I help you with something?"

"No…I…Miss Darcy forgot her shawl, and I came to find it."

"Oh, let me look for it, and I will take it to Miss Darcy's room right away. There is no need for you to wait here."

"Of course. Thank you," she answered and left in haste, surprised by the conversation she overheard. A clap of thunder near the inn let her know that the rain had started.

ALTHOUGH HE LEFT THE DINNER TABLE RATHER EARLY, DARCY SPENT almost two more hours with the colonel, talking and enjoying Mr. Nott's finest brandy.

"This room is pretty small," the colonel said as he sipped his drink.

"It is; it was the only one available, so I offered mine to Miss Bennet, and I moved here. It will do for one night."

"True. But the brandy is good."

"It is; Nott always provides good food and drink," Darcy declared.

"Dinner was excellent indeed," the colonel admitted. "A pity it did not last longer."

"An unfortunate conversation always ruins any dinner," Darcy answered coldly.

"Agreed, but you must know that, once you departed, Lady Hardwick scolded Emmeline quite harshly."

"That is little compensation for her rudeness. If it were not for the embarrassment it would cause Miss Bennet and Georgiana, I would have censured her myself. I know I am not the most amiable person, and my manners are neither easy nor pleasant most of the time. There have been times when I preferred not to engage in conversation with people who happened to be nearby. But I hope I never found pleasure in offending someone gratuitously."

"You have not; although, your manners could use improvement and softness on occasion."

"I am glad you are amused; at least one of us is. Surely, Miss Bennet is not inclined to laugh at her own expense," Darcy replied.

"Well, I would say she is inclined to do just that. Miss Bennet is a young lady with an excellent sense of humour."

"She is, but rudeness is never humorous. I cannot possibly understand how Emmeline came to behave in such a way. How is it her business that Miss Bennet was invited to Pemberley?"

"Well...she might be jealous," the colonel said tentatively.

"Jealous because Georgiana preferred Miss Bennet to her? That is ridiculous."

"Not quite. I believe she feels Miss Bennet might be a rival for your favours. I have seen such behaviour in ladies many times."

Darcy filled his glass and remained with his back to his cousin so as not to face him.

"That is even more ridiculous. Does any woman believe that rude behaviour and offensive manners are an inducement to gain a man's attention?"

"Well, they must try something, especially with a man as aloof and haughty as you are."

"Even more reason for a woman not to want my attention. Let us end this discussion. Tomorrow I intend to leave very early. Will you join us since your destination is closer to ours than to the Livingston estate?"

"Yes; I will inform the others and come with you. But I hope that, tomorrow at breakfast, Emmeline changes her behaviour and maybe even apologises to Miss Bennet."

"Perhaps. I forgot to ask: How are your parents? And your brother?"

Their discussion continued until fatigue and brandy overcame them. The rain had begun, and its patter, together with a lack of sleep the previous nights, soon threw Darcy into a deep sleep.

It did not last long, however. Rest was replaced by agitation just as the sound of the rain became silence, and he woke up. His head was still foggy, and he felt unbearably warm. He tried to remove the blankets from around him, but something prevented his doing so. He stretched his hand to remove the obstacle, and he froze when his hand touched the softness of a gown. He slowly rose on his elbow and glanced at the silhouette in a deep, peaceful sleep. He could only see a back with long, thick brown hair falling loosely on the shoulders. Warmth increased, as did an intoxicating scent. His breath caught as he had no doubt it was Elizabeth. Somehow, he must have left his room and mistakenly entered the one he was accustomed to.

Darcy dared not move, but he knew he must. Slowly, he attempted to leave the bed. He threw a last glance at the soft form in the bed, and panic made him still. She was turning to him, moaning sweetly through her sleep until she woke up. Her eyes glittered from behind long eyelashes, and a shy smile greeted him.

"Do not leave…stay a little longer," she whispered, and amazement stilled him. Her breathing became irregular, moving her throat and breasts enchantingly. Her lips parted, and she stretched her hand to him. The nightgown glided from her shoulders, and only the locks of hair sheltered her skin from his greedy eyes. He knew he should leave—he should run—instead, he leant towards her until they almost touched. His lips brushed hers as his torso pressed against her until their bodies touched and their hearts started to beat together. Her tentative fingers caressed his hair and moved around his neck. Then his mouth captured hers, tasted it, savoured it, until the need for air made him stop and withdraw from her reluctantly in painful sorrow…

Darcy woke almost violently from his tormenting dream. The awakening was so abrupt that he nearly fell from the bed. He looked around in complete panic and realised he was alone in the small room. Of course she was not there. Of course it was only another mortifying fabrication of his troubled mind.

He rushed to wash his face then opened the window widely. The rain had stopped—that was the only fact. He opened his shirt as he still felt he could not breathe. A gentle breeze was blowing, and he leant out the window as much as he could, allowing the wind to chill his inner heat.

Everything was dark except for the torches that guarded the inn. To his left on the lower floor, another window was open. He remained still, and his knees weakened as he recognised Elizabeth's figure wearing nothing but a nightgown, her hair playing in the wind. He wished to withdraw but had not the strength to abandon the bewitching image. When she turned to him, their eyes met; it was too dark for him to read the expression on her face, but she did not avert her gaze. He knew he should say something, or at least wave to her or give the reasonable response of a proper gentleman. But he could not; the taste of her lips and the memory of her scent —though not real, just the result of his imagination—were too vivid to allow him to think rationally. So he just took a step back and closed the window. The room became unbearably warm, and it appeared to shrink, weighing heavily on his shoulders. So he opened the window again but remained away from its frame. Finally, he dared to steal a glance; the window of Elizabeth's room was closed.

THE NIGHT WAS LATE AND DARK; THE PATTER OF RAIN HAD STOPPED AFter hours of splashing rhythmically on the window, and it was the perfect, complete silence that awoke Elizabeth. At first, she was confused about her location. She felt herself shivering and wrapped herself in the blankets. But then she became warm and thirsty and went to the small table to pour herself some water.

She glanced back at the large bed with its four pillows. Two of them were not even used. Both the bed and the pillows were too large for her, just as the bed in the smaller chamber was probably too small for Darcy. She should have taken the other room, but he would brook no argument. He wished to be certain she was comfortable, but she was not, and her sleep was restless. The image of him sleeping in the same bed on another night was disturbing. Not unpleasant. Not distressful. Only disturbing, thrilling, stirring. She knew that her thoughts were unreasonable, embarrassing, even shameful, but she could not escape them. Just as she could not escape the recollection of his closeness, his touch, or his scent that had troubled her since dinnertime. She had never known such a storm of feelings from the mere nearness to a man. She could have moved her chair a few inches away to be sure their bodies would not brush against each other. But she did not. He could have done the same if he wished. He was at the end of the table—for him it would have been even easier. And yet, he preferred not to.

What was happening to her? She was there to keep Georgiana company. To take care of her. To provide that sweet girl the peace, comfort, and support she needed. Instead, she was making a fool of herself. She must gather herself and keep her head clear. She had to be more careful. She should avoid being too close to him. Her behaviour was neither proper nor reasonable in his presence.

She turned to the bed again, and a sense of panic enveloped her. Should she go back to sleep? Or perhaps just wait for morning to come?

Elizabeth opened the window, yearning for fresh air, and she breathed deeply the scent of early autumn washed by the rain. There was little to be seen as the moon and the stars were hidden by the clouds. A few torches lit the yard of the inn, their fire flickering with the breeze. A sense of calm enveloped her, and she closed her eyes, bending out over the window frame. Then a shiver ran down her spine, and her heart fluttered for no apparent reason. She opened her eyes and glanced up the dark wall of the building. She startled then remained still, astounded, her gaze frozen. On the upper floor—at a small window lit by the torch burning behind it—stood Darcy. He was looking outside, his white shirt unbuttoned and his hair in disorder. Mesmerised, Elizabeth watched his head slowly turn, his gaze falling upon her and seeming to burn her face. Their eyes met and held for a long, heavy moment; then he gradually retired and closed the window.

She needed time to regain her composure and reluctantly do the same. With hesitant steps, she returned to the bed, lay down, and pulled the blankets around her. A few minutes later, she took one of the extra pillows and embraced it, but the tremor inside her was not to be soothed until dawn.

Chapter 20

To Darcy's surprise, the next morning at breakfast, everyone was present. However, the conversation was sparse, and the extended party soon continued their journey together.

After the torment of the previous night, Darcy felt uneasy at the notion of being trapped inside the carriage so close to Elizabeth. Therefore, he decided to ride horseback, and the colonel joined him.

Elizabeth was also relieved by the gentleman's absence. Her sleep had been poor and restless, so the morning found her tired but also anxious and embarrassed by her own feelings.

"My dear, I hope Emmeline's remarks did not upset you," Lady Hardwick said. "Please do not take them to heart."

"Your ladyship must not worry—that is truly the least of my concerns." Elizabeth knew she was speaking the truth. A mere glance from Darcy disturbed her more than the entire conversation of the previous evening.

"Well, I am glad to see a young woman who is wise and reasonable for a change," the countess continued. "I wonder whether I was as insensible and arrogant forty years ago. Probably not, as these unpleasant traits do not necessarily persist as one ages," she concluded philosophically.

Elizabeth laughed. "Then I am happy to know your ladyship when you are kind and generous."

"I tell you, my dear, a woman who is desperate to secure a husband often loses her reason. Thank God I am over that too."

"I confess I am worried about whom William will finally choose to marry," Georgiana whispered. "I hope and pray it will be someone kind and gentle—and worthy of him. Mrs. Reynolds has said the same. Lizzy, Mrs.

Reynolds is our housekeeper at Pemberley, and she has been with us since my brother was four."

It was the countess's turn to laugh. "If it were up to Mrs. Reynolds, nobody would be worthy of your brother. She is more protective of him than anyone else."

"True. But indeed I am sure there cannot be a better man than William. He is excellent in everything he does."

"Except for his manners in certain circumstances." Lady Hardwick laughed again. "By the way, Elizabeth, I still need to hear the story of his refusing to dance with you. This would be the perfect time to share it."

Elizabeth blushed then tried to sound whimsical. "I am afraid I cannot do that. If the story is shared, Mr. Darcy should be present too. I cannot possibly speak behind his back, especially since I will live in his house for a time."

"Do not worry, dear; if he throws you out, I will take you to live with me."

"Aunt Amelia!" Georgiana cried in genuine distress, frightened that the joke might upset Elizabeth. "Why does everyone speak of William as if he were an ogre?"

"I do not know, dearest. It might be something he does to evoke such a common opinion," the countess replied with amusement. "It is strange that a young man with an excellent character and a kind heart has manners that rarely show it—unlike most men who pretend and show themselves to be better than they truly are."

"Your ladyship is right," Elizabeth replied thoughtfully.

Two hours later, the party stopped at an inn to have tea and change horses. Lord Mowbray and the colonel immediately helped the ladies out of the carriages while Darcy went inside to speak with the innkeeper.

Georgiana held the basket with Mist while Didi ran happily between their feet.

Still uncomfortable at the thought of facing Darcy, Elizabeth felt at ease in the company of the earl and the colonel. Since neither her heart nor her mind was in any way engaged with them, her wit was sparkling, and the conversation flowed easily.

Lady Emmeline was considerably less talkative than on the previous evening. She ceased her rudeness towards Elizabeth but spoke no more than a few words to her. Instead, she focused her attention upon Darcy, to whom she directed a question every few minutes.

Again, Elizabeth and Darcy exchanged few glances and not a single word. Both were distressed by their own thoughts and reluctant to face the other.

"Mr. Darcy, we host a ball in two weeks. Will you join us?" Lady Livingston inquired.

"I thank you for your kind invitation, but I see little chance for that to happen," he replied.

"You should have expected such an answer," Lord Mowbray said then turned to Darcy. "But perhaps you can host a ball at Pemberley that we could attend?"

Darcy threw him a stern glance. "That is even less likely to happen."

"Well, there will be a large party at Pemberley for Christmas, we hope," the countess interjected. "If you happen to be in the neighbourhood, I am sure we will be pleased to see you again."

"I might take your invitation to heart, Lady Hardwick," the earl said. "That is—if Darcy approves."

"You would, of course, be most welcome," Darcy responded. "Now, I suggest we leave; it is already late."

"Where will you spend the night?" Lady Emmeline asked daringly. Darcy appeared disconcerted, and he stole a look at Elizabeth, who pretended to be engaged with Mist.

"As soon as we pass Birmingham, we will rest at the Wood Inn. We always stop there."

"Why would you not come to my brother-in-law's estate? Livingston's residence is only half an hour ride by carriage," Lady Emmeline continued, and Lord Livingston approved the suggestion enthusiastically.

"You are very kind, and I appreciate your generosity, but we will proceed according to our plan," Darcy declared. "I am rather strict with travelling plans on long journeys."

"It is such a pity," Lady Emmeline continued. "A gentleman should change his plans when opportunities arise."

"He should, my dear Emmeline, if he feels the opportunities are more tempting than his plans," Lady Hardwick responded. "If not, as much as others might point it out to him, his firmness remains unmoved."

"However enjoyable this conversation might be, we must leave," Darcy interrupted the discussion, and the countess laughed, nodding towards Lady Emmeline.

"And here is your proof, dear niece. Yes, let us leave. I am eager to arrive at Pemberley. Long trips in a carriage have never been my favourite diversion."

The party resumed their travels—the gentlemen still on horseback. Elizabeth was intrigued and abashed by the troubling conversation between Darcy and Lady Emmeline. Her stomach was tight and unsettled. How could a young lady be so easy in manners with a gentleman in public? Not even Miss Bingley had ever dared so much—unless, of course, they had a previous friendship. Certainly, such a friendship was not her concern. And yet, she could think of nothing else. Therefore, she remained oblivious to Georgiana's question until the girl repeated it several times.

DARCY WAS RELIEVED AT THE PROSPECT OF SEPARATING SOON FROM THE other party. Emmeline's manner had become more familiar than ever before. It was likely due to the presence of Lady Hardwick, who was related to everyone in the group. Still, he was displeased with any flirtatious display in the presence of his sister—and Elizabeth.

However, Elizabeth appeared to give it little interest. Her attention seemed engaged by the presence of the colonel and of Lord Mowbray, who was open in his admiration for her.

Mowbray's easy conversation with Elizabeth troubled Darcy even more than Emmeline's forwardness although there was nothing improper in the earl's manners. Darcy avoided staring at Elizabeth to ease her comfort, but it was a struggle as his dream from the previous night and her enchanting image glowing in the light of the torches were painfully vivid in his mind. Her hair was now perfectly arranged, but he remembered it falling loose. She was now properly dressed, but he recollected her neck, shoulders, and arms barely covered by the thin fabric of her nightgown.

"So I will come with you," the colonel said, and Darcy turned to him in puzzlement.

"Forgive me, did you say something?"

"Yes—I said I will stay with you at the Wood Inn tonight, perhaps remaining at Pemberley tomorrow night if that is convenient for you, and I will be at the regiment the day after tomorrow."

"It sounds perfect," Darcy approved.

"I might stop and check on Wickham on my way back."

"That should be interesting."

"Do you still have him supervised?"

"Of course. I will until I am sure I have no reason for concern."

"That might never happen with Wickham."

"I am aware of that, Richard."

Another break in their journey followed around noon and a third one late in the afternoon when the group parted—to the disappointment of some and the relief of others. A warm farewell was taken, and hopes of a forthcoming meeting expressed. Lord Mowbray mentioned several times how delighted he was to make Elizabeth's acquaintance while Lady Emmeline flirtatiously accused the colonel of betrayal and Darcy of ingratitude for her efforts to leave London a day early with the particular purpose of meeting him. Both gentlemen apologised politely.

The party split with some delay, and Darcy's group increased its speed to recover the lost time. Half an hour later, rain and wind began again, so the horsemen joined the ladies in the carriage.

"May I sit by you, Miss Bennet?" the colonel inquired, and at her ready acceptance, he took the place next to her.

Darcy sat on his aunt's side, occupying the space previously claimed by Didi.

"I do hope it is not raining tomorrow when we arrive home," Georgiana said. "I would really like to show Pemberley to Lizzy on a sunny day."

"I am sure I will love Pemberley on any day from everything you have told me about it," Elizabeth answered then blushed as she felt Darcy's gaze on her. Somehow, speaking favourably about his estate was as uncomfortable as if she had criticised it.

"I am sure you will, my dear," the countess replied. "I confess, I am very proud of Tidestone—the Hardwick residence—but Pemberley has held a special place in my heart since I was a child."

"Matlock, my parents' estate, is also beautifully situated and rather close to Pemberley. You should visit it too, Miss Bennet."

"Thank you for suggesting it, Colonel. I will certainly do so as soon as the opportunity arises. And I would also like to see Tidestone."

"Both of them are not more than an hour's ride from Pemberley on a good day with a good horse," the colonel continued, and Elizabeth laughed nervously.

"Well, that is not a very helpful recommendation for me, sir. I see no possibility of my riding in any direction anytime soon."

"Oh yes, I remember, you delight in walking. I fondly recall our strolls in the Rosings gardens."

"You are too kind, sir," Elizabeth answered, struggling to sound easier than she felt. Recollections of Rosings strolls included the day she had confirmation of Darcy's intervention in separating Jane and Bingley, awkward meetings with Darcy, and a letter offered and ripped apart—all painful and unpleasant images.

"Despite the weather tomorrow, Miss Bennet will stay at Pemberley long enough that you could show it to her on all sorts of days, from sunny to snowy," Darcy addressed his sister.

"True," the girl answered animatedly. "Oh, I just realised we have not decided which rooms we will give to Lizzy."

"She should take the chambers next to yours," Lady Hardwick said in earnest as if this were a significant decision. Elizabeth could hardly keep her countenance, considering the reaction of her mother, Mrs. Phillips, and Lady Lucas had they known a young heiress and a countess were preoccupied with which rooms to offer her at one of the largest estates in the North.

"I think Miss Bennet should visit several available rooms in the family wing and choose for herself," Darcy intervened.

"Yes, of course; that is what we shall do," Georgiana agreed.

"Oh, there is no need, sir." Elizabeth ventured to meet Darcy's gaze. "Any room will be perfect, I am sure. I would like to be as close as possible to Georgiana if that is convenient for you."

"Of course it is convenient, Lizzy; it would be perfect."

"Then no other choice is necessary. I am sure all the rooms are perfectly comfortable and beautifully furnished."

"I would hope they are," Darcy responded, his eyes now holding Elizabeth's. "But it might be the view that makes the difference. Each room has a balcony from which the sight of the estate can be admired."

"You are very considerate, sir," she replied, flustered. "I have no doubt that all the views are wonderful at Pemberley, though. That would certainly make my choice even more difficult. It is a tragedy, indeed, to be forced to choose between several versions of perfection. I am afraid I will become quite spoiled," she joked.

"You should take this opportunity to make your choice, Miss Bennet, while Darcy offers it to you. It will rarely happen again. As I mentioned several months ago during our lovely walks at Rosings, Darcy arranges things just as he pleases," the colonel teased his cousin.

Darcy's countenance remained serious, and Elizabeth became uneasy at the prospect of his believing she had gossiped with the colonel at his expense. It was not entirely untrue, but she wondered that the colonel mentioned it. It happened at another place, another time, with another Elizabeth...

"I do remember what you told me, Colonel," she answered. "However, what I did not know then and I do know now, as I begin to know Mr. Darcy better, is that most of the time he makes arrangements not so much for his own liking but for the safety and well-being of the people in his care."

She observed that Darcy was surprised by her small praise; their eyes locked again for a moment, and his expression slowly softened.

"'That is so true," the countess responded. "I admit that my two estates are better managed by my nephew than they were by my beloved late husband. And while I did appreciate surprises and the unexpected when I was much younger, now I feel safe and at peace every time this young man here makes plans that involve me. I can scarcely remember more than two occasions when he has been wrong about something."

Darcy smiled and kissed his aunt's hand. "You are too kind, dear aunt; I have been wrong more times than I like to admit. And I do appreciate surprises and the unexpected too, as long as they do not mean any possible harm for those in my care. When I am alone, I do tend to do foolish things, I assure you."

A shiver ran along Elizabeth's arms, and a lump in her throat kept her silent; she knew he was right. She was perfectly aware of several circumstances when he had done things that he might call foolish, and she also had the chance to experience the benefit of his actions and his plans.

"Well, the ladies seem determined to praise you while you can only blame yourself, and neither opinion is wrong," the colonel added. "If you ask me, after knowing you for eight and twenty years, I might say that your virtues spring from your character and your faults from your manners."

"Excellent description," Lady Hardwick agreed. "That is Darcy indeed."

"Most of the things I do and say are excellent," the colonel replied, laughing. "As you see, I am not at all willing to point out any of my own deficiencies."

Elizabeth said nothing, but her eyes returned to Darcy and held his again.

He appeared discomposed and reluctant to receive praise, and his uneasiness touched her heart.

Yes, she could see the truth in the colonel's description—which was why she had only seen his faults and had remained oblivious to his merits. It was much easier for her—and for everybody in Meryton—to observe his manners than to understand his character.

"So, speaking of manners less seriously and gravely, you still owe Georgiana and me a story, my dear nephew." The countess smiled mischievously.

Darcy was puzzled. "What story?"

"The story of your calling Miss Bennet 'tolerable' and refusing to dance with her. I asked her earlier, but she insisted you should be present when that tale is disclosed. It must be very grave," the countess said mockingly.

The colonel was dumbfounded, and Georgiana blushed with worry for the discomfort of her brother and her friend.

"Aunt Amelia…"

"Oh hush, dearest." The countess waved her hand, refusing to be deterred from her purpose.

Elizabeth flushed, torn between amusement and embarrassment, and wondered what Darcy would say. To her complete disbelief, a small smile narrowed his eyes and twisted his lips.

"Yes…that story; do I have any chance of refusing you, Aunt?"

"Not a single one, my dear."

"Very well—I see you cruelly insist on laughing at my expense. Then it depends on Miss Bennet; if she agrees, I will tell it."

"Do tell, sir. I have nothing against it. Why should we keep a secret that is disclosed by my mother at every opportunity and discussed frequently?" Elizabeth responded, still in jest.

Darcy breathed deeply then met Elizabeth's gaze another moment, and his smile widened.

"It was the middle of October last year about three weeks after Bingley took possession of Netherfield. An assembly was held in Meryton. Bingley insisted I should go with them, and I had no argument to resist him. I confess that I found little enjoyment in the event for personal reasons," he admitted, and everyone knew to what he referred. He paused for an instant then continued in a tone that obviously struggled to remain easy.

"So, to end any argument, I attended, but my mood was not suitable for the occasion, and I am sure my behaviour clearly showed it. Once there, Bingley went on and on, insisting on my dancing. I struggled to deter him but with little success. I must also mention that I had danced with Miss Bingley and Mrs. Hurst and had every intention of avoiding a repetition."

"Well, I can empathise with that," the colonel intervened. "I have rarely seen a lady as handsome and smart—and as unpleasant—as Miss Bingley."

"As I said, at that time, the only fault for my vexation belonged to my mood; Miss Bingley was not to blame. But instead of leaving me alone, Bingley returned to me after each dance and insisted that I dance. In the midst of our debate, he pointed out Miss Bennet to me—whom, I confess, I barely noticed until that moment. I surely did not remember anything about her, but in order to escape Bingley's annoying solicitation, I told him that Miss Bennet was tolerable but not handsome enough to tempt me! Of course, I was not aware that, sadly, Miss Bennet heard me—and was rightfully offended by my words—until much later when I discovered that all of Meryton was speaking of the incident."

"You did not!" the countess exclaimed.

"Oh, dear Lord," Georgiana whispered.

Elizabeth forced a laugh. She was less distressed by the story itself than by the recollection of that crucial moment that marked the development of their acquaintance and led to the dreadful day at the Parsonage.

"It is truly not a reason for distress now. But yes, I confess that, back then, my pride was offended. There is nothing a girl wants more at a ball than to dance."

"That is correct," Lady Hardwick agreed. "Such behaviour is unacceptable. What was wrong with you, young man?"

The colonel hurried to take his cousin's side, laughing loudly. "Well, although I cannot understand why anyone would ever refuse to dance with Miss Bennet, I can sympathise with Darcy. Upon my word, Bingley is sometimes so annoying in his persistence that even I would say anything to get rid of him."

"It seems his persistence ensured him a most fortunate marriage, so in the end, it turned out well. But that was the story Mrs. Bennet mentioned with understandable resentment. I take this opportunity to publicly and officially beg Miss Bennet to forgive my rudeness," Darcy bowed towards her solemnly, his voice half grave, half in jest.

Elizabeth blushed, but her discomfort vanished. "Gladly, sir. Your care in choosing a room with the perfect view for me at Pemberley surely compensates for your refusal to dance with me the first time we met, even more so as it eventually happened the second time."

"I am grateful for your generosity. But our dance together occurred the *third* time I asked. You refused me twice: at Sir William's party and one evening at Netherfield," he replied teasingly.

It was Elizabeth's turn to remain silent in astonishment.

"Is there another story I should know about?" the countess inquired. Georgiana chuckled while Darcy hurried to deny it with a firm shake of his head.

When the conversation on that subject seemed finally ended, the colonel turned to Darcy and said with apparent secrecy. "Cousin, once we arrive at Pemberley, remind me to explain to you that dancing with a lovely lady at a ball *alleviates* distress and does not increase it. I wish I had taught it to you years ago so you could have avoided such awkward moments as you just related. But it is never too late to improve one's knowledge and manners on the subject."

Chapter 21

The evening was spent at the Wood Inn as planned. The inn was sparsely occupied, so finding rooms for Elizabeth and the colonel was an easy business, and dinner was peaceful. The party resumed their journey early next morning to ensure they would arrive at Pemberley by evening. As the day was beautiful, the gentlemen again preferred their horses. Inside the carriage, the ladies, accompanied by Didi and Mist, amused themselves with stories of the past and plans for the future.

After noon, following their second stop on the road, a brief rain began, so the gentlemen sheltered again in the carriage.

"I am so happy to be home soon," Georgiana exclaimed.

"As am I," Lady Hardwick answered. "I believe I shall sleep a few days and nights in a row."

"I confess I am anxious to see Pemberley, and I am afraid I will not be able to sleep at all for a few days at least. Dear Georgiana's eagerness and enthusiasm are contagious," Elizabeth said. "I hope we visit as much of it as possible tomorrow."

"My dear, you will need at least a week to visit it. The park alone is about ten miles 'round, is it not, Darcy?" the countess replied.

"Yes it is, Aunt."

"Truly? That is overwhelming indeed," Elizabeth said with a smile.

"Yes, but we can start tomorrow morning," Georgiana continued. "I will ask Mr. Slade to have a phaeton prepared for you. Do you know how to drive? If not, Luke or one of the other stable boys will join you. I would really like to ride if you do not mind. But do not worry, Lizzy; I will stay close to you."

Georgiana's eyes glowed with anticipation, and her voice was filled with joy. Darcy's heart melted; he gazed at his aunt and could see her contentment. The shy, silent, fearful girl, who was afraid to face the world and the daylight in London, seemed replaced by this witty, voluble, lively Georgiana, who was ready—and eager—to enjoy life in all its beauty. Darcy ventured a brief look at Elizabeth; he knew how much he owed her for this change. The distress of Elizabeth's nearness was endurable when compared to the extraordinary benefit of her friendship with Georgiana. His own feelings were insignificant under the present circumstances. His job—his duty —was to make certain this friendship was sheltered, and he would refrain from any gestures—including thoughts—that might make Miss Bennet uncomfortable.

"Who is Mr. Slade if I may ask?" he heard Elizabeth inquiring.

"Oh, he is a dear friend of our family. He lives in a cottage less than a mile from Pemberley House. He is also in charge of our horses and stables. Just wait 'til you meet him. I am sure you will like him as much as I do," Georgiana responded with the same enthusiasm.

With a calmer voice and a little smile, Darcy added, "Mr. Slade is indeed a dear friend of our family. His father was at Pemberley when my grandfather was young. He was in the army for many years, and after he suffered a dangerous wound fifteen years ago, he decided to return to Pemberley. We happily welcomed him as he is a great help and comfort to us."

"Oh, what an exciting story. I look forward to meeting him," Elizabeth said.

"Mr. Slade is also an excellent rider and fencer. He taught Richard and me to ride and handle a sword," Darcy continued.

"True," the colonel agreed. "Even to this day, though he must be in his early sixties, I am not certain I could defeat him in a horse race or a duel."

"Not to mention he was an exceedingly good looking man; no other was more handsome than he was," the countess whispered to Elizabeth, whose cheeks coloured. Georgiana also blushed and chuckled while the two gentlemen stared in surprise at such a statement.

Lady Hardwick had more to reveal. "I confess I lost my heart to him years ago. He did not know any of this of course. I used to watch him with Darcy's father as they rode through the fields or fenced in the back garden. He was a great favourite of many ladies, but for some reason, he chose not to marry. Then he joined the army and now is alone with no family. Of course, I was married twice, and I am in a similar position. Strange, is it not? Oh well, I confess I am still a little unsettled when I see him." She laughed, much to the others' astonishment.

Elizabeth did not know what to do with such a statement, except to consider it another proof that the countess was a most unpredictable lady and one should never be alarmed about what to expect from her next. That, together with her keen sense of observation and sharp intelligence, made her an equally admirable and frightening companion.

"Lady Hardwick, you never cease to amaze me," the colonel said with a laugh as if reading Elizabeth's mind.

"Well, my dear, at my age, amazement is one of the few feelings I might hope to arouse in a young gentleman," she replied, and the colonel laughed even louder, kissing her hand. Darcy struggled to remain stern as he noted the mirth in Elizabeth's' eyes and the amusement on Georgiana's flushed cheeks.

THE SUN WAS SLOWLY SINKING WHEN THE CARRIAGE REACHED A CROSSROAD.

Lady Hardwick pointed it out to Elizabeth. "Look, my dear, if we continued to the left, we would reach Tidestone in about an hour and a half."

"And this is where Pemberley begins. We will be home soon," Georgiana said. "I am so happy we arrived before dark."

"Yes, it was worth hurrying a bit. It seemed Darcy's travelling schedule worked perfectly," the countess teased her nephew.

Darcy bore her jest with an unmoved expression. He knew he hurried the party more than necessary with the sole purpose of allowing Elizabeth a glimpse of Pemberley in daylight. His goal was achieved when he saw her lean on the carriage window and gaze outside, unwilling to miss the view for a single moment. However, for the time being, there was little to see but the dense wood, its large trees coloured with the rust of autumn.

The sun had almost set, and the redness of the fields matched the crimson of the sky when Pemberley finally appeared in the valley, majestically guarding the lakes, the gardens, and the groves that surrounded it.

The expression of utter delight and profound amazement on Elizabeth's face was Darcy's reward. She continually whispered her admiration for the beauty before them, and Georgiana leant near her. He smiled as he watched them share the same joy and wonder.

"It takes my breath away every time I see it. I cannot believe it is my home, and I deeply miss it when I am away," Georgiana whispered.

"I can well understand. I do not think I have ever seen a more beautiful place. Nothing I have heard about Pemberley does it justice. Thank you for inviting me here, dear Georgiana."

As the hoof-beats brought them closer to the main entrance, silence took the place of words inadequate to express Elizabeth's admiration.

When they finally stopped in front of the building, Darcy and the colonel hurried out and helped the ladies. Lady Hardwick remained on the arm of her nephew while Elizabeth and Georgiana slowly walked together.

Darcy was amused and pleased to see Elizabeth lost in delight, her head turning rapidly in an attempt to see everything at once.

Mrs. Reynolds hastened to greet them, followed by several servants.

"Welcome, welcome! Master, what a joyful day for us to have you finally here! Lady Hardwick! Colonel Fitzwilliam! Miss Georgiana—how much you have grown and how beautiful you are! Oh, you have been dearly missed."

"Mrs. Reynolds, we are happy to be here," Darcy said as Georgiana embraced the woman whose eyes were moist with tears. "Allow me to introduce Miss Elizabeth Bennet. She is a close friend of Georgiana, and she will be a lovely addition to our family for the next months."

"Miss Bennet, we are so pleased to have you here. Come, come—let us enter. Everything is prepared. We will take you to your rooms first. Dinner is ready when you are."

Lady Hardwick was the first to be helped to her apartment. Georgiana held Elizabeth's arm and continued to speak as they headed towards the stairs to reach the other bedchambers.

"I could take you on a tour of the house now if you want. Or tomorrow. You must see the music room; the pianoforte is exquisite. It was a gift from William."

Darcy gently touched his sister's shoulder. "Dearest, let us take things slowly. You will have plenty of time. For now, we should settle and eat something. This has been a long and tiring journey."

"And drink something," the colonel added. "I will take my usual room and see you in the library in half an hour, Darcy."

"Very well. Now, it is Miss Bennet's turn to choose her chamber," Darcy said.

"Come, Lizzy, let me show you. Aunt Amelia has a suite downstairs on the first floor; she cannot tolerate the stairs. Here is my apartment; William's is at the end of the hall. And these three are the available rooms in the family wing. Of course, there are many others, but I thought you would like to stay closer to me. Two of these have a view towards the back and one towards the front, but I believe it is a little smaller."

Elizabeth felt slightly overwhelmed by the situation. Everything was so beautiful yet so solemn and silent that it was intimidating. She was reluctant to enter the rooms as Georgiana opened them one by one by. They were all large and exquisitely furnished. Each had an impressive bed, twice as big as the one she had at Longbourn, very high windows, a fire in the fireplace, and many other things upon which Elizabeth barely had time to rest her eyes. She turned towards Darcy, who was waiting a little distance away as if he did not want to enter a room she might occupy.

"Sir, which would you recommend? They are all so beautiful that I cannot possibly know how to choose."

He was so surprised that he needed a moment to form a reply. He could see Elizabeth was a little lost and uncomfortable, but the notion that she asked his advice in selecting the place she would stay for several months raised a strange feeling inside him.

"I suggest the room towards the front. From the balcony, there is a beautiful view of the lake. I believe you will enjoy it."

Her eyes held his only an instant. "I am sure I will; my decision is made. I thank you for your help."

He bowed then stepped away, entering his apartment while Elizabeth entered her chamber, followed by Georgiana. She wondered what his room was like and despised herself for such thoughts while Georgiana continued to speak.

"Lizzy, this is a lovely room, and the view is truly beautiful. Let me show you: here is another small chamber for bathing, here is your dressing table, and here is the armoire. Your luggage will be brought immediately, and a maid will be at your service all the time. And if you need anything else just let us know…"

Elizabeth held the girl's hands tightly and smiled at her. "Dearest Georgiana, please calm yourself. Everything is perfect; I need nothing else. I am just glad to be here."

"So am I," Georgiana answered with a thrill. "Very glad indeed."

"Oh, and since you ask: I would be grateful if I could write a letter to

Jane, just to let her know we arrived safely."

"Of course; everything you need must be here," Georgiana answered, pleased that she could address her friend's wish. She opened the drawer of a small desk in the corner of the room by the window, revealing paper, pens, and ink.

"Everything we need is always available in these rooms in the family wing," Georgiana explained. "William requires that."

"Mr. Darcy seems to take care of everything," Elizabeth said with a smile.

"He does; I believe he must since there are so many responsibilities on his shoulders: several proprieties, the tenants, the staff, and me...when I am doing silly things. Sometimes I wonder how he can handle everything."

The conversation was becoming emotional when a fortunate knock on the door interrupted it. Mrs. Reynolds entered, leading a young maid and several servants who carried Elizabeth's belongings and two pots of hot water.

"Miss Bennet, this is Sarah; she will be your maid during your stay here. Of course, for anything else you might need, you may ask any of the staff."

"Thank you, Mrs. Reynolds."

"Mr. Darcy said dinner should be ready in an hour if that is convenient for you."

"Very much so. I only need to change and refresh myself a little."

"Lizzy, I am leaving now, but I will come to take you downstairs shortly."

Elizabeth laughed. "Very well, my dear; I will wait for you."

The next half hour flew with an efficiency that amused and impressed Elizabeth. Sarah helped her wash and change her gown then arranged her hair. Another two maids entered to put her clothes away, throw another log on the fire, and take out the used water while Elizabeth glanced from one to the other in silence.

She even had a few minutes to quickly write to Jane. She felt tired and unsettled, and her thoughts were too affected for a longer letter, but she knew her family would be eager to receive news from her.

Georgiana retrieved her right on time. Before entering the dining room, Georgiana took her on a quick tour to show Elizabeth the music room then stopped in front of a massive wooden door.

"Here is the library; let us see if my brother and cousin are still here."

She struggled to push open the door and revealed to Elizabeth's eyes a place whose grandeur astounded her. It was significantly larger than the library in Darcy's townhouse, and three of the walls were lined with ceiling-high wooden shelves completely filled with books.

Elizabeth stepped inside, mesmerised, and glanced around.

"Good—you are here. Dinner must be ready." Darcy's voice startled her; only then did she observe the two gentlemen resting on a couch, holding their drinks.

"This is magnificent," Elizabeth whispered.

"I am glad you approve of it," Darcy replied.

"Approve of it? I am truly amazed."

"William, Lizzy wrote a letter for Mrs. Bingley; how can we have it delivered? They must be eager to have news of our arrival."

"I wrote a few words to Mr. Bennet too," Darcy answered his sister. "They will both be sent express tonight."

"Thank you, sir," Elizabeth replied, handing Darcy the letter. She hesitated a moment then continued, trying to hide a smile. "I know this is ridiculous, but may I add two lines for my father? About the library…"

Darcy laughed, surprised by the request. "Of course. Please sit here at the desk," he offered, helping Elizabeth to his armchair. She hesitantly followed his lead, and a strange feeling enveloped her knowing that place was usually his.

He offered her pen and ink and talked with his sister and cousin while Elizabeth finished the letter and sealed it.

A few minutes later, the small group walked towards the dining room. The colonel offered his arm to both Elizabeth and Georgiana, and Darcy went to retrieve the countess.

Dinner arrangements were elegant but informal. There were no fixed places, and Elizabeth sat by Georgiana, facing the colonel.

She was not completely at ease, and she could see that Darcy was not perfectly composed either. They glanced at each other from time to time, but mostly the conversation was carried by Colonel Fitzwilliam and Lady Hardwick. Georgiana was also more animated than usual while Elizabeth found little to say.

"Miss Bennet, is the room to your liking?" Darcy eventually asked her.

She raised her eyes to him. "Yes, thank you. Very much so."

The discussion next moved to the colonel's departure next morning and his return next week, then to the weather, and continued in the same manner until dinner ended.

All three ladies preferred to retire immediately afterwards, allowing the gentlemen to enjoy their drinks and amuse themselves.

The countess returned to her room, joined by Didi; Elizabeth and Georgiana spent another hour together, talking and petting the much-spoiled Mist.

It was rather late when fatigue overcame Georgiana, and Elizabeth finally was alone in her room.

But in the solitude and silence, Elizabeth's distress returned. She opened the window widely, allowing the cold breeze to chill her. He was right—the view was splendid, and she would see it every morning for the next several months.

Elizabeth knew she should be tired, more than she felt. Her restlessness was such that sleep was impossible, but she changed into her nightgown, loosened her hair, and lay in bed, looking around the room. She knew her presence in the family wing was likely a privilege rarely offered to guests.

The beauty around her was still new and overwhelming. And on top of everything, a thought spun in her head: *of this place, I might have been the mistress! With these rooms, I might now have been familiarly acquainted! Instead of staying here as a guest, I might have occupied the mistress's apartment.* The mere notion of her being the mistress—his wife—spread cold shivers inside her for reasons she refused to analyse closely. Seeing for herself what Pemberley meant—his desire to marry her, his decision to choose her as his partner for life in everything he was and everything he owned—increased its importance and weight tenfold. It was not about wealth; it was not about the pin money, balls, parties, or connections. It was about the responsibilities attached to that life and about his belief that she was worthy and capable of accomplishing them.

In April, her opinion of him was such that not even the King himself could have persuaded her to change her mind. Neither Pemberley nor all of Derbyshire would have convinced her to marry him. And the manner in which he now addressed her made everything worse. Painfully worse.

As she had come to know him better these last months and to discover and accept his qualities together with his faults, the consequences of her refusal burdened her. And the admission that she had grown more partial to him and drawn to him—as he became more polite and friendly but more indifferent and distant—shattered her soul and filled it with bitterness. Yet, she had no choice but to become accustomed to the present situation and dared not consider whether she would have liked it to be different.

She rose from the bed and wrapped herself tightly in her robe, placed a chair on the balcony, and sat down to admire the stars and the full moon shining over Pemberley. The wind played with her hair, and she closed her eyes, imagining it was a tender caress.

She briefly wondered which side of the house his windows faced then banished the thought when another one intruded: Georgiana's worry about his potential future wife. It would be expected for him to find someone else soon to fill the mistress's apartment. Lady Emmeline was surely ready and eager to occupy that place by his side, along with many others. It was only natural, and it was surely not her business since she had refused his proposal.

The wind intensified, and she wrapped her arms around herself, entranced by the sparkle of the water reflecting the moon.

Her attention was suddenly drawn by the sound of a horse. Through the trees, she spotted a horseman—whose identity was no mystery—and his stallion racing past the lake like a hasty, dark chimera breaking through the night.

Her heart tightened and ached because she felt as though he were running away from her and from her hopes—hopes that she had not known to exist until that very night, her first night spent at Pemberley.

Chapter 22

aylight found Elizabeth deep in a dreamless sleep. Reluctantly, she moved under the blankets when she heard whispers and footsteps around the bed. She needed several moments to fully awaken and to realise where she was. Then she opened her eyes to meet Georgiana's smile and Sarah's serious expression.

"Dear Lizzy, forgive me for disturbing you, but breakfast is ready, and I thought you would like to join us before Richard leaves."

"Oh dear." Elizabeth almost jumped out of bed. "How did I sleep so late? Forgive me; I will be ready immediately."

"Do not worry; we are all happy that you rested. William said that you must be tired after our long journey and the excitement of last evening. Take your time. I will wait for you in my chamber so I can show you to the small room where we like to have family breakfasts. It was my mother's favourite."

With the maid's help, Elizabeth dressed quickly. Before leaving her chamber, she briefly went onto the balcony, her eyes rejoicing in the beauty of the view. She breathed deeply, allowing her mind and heart to be revived by the fresh air. Darcy was right when he suggested this room—there could not be a better prospect.

In the small saloon, Darcy, the colonel, and Lady Hardwick were already gathered. After greetings were exchanged, the colonel addressed Elizabeth.

"Miss Bennet, I am happy to see you if only for a few minutes before I leave."

"I wish you a safe journey, sir. I hope to see you in good health very soon."

"As do I, Miss Bennet. I expect that, by the time I return, you will be familiar with Pemberley's surroundings, and we will enjoy pleasant walks together."

"I look forward to it, sir."

The colonel's departure diminished conversation for some time. Elizabeth could not gather herself enough to begin a new subject. She ate little but had a cup each of tea and coffee.

From the head of the table, Darcy glanced often at Elizabeth and noticed her lack of spirits following the colonel's departure. There was no doubt that she enjoyed his cousin's company and missed his presence. This revelation did not pain him as much as before. It was a fact to which he resigned himself—or at least pretended to.

The silence became heavy, so he broke it, addressing the ladies.

"Around noon, Mrs. Weston will visit you. Since we plan to stay here until spring, she will be happy to find that she must provide gowns for three ladies—and for three seasons."

He then turned to Elizabeth with further details. "Mrs. Weston owns a shop in Lambton. She is an experienced dressmaker—or so I was told by my mother, my aunt, and my sister. It is a custom that the Darcy ladies order gowns from her during their stay at Pemberley."

Elizabeth's face coloured slightly. "I see. But, sir, I assure you that I do not need new gowns. The ones I have are satisfactory, and—"

He interrupted her in a friendly yet determined tone. "Miss Bennet, I beg you not to debate this subject. We decided some time ago that you would be treated like family. Therefore, anything related to Georgiana will also apply to you unless, of course, you disapprove of it. I dare say neither my sister nor my aunt needs new dresses, but for many years, we have endeavoured to support the people in our area by any means available. So every purchase we make is ordered from the shops in Lambton."

She was surprised and embarrassed by her thoughtlessness. As usual, she was tempted to believe that he was doing her a favour when, in truth, his gesture was intended not to feed her vanity but to help those in need.

"I see...I thank you for your consideration, sir," she finally answered, venturing a look at him.

"Aunt Amelia, will you join Lizzy and me for a short ride before noon? I sent word to Mr. Slade to prepare my horse and a phaeton. William is coming too."

"Dearest, not today...perhaps tomorrow. I am not completely rested, and I would only slow you down. Maybe a short stroll in the garden later if you and Miss Bennet will keep me company."

"Of course," both hurried to accept then Georgiana continued. "We can stay with you if you wish. There is no urgency; we can go out another day."

"Nonsense, my dear...I will be perfectly fine; I intend to sleep. Just have someone care for our pets."

When breakfast was almost finished, a surprising entrance brought liveliness and joy to the group. A gentleman of middle age bowed ceremoniously and stopped some distance from the table. Elizabeth observed him closely, intrigued by the unusual strength he conveyed. He had handsome yet austere features and sharp blue eyes, and he was dressed informally, his long, loose hair falling freely on his shoulders.

Darcy hurried to shake his hand, and Georgiana rose to embrace him tenderly, much to Elizabeth's astonishment.

"Mr. Slade—such a pleasure to see you," both siblings declared warmly.

"What a joy to see you finally home," he answered with a deep, hoarse voice. "Forgive me, I came too early and interrupted your breakfast. I will return later."

"You will do no such thing, sir," Lady Hardwick intervened with apparent severity. A smile seemed to soften Mr. Slade's countenance. As Darcy insisted he stay and join them, the man stepped forward and bowed to the countess. She stretched her hand to him; he took it and placed a reverent kiss upon it.

"Lady Hardwick, we are as honoured as we are pleased by your presence. Your ladyship seems not to age at all. You are still the most beautiful woman I have ever seen."

"Nonsense, nonsense! You are the one who appears unchanged for the last two decades, Mr. Slade. I am very happy to see you too. Come, sit by me."

He seemed to reluctantly accept when his attention was drawn by Elizabeth.

"And may I ask who this lovely young lady might be? Dare I hope that someone has finally stolen the master's heart?"

Elizabeth's cheeks turned crimson, and embarrassment took away both her breath and her voice. She glanced at Darcy and saw him equally troubled; even worse, she sensed Mr. Slade's scrutiny of her face, so she struggled to smile and form a jesting reply.

The countess, however, spoke first. "Sadly, no—rather the young mistress's heart. Miss Bennet is Miss Darcy's dear friend, and she will spend the next months with us."

"It is a pleasure to make your acquaintance, Miss Bennet. I must apologise; I did not saddle a mount for you, but I will do so at once. Just let me know what kind of horse you prefer."

"I prefer any horse to keep its distance from me," Elizabeth joked. "I am a poor rider, I am sorry to admit. I learned to ride when I was a young girl, but have not done so in the last ten years. I much prefer to walk."

"Indeed, I regret hearing that—not that you like to walk but that you dislike riding. I hope you will change your mind very soon. There is nothing more pleasurable then discovering the beauty of Pemberley on horseback. Besides, Miss Darcy is a most proficient rider—as is Lady Hardwick."

"I *was*, my dear Mr. Slade; now I am fond of neither riding nor walking. I much prefer the phaeton. Things change."

"Perhaps, but the spirit remains as young and as brave as ever. Your ladyship proves it. And I did remember your preference for the phaeton. I had it prepared with two white horses, and I will be honoured to drive it for you."

"My dear Mr. Slade, your gentlemanlike manners are dangerous for a lady's heart. But the phaeton is for Miss Bennet as I was determined to spend the day in my chambers; now I am reconsidering."

"Aunt Amelia, since Mr. Slade will join us, you have nothing to worry about. You should come if you feel well enough," Georgiana pleaded.

The countess hesitated for a moment. "Very well, I cannot argue with you all. I will come. I need refreshments and a little port for later, and a comfortable blanket to rest upon. And Miss Bennet—you will need a heavy gown. The drive will take more than two hours, and it is rather chilly outside."

"Your wishes are my command, dear Aunt," said Darcy. "Everything will be arranged to your liking."

As Elizabeth returned to her room to change, she thought of the enjoyment both Darcy and Lady Hardwick had in making plans and the persuasion Mr. Slade had over the countess. She had to admit, though, that her ladyship was right: Mr. Slade looked as handsome as he was powerful, and he seemed a difficult man to refuse.

THE RIDE ALONG THE LANES OF PEMBERLEY WAS THE MOST PLEASANT ELIZAbeth had ever enjoyed. The beauty of the park amazed her, and the company of the countess—under the lead of Mr. Slade—was simply joyous.

The Darcy siblings trotted in front of them, and once again, Elizabeth marvelled at Georgiana's skills. In riding, the girl looked the embodiment of confidence and bravery. Her delicate figure on a white and chestnut horse contrasted with the impressive stature of her brother, who rode a stately black stallion. He looked powerful; she looked agile.

From time to time, Georgiana would return to the phaeton to be certain Elizabeth was having a pleasant time; and indeed, she was.

Mr. Slade kept the phaeton at a higher speed than Elizabeth was accustomed to, and yet she felt completely safe as the man held the reins with strength and confidence, careful of his passengers' comfort. Lady Hardwick also appeared in an excellent mood, and she seemed to shed her earlier fatigue and enjoy the ride.

The novelty of the wind playing in her hair and caressing her face, as the horses moved through the beautiful grounds, created an intoxicating sensation within Elizabeth. And when they were again in sight of Pemberley House, the image of the impressive building—perfectly surrounded by nature's beauties—added to her exhilaration.

The joy of her first day at Pemberley did not diminish for Elizabeth in the following weeks—quite the contrary. During the day, she spent all her time with Georgiana and Lady Hardwick. Her ladyship was now also calling her "Lizzy," as the familiarity between them grew and deepened. They visited Lambton almost daily, and Elizabeth soon became as well known in the small village as was Miss Darcy herself. And Sunday's service at church gave Elizabeth the chance to meet Pemberley's tenants.

Mr. Darcy was almost never with them, and Elizabeth felt he avoided her on purpose. He did not want to be seen in her company or even to be in the same room with her except during breakfast or dinner. However, she felt he was as careful and protective of her as he was with his sister. Not once did Elizabeth feel an outsider or unvalued or disrespected.

An exception to their distant interactions occurred in the library. Occasionally, it happened that Elizabeth entered the room to choose a book, and he always helped her to pick the one she liked from a higher shelf or recommended something she had not discovered herself from the impressive collection. But they never spent time alone, not even reading at the same time in the same room.

Elizabeth carried on a regular correspondence with Jane—whose happiness beamed through her letters—and with her father. She wrote them every other day, sharing from afar everything she lived, learned, and discovered. To Mrs. Gardiner, Elizabeth sent her admiration of Pemberley and approval of Lambton together with news and greetings from friends and relatives.

Almost a month into her visit, a rainy day kept Elizabeth and Georgiana in the latter's room. Georgiana's spirits seemed lower than Elizabeth had seen in a long while, and nothing appeared to amuse her—not even Mist and Didi chasing each other.

"My dear, is anything wrong? You look preoccupied and a little sad, or I am wrong?"

"You are not wrong…you know me too well. It is just that…Lizzy, you have been with us for a month now. Do you believe that William is upset with me—that he avoids my company?"

The question took Elizabeth completely by surprise, and the pain in the girl's voice cut her heart. She searched for a response carefully and cleared her throat.

"What do you mean, dearest?"

"Have you not seen how little time he spends with me? I mean that, except for riding a few times together, we only meet at the beginning and the end of the day. I know there must be something wrong."

"But…is this unexpected? Was it different before?"

"Oh yes…until last summer…we were together much of the time…until I disappointed him so deeply with my attempt to elope. I believe his generosity made him forgive me, but I fear he will never forget…and therefore he cannot bear to be in my presence for too long…"

"My dear, I cannot believe this to be true! It is nonsense—as your aunt used to say." She attempted a joke as she embraced the girl tightly and caressed her hair.

"It is true, dear Lizzy, I know it…I feel it. And I do not know what to do to change things. My reckless actions troubled my brother so much…I understand why. He tried to raise me, he offered me everything…I was such a disappointment…"

"Georgiana, never say that again! How can you not see the obvious? How can you not feel how much your brother loves you?"

"I do know he loves me, Lizzy. I just wish him to be proud of me…or at least content…to wish to be with me…"

"Dearest, I have heard him declare many times that your happiness is the most important thing to him…that he would do anything to see you happy…"

Georgiana looked at her with heavy, tearful blue eyes. "Of that, I have no doubt. I just hoped that my presence would give him as much happiness as his presence gives me…"

"But have you considered that I—not you—might be the reason for Mr. Darcy's avoiding us? You know our acquaintance was always…rather challenging. Neither of us is comfortable in the other's presence. We have argued so many times in the past that we still find it difficult to be at peace in each other's company. I came to Pemberley for you, and he surely accepts my presence here for your benefit because he knows it makes you happy. He would do anything for your happiness—even accept someone with whom he is uncomfortable. So it is little wonder that he has no wish to see me. It surely has nothing to do with you, dearest."

"Perhaps…I know you and he are not good friends although I cannot possibly imagine why…but…his preference for my absence started long before your arrival here. It started in the winter, and it became unbearable in the spring. If I could only dare tell you…"

"What are you saying, my darling? Tell me what?"

"Forgive me, I should not have said anything. It was selfish of me to burden you with my foolishness. Shall we go downstairs and play some music?"

"Georgiana, we will go nowhere until you explain to me. I must know what troubles you so I can help you. I beg you…"

"It is not I who needs help, but my brother. I thought things would be better as time went by. Last autumn, after he wrote to George Wickham… everything seemed fine. William wrote to me every day from Netherfield…I was living with Mrs. Annesley—she was so kind to me—but then William returned from Hertfordshire, and I noticed he was more preoccupied, more silent than usual. And then he visited Aunt Catherine…with Richard. When he returned, he was another man. I did not see him smile for months…he was so troubled…he used to lock himself in the library. I rarely saw him the entire day…he barely spoke to me. He never walked with me or joined me at the theatre or opera or anywhere. He listened to my music absently… looking at me without seeing me. I knew he was still pained…still disappointed in me…that things would never be the same. I wondered what would happen if anyone ever discovered my attempt…how this secret, if revealed, would harm my brother…and my family name…and…I wanted to forget. I found some…there was…in one of the guest's rooms…I took some opium. I do not know what was in my mind…I thought of nothing…I just wished to forget for a while…"

Her confession struck Elizabeth like lightning. As much as she fought to deny the obvious and to believe she had misunderstood what she heard, the truth became grievously clear with every word. Her entire body felt trapped in a block of ice; her chest was caged, and she ceased breathing, wondering what she could say—how she could take Georgiana's burden on her shoulders. Because the burden was hers. And his. The girl's distress and the turmoil that had tortured her for many months were not even related to her, and Elizabeth knew it.

Georgiana said her brother's state worsened when he returned from Rosings… *"In vain I have struggled…"*

She finally began to see the complete picture of the effects of that day in Kent. Just as weeks before when her family struggled during those desperate days and she considered the consequences to her parents and sisters of her refusal, she now saw the despair and sorrow in Georgiana's sad eyes.

Elizabeth was devastated by self-reproach and guilt. She never imagined that his pride, her prejudice, and their equally bad tempers could have such a devastating influence on someone completely innocent. She felt Georgiana trembling in her arms; the girl was not even crying—only lost in a deep silence.

"My dear Georgiana, I would not dare to say I understand your sorrow… but not for one moment can I believe that your brother is upset with you or avoids your presence. I strongly believe that, whatever might have troubled him, it is in no way related to you. Have you asked him about this?"

"I have…in a way. He always tries to make me feel better… says he is fine… nothing is wrong. But something must be wrong. I feel he is keeping his true feelings from me…things that trouble him. He still believes me a child…"

"My dear, he will always do so. You will always be his younger sister; that can never change. But if he assures you that you have no reason for concern, why do you not trust him?"

"Because he wishes to protect me…"

"Of course he does, but you cannot continue to torment yourself in this way. You must speak of all these things to him. I am certain he is equally worried about you...about your restraint towards him. You must tell him what you feel, and perhaps you will see that your distress is unfounded. Since you do not doubt your brother's affection, you cannot refuse him your trust, even more so as he has never disappointed you. Has he?"

"No, never. You are right of course, Lizzy. Perhaps I will do just that. Perhaps I should speak to him. But I am afraid I might sadden him even more..."

"Nothing could sadden him more than his sister's sorrow. I have no doubt that he would rather bear any pain of his own than witness yours. You must speak to him."

"I will try. Let us see how things go in the next few days...then I will talk to him..."

"Very well, as you wish..."

"Now, if you do not mind, I would like to rest for a while. It is still raining," Georgiana said and lay back on the pillows.

Elizabeth caressed her hair and pulled the bedclothes around her.

"I believe that is an excellent idea...and I will bring a book and read near you just here by the window. I will take care of Didi and Mist, who seem to be in no mood for sleep."

Georgiana held her hand. "Lizzy, I am not a silly child, you know. I know you wish to stay here because you are worried for me. I am fine, I promise you."

Elizabeth smiled. "I know you are not a silly child, and I cannot deny that I shall stay here because I am worried about you. We always watched each other at Longbourn when one of us was unwell. I did that with my sisters, and I will do so with you. Nothing you say will change my mind."

Georgiana returned the smile. "Very well, I dare not argue with a guest. Do as you wish."

Chapter 23

For the rest of the afternoon, Georgiana fell into a deep sleep, as if her body and mind needed rest. From time to time, she opened her eyes, glanced at Elizabeth reading by the window, exchanged a smile, and returned to her dreams.

Elizabeth's torment was not diminished in the slightest. Although she held a book, the pages were seldom turned, and she retained nothing from the few words she read. Even Mist and Didi felt the tension and stopped playing, sleeping peacefully in their baskets.

At dinner, Georgiana looked rested and wore a large smile—so large that Elizabeth wondered whether it was genuine.

"My dear, do you have any fixed plans tomorrow?" the countess asked.

"Yes, we have, Aunt. Our tenant Mr. Burk is not feeling well. And Mrs. Burk just gave birth to her fourth child; she is still in bed. Lizzy and I will visit them and take them a needed basket of food. And then we will stop in Lambton at Mr. Dunn's shop."

"That is lovely. But how does it happen that you know about Mr. and Mrs. Burk? I must say, I am impressed with you—a perfect mistress of Pemberley."

Both girls smiled and blushed before Georgiana explained. "Oh, I deserve no praise. William tells me everything that occurs on the estate. And Lizzy is my support in everything. Whenever I discover a problem, she has a suggestion to solve it. I believe Lizzy is the one who acts like the mistress of Pemberley."

Elizabeth paled, and her nervous fingers were unsteady on her glass, which she raised hesitantly to her lips. She felt—as she dared not actually meet—Darcy's eyes. She gulped some fresh water then finally spoke.

"The praise all belongs to you, dear Georgiana. I did nothing but provide ideas from time to time. But you are the one who employed them, and your generosity is what helps the people around you."

"We are impressed with your achievements, dearest," Darcy addressed his sister. "But we also appreciate Miss Bennet's support of you, and we are grateful for it. I believe her friendship is beneficial not just to you, but to many others."

Elizabeth ventured a glance at him then added, "Everything Georgiana does is the result of her excellent character, generous manners, and lofty education. She would have done all these things with the guidance and support of her brother."

The countess laughed. "Well, well—such a burst of modesty! Do none of you desire credit for the good things you do? You know—young ladies —you both must learn to boast of your merits. Otherwise, how will handsome, eligible gentlemen hear of you?"

Elizabeth smiled, but Georgiana paled, and her discomfort was obvious. "Aunt, I have no interest in any gentlemen, and I never will. I would be perfectly happy if none of them ever heard of me."

The countess reached across the table to caress her hand. "Do not worry, dearest, that will change soon; I promise you that."

"But until then, shall we change the subject, please?" Darcy intervened. "So you will visit the Burk family tomorrow morning?"

"Yes. Would you like to come with us, Brother?" Georgiana inquired.

He hesitated a moment. "I do not want to disturb your and Miss Bennet's plans, my dear. I have several things to attend to tomorrow, but later in the afternoon, I will stop by the Burks'."

A trace of sadness shadowed Georgiana's eyes that Darcy seemed to miss as the fireplace held his attention. "Very well...as you wish...perhaps another time..."

"My dear, if there is anything you might need, just let me know. Who is driving Miss Bennet's phaeton? Tell Mr. Slade I would prefer Todd. He is older and wiser than the other boys."

"Thank you, we will," Georgiana replied.

"And would you and Miss Bennet be so kind as to play for us after dinner?"

"Of course," they responded.

That evening and the next two days, Elizabeth witnessed Georgiana's struggles: she invited Darcy to join them in various activities, and he constantly refused. He was always warm, caring, and willing to listen to anything she said. He encouraged and praised her but avoided being in her company unless absolutely necessary—or rather, in *their* company. Even more worrisome to Elizabeth was Georgiana's attempt to hide her distress, struggling to maintain a bright smile and an amiable countenance.

After dinner on the third day, the three ladies retired for the night, but Darcy declared he still had business to finish in the library.

Half an hour later, with Georgiana well settled in her room, Elizabeth lost the fight between her reason and her heart. With little forethought, she returned downstairs and, despite the lateness of the hour, knocked on the library door.

She heard Darcy's voice bid her enter, and she did so—tentatively—then stopped. He appeared so surprised that he rose from his chair in haste and hurried to her.

"Miss Bennet? What has happened? Are you unwell? Or Georgiana?"

"No—no sir, all is well. Forgive me for intruding...it is just...there is something I wish to discuss with you...about Georgiana..."

He looked intrigued, watching her intently. He surely wondered what she could possibly wish to talk to him about at that hour, and suddenly her gesture seemed strange even to her.

"Please take a seat. May I offer you a glass of water? You look rather distressed."

"No...yes...thank you...I am not sure how to explain...this is quite difficult..."

"Is someone ill or in danger?"

"Oh no, sir."

"Then please let me know how I may be of service to you. It is rather late, and you should not be alone with me. Can this conversation not wait until morning?"

"Forgive me for the intrusion. It is about Georgiana—about a conversation I had with her. She made a painful confession to me, and I do not know what to make of it in order to help her. I do not even know if I should be here..."

She sat and so did he, his eyes never leaving her.

"Yes...?"

"I really do not know how to say this...nor am I sure whether I am being a good friend or betraying her trust. I am only looking for the best way to help her."

"I have no doubt of your good intentions—nor would my sister."

"Mr. Darcy, I am sure you know of Georgiana's great affection for you. In everything she does, she is preoccupied with your opinion and your approval. And lately...she is worried because she feels you avoid her company...that you prefer to be with her as little as possible..."

Darcy frowned in astonishment. "How could she believe such a thing? I am always here; I am with her every single day—"

"But, sir, except for riding with her a few times a week, you do nothing with her. She invites you to join her in visiting tenants...and many other things... and you refuse her..."

His eyes, narrowed in disbelief and disapproval, held hers briefly; then he rose to pour himself a drink.

"I tried to convince her otherwise. I know very well that you do not avoid her presence, but mine. I even mentioned it to her— mentioned that you and I had many disagreements in the past so you likely prefer to be in my company as little as possible..."

She paused a moment; he made no reply—no attempt to contradict her.

"But she disagreed with me, saying you started to distance yourself from her last winter...and that things had turned worse since April..."

His glare returned to her, and she could see his distress slowly become smouldering anger.

"I see. Miss Bennet, my sister went through a most difficult time. I am doing everything I can to help her, and I hope I am correct in sensing an improvement in her spirits. I admit that the friendship she has developed with you and your presence here were very helpful."

"My friendship cannot replace the affection of a brother she feels she has lost..."

He began to pace the room. "I cannot accept the blame for not behaving properly with my sister...of not knowing what is best for her. She must know how important she is to me...and that I am doing everything for her..."

"She does know of your affection and your concern for her...but her feelings were...she...confessed to me about the incident...with the opium..."

He was dumbfounded for a moment then continued his tirade and his pacing.

"I am not as insensitive and oblivious to my sister's distress as you are inclined to believe. Her generous heart was broken after that scoundrel's treacherous deceit. The more genuine her affection, the more she suffers. Her kind and generous nature did not allow her to blame anybody, so she blamed herself until her own feelings became too much to bear. I do understand her quite well, and I suffered with her, knowing that she bestowed her affection upon the most undeserving of men. Wickham is not worthy of a single moment of suffering by my sister."

"Sir, I do not believe you to be insensitive—quite the contrary. But in some respects, you are wrong: Wickham is not the reason for Georgiana's torment. There is someone she loves much more, someone for whose approval she would do anything, someone whose good opinion she feared she had lost forever. She lost hope when she thought she had disappointed her brother—the most beloved person in the world to her. She felt he was ashamed of her."

Darcy's eyes were as dark as his countenance. "I do not fully understand your meaning, Miss Bennet, and I do not appreciate this image you have concocted."

"Sir, Georgiana confessed to me that she felt she had slowly lost your affection. Since last winter, she has noticed you spend less time with her. She thought her company was no longer pleasant to you. And then, last April you removed yourself from her presence permanently. She was certain you were still ashamed of her behaviour...of her attempt to elope. You refused to be seen with her at the opera or theatre; you never kept her company when visiting your relatives. Forgive me; I do not want to pain you, and I would not dare to assume anything, but...I fear there might be some misunderstanding here. I feel that she might have misinterpreted the reason for your...distraction, as I find it difficult to believe that you would maintain any grudge against a sister you love and cherish. But somehow, this is what she feels and...I would not dare to tell you all this, but she is uncertain of your feelings. She does know you love her, and she hopes you have forgiven her, but she is still concerned that the disappointment and shame are not forgotten. It pains me to see her suffering, and I would do anything to release her pain..."

He stopped in front of her; she was sitting, and he was standing—tall, dark, unmoved, struggling to breathe. Her own breathing was irregular, and she clasped her hands together to stop their trembling. She licked her dry lips and spoke hesitantly.

"Perhaps she should know the truth...about the reason for your distress...to be told it is not her fault. Her suffering should be stopped without delay. She confided so much to me that I feel pained and helpless to keep such a secret from her. If the secret were only mine, I would have confessed it to her while we were still at Longbourn...but I did not imagine... how could I have...?"

Her voice became weaker, and his pacing resumed.

"And pray tell me, Miss Bennet, do you believe my sister would feel better if she knew that her brother offered the the most wretched marriage proposal in the world, was refused in the worst possible manner, and then spent the next month behaving like the most ridiculous fool who ever existed? And that her closest friend was involved? Can you be certain that such an endeavour would be successful?"

His voice bore equal anger and bitterness, and Elizabeth was reminded of the day she appeared at his house, asking for help in finding Lydia.

"I am the last man in the world to share such a story with his sister—or any living creature. I wish nothing more than to forget that day and its consequences. How could I possibly relate it to anyone else? And can you imagine what Georgiana might think of you—how this might harm her and make her lose her barely found tranquillity?"

"Mr. Darcy, I was only suggesting that...I do not know...I might be wrong. I did not think of all this. You might be right...I might have only made things worse. I apologise...I should leave now..."

Elizabeth slowly stepped towards the door, unsteady on her feet. Her intervention had done more harm than good. She had betrayed Georgiana and only revived tormenting memories for Darcy—and for her. His reaction was stronger—in a different and painful way—than she ever imagined. He had not forgotten or forgiven anything; Georgiana was right about that. Except for the identity of the event that seemed to remain forever vivid in his mind—on that, the girl's assumption was wrong.

Elizabeth climbed the stairs to her room and walked along the hall, barely supporting herself, so heavy was the burden his words had put on her shoulders. How could she free herself from it? His torment was still so strong, so overwhelming, that she was certain he still hated her; she could sense his resentment. She did not miss his reference to "the last man in the world" that she had thrown in his face.

She closed the door to her chamber and sat by the window, staring outside absently.

Why could he not just put aside what had happened? She did not expect him to forgive her but to forget or dismiss the memories for his own peace of mind. What kept his anger alive after six months? Would it only disappear after six *years*? Perhaps not. If nothing else, it was his ego, his pride that did not allow him to move forward.

As these thoughts spun in her mind, she grew angry with herself. How dare she judge him? It was impertinent to question his reaction when she herself could not forget—for six months—his calling her "tolerable" and refusing to dance with her. When they met in Kent, she still held a grudge against him. Yes, there had been other things that contributed to her low opinion, but she had never let go of the recollection from that evening. She had felt offended and slighted, and her ego and pride had been hurt.

What was she to do now? She raised his ire, but he still refused to make any amends to Georgiana. She wished to help her friend but only made things worse. Surely, from now on, he would be even less desirous of seeing her, and he would avoid being in her company—and consequently in his sister's—as long as she remained at Pemberley. Might it be better if she returned to Longbourn? Might the siblings manage to strengthen their bond, to understand each other, and to support each other's happiness once her disturbing presence was gone?

Tears stung her eyes, and she wiped them nervously then took the pins from her hair and pushed the loose strands to her back with the same abrupt gestures.

She put another log in the fireplace then placed her nightgown on the bed. A gentle knock on the door startled her, and for a moment, she thought it was only her imagination. The sound repeated, and she opened the door, intrigued, then remained still, any words frozen on her lips, which parted in disbelief.

"May I come in for a brief moment?" Darcy whispered, and she stepped back, still dumbfounded, allowing him to enter.

"Forgive me, Miss Bennet; I will stay only a moment. I know it is preposterous to be here at this hour. If you would only allow me a couple of minutes…"

She swallowed the sudden lump in her throat and nodded in agreement.

"Forgive me for entering your chamber, but I was afraid we might be heard...or seen..."

"It is fine, sir; do not worry..." she finally murmured.

"Miss Bennet, I must beg your forgiveness for my behaviour...and for my thoughtless reply to your genuine concern for my sister's well-being. I had no right to say those things...they are of no help to anyone..."

"Sir, I—"

"I spent many months worrying about Georgiana...but I could not force her to confess to me what was troubling her. I reproached myself many times...all the time...for not being more careful with her...for not guessing the degree of her turmoil. I withdrew from her because I knew I was a horrible companion to her. I did not want to distress her even more with my poor mood. I did not realise that my behaviour was precisely the reason for her torment..."

He spoke while looking from her to the fireplace, then to the window, then back to her again, as if he could not bear to hold her eyes for too long. And her feelings were the same. She was grateful when his glance freed hers so that she could observe his pale countenance and fallen shoulders.

"Sir, I know self-reproach only too well. We need not speak of it anymore; nor should we mention forgiveness or apologies. All I wish is to make certain Georgiana is well..."

"And I thank you for that. I am truly grateful for the affection you have for my sister despite everything that has occurred between us—and at times, still does. I know it is my fault—"

"We should not speak of faults either—yours or mine—or we will not end this conversation before breakfast," she interrupted him, attempting a jest to alleviate his distress.

"Yes, well...I should leave now..."

"Yes...it is very late. I thank you for coming here...to clarify the misunderstanding..."

"I did it only for selfish reasons. I could not possibly have slept a single minute after our conversation...after my reaction..."

"Your reason might have been selfish, sir, but I assure you I benefited from it at least as much as you did."

"Very well then...I shall see you in the morning. Good night, Miss Bennet."

"Good night, Mr. Darcy."

He left and closed the door behind him slowly. The silence of the room enveloped Elizabeth again, but this time her soul was light, and the storm inside her mind quieted. She glanced at the closed door then at her own image in the mirror, and only then did she notice her hair falling freely down her back and the dress lowered from her right shoulder.

Her cheeks and neck turned crimson, and her skin shivered at the mere thought that he had seen her in such disorder. She changed her clothes, still flushed, and quickly lay in bed, wrapping herself in the bedclothes.

How easily he could change her state of mind and heart; how little was needed for him to free her from that weight. With a few words, he placed the burden on her shoulders, and with a few words, he removed it. If he had not come, her night and likely future days and nights would have been filled with sorrow. How different everything was—she was—after spending only a few moments with him. He said he had come for selfish reasons, and he admitted he could not have found rest otherwise. He seemed to feel the same way she did. But did he truly? And had he come only for his own peace of mind, or did he consider hers too?

She closed her eyes, thinking of the impropriety of his being in her room in the middle of the night. That alone would be reason for distress when they met again in daylight. But even more embarrassing was the recollection that she had presented him an improper picture of herself. However, she likely worried for no reason. Surely, he never noticed her appearance, as preoccupied as he was with his apology.

At that comforting thought, she finally fell asleep without imagining that, only a short distance away, Darcy spent another restless night, haunted by a painful conversation and by long, dark hair caressing a bare shoulder.

Chapter 24

Darcy met the first glimpse of day with gratitude and relief. His night had been as difficult as many others in the last year.

The previous evening, when Elizabeth entered his library at a late hour, he was surprised and concerned. Then, as had happened many times before, his temper betrayed him during their conversation. Her words cut his heart, even more so as he knew the justice of her statements. His responses expressed personal anger and disappointment; in only a few months of friendship, Georgiana had opened herself to Elizabeth more than with anyone else in their family. He was happy—for his sister's sake—but also sad, and it left him bewildered about how to proceed.

Yes, he had selfishly tormented his sister all those months, and if not for Elizabeth, he likely would have continued to do so without understanding the consequences.

The moment Elizabeth left the library, he understood that his fury —meant for himself—had harmed her too, and she did not deserve to be touched by his self-reproach. In rage born of his recollections of the agonising past, he cast the blame on Elizabeth's shoulders as bitter retribution for her sincere willingness to help Georgiana.

Elizabeth's accusations from that day at the Parsonage were partially right, partially wrong, and she had already confessed to him that she regretted her words as well as her destruction of his letter. But Georgiana's pain was entirely his fault. His reactions and behaviour alone were responsible—just as he was responsible for deciding what to do next: to take Elizabeth's words to heart and make amends or to persist in his proud conceit. The choice was easily made, but as he walked to his room, something drew him to Elizabeth's chamber. She was unlikely to be asleep after the harshness of their recent conversation. He knocked with a heavy heart, but he knew he must apologise and settle things immediately, or he might not soon find another opportunity. If it were for his torment alone, he would not dare make the extraordinary gesture of entering her room in the middle of the night. But he suspected she was not at peace either, and he could not allow her distress to continue.

In the first moments of their reconciliation, he was oblivious to everything around him. When her soft, gentle voice told him that she forgave him and generously rejected his attempt to take the entire blame on himself, he finally found a bit of calm.

Only then did he observe her ravishing appearance, the same picture of pure beauty he had seen that night at the inn. The only difference was the closeness that allowed him to enjoy her scent and warmth and permitted his eyes to caress the skin of her shoulder, covered only by thick strands of silky brown hair. He hoped his stare was no longer than a heartbeat. But he was so desirous of her and his thirst was so powerful that an instant was enough to imprint every detail of her beauty on his heart and mind. He would remember them repeatedly in the loneliness of his room.

At dawn, he hastily dressed and left his apartment then the house. He was too restless to stay inside, so his destination was the stables.

All was silent and still; the horses neighed at his entrance while the dogs came to greet him. As expected, a moment later Todd—the main stable boy—appeared.

"Good morning, master; forgive me, I did not know you were to come so early. How may I serve you?"

"It is nothing, Todd, you may return to your rest. I just need a ride. I will prepare Black Runner myself. I have not ridden him this week, have I?"

"No indeed, master; he will be happy to join you. But will you not let me saddle him?"

"That will not be necessary; as I said, you may go back to sleep."

"Yes master," the young man replied, but he remained a few steps away until Darcy jumped into the saddle and Black Runner eagerly hastened his pace. The dogs attempted to follow, but Todd called them back harshly. If the master wanted their company, he would have invited them himself—that was the rule Todd had learnt years ago.

THE NIGHT BROUGHT MORE REST THAN ELIZABETH EXPECTED AFTER SUCH a distressing evening. She awoke light of heart with her strength and spirits high. She opened the window widely and looked outside. It was too early to guess at the weather, but the fresh breeze brushed her face and made her smile. The house was silent and breakfast still hours away, so she dressed and slipped out the door for a stroll.

It was not the first time she had done so. In a month, Pemberley had become as familiar as her own home, and she frequently took a solitary walk before Georgiana awoke. She would always greet Darcy's staff and exchange a few words with them. She knew each of the servants quite well, just as she knew the tenants and most of the people in Lambton. She realised how much she would miss all of them when she returned to Longbourn.

"Miss Bennet! Good morning."

She heard a voice then hoof-beats and saw Mr. Slade's friendly figure dismount and bow to her.

"Good morning, sir."

"You will not need the phaeton until after breakfast, will you? I hope I understood correctly."

She laughed. "Yes, Mr. Slade; do not worry. I am only taking an early stroll before Miss Darcy and Lady Hardwick rise for the day."

"Ah—I see. Walking is excellent exercise. May I join you?"

"Of course—it would be my pleasure."

Mr. Slade dropped the horse's reins then caressed his crest, spanked his hip, and pushed him gently until he started to run. Elizabeth's astonishment met her companion's smile.

"Do not worry—he will return to the stables. The boys will take care of him."

"What if he runs away?" she inquired with concern.

"Why would he? He knows the way perfectly well, and everything he likes is there."

Elizabeth glanced at the gentleman, who was still wearing a wide smile. She admitted that the countess was right: Mr. Slade was one of the most handsome and impressive men she had ever met. He must have been of her father's age, but his strength, self-confidence, and vigour made him look completely different.

"How do you like Pemberley, Miss Bennet?"

"Exceedingly well. It is truly the most wonderful place, and I am sure I will greatly miss it."

"Oh—will you leave soon?"

"I am not certain…not too soon…my sister and her husband—Mr. Bingley—will visit for Christmas, so I dare say I will not leave until then."

"That is welcome news—to see Mr. and Mrs. Bingley soon and to know you will not leave Pemberley in the near future. I am sure Miss Darcy and Lady Hardwick will be content to have you here for as long as possible—as would we all."

"Thank you, sir, you are too kind. It is I who feel privileged to be here and to have their friendship," she replied warmly.

"You know, Miss Bennet, many young ladies have visited Pemberley in the last fifty years, but none has ever spoken more than a word of greeting to me—or with anyone on the staff."

"Well, sir—that was certainly their loss," she said with a smile, and Mr. Slade laughed.

"Now you are too kind, Miss Bennet—but your little compliment gives me pleasure, I confess, although it was more a comment than a complaint. I am perfectly content with my life, and I surely do not need more attention."

"I know that Mr. Darcy, Miss Darcy, and Lady Hardwick consider you part of the family. They speak very highly of you; I am sure you know that."

"Indeed—they are very generous to me. All the Darcys have been the same: generous, kind-hearted, upright, and not easy with strangers."

Elizabeth felt slightly uneasy as if the statement were meant for her.

"True…the better one comes to know Mr. Darcy, the more evident is the excellence of his character," she said.

Mr. Sloane looked at her briefly. "Yes, he is much like his father and his grandfather—only slightly better skilled in the management of the estates and a little more handsome."

It was Elizabeth's turn to laugh, trying to conceal her uneasiness. "On this, I must take your word, sir, as I was not fortunate enough to meet the other two Darcy gentlemen. I understand you have been with the family since Mr. Darcy's grandfather? An extraordinary attachment to the family, I would say."

"Yes…for fifty years…a lifetime. My attachment to them meant little compared to their lavish generosity to me. My father took care of old Mr.

Darcy's stables and horses—I mean the master's grandfather. He was content with my father's services, and in exchange, he paid for my attending school. After I graduated, he purchased me a commission in the army. Even more, I was granted the friendship of the next Mr. Darcy. Who would have done that for the son of a servant?"

Elizabeth immediately thought of Wickham and his godfather—but kept the thoughts to herself. He likely attempted to follow his father's example and show the same generosity to another young man he considered worthy of his support. Similar situations, different characters, such different outcomes.

"I understand you were severely wounded. Lady Hardwick told me…"

"Yes…by that time, I had the means to choose where I wished to spend the rest of my life, but I spoke to the late Mr. Darcy, and I returned to Pemberley. His death was a real tragedy, just as painful as Mrs. Darcy's. It is tragic that such wonderful people were gone too soon. I have nothing left but to see their children continue their legacy."

Mr. Slade's voice was so weighted by sadness that Elizabeth could barely hear him. The gentleman's pain overwhelmed her, and she wondered what she could say to comfort him. But he continued to speak.

"I am glad Lady Hardwick moved here to stay with Mr. and Miss Darcy. The three of them are the last Darcys left. I hope and pray the master will soon marry and have children. If only he could find a lady to deserve such a man."

Again, Elizabeth said nothing, but her face coloured.

"By the way, I understand Mr. Bingley has been exceedingly fortunate in choosing his wife. I heard Mrs. Bingley's beauty is as great as her character."

"Given that she is my beloved sister, I cannot but agree with such praise. I am not certain who is responsible for providing you with such a generous description, but I thank you both. Indeed, I am sure the Bingleys' marriage will be a blissful one."

"Happiness in marriage is a rare gift. One must treasure it if one has the good luck to find it. I know Mr. Bingley will. He is an excellent man."

"He is indeed; my sister was fortunate too. Happiness in marriage is also a matter of luck—a good friend of mine used to say."

"I shall not debate that. For a woman—however accomplished she might be—happiness in marriage is even harder to achieve as she does not have the full power of choosing. Men have that privilege, and they often waste it. The woman can only refuse—but few dare consider whether the suitor is acceptable. Marriage is a goal itself in society—more often pursued than happiness."

"I cannot but agree with you. I confess I am a little disconcerted to hear a gentleman speak with such fair consideration about marriage and happiness. It is an interesting and rare conversation for a woman to have with a man."

"My dear Miss Bennet—at my age, one should better use the experience of a lifetime to at least carry on an interesting conversation when one is lucky enough to be in the company of a beautiful young woman," he replied with amusement. Elizabeth laughed as she recollected the countess's similar reply to Colonel Fitzwilliam at the inn.

"So, Miss Bennet, have you changed your opinion about riding?" Mr. Slade suddenly changed the subject as they approached the stables.

"I am sorry to say—but no. My sister Jane, on the other hand, is an excellent rider."

"Would you at least like to greet my wordless friends? I do not believe you have visited the stables yet. We have some of the best horses in the country."

"Indeed, I have not. I will join you—if you promise to share some stories about them and not allow them to get too close."

Mr. Slade invited her inside, and two boys greeted her happily; also, the dogs—met many times on the lawn—approached to demand attention.

Elizabeth petted the dogs then looked around, again impressed by the splendid animals that stared at her from their stalls.

Under the guidance of Mr. Slade but still reluctant, Elizabeth moved from one to another while Mr. Slade provided details about each horse.

"This is Moon. She is one of the oldest and most gentle horses in our stable. Both the master and Miss Darcy learnt to ride on her. This is Fate, Moon's daughter—speedy and smart but also gentle. And this is Storm, one of the master's favourites." Elizabeth recognised the horse—or at least she thought she did—as she was overwhelmed by his shining black colour and imposing stature.

Mr. Slade continued. "From the age of fourteen, the master has been the only one to ride him. Although I have ridden him at times when the master is not at home, he accepts no one else. He is very clever, powerful, stubborn, and not at all friendly to strangers."

"Do you speak of Storm or Mr. Darcy?" Elizabeth inquired, and Mr.

Slade turned to her with obvious surprise then laughed.

"I do not remember being compared to Storm before, but I can see a certain resemblance," a voice interrupted them, and Elizabeth startled then flushed. She turned to the new arrival and saw Mr. Darcy smile, his eyes full of mirth.

"I can see the resemblance too," Mr. Slade joked. "Good morning, sir. I was showing Miss Bennet our beautiful horses."

"I did not know Miss Bennet had an interest in horses," Darcy replied, his voice almost flirtatious. His eyes met and held hers; his smile widened and made her shiver.

"Well, sir, a gentleman must be diligent in discovering a lady's true interests and behaving accordingly," Mr. Slade continued.

"True; you are always right, Mr. Slade, I must give you that. Miss Bennet, I do not know whether I said good morning yet. Are you well?"

"Good morning, sir. Very well indeed. I had a lovely walk in the most pleasant company a lady can desire. And Mr. Slade was just telling me about the family's horses. I believe he has a secret pact with Georgiana to convince me to ride." She released a nervous laugh as she tried to jest.

Storm noticed his master and became restless, demanding attention. Darcy moved closer and gently caressed his neck and forelock. Storm leant his head in obvious delight while Elizabeth watched them, mesmerised.

"Would you like to touch him?" Darcy asked her, and Elizabeth stared at him in surprise.

"Oh, I would not dare do that...I mean...I would like that, but..."

Darcy took off his riding gloves and stretched his hand to Elizabeth; first, she did not understand what he intended. Eventually, she brought her gloved hand to his a few inches from Storm.

"Please allow me. It feels better this way," Darcy continued and, without giving her time to answer, removed her glove too.

The feel of his bare fingers on hers weakened Elizabeth's knees, and a wave of warmth stirred inside her. She held her breath and remained still as he slowly took their joined hands and rested them on Storm's forehead. His fingers lingered on hers a little while, showing her how to caress the horse's soft hair then withdrew, leaving hers alone. With her hand near the impressive stallion's muzzle and with Darcy just behind her, Elizabeth did not dare move—or even breathe. Storm also remained still, looking at her as if encouraging her to continue. Fearfully, she began to move her fingers a little at a time. Storm lowered his head to make it easier for her to reach him. She laughed at that incredible proof of understanding from the beautiful steed, and she gathered more courage. She caressed him gently then suddenly took off her other glove and handed it to Darcy without realizing what she was doing. Her full attention was on Storm, and she resumed the caresses, now with both gentle hands. Storm shook his head, and his forelock flicked at Elizabeth, making her laugh again.

From the near stalls, Moon and Fate seemed to protest the lack of attention. Elizabeth looked inquiringly at Darcy, and at his approving nod, she moved towards them, sharing the same gentle touch.

So preoccupied was she with this newly discovered enjoyment, that she completely missed Darcy's enchanted gaze and the expression of utter delight on his face, as well as Mr. Slade's contentment as he watched his master with keen interest.

THE MORNING OF ELIZABETH'S FIRST VISIT TO THE STABLES MARKED A change in relationships at Pemberley. Georgiana was beside herself with happiness when she heard about her friend's excited admiration of the horses. Lady Hardwick laughed and declared that surely it was the influence of Mr. Slade's charms.

From that day, Mr. Darcy began to join his sister in visits to tenants. They also decided to spend an hour riding together each day while Elizabeth declared she would be happy to use that time to walk.

By the middle of November, at Georgiana's insistence, Elizabeth finally agreed to take riding lessons.

"Lizzy, this is so wonderful! I cannot wait! You will like it so much—I promise you."

"Dearest, I doubt I will ever be a good rider, but hopefully I will be able to seat myself on a horse when necessary. And I will spend more time with Mr. Slade's wordless friends, which cannot be other than fabulous."

"William will teach you to ride! Won't you, Brother?"

Elizabeth panicked as she awaited Darcy's answer, which did not come immediately. In the last few days, Darcy had been more in their company; however, except for that first morning at the stables, he had made no intimate gesture and spent no private moment with her.

"I believe Mr. Slade will be a better teacher. I am afraid that I have neither the patience nor the time to dedicate to Miss Bennet as she deserves," he finally replied, avoiding the ladies' gazes.

"Well, that will be much to Miss Bennet's benefit, I am sure," the countess said teasingly.

"However, I am more than happy to help Miss Bennet with anything she might need. First, we must choose the proper horse. We can visit the stables after breakfast and select one."

"Oh yes—I will loan Lizzy a riding habit. This is wonderful," Georgiana replied after the first moment of disappointment at her brother's refusal.

Darcy's willingness to support Elizabeth was as obvious to his companions as was his struggle to avoid being directly involved in that long-term activity. However, he joined them in choosing a horse for her—Sunset, a beautiful mare of fifteen years, chestnut with white spots, gentle, and obedient. And, much to Elizabeth's surprise, he remained for the first lesson, personally arranging Elizabeth's saddle and making certain she was safe in it. He also suggested the correct position of her back, her legs, and her hands on the reins. He walked the horse in the stable yard, watching Elizabeth intently while Georgiana followed them cheerfully.

The first hour of riding was disturbing for Elizabeth—because of the horse, of course, but more so because of Darcy. He helped her climb onto the saddle, and his hands held her waist for a few moments; then he arranged her legs, straightened her shoulders, and put the reins in her hands. Every gesture—natural and useful—was equally pleasant and embarrassing and gave her countless shivers. By the time the first lesson ended, Elizabeth was grateful that Darcy had passed the role of teacher to Mr. Slade; this would surely allow her to concentrate more on the horse and reduce her agitation.

She was proved correct in the following days as she slowly became more at ease then even eager to exercise, and she extended her time atop Sunset. Soon, she was riding at a slow pace in the back garden, together with Georgiana, each on her own mount. Darcy came to witness the progress every day; he congratulated her but remained at a distance. When Georgiana suggested extending the ride outside the garden along the path by the lake, Darcy tempered his sister's enthusiasm and recommended patience and caution as well as several more lessons under Mr. Slade's supervision.

One evening, during a pleasant and animated dinner, a servant entered to bring Darcy what he called "an important express," informing him the messenger awaited a reply. The late hour and the urgency worried Elizabeth and Georgiana and intrigued the countess, all three gazing at Darcy with curiosity.

"It must be from Colonel Fitzwilliam. His business kept him in the north much longer than he anticipated, and I expect him to announce his return any time now."

He opened the letter, cast his eyes over it, and appeared to be amused as he read, then his countenance suddenly darkened. He observed the others' preoccupied faces, so he explained.

"It is from Lady Catherine. Nothing urgent or important. I shall answer her later."

"Oh, I hope my aunt and Anne are in good health," Georgiana said.

"I believe they are; the letter gives me no reason to believe otherwise. Let us eat—it is not worth interrupting our dinner."

The next course was served, but all conversation ceased; Darcy's repressed anger was obvious, and while none dared inquire about it, his tense state affected them all.

Later, Darcy excused himself and retired to the library, wishing them all good night—a clear sign that he did not intend to return to their company. He offered no other explanation, nor did he attempt to conceal his haste. Georgiana's eyes filled with worry as they followed her brother's departure, and she held Elizabeth's hand tightly.

Lady Hardwick slowly rose from her chair then turned to her niece. "I will see you in a little while, my dear. I must have a drink and a word with your brother."

Chapter 25

The first thing Darcy did in the solitude of the library was to throw the letter onto the desk, pour a glass of brandy, and empty it in one gulp. He should have guessed such a letter would come.

The last weeks had been more calm, pleasant, and joyful than he could remember in a long while.

He did not confess the events of the last year to Georgiana, but he followed Elizabeth's advice and spent as much time as he could with his sister. Slowly, Georgiana seemed to take one step at a time towards him to begin opening her heart to him. For the first time in years, he heard her laugh wholeheartedly as they raced their horses one morning. And he promised her—during one amusing conversation about the ladies' sports and competitiveness—that he would ask Mr. Slade to teach both her and Elizabeth the mysteries of archery and fencing; then he teased her for days, suggesting she should join the army and lead a regiment.

Elizabeth's presence—although disturbing—became a constant in his life, and he struggled to accustom himself to it. He could feel her approach from afar, he sensed her presence before he noticed it, and he dreamt of her every night. Her nearness caused him to boil inside and made his skin shiver. He found himself glancing at her lips, her neck, her shoulders, or at the garnet cross that sparkled on her neck and touched the edge of her gown, but his self-control learnt to better guard his temper and his temptation.

He did not allow himself to think of anything—to hope for anything. He had to live the days one by one and take the best of each of them—just as he did that morning in the stables when he caressed Elizabeth's bare fingers and helped her overcome her fear of horses. He smiled as he considered how easily Storm—usually reluctant with strangers and unwilling to allow a new acquaintance to approach him—accepted her. Perhaps his longtime friend could see into his heart and sense the depth of his affection for Elizabeth. Perhaps she had charmed Storm as quickly as she did him; after all, she herself suggested the similarities between them.

The door of the library opened and brought Darcy back from his musings; he was ready to dismiss the unwelcome visitor when he recognised his aunt moving towards him decidedly.

The countess took a seat on the couch before he had time to invite her.

"What is the matter?" she asked unceremoniously. "And before answering me, please be so kind as to pour me a glass of that port. I feel I will need it."

"Of course, Aunt. I am sorry if I worried you; everything is fine, I assure you."

"Then let me read what Catherine has to say."

He hesitated a moment. "I would rather not have you read it. Lady Catherine is displeased with Miss Bennet's presence at Pemberley. She scolded me for accepting Georgiana's request to invite Miss Bennet. And she...she speaks very harshly of Miss Bennet. She accuses her of schemes and allurements...and considers this situation to be highly improper and compromising. I will burn the letter; I dare not risk that Georgiana or even Miss Bennet should ever lay eyes on it."

Darcy felt so embarrassed and angry at what he had read that he could barely look at his aunt. So the countess just pulled the letter from his hand.

"Oh, stop rambling and let me read it..."

A few minutes later, Lady Hardwick rolled her eyes in exasperation.

"Dear Lord, this woman is getting worse with age. How can anyone write so much nonsense in only a few lines? I will write her back. She will have a piece of my mind too."

"I beg you, let us be wise and put an end to this sooner rather than later. I shall reply to Aunt Catherine accordingly."

"Well, at least do me this favour. Write: 'Dear Aunt, I never thought that Miss Bennet's presence as Georgiana's friend might be a compromising situation. I thank you for bringing it to my attention. I assure you I will take the proper course and propose marriage to Miss Bennet right away.' Dear God, that would surely kill Catherine." Lady Hardwick laughed loudly before drinking a little port.

Darcy struggled to display a large smile although his discomfort was greater than his amusement. Still, he did wonder how Lady Catherine would have reacted had she ever received such a letter—not unlike the one that he had expected to write to her last April.

"You know, that is not such a bad idea," Lady Hardwick continued with prudence and a scrutinising gaze.

"Which idea? Writing to Lady Catherine?"

"Marrying Miss Bennet…"

He glanced at his aunt a moment then averted his eyes and remained silent.

"Miss Bennet has everything needed to be an excellent mistress of Pemberley," the countess continued. "More than any other woman I have seen with you—including my niece Emmeline."

"Yes…" he replied sternly without missing his aunt's surprise.

"So, you do not disagree? I have been struggling to discover your true opinion of Miss Bennet for more than three months now. I see such different and puzzling things that I am unable to come to any conclusion."

"My opinion of Miss Bennet is a positive one; you should not doubt that. Could we please drop this subject?"

"My dear boy, I can scarcely understand what is happening in your heart. I see you doing everything right—taking care of everything and everyone around you. I see your brilliant mind making decisions, but I am worried about your heart."

"Dear Aunt, you are undeservedly generous to me. I am sorry to admit that I am doing more things wrong than right…and please do not worry about me. I am fine."

"You are fine, but do I ask too much to wish you to be happy? You are already eight and twenty and seem to be rather lonely."

Darcy took his aunt's hand, kissed it tenderly, and then held it in his.

"I understand your meaning. I know I should marry and provide an heir for Pemberley. I know I must find someone worthy of Mrs. Darcy's position and who will also be a good sister for Georgiana."

"No, no, my dear—no! There is nothing you need do except what your heart tells you. I do not intend to induce you into marriage just because your age and duty demand it."

"Do you remember my parents talking about their desire that I should marry Anne?"

"Not your father—and I am certain he had no such wish. He would never impose the burden of an arranged marriage on you. As for your mother, she is unlikely to have made such a plan with Catherine—all for your benefit, I am sure. This sort of engagement is rather common within the ton. But to me or in my presence she never mentioned such a plan. If she had, I certainly would have disapproved of it."

"I was only asking out of curiosity. I had not intended to accept such an engagement before now. I have never given Anne any hope for our marriage. Quite the contrary—we discussed many times that I would always take care of her in every possible way, but a bond of any other kind between us should not to be expected—except by Aunt Catherine. And yet, lately I have given it more consideration. What if I should do what so many others are doing? I have affection and respect for Anne. She is a good person, and she and Georgiana are fond of each other. Perhaps that is the answer. If—with God's will—she provided me with an heir, I would ask for nothing more."

"Nothing more? Do you expect so little from your life? Do you not want to feel the bliss that brightened Bingley's face? To feel lively? To laugh out loud? To shiver every time you look into the eyes of the woman you love? To share your passion with her in the marriage bed?"

"I do want that," he admitted after a brief hesitation. "But what if it is not meant for me to have these things? What if they are only foolish dreams? If such bliss were easy to find, there would be fewer arranged marriages. Maybe real day-to-day happiness means being content that you provide for your family, keep it safe, and accomplish your duty."

"Oh!—what nonsense. Happiness means locking yourself alone with the woman you love and needing nothing and no one else except her—along with many things you must *feel* to understand them. I shall not allow you make the same error as your father. You are much like him, and you tend to repeat his mistakes."

"Aunt Amelia, why do you bring this up again; I must say it pains me. I know—and I never heard anyone declare otherwise—that my parents were excellent people who shared an excellent marriage—sadly too short."

"My dear, I surely do not want to pain you or to contradict this belief. Everything you say is perfectly true. They were wonderful people. Your father was the quintessence of goodness and generosity, and your mother was one of the most accomplished and admired women I have ever met. Their marriage was indeed an excellent one by the standards of society—just as was my first marriage, the one the Matlocks have shared for six and thirty years, and so many others...and yet..."

"You must tell me the truth since you have stirred up this subject. I beg you—let us clear the air once for all and never discuss it again."

"I do not know how to tell you—or whether I should. Damned port—it is too strong for me. I should cease drinking it when I want to conduct a rational conversation. What I mean is...your mother liked balls and parties and perfect society; her hair and gowns were always perfectly arranged. Her manners were perfect; her performance at the piano was perfect. She was perfect; nobody ever found anything wanting in her. And she was as good a wife as she could be. She did everything she was taught to comply with society's demands."

"She was also kind and gentle. Her presence was always a comfort to me."

"Indeed, she was a loving mother. As for your father, I heard him laugh and saw him party, hunt, ride, and fence many times...before he married. Afterwards, he forced himself to fit into the confines of propriety and decorum of which your mother was so fond—and to become the perfect father for his children."

"That is very much what I remember. I also recollect how devoted my father was to my mother."

"He was...the moment he made vows to her, he dedicated his life to her and his children. But...his heart remained elsewhere..."

"Aunt, what on earth do you mean? Surely you cannot imply that—"

"But I do. You see, my dear, when we speak of arranged marriages, everything is settled except for the heart. It remains alone, outside the arrangements; and we often see that, before or after the wedding, the heart becomes engaged to someone else. In your father's case, it was the daughter of a shop owner from Lambton. He left the neighbourhood before you were born. His daughter, Jenney Morton, was the loveliest girl that ever existed. She was your father's age, and they grew up together."

"I never heard that name—Morton. Did my father make a promise to another woman?"

"He did not. Back then, Pemberley was not as successful as it is today. Your grandfather—God rest his soul—was more kind and generous than he was an efficient landlord. And your father knew that he had to bond his family to a titled one with excellent connections to ensure his heirs a prosperous life. Marriage to Jenney was never discussed…not even considered…everybody knew that, including the two of them. Only their hearts refused to listen…"

"I have never heard such a story. So…what happened? Do you suggest that my father kept a mistress all those years?"

"Of course not. He was entirely devoted to your mother the moment he married her. He simply…he never broke his vows to his wife. He ignored his heart and followed his duty. He was that kind of man—and I am afraid you are too much like him."

"And do you know what happened to Jenney Morton? Where is she now?"

"Of course I do; I even met her a few times. She moved with her family to Oxfordshire to be with relatives. She had a very comfortable situation and several suitors whom she refused. Sadly, she died six years after your father's marriage. Nobody knew the reason for her illness. Her family had means enough to provide good doctors and the best care but…it seems it was her lungs…there was nothing to be done…"

"Goodness…such a sad story of which I was oblivious all these years. My father must have suffered so much."

"George's pain was terrible; although he never saw her after his marriage, the news of her death broke him. He trusted me enough to confess it to me…and I believe Mr. Slade knew too. George was never able to forgive himself. He could not allow anyone to see his suffering, so he locked in his pain and disguised his feelings. From a lively, joyful man, he became an aloof and haughty one. He gradually forbade himself to enjoy life, but he carried on, serving his wife and accomplishing his duty while he grieved for his lost love. The truth is that Jenney Morton probably would have died even if she had married George, but they would have had a few years of happiness—the happiness I told you about. But then, perhaps he would have suffered even more, knowing exactly what he had lost. Only God knows whether it would have been better…"

"And—you think my mother did not know? Did not feel it?"

"I cannot say, my dear. George's behaviour towards her was impeccable. He complied with her every demand and wish; he gave her everything he could. When she fell ill, he was not away from her a single day. Her death devastated him…and I believe it increased his feelings of blame towards himself. Until the end, I fear he considered himself guilty of disappointing and failing both women in his life."

The countess's eyes shadowed with tears, and she drowned her last words in another swallow of port.

Darcy found no strength to speak or move. He could feel his father's turmoil and self-blame, the burden of the faults he carried so many years, the devastating struggle his heart had to bear against his mind and the demands of his duty. The picture of the perfect gentleman he had always looked up to was slowly erased and redrawn until it revealed a more human—and even more admirable—man with his faults and virtues, trapped in a battle impossible to win from which he had no escape.

"I did not know...I never imagined..."

"I am very sorry, my dear, if I hurt you. I will probably hate myself tomorrow for everything I told you today. I beg your forgiveness..."

Darcy kissed her hand again. "Such suffering I have not felt for some time...but I am grateful to you for telling me. It helps me better understand some things...about my father and myself..."

"I hope and pray that you will not think less of George now...that you are not disappointed in him..."

"No—how could I? I know now that he is everything I knew him to be... and much more. He taught me everything I am today."

"You must keep everything that is good from what he taught you and avoid his mistakes. And when it comes to your future life, you have an advantage that George lacked: you may choose for yourself. You have mastered Pemberley in an efficient way, and now you may do whatever you please; all decisions are yours. Choose wisely with an open mind and heart. If George were here now, I am sure he would tell you the same."

The countess slowly rose from the chair, and Darcy followed her. She reached to embrace him, and he kissed her hands then put her hand on his arm.

"Come, let me accompany you back to the music room. I hear Georgiana and Miss Bennet playing. I will write to Lady Catherine later."

"Yes, yes, she can wait. By the way, how does she know Miss Bennet?"

"Miss Bennet's cousin is the parson of Hunsford parish; he married Miss Bennet's friend, and she visited them last spring. I believe Lady Catherine found Miss Bennet too opinionated for her taste," he attempted to jest.

He knew Lady Hardwick had changed the subject to dissipate some of the burdening grief that overwhelmed them both, and he tried to do the same.

"Of that, I have no doubt. It must have been entertaining to watch them together."

"Quite; and if you knew Mr. Collins—the clergyman—you would have a better understanding of the entire picture."

"So, that was where the colonel first met Miss Bennet."

"Yes…"

"They seemed to enjoy each other's company very much; they are rather alike in manners."

"Yes…"

"Mr. Slade also admires Miss Bennet. He confessed to me while we walked together a few days ago. He said she is the most pleasant lady guest he has seen at Pemberley."

"Truly? I was not aware that you enjoyed private walks with Mr. Slade," Darcy teased his aunt.

"You are not entitled to know what kind of activities I enjoy privately with Mr. Slade, young man. That is entirely my business," she replied in complete seriousness, and Darcy laughed aloud.

"And you should laugh more. Laughing makes you more handsome," she concluded as they entered the music room together.

Recollection of the story about his parents haunted Darcy. For days, he struggled to remember small details about his parents that would allow him to better understand the truth hidden within their perfect manners.

He started to consider the marriages of his relatives with different eyes —from another perspective. He then remembered Bingley's broad smile every time he was in his wife's presence—always near her, touching her arm, losing himself in her eyes, and worrying about his ability to make his wife the happiest woman in the world. And he understood that, of all his acquaintances, his young friend Bingley was likely the only one who married for love.

One day after Lady Catherine's letter arrived, Colonel Fitzwilliam returned on his way back to London. He remained overnight, much to the ladies' pleasure. He also informed Elizabeth—privately—that he had briefly met Mrs. Wickham, who looked remarkably well and seemed to enjoy her new friends, new life, and all the balls and parties to which she was often invited. Lydia had no time to write a letter to Elizabeth, but she did send her best wishes to her sister.

The colonel departed for London shortly without fixed plans for seeing them again, and the four residents of Pemberley returned to their normal routine. Elizabeth's riding lessons brought the desired results, and she was able to ride daily on the paths along the lake, together with Georgiana. Darcy joined them from time to time, but the cold weather kept Lady Hardwick mostly inside. Plans for Christmas were made, and the arrival of the Bingleys was eagerly anticipated.

Then one night, the beauty of the estate was suddenly coloured in white. Winter had come, freezing the roads, the fields, and the lakes, shortening the daylight and extending the darkness, and changing habits and plans. The time spent outside diminished; however, the winter season gave Pemberley a new face worthy of being admired, and Elizabeth was ready to discover it. She did not trust her new skill enough to ride on frozen roads, so she returned to walking, and the phaeton was replaced by a carriage.

Trapped inside the house, Elizabeth and Darcy found themselves more frequently in each other's company. Either for Georgiana's sake or because they slowly made peace with their own feelings, they learnt to be more at ease with each other. Consequently, conversations became more animated, and little debates and arguments that had enchanted Darcy during his first stay at Netherfield returned.

"I wonder if you two ever agree on anything. I would wager you do not," Lady Hardwick inquired one evening when Mr. Slade was also invited for dinner.

The two seemed puzzled by the statement and exchanged a look.

"Of course, we do," Darcy eventually declared.

Elizabeth blushed and released a small laugh.

"And may I ask on which matters you agree?" the countess continued her questions to Darcy.

"Well, I believe we both appreciate good music, good books, good plays…"

"Of course you do—you and half the population of England. Can you be more specific? Or should we drop the subject and admit I am right?"

"We both like Georgiana and your ladyship—and Mr. Slade and Pemberley." Elizabeth decided to be of help, venturing another glance at Darcy.

Lady Hardwick rolled her eyes. "Of course, you do. Georgiana, Mr.

Slade, and I are very pleasant people. Everybody likes us. That only points out that I am right once again."

This final statement raised peals of laughter from around the dinner table.

"Disagreements bring out the most interesting conversations," Mr. Slade declared. "I believe Mr. Darcy is accustomed to everyone always agreeing with him. He looks more...animated since he has the opportunity to debate more often."

Darcy's face coloured slightly while Elizabeth hurriedly raised a napkin to her mouth to conceal her sudden flush. Their eyes met, filled with mirth.

Without much consideration, Elizabeth turned to her other companions. "Perhaps people have not argued with Mr. Darcy until now because everybody knows he is always right. That was common knowledge even in Hertfordshire. I must be the only one who ignored this universal truth."

Darcy's eyebrow rose in challenge, and he held her gaze for a moment then answered with pretended arrogance, "I am not always right—just most of the time. It is a burden with which I must learn to live, and it is my goal to convince even you of this, Miss Bennet."

His stern reply provoked laughter again; he was the only one who remained serious, trying to suppress the smile that narrowed his lips.

Elizabeth's amusement was overcome by her embarrassment. She could not believe that she had teased him so in front of his relatives nor that he had answered in such a manner. Still, the exchange pleased her and made her heart race. She stole a look at him then turned her attention towards her plate.

Georgiana gazed at her brother with keen interest and such curiosity that it finally drew his attention.

He smiled at her. "Is everything well, dearest?"

"Oh yes, of course...I was thinking...you look very different when you smile," she confessed genuinely.

"Yes, he does—he should smile more," the countess agreed.

Darcy appeared confused and slightly uncomfortable, and Mr. Slade intervened again.

"A man cannot smile all the time; he must have good reason to do so, or else he looks ridiculous."

"I disagree," the countess interfered. "An amiable man with a pleasant smile is much more to the liking of all ladies."

"He might be; but for some gentlemen—not many, I admit—being to the liking of all ladies is not a goal, not a purpose in itself," Mr. Slade replied.

Elizabeth decided to take a side in the debate. "While I agree with Lady Hardwick about amiable gentlemen, a sincere smile on the face of a man who is usually stern and aloof might be more appreciated. An excess of smiles, meant only to charm the ladies, might be as unpleasant as continual haughtiness."

"I am happy to discover a new subject on which Miss Bennet and I agree," Darcy concluded then changed the subject, asking Elizabeth whether she had recent news from Mrs. Bingley.

"Lizzy, do you know how to skate?" Georgiana asked when desert was served.

"I do, indeed. In fact, Miss Darcy, I daresay I am quite good at it. Perhaps that is one sport in which I am better than you."

Georgiana smiled, amused by her friend's challenging tone.

"Well, we shall see. I have skated since I was four years old."

"I must say, you are a little annoying, you know. I have never met anyone so talented and proficient in everything she does," Elizabeth declared in mock frustration.

"It is not that I am talented, but I had the good fortune to have an excellent teacher and to practice with him quite a lot," the girl answered, gazing lovingly at her brother.

"Yet another reason that I regret not having a brother," Elizabeth replied, her smile widening.

"Well, I am sure Georgiana would not mind sharing hers with you," Lady Hardwick said between sips of wine.

The statement dumbfounded Darcy for several moments; then he elegantly ignored his aunt's last words and moved the conversation to safer ground. He did not miss Elizabeth's embarrassment, so he attempted to put her at ease with a friendly smile.

"I am glad to discover another matter on which I completely agree with Miss Bennet. You are indeed very talented, dear Georgiana, and your accomplishments are all yours. And speaking of talent—may we have some music, please?"

The evening ended pleasantly with Georgiana and Elizabeth playing,

Lady Hardwick and Mr. Slade sitting on the couch, enjoying music and drinks, and Darcy alone on the settee, staring at the pianoforte and lost in his thoughts.

The countess's statement distressed and amused him at the same time. He could easily read his aunt's intentions, and he knew she would not hesitate to do or say anything to reach her desired result. On this, she was not all that different from Lady Catherine except that she had in mind his well-being and future felicity. Of course, the countess did not know that such an outcome had little chance of occurring.

He could easily see that Elizabeth's manners towards him had become warmer. Also, he had no doubt that her opinion of him had improved, not just because of her affection for Georgiana but also because of her better knowledge of him. He was almost sure that, if he proposed to her again, she would agree to be his wife. And they would—likely—have a good marriage, ensuring a worthy mistress for Pemberley and a beloved sister for Georgiana.

However, now he could not settle for so little. After the distressing conversation with his aunt and the tormenting discovery about his father, he knew he had the right to more—at least to hope for more. And if he was eventually forced to settle for a "convenient" marriage, it could not possibly be with a woman he loved more every moment, a woman whose laughing eyes brightened his days and whose lips and skin he dreamt to savour every night.

With Elizabeth, he could not accept sharing less than a complete, blissful, passionate love. With any other woman, he would be content with less as he had little left to offer.

THE FOLLOWING MORNING, IMMEDIATELY AFTER BREAKFAST, DARCY LEFT to attend to estate business. The countess returned to her room while Elizabeth and Georgiana went to the library. They wrote letters, then chose a book, and read for half an hour until Georgiana became restless.

"Lizzy, would you like to go skating? The weather is too pleasant to stay indoors. I will inform Mrs. Reynolds, and by the time William returns, we will be home."

"That would be lovely, but where will we skate? The weather is too mild to freeze the lake."

"There is a swamp not more than a mile away. It is right by the bridge

—I am sure you remember it. The water is not deeper than twenty inches; it should be frozen. It is the place I have skated since I was very young."

"I believe I remember it. It will not take us more than a quarter of an hour to walk there."

Dressed properly—arm in arm and holding the skates—they left the house at a rapid pace. By the time they reached the swamp, it had turned even colder as the sun slid behind the clouds. A chill breeze blew the snow from the trees.

They held hands and stepped tentatively onto the slippery surface; there was no doubt that it was solidly frozen.

Elizabeth and Georgiana brushed the snow from a fallen tree limb, sat on it, and helped each other put on the skates.

"Lizzy?"

"Yes, my dear."

"Are you and William on friendlier terms now? He seems not to avoid either of us as much lately, and you look more comfortable in his presence."

Georgiana's question startled Elizabeth, and she tried to find the most suitable answer.

"Mr. Darcy's manners towards me are beyond reproach. I have no complaint. He is respectful and kind," she answered after a brief hesitation.

"He is exceedingly handsome too; would you not agree?"

"Yes, he is…"

"Better looking than Lord Mowbray and Cousin Richard?"

Elizabeth laughed nervously. "Dearest, are we ranking the gentlemen's handsomeness?"

To her complete disbelief, Georgiana replied with serenity, "Yes, we are. So who is your favourite?"

Elizabeth laughed wholeheartedly then glided onto the ice. "Come, let us race. I wager I am at least better than you are on skates. I am tired of seeing you more proficient than me in everything we do."

"Lizzy, do not change the subject! I am sure my brother is the most handsome. And although he is not titled, his fortune is at least as large as Lord Mowbray's. And Richard must marry a woman with great wealth; I have heard him say that many times."

The girl slid elegantly and stopped next to Elizabeth, who met her with mock severity.

"From what I see, I fear I might not defeat you in this sport either. Now —may I ask what the purpose of this conversation might be, Miss Darcy?"

"I do not want you ever to leave us, Lizzy…" the girl whispered.

"My darling…" Elizabeth embraced her tenderly and held her tight.

"Come now, let us skate. I am sorry I troubled you with my silliness." Georgiana suddenly withdrew from her.

"You never trouble me, dearest," Elizabeth replied, but the girl was already away, gliding speedily over the frozen swamp.

With joyful cries and laughter, the time flew. It started to snow again, and the increasing wind intensified the cold, but so caught up were they in their joyful play, they did not even notice it.

They made a few final rounds, racing side by side. Then a strange noise, partially covered by the sound of the wind, alerted Elizabeth, and she looked down to avoid a possible obstacle. With horror, she saw the ice cracking under their skates, and panic momentarily froze her. She stopped and grabbed Georgiana's arm so quickly that they both fell and the cracking widened. On her knees, Elizabeth pushed Georgiana with all her strength, so violently that the girl slid in disorder to the edge of the swamp. Then the ice broke completely, and Elizabeth's feet sank into the water.

It seemed that hundreds of knives cut her feet to the bone, holding her prisoner.

"Lizzy!" cried Georgiana and hurried to her.

"No! Do not come closer—you will fall in too," Elizabeth yelled at her. "The water is very shallow—look, it is below my knees. Search for a branch, a stick—something to help me out."

"Yes…I will find something. Can you take my hand? I will pull you out, and we will run home…"

"No, do not come here; we will both become stuck!" Elizabeth shouted again.

With the skates on her feet, clumsy and scared, Georgiana crawled through the fresh snow, searching for something to help her friend. Then she started to cry for help, hoping the wind would carry her voice and someone from the house or the stables might hear her.

Fighting the freezing water, Elizabeth managed to move her feet a few more steps. She was also wearing the skates, and her gown was heavy, soaked with dirty, cold water that started to freeze around her legs. She put one knee up, but the ice broke again. Fortunately, she was close to the edge, so she took Georgiana's hand, grabbed some protruding reeds with the other hand, and pulled herself out of the water. The girls embraced, resting their heads against each for a few moments, struggling to breathe.

"Lizzy, are you hurt? Do you feel any pain? Can you move?"

"Dearest, listen to me. You must take off your skates at once and run home. I will try to follow you, but you must bring help because I do not know whether I can walk."

As she spoke, Elizabeth started to untie the girl's skates, but her frozen fingers were so numb that she could barely move them. Georgiana was more successful, and she had removed one skate when the sound of footsteps broke through the noise of the wind and a voice shouted:

"Georgiana, Miss Bennet! Dear Lord, what are you doing here?"

Chapter 26

As Darcy rode back to Pemberley after a day spent with two of his tenants, the snow and wind intensified, and he hurried the pace of his horse. The first cries for help were far away—so weak that he barely heard them—but he reacted immediately, struggling to discern their location and to whom they might belong. He followed the sounds towards the bridge with fear and disbelief as he recognised Georgiana's voice. Alarm froze him more than the cold as he saw Georgiana and Elizabeth on the ground, holding each other and talking incoherently, their gestures erratic.

He dismounted and ran to them. As he got closer, he noticed the skates on their half boots then Elizabeth's wet dress and feet. Her lips were purple and trembling.

"The ice broke," Georgiana cried. "I believe Lizzy is hurt. She pushed me away, but she fell into the water…"

He quickly removed Georgiana's remaining skate then grabbed her arms.

"Georgiana, listen to me: you must take my horse and go to Mr. Slade. Tell him to bring a carriage…something…to carry Miss Bennet. Then go home and change your clothes. Do you understand me? I will see to Miss Bennet—go now!"

The girl nodded, tears falling down her face. Darcy nearly tossed her onto the saddle then returned to Elizabeth who looked at him abashed, a tentative smile on her shivering lips.

"I will take off your boots," he explained as he removed his gloves and began the task. Delicately, he unlaced and pulled off the first boot. As he feared, it had already started to freeze, and as her foot was swollen, she moaned in obvious discomfort. He then immediately removed the other boot. Her stockings were soaking wet, as was her gown.

"We should take shelter under the bridge. Do not worry; help will arrive in a few minutes."

She nodded and attempted to rise, but her feet slipped.

"I will carry you," he said and lifted her in his arms before she could respond; she instinctively put her hands around his neck. A minute later, he sat her on the ground under the bridge, her back against its wall of dirty snow.

"Your feet are in the greatest danger of being harmed. How long were you in the water?"

"A few minutes…it happened just before you arrived…"

He then took off his greatcoat, jacket, and waistcoat. To Elizabeth's astonishment, he pulled off her stockings, exposed her reddened wet feet, and began to gently massage them. Surprisingly, he then held them in his palms to warm them a moment before wrapping them tightly in his waistcoat and jacket.

He put his thick greatcoat back on and sat next to Elizabeth. She had already thrown away her wet, dirty gloves and was rubbing her hands together.

Unceremoniously, he picked her up and placed her in his lap.

She cried out and glared at him, placing her hands between their bodies.

"Miss Bennet, you cannot stay on the ground; your gown is wet, and it will freeze. Please understand: I am doing this for your safety. We must keep you warm…"

"I know…it is just that…you are right of course…thank you…"

He put his arms around her, and she reluctantly leant against his torso. He began to rub her back, her arms, and her feet still wrapped in his clothing. Slowly, she started to warm, and the shivers inside and outside her body ceased. There was nothing improper, nothing romantic in his touch —she understood that. He only wanted to protect her from freezing until help arrived.

He opened his greatcoat, pulled her closer, and struggled—unsuccessfully—to wrap it around her. His body's heat warmed her through the thin lawn of his shirt, and without thinking, she rested her head on the base of his neck, sliding her hands around his waist.

"Is it better now?" he asked softly, his voice barely audible above the sound of the wind.

"Yes…thank you…much better…I might fall asleep soon…"

"No, please do not fall asleep. It will only take a few moments to return home. We will have hot tea and soup very soon…"

His voice comforted her, his arms protected her, and his strength allowed her to relax under his care. She heard his heart beating and wondered why it was racing so. She moved her head, then raised her eyes to him and met his worried gaze.

"I hope Georgiana arrived safely…" she murmured.

"I am sure she did. Even you said my sister is an experienced rider. Someone should come very soon."

"Yes…I am very sorry for my silly accident. I am giving everyone so much trouble…"

"You protected Georgiana from falling, did you not?"

"I am glad she is safe. I should have been more careful but…I have skated all my life, and such a thing has never occurred…so silly of me to fall in such shallow water."

"You avoided my question," he said, and her heart skipped a beat when a smile appeared on his face and his fingers gently stroked her face. She closed her eyes to enjoy the caress, and his fingers slowly moved to her forehead.

"Your face is freezing," he whispered.

She smiled and lifted her hand from behind him, brushing her fingers over his face.

"Your face is frozen too…"

They were inches from each other, their hot breath meeting, their lips almost touching.

"I thank you for finding us…for saving me again. I might become accustomed to your saving me. What will I do when that does not happen?"

"Most of the time, you were in danger because of me…or someone from my family…"

"Oh—that is truly nonsensical, sir. You receive gratitude poorly."

"You are no better at it, Miss Bennet."

"You have frozen snowflakes on your eyelids," she replied then pressed gentle fingers over his closed eyes. He moved his head a little, and his lips touched her wrist. Both remained still, and his lips lingered against her cold skin. She slowly withdrew her hand, and her fingers brushed his face while his lips traced a burning line towards her palm.

Gazing into each other's eyes, their faces moved closer, their lips almost touching—their desire stronger than the danger and their tenderness more powerful than their fear.

A sound startled Darcy and brought him back to the present. Dazed, he saw Georgiana a short distance away, staring at them in bewilderment. Distressed, he gathered himself, put Elizabeth down, and rose.

"My dear, what are you doing here? You are still wet! You will freeze to death!"

"Mr. Slade is coming with a carriage…in a few minutes. I brought a blanket…for Lizzy…and some brandy to warm you—Mr. Slade said. Is Lizzy harmed?" she whispered in apparent turmoil.

Darcy took the blanket, hastily wrapped it around Elizabeth, and helped her take a swallow of brandy.

"I am not harmed, dearest," Elizabeth said, grimacing from the strong drink. "My feet were hurt and frozen, and Mr. Darcy took my boots off. Oh, look at you, my darling…the edge of your dress and shoes are wet—"

Mr. Slade's strong voice made his arrival known. He stepped down under the bridge and, together with Darcy, picked up Elizabeth and took her to the carriage.

"Georgiana, come," Darcy invited his sister, but she shook her head. "No, I will ride back home—much quicker than by carriage." She hurried to the saddle, and in the blink of an eye, she disappeared into a curtain of snow.

Inside the carriage, Darcy arranged the blanket around Elizabeth and sat opposite her while Mr. Slade hurried the horses. Their moment of complete intimacy was gone, and its consequences appeared. His body ached for her closeness, and his lips were starving for the touch and taste that fate intended never to happen.

Elizabeth had looked troubled and Georgiana desolated. His worry for Elizabeth was now equalled by his concern for his sister and the questions that might arise.

"Are you well?" he inquired, and Elizabeth nodded.

"Georgiana is upset," she whispered. "She saw us and…she will imagine that…dear Lord, she seemed so grieved. I could not bear to know she is disappointed in me…"

"I will talk to her. I shall explain and…she must know that nothing happened. It was my fault that I lost self-control in a distressing situation…"

She looked at him intently, attempting to understand his words, then averted her eyes.

"We should not have lied to her. Half-truths only make her feel betrayed. I should have thought longer before I agreed to come here…"

"Miss Bennet, I—"

Their discussion was interrupted as the carriage stopped and Mr. Slade opened the door in haste. Both gentlemen took Elizabeth inside the house. Mrs. Reynolds and two maids were waiting.

"Mrs. Reynolds, how is Georgiana?"

"Miss Darcy is well-attended in her apartment. She seems unharmed. Lady Hardwick and her maid are with her. Oh, dear Lord! Miss Bennet, you have no shoes or stockings! Come, make haste!"

The uproar at Pemberley lasted all afternoon; as darkness fell, it continued to snow.

Darcy quickly changed his clothes and eliminated his chill with a glass of brandy; he was less successful with his distress.

What might have happened if he had been late or not heard Georgiana's cries? Without his horse, Georgiana would have needed half an hour to reach Pemberley in such weather. Would Elizabeth have been found in time? Could she have been lost because of a silly accident? And how did it happen that they were outside alone? Why did he not remember to warn them about skating? He was both grateful and frightened as he considered the slight coincidence by which she was saved.

Darcy combed his fingers through his hair, shivering from the recollection of Elizabeth's nearness; then he despised himself for having frivolous thoughts during such a serious situation.

He thanked the Lord for the fortunate outcome; yet, he knew there was still much to remedy. First, he had to speak to his sister—to explain to her something of which not even he was certain.

There was a moment, when he held Elizabeth in his arms, that he forgot himself; caught in the tumult of a dangerous accident, she was not sensible to propriety. He knew her gesture was caused by her fear and gratitude for his having saved her. Still, he shamelessly admitted that the instant he almost kissed Elizabeth gave him the most intense delight he could remember.

But his sister had seen them, and he hoped never to see such distress again. He could not allow her torment to last; he had to speak to Georgiana without delay.

He knocked on her door and, not surprisingly, heard the countess's voice invite him to enter. His aunt and his sister were alone, talking on the couch.

"How are you feeling, dearest?"

"I am fine, Brother. I am a little tired; I believe I will retire early."

"Should we not fetch a doctor?"

"For me? But I am unharmed. Perhaps for *Miss Bennet*...she might be hurt or might catch a very bad cold..."

"My dear, we must talk..."

"I know you must be upset with me...for being unwise with the skating. I should have brought someone with us...and I should not have returned when you asked me to go home. I am frequently incautious as we both know..."

The girl's voice was sharp and carried a poorly disguised anger that he had never heard before in his sister. He noticed that she called Elizabeth "Miss Bennet" and she was fighting tears.

"Georgiana, I would never reproach you for an accident...and it pains me that you believe I would. Have I been so unreasonable in my behaviour to you? Have I ever called you incautious?"

"I am sorry for your pain, Brother, but it cannot be worse than mine."

"Which is why we should talk, my dear," he continued while Lady Hardwick sat on the couch in complete silence, not attempting to intervene.

"I cannot talk now; forgive me, I am not feeling well."

Her rejection cut him more than anything could. He did not understand what she saw, what she believed, or what upset her so, but her grief seemed to return, along with an unwillingness to talk to him.

"Very well, I shall wait for you to feel better. But we cannot delay for long. Any questions you have, we must clear up. You cannot judge things without knowing the truth."

"The only truth I know is what was told to me. And if I have questions, how can I know whether I will be told the truth?"

"Georgiana..."

"Forgive me, Brother; I need to rest."

Elizabeth was in bed, blankets wrapped tightly around her. She felt exhausted; her body was weak and her mind restless. She had been cleaned, warmed, and fed, but she felt worse than when she shivered from cold under the bridge.

Of the few minutes she spent with Darcy—in his arms—and of what she did and said, she dared not remember. Her worry and torment now were entirely related to Georgiana. Her heart ached as she wondered what the girl might have seen and—more importantly—how she felt.

Maids were still moving around the room, and Elizabeth kindly asked them to let her rest. When they finally left, Elizabeth flushed as she saw Georgiana enter. She rose to sit and stretched her hand to the girl, who remained at a distance from the bed.

"Georgiana…how are you, my dear? Please come and sit with me…"

"No…I cannot stay. I only came to see if you are well. I hope you were not harmed?"

"I am fine…only worried that you seem upset with me. Your distress pains me more than anything else…"

"You should not think of my distress; it will go away as it did before."

"My dear, if you tell me what you believe, I might explain to you…if you will only speak to me…"

"My brother keeps telling me I should speak to him too. But I do not wish to. I cannot. He seems more desirous to speak to me now than he ever did before."

"My dear, that is not fair…"

"It is strange to hear you speak of fairness to me, Lizzy, when I have never been unfair to you."

"Nor have I been unfair to you," Elizabeth whispered.

"Yes, you have! I know that you put your life in danger for me today as you have before. I know you put aside your family to visit with me! I know how much you have done for me; yet, you did not trust me enough to tell me what was happening between you and my brother! You deceived me —both of you!"

"Georgiana, we never deceived you. Nothing improper has happened between Mr. Darcy and me."

"If you did not deceive me, you surely distrusted me. I saw you embrace, Lizzy. I saw you kiss each other while for months you let me believe you can barely stand each other."

"We were not kissing…it was just a gesture of comfort that never would have taken place if not for the distressing situation. I do not know what happened...I was so cold and I think a little frightened..." Elizabeth attempted to explain, ashamed, sad, and uncertain of her own words and feelings. The girl seemed not to listen to her.

"I cannot understand. You kept such a secret from me for no reason! I would never blame you for a having a relationship with my brother. Quite the opposite; it was I who suggested it several times. But you both let me believe you loathed each other. You refused to spend time in each other's company. What was the purpose of such deception?"

"Neither of us would mislead you on purpose. You must know the strength of our affection for you..."

"I do not question your friendship, Lizzy. You have proved it to me many times. You often thought more of my safety than your own. But you did not confide in me. What are your plans? And when did you intend to tell me?"

"There are no plans. Dearest, please, I beg you—just speak to your brother. Do that for me, for him, and for your own peace of mind. You have said many times that you owe me—please let this be your repayment."

Georgiana looked at her for a long moment, her eyes filled with tears she did not attempt to hide. "You are still not telling me the truth; I can see it. You still do not trust me. You have saved my life in many ways, Lizzy, but you have broken my heart..."

She hastily left the room, slamming the door behind her.

Elizabeth's torment burst from her soul into her eyes and fell on her cheeks in heavy, painful tears. The notion that she had brought so much pain to Georgiana—justified or not—was unbearable. She knew there would be no good resolution to this. Nothing they could tell Georgiana would calm her unless they wished to continue lying to her. How could the girl understand their burdensome present unless she knew their anguished past?

But more agonising was the memory of what had actually happened and how she felt about it.

It was true that she deceived her friend. Something was indeed happening—at least on her part. The comfort of being held tightly in his arms—his hands warming her feet, his whispers to her ears, his lips almost touching hers, their hands entwined, their lips almost touching—remained deeply burned into her heart, and the sorrow of knowing it would never happen again threw her into a pit of despair colder than any frozen swamp.

WHEN GEORGIANA DISMISSED HIM, DARCY COULD NOT BEAR TO RETURN to his apartment, so he headed to the library. A glass of brandy later, his restlessness increased. He was tempted to go for a walk or a ride, but the weather had worsened. Dinner was still three hours away, and he was alone and lonely, struggling to solve a situation that again occurred because of him.

He was surprised to see Watts, his valet, enter and bow to him.

"Sir, Miss Darcy is asking whether you have a moment. She wishes to speak to you if you are available."

"Yes, of course. Is she in her apartment?"

"No—in Lady Hardwick's."

"Very well, I will go there."

Darcy had only a minute to wonder what his sister wished to talk to him about. She had obviously changed her mind after the earlier refusal. He was at least content that she did not keep her distance from him, but he feared the turn such a conversation might take. And he felt deeply embarrassed at the mere thought of discussing such a subject with his sister and his aunt.

Georgiana met him with restraint, her face pale and her eyes still teary.

"Are you well?" he inquired.

"I am not," she whispered, her eyes avoiding his. "But Elizabeth begged me to speak to you. And Aunt Amelia said I should."

"You talked to Miss Bennet then?"

"I did. I told her how upset and disappointed I am with her."

"Miss Bennet is not to be blamed for anything," he said decidedly.

"She is my friend, and she betrayed my trust—and so did you. You pretended to disapprove of her... disguised your feelings and concealed them from me...and now you suddenly seem to protect her."

"You have reasons to be disappointed in me...but Miss Bennet is not to blame," he repeated. "She thought only of your well-being. Her affection for you is deep and genuine."

"I do not doubt that. But I was persuaded to believe you and she are enemies, only to discover what was truly happening between you."

"My dear, nothing is happening between Miss Bennet and me."

"She said the same...but if I trust you, I must presume that my eyes are deceiving me."

"Do you suspect that I would involve myself in an improper relationship with a young lady under my protection—one who came into my house as my sister's friend? And even if I were such a low sort of man, is Miss Bennet that sort of lady?"

Georgiana paled further; her lips trembled, and tears rolled from her eyes.

"No...of course not...but then what should I believe?"

He paced the room, glancing from his sister to his aunt. He had little courage to speak, yet he dared not remain silent.

"There are things that must be told...delicate things. It is a story no man should ever share with his young sister or his aunt. And yet, it must be related from the beginning, or else trust and sincerity will disappear forever."

"You are frightening us," Lady Hardwick said. "Let us have tea and speak calmly."

"First, I must repeat that nothing improper happened between Miss Bennet and me today. After you left, I observed the gravity of her situation and the possible consequences. I was grateful to her for helping you and afraid that she might be in danger. I confess I would do anything to keep her safe —this I cannot deny. Perhaps holding her as I did was not the most proper behaviour, but it was surely the best solution for warming her..."

He paused again, tormented by the words he had said and by those that would follow.

"However, dearest, the truth is I did deceive you by keeping you ignorant about a delicate, painful, and shameful subject. Miss Bennet insisted on my telling you long ago, but I refused. I found it inappropriate and disturbing to discuss with you."

"Dear Lord...what is the matter, Brother?"

"It all began the evening of the Meryton assembly when I called Miss Bennet 'tolerable.' After the ball I even jested at her expense with Miss Bingley and Mrs. Hurst. During subsequent visits, I found reasons to condemn the Bennet family for their improper manners and lack of decorum. But in my struggle to judge Miss Bennet, I did not notice when my opinion changed. I began to admire her wit, her genuine affection for her sisters, her knowledge, her deep understanding, and her delight in doing things that other young ladies her age would never do. Most of all, I enjoyed her tendency to tease me, disagree with me, and point out my deficiencies when it was deserved."

"Yes, we do recognise her in your description," Lady Hardwick intervened. "But it is quite astonishing to hear of your admiration when we only knew of your disapproval."

"It was equally astonishing and distressing to me. I knew I could never attach myself to a woman whose situation in life was so far below mine. Since I did not wish to give Miss Bennet any sign of my inclination or to raise false expectations, I made it my goal to keep myself at a distance from her. At the same time, Bingley grew very fond of Miss Jane Bennet, and his intention to deepen their acquaintance was obvious to me and to everyone else in Meryton..."

"And?" Georgiana's eyes widened with eager curiosity.

"And, to complete the picture, it was at this time that Wickham appeared in the village. He immediately became friendly with Miss Elizabeth and related to her his own version of events to malign my name. I suspected he would do so, and I was aware that his presence in the peaceful neighbourhood would cause problems. But I chose to do nothing, to withdraw even further, and to act indifferent. Even worse..."

"Yes?" his sister asked again during his short pause.

"It was I who convinced Bingley that a marriage to Jane Bennet would bring him only disadvantages. I expressed my certainty that she did not return his affection. Bingley did not return to Netherfield although his heart was broken. His happiness would have been ruined forever if he had not visited you that day and Aunt Amelia had not encouraged him to return to Hertfordshire."

"But, Brother, why were you opposed to Miss Jane Bennet? Even you admitted several times that she was perfect for him. And her affections seem so strong. Poor Jane..."

"At that time, I was not capable of seeing the truth. I was arrogant and selfish and inconsiderate in my assumptions."

"Oh dear..." the countess said. "Does Bingley know all of this?"

"He does. I confessed everything to him in August. As always, he was extraordinarily generous to me. I did not deserve it."

"William, what about Lizzy...?"

"I met Miss Elizabeth again in Kent last April. For a fortnight, we saw each other almost every day. I was certain she returned my feelings and desired my attentions...so...I proposed to her..."

Two astounded sets of eyes searched his incredulously as he struggled to continue.

"I spoke to her of my feelings and my affection, and I asked her to marry me. I also told her about my sense of her inferiority, her family obstacles that had opposed my inclination, and my decision to marry her against my duty and family's expectations and despite my own sense and judgement."

Astonishment and disbelief brought a grimace to Georgiana's face; the countess put down her cup of tea, staring at her nephew with widened eyes and mouth.

He smiled bitterly. "You can surely guess what followed: I was rejected with the harshest words a man could hear. She accused me of many things —most of them just—including that I separated her sister from Bingley and ruined Wickham's fortunes by refusing him the living left by my father."

"Oh, William...and what did you answer? What did you do?"

"I answered by offending her. I lost my temper of course...and I left after a terrible argument...terrible indeed. But later that night I wrote her a letter, giving my side of the story to all her accusations...but she refused to read it and tore it up..."

"Dear Lord!" both ladies exclaimed at once.

"Yes...during the months that followed, I was furious with myself, disappointed by my weakness in proposing to her, and angry and resentful towards her for her rejection, her accusations, and her refusal to read my letter. I never considered the justice of her reproaches until much, much later..."

Georgiana's face was now darkened by distress, and her hands trembled; she spoke, but her words were filled with tears.

"So that was the reason for your distant behaviour? I thought it was me... that you were disappointed in me for almost eloping, and that my mere presence was painful to you. I thought you avoided me. That is why I preferred to stay with Aunt Amelia."

"I know, dearest...but in my miserable selfishness, I did not think of that. I did not consider how much I hurt you...how much pain I brought to you. I was only made aware of it a few weeks ago by Miss Bennet herself. Please do not blame her for telling me; she did it to convince me to tell you the truth and to release the sorrow that was troubling you. She was willing to risk her good name—and even your friendship—so that you could be at peace and cease blaming yourself with a guilt that should not exist. She was much more considerate and generous than I was to my own beloved sister. I have said many times that I would do anything for your happiness, but I was fool enough to become the precise cause of your unhappiness."

Silence fell over them, adding more weight to the guilt, pain, sorrow, disappointment, and remorse filling the room. Georgiana fell into the depths of grief, the storm of feelings apparent on her face. The countess remained distant and impartial as if she were afraid to intervene between the siblings. Darcy stood by the window, glass in hand, caged in his own self-blame.

"Brother, I find it difficult to understand everything you told me. So many things appear different now. And I still cannot believe that Lizzy refused to marry you...and that you offended her so deeply. That is not the man I love and admire..."

"I am ashamed to confess how far I am from the man you thought I was. I have so many faults, and I have done so many headstrong things that deeply hurt people who had the misfortune to know me. I surely do not deserve your admiration, but I cannot help feeling sad for losing it..."

"I am not surprised that you did not wish to relate this story...it is better kept private," Lady Hardwick finally said. "And I share Georgiana's astonishment at Elizabeth's refusal. I wonder whether another woman in her position, with the lack of family connections and dowry plus the future threat of the family losing their home, would reject a man in your position—even more so since you could have no other reason to marry her than genuine affection."

"It was a response consistent with her poor opinion of me. Her disdain for me was stronger than any worry for her family's future—and rightfully so, one could argue."

"That is debatable, my dear," the countess retorted. "But she was true to herself and did not hesitate to express it, regardless of the consequences. I am not certain whether this is proof of bravery or foolishness. Regardless, Elizabeth is a woman to be admired."

"William, when did you meet with Lizzy again?"

"When she came to ask for my help after her sister's elopement."

"Were you still angry with her at that time?"

"Yes..."

"But you still helped her?"

"I did..."

"I am glad. How ashamed she must have felt to be forced to beg you... and how difficult for you to offer your help against your own feelings. Then I invited her to Pemberley...and you both looked so distressed...now

I see everything more clearly. You approved of my invitation to her…accepted that you would see her every day. That is why you avoided being in our company…"

"My dear, I shall not deny that your invitation was agonizing both for me and for Miss Bennet. And I shall not conceal from you that we spoke of it before her visit…because we both care for you. It seems a fortunate decision as I can see how wonderfully your friendship has grown. And I dare say Miss Bennet has few regrets about coming to Pemberley."

"Does Lizzy know the truth now—about George's deceptions and lies?"

"She does; I have reason to believe she came to understand the truth on her own some time ago."

"Surely, her opinion of you has improved significantly. She certainly does not despise you now. She expressed her admiration for you on several occasions; I have heard her myself. And she is not displeased with your company, I know that."

"I hope she is not. I hope we can be civil in each other's company as there are three people who are dear to both of us. If for no other reason, at least for Bingley, for her sister, and for mine we must be on friendly terms."

"Brother…I must ask: Have your feelings for Lizzy changed?" she asked shyly.

The answer came reluctantly. "They have."

Darcy hoped his sister would be content with that answer and cease the inquiry, but to his surprise, she continued with a wisdom that flustered him.

"But…has your affection for Lizzy diminished?"

"Dearest, I cannot lie to you; neither do I wish to speak of this. Please ask no more and let us end the subject here. You must keep Miss Bennet as the dear, loyal friend she has been to you all this time; the past should be completely forgotten."

"Neither the past nor the present will be easily forgotten. I offended Lizzy today…I saw her so troubled, so pained, and I still hurt her with my suspicions. I accused her of betraying my trust although I knew she put herself in danger to protect me. How can I ever apologise to her?"

Darcy kissed her hand and stroked her hair. "She will not hold it against you. She will surely understand the reason behind your words, despite their injustice. It was my concern for her safety that made me behave improperly, but that will never be repeated. I will never again allow circumstances to interfere and put me, you, or Miss Bennet in a distressful situation."

Georgiana embraced her brother, and he held her tight, stroking her hair.

"Dear brother, I hope I will not have to choose between you and Lizzy. I hope you can become friends. I cannot reconcile myself to the thought that each of you is distressed by the other's presence and that I forced you into this upsetting situation. If I could only do something…I feel as if I traded my grief for yours…"

"Dearest, Miss Bennet told me one day that nothing is more important to her than your peace of mind. We both feel the same on this matter—do not doubt it."

"I am well now—I hope I will be even better soon—but I wish nothing more than to see you happy. And Lizzy…"

"I wish Miss Bennet every happiness too. Never doubt that."

THERE WAS NO FORMAL DINNER AT PEMBERLEY THAT EVENING; THE TOR-ment of the day was too intense, and more time and rest were needed to calm the spirits that had been stirred.

After his startling confession, Darcy retired to his apartment while Georgiana and the countess discussed the matter for another hour. Later in the evening, their aunt returned to her rooms, hoping she had left her niece a little more tranquil and on the edge of sleep. But as soon as she was alone, Georgiana went to Elizabeth's rooms. She entered slowly and found her friend already asleep. She crept closer to the bed, and for a few minutes, she stared in silence at the woman who had so dramatically changed their lives, wondering what was in the mind and heart of Miss Elizabeth Bennet.

Chapter 27

His confession drained Darcy's strength. Once he related the history of the past year, his turmoil increased. He was grateful for the embrace Georgiana offered him at the end. The relief of knowing that his sister could show her affection, despite the suffering she had gone through, was a blessing.

He also had reason to hope that her friendship with Elizabeth would survive that dreadful moment. But, now the secret was known, he wondered whether the relationship between the two would remain as strong and deep as before.

As for his own relationship with Elizabeth—he dared not consider how they would face each other the next day. The knowledge that their past was now revealed must trouble Elizabeth and place her in a distressful position that no honourable lady should suffer. Even though she was the one who asked for it, she would feel the burden of it; he felt it himself. Even worse, he could not offer her comfort, even the innocent comfort of a friend. Every word—every gesture—would now be closely observed and likely misinterpreted by his sister and his aunt. Surely, there could not be a peaceful friendship between them. He worried that Elizabeth would feel the close scrutiny. If the situation were difficult for her at the beginning of her stay, now it would be worse.

He also knew that he was disguising his own feelings. Friendship with Elizabeth was as impossible as it was unbearable. The moment he held her in his arms, any doubt or unreasonable hope of such an outcome vanished. Her arms around his waist, her head resting on his chest, her fingers touching his face, her soft lips almost touching his made him burn inside. He was no fool; he knew the gestures were made of her own will. She wanted to touch his face, and she put her arms around him because his presence gave her comfort and, perhaps, even pleasure. She leant towards him because she wished for a kiss that never happened.

But, while his heart desperately begged for a deeper meaning to her gestures, his reason knew it was foolish to imagine more than it was. Just as he had repeated to Georgiana, if not for those dangerous circumstances that threatened her life and her gratitude for the man who offered her support and warmth, such intimacy never would have occurred. And he promised his sister that it never would again.

But every fibre of his body yearned for her touch and craved more—much more. He said last April that he loved her *ardently*, but every time he was near her, he discovered new and deeper meanings for that word.

His desire and passion shadowed his reasoning so that he could not —dared not—discover the truth behind her gestures. If any other woman had been in his arms and touched him the way she did, he would have been certain of what she wanted and expected from him. But with her, everything was different. She was different.

What would happen the next morning when they all met at breakfast? What would happen in the next weeks? How long would they be in such unbearable confines? Would she be desirous to leave? Would Georgiana prefer not to prolong a situation that had become so odious to them all?

His thoughts grew into a violent storm, stronger than the wind that blew outside. A fierce headache sliced his temples, and he opened the window widely, the snow hitting his face. Melting snow dripped down his face like frozen tears from beyond his eyes. He remained there for a long while, scarcely feeling the piercing cold.

When he withdrew into the room, closed the window, and poured himself a glass of brandy, he knew what he had to do.

WIND SHOOK THE WINDOWS, AND ELIZABETH STARTLED, FRIGHTENED and confused, looking around her. She was uncertain of the hour. How was it possible that she slept so deeply? It must have been Mrs. Reynolds's tea. She left the bed and put on her robe. Her feet hurt slightly, but she ignored them. Greater pains troubled her. How much time had passed since her conversation with Georgiana? Was it already dinnertime? The mere thought of eating made her cringe, but she wished to know where the others were gathered.

She rang, and Sarah arrived immediately.

"Miss Bennet, how are you feeling? Are you well?"

"I am very well," she said with a weak smile. "Would you please tell me the time? And how is Miss Darcy?"

"It is around eight o'clock, ma'am. Mrs. Reynolds says there will be no formal dinner tonight as the family has already retired. But I can bring you something to eat. Just let me know...the cook made some fresh soup...warm..."

"A little soup sounds lovely. But would you be so kind as to inquire whether Miss Darcy is unharmed? And Mr. Darcy of course. No need to bother any of them; only ask and let me know."

"Of course ma'am—at once."

Time passed, but the maid did not return. Elizabeth sat in the chair, her feet up with her arms wrapped around her legs. She stroked her still-aching toes, and she felt herself blush as she recollected the touch of Darcy's fingers on her feet and his palms sheltering her frozen feet.

Elizabeth turned towards the opening door, eager to hear some news. But instead of the maid, Georgiana entered. Pale and grave, she walked in reluctantly, her blue eyes shadowed by dark circles.

"May I come in?" she asked diffidently.

"Of course—please come in," Elizabeth invited her, hurrying to her.

They sat on the bed at a polite distance.

"How are you feeling, Lizzy?"

"I am as well as I can be if you refer to my health. Please do not worry."

"I do worry...how could I not?"

"I can see you are upset..."

"I am not upset—only a little worried and sad. I talked with William. He told us..."

"Oh. Is there...do you wish to ask me anything?"

"No. I imagine it must be hard for you to speak of it. It has been a year of distress for all three of us."

"Yes..."

"My brother said he offended you...but you must believe me: I have never heard William offend anyone before. He is sometimes aloof and restrained, but I never heard a cross word from him addressed to either the family or the tenants or even the servants. Everybody agrees that he is the best master and the best landlord."

"My dear, I do know that now. You must understand that Mr. Darcy and I had a violent argument. We were both angry and unfair, and we said things that we have come to repent. But I dare say we have discussed this matter, and we agreed that we both share the blame. On this subject, there is little else to be said."

"Lizzy, I know you insisted William reveal your secret to put me at ease. You exchanged your comfort for mine. I cannot even imagine how difficult it was for you to come to Pemberley."

"My tranquillity was not complete without yours, my dear. And the weeks I have spent at Pemberley with you were truly wonderful."

"Oh, Lizzy, what are you saying? You do not plan to leave, I hope?"

"I am not certain yet…but perhaps it is time for me to return home so you and your brother can spend some time together. I do not want to create more distress for anyone."

"I will not insist on your doing any less than you want. But I would be happy if you were to stay at Pemberley forever. And if you decide otherwise, you must remember that Pemberley will always be your home."

THE FOLLOWING DAY, ELIZABETH WENT TO BREAKFAST WITH A HEAVY HEART and unsteady thoughts. She was abashed at the prospect of seeing Lady Hardwick and Darcy for the first time since the incident at the swamp and his confession.

Her ladyship smiled at her, inquired after her health, and then thanked her for protecting Georgiana. They sat at the table, but she noticed Darcy was not there. When he appeared a few minutes later, he greeted them briefly, and his gaze lingered on Elizabeth's face for a moment.

Formally attired and his countenance severe, he wore obvious signs of a lack of sleep.

"I hope you had a good night. Did you rest well?" he asked politely.

"We did, Brother. Although Lizzy and I went to sleep rather late, we talked until near midnight." The reason for Georgiana's statement was no mystery to anyone.

"I am glad to hear it. There is something I must tell you—something I considered thoroughly and decided after weighing all the details very carefully."

Darcy's hoarse voice startled his companions. They stared at him, intrigued and impatient.

"I have long intended to visit our other property in Cambridgeshire and Lady Hardwick's two in Oxfordshire and Birmingham. I believe this is the time to do so. I might also stop briefly at Newcastle. My luggage is packed, and everything is prepared. I will leave after breakfast."

Elizabeth dropped her cup and spilt hot tea on the table, a few drops burning her hand. Darcy hurried to help her, but she hastily wiped the table with a napkin, struggling to keep her eyes from him.

He resumed his place, followed by the gazes of his sister and aunt.

"Brother, what are you saying? Surely, you cannot leave Pemberley!"

"I am, my darling. Just as last autumn I spent a few months with Bingley at Netherfield, I have to attend to business for a while."

"But…Mr. and Mrs. Bingley arrive next week!"

"I know…I will inform Bingley. I have no doubt he will understand. They come to visit you and Miss Bennet. I am sure you will be a perfect hostess and show them a pleasant time."

"So you wish to leave today? Now? In winter—it could be so dangerous! You have said so many times!"

"I will have Watts and four other men with me. We will stop and rest frequently, I promise. And I will write you from each destination." He smiled at her.

"Brother, how can I convince you to reconsider your plans?"

"Mr. Darcy, please do not leave because of me. I beg you, sir. I should return to Longbourn—I believe it is time," Elizabeth whispered, fighting to maintain her composure and speak coherently as she squeezed her wet napkin with trembling hands.

Darcy raised his eyes to her; their gazes met and held, and he answered only to her, oblivious to everything else.

"I am not leaving because of you; I am leaving because of me. Please rest assured that your presence at Pemberley is a great benefit for everyone, and I trust you will have no reason to leave soon."

She understood that he was pleading for her to remain with Georgiana while he was away. The depths of his gaze and the severity of his countenance showed her that his decision was made and he would not change it, regardless of their objections.

She could only nod silently.

They spoke little during the meal. Words that needed to be said were withheld; any others were useless.

When Darcy finished breakfast and declared he must finish his preparation, the countess demanded to speak to him privately. He reluctantly agreed, having no other choice; it was not a request.

"I wish to know what is behind all this," Lady Hardwick insisted when they were alone.

"Aunt, let us not have a debate. My decision is unmovable."

"I am trying to understand you. I have been in situations, delicate for the mind and the heart, which tormented me in my life, so I am not unsympathetic. But you must be aware that this departure is akin to running away."

"I am aware."

"And that is what worries me. You never avoid a challenge, but it seems that you are doing so now."

"I am not avoiding the challenge, Aunt; I intended to fight. But now, my adversary is myself. Therefore, I need time and distance to carry out this battle so that I do not risk hurting you too."

"But why are you having this fight? What is it that you want to accomplish?"

"Peace...and happiness."

"My dear boy, what am I to do with you? You carry on a struggle that could be won easily by other means. You choose a more difficult and painful strategy than is necessary."

"Perhaps, but I shall discover it myself and make amends if necessary."

Darcy embraced his aunt lovingly, and she placed a tender kiss on both cheeks.

"I feel you are a fool, and I wish I could prove it to you. Do return home soon."

Around noon, Darcy was ready to leave, and he stopped at the stables to speak to Mr. Slade.

"I will not take Storm with me," he said.

Mr. Slade's amazement was apparent. "You will not?"

"No...I am not certain of my travelling plans, and I do not want to drag him around the country in such weather."

He did not want to take Storm because he would always remind him of Elizabeth, of the day he helped her to step beyond her apprehension and pet the horse—the day their bare fingers touched. That image was agonising, and he needed to detach himself from it.

"I beg your forgiveness, but I find it strange that you are more preoccupied with the horse's well-being than your own, Mr. Darcy."

"I do not neglect my well-being either, Mr. Slade. But I must leave."

The elder gentleman threw Darcy a scrutinising look. "The master of Pemberley *must* not do anything. He is free to choose."

Darcy smiled at the gentleman's veiled reproach. "Unless his reason and duty demand it."

Mr. Slade's eyebrow rose. "Then perhaps he should listen to his heart more. Sometimes, even the brightest of men is deceived by his feelings. At times, the mind cannot understand properly what the eyes see clearly. Reason must keep the heart under good regulation but not stifle it."

The statement surprised Darcy and discomposed him. Their gazes confronted each other, neither man abandoning the silent duel.

Then Darcy chose not to further the debate. "Mr. Slade, I count on you to watch over my family. I will be in touch, but I will not be close enough for some time. My friend Bingley will be here for a month or so."

"Very well, Mr. Darcy. We shall do as you ask."

THE DAY OF DARCY'S DEPARTURE AND THE NEXT WERE A STRUGGLE FOR Elizabeth and Georgiana. The girl tried to be cheerful, and Elizabeth supported her. They played and sang together, walked in the gardens, and read in the library—now desolate. They spoke of everything but most often of Darcy. Georgiana recollected countless stories from their childhood, and Elizabeth was happy to listen.

In Darcy's absence, Elizabeth's feelings for him seemed to strengthen and become clearer. Every Pemberley location, no matter how insignificant, reminded her of him, and her heart was burdened by a sorrow she had never felt before. She had missed her sisters, her parents, and her relatives many times, but this was the first time that such an intense longing afflicted her. To this was added her fear that his interest might be drawn to someone else—that he might choose a Mrs. Darcy ideally suited for the position. His cousin Anne, Lady Emmeline, or someone else—someone to make him as happy as he deserved.

She was humbled, and she was grieved; she repented. She became jealous of anyone who might have his esteem. While she missed his presence, she admitted what she had long suspected: that he was exactly the man who, in disposition and talents, would most suit her. She was now convinced that she could have been happy with him when there was little chance of this happening. But at least, she could keep him vividly in her mind through the conversations she shared with Georgiana and Lady Hardwick.

All three were worried and eager to hear of him, so when a letter arrived for Georgiana on the second afternoon, it was shared with great curiosity.

"It is dated last night. It seems William travelled faster than we did. He always does that," the girl explained to Elizabeth; then she read on.

Dearest,

I hope that you, Lady Hardwick, and Miss Bennet are all in good health.

I have arrived in Birmingham reasonably quickly, and I am staying at the Wood Inn. The weather is as good as can be expected. I will continue my travel towards London tomorrow morning, but I have two pieces of news to share with you, both of them related to Miss Bennet.

First, I sent an express to Bingley, which will hopefully arrive before they leave Netherfield. I explained to him my absence but also extended the invitation to Pemberley to both Miss Mary and Miss Kitty. Mr. Bennet already declined to travel in the winter, but he might allow his daughters the opportunity. If so, you will soon have two more friends with whom to celebrate.

Georgiana stopped and looked at Elizabeth with genuine delight. "Oh, Lizzy, is this not excellent news? It would be such a pleasure for us all to be together. I only hope your parents will not mind being alone during Christmas."

"Yes, this is wonderful news; I cannot wait to see my sisters. Mr. Darcy is very generous—as always. And...what is the second item?"

"Let me see; I will read further:

As I found the Livingstons returned to their estate, I briefly called on them. Lord Mowbray was also there, and he asked me to convey his warm regards to Miss Bennet. He also said he would be delighted to visit you all at Pemberley soon if it is convenient for you.

I will write you again from my next stop. Please take good care of yourself and send my best regards to Aunt Amelia and Miss Bennet.

Your loving brother.

Georgiana finished the letter, and Elizabeth remained lost in her thoughts. She was grateful for his consideration in inviting Kitty and Mary. They would both be excited, and she dearly wanted to see them. But what troubled her more was the knowledge that he visited the Livingstons' estate. Was Lady Emmeline there too? Was that the main reason for his visit?

"Lizzy? Are you unwell?" Georgiana called to her several times before she finally noticed.

"Yes—forgive me. I mean no—I am not unwell. I was just thinking."

"So what do you say of Lord Mowbray?"

"In what respect?"

Lady Hardwick seemed disconcerted. "In what respect? My dear, Lord Mowbray is one of the most eligible men of the ton. He is wealthy, handsome, and amiable. He just sent you his warm regards and asked for your approval to visit us. Any young woman would be thrilled with such proof of admiration."

"Oh...yes, forgive me. I am sure Lord Mowbray is an admirable gentleman. I was pleasantly impressed by him. He is very handsome too. If he should come to visit Georgiana and your ladyship, I would be pleased to see him again."

She paused briefly then spoke to Georgiana, oblivious to Lady Hardwick's puzzled countenance. "Do you think Mr. Darcy will stay in Birmingham long? Oh, he did mention he would leave next morning. That would be this morning...so he must already be far along."

"Yes, he should arrive at Nott Inn tonight if he keeps to his usual schedule. Lizzy, would you like to play with me? I intend to practice for an hour or so."

"Dearest, would you mind if I rest a while? I am a little tired."

"Of course—I will see you later," the girl answered, exchanging a worried glance with her aunt. She did not remember her friend ever resting at noon.

Elizabeth hurried to her room for no other reason than to be alone with her thoughts. Yet, her solitude was disturbed a few minutes later when Sarah entered with a note from Lady Hardwick, inviting her to her apartment.

Surprised, she accepted the invitation and knocked on the countess's door, stepping in hesitantly.

"Elizabeth, please take a seat and have some tea with me. We must talk on a subject that is difficult to approach but even more difficult to ignore. That is why I preferred to have this discussion without Georgiana; the matter is too delicate for her."

Elizabeth looked with unaffected astonishment. "Would your ladyship be so kind as to be more specific?"

"My dear, you can be at no loss as to what I am referring. We face a situation that makes all of us miserable. I admit it chiefly affects you and my nephew, but it also pains Georgiana just when she has found some peace. Not to mention that it annoys me exceedingly."

"I am aware of that, and I cannot say how much I regret it; it is entirely my fault, and I am ready to do anything to remedy it."

"Oh, enough with this fault and to whom it belongs! Both you and Darcy accept the blame but neither of you takes proper action, and the situation only worsens. Of course, my nephew is more proficient at this than you are: you take no action while he takes the wrong ones."

Elizabeth blushed with embarrassment. "I do not know how to respond to this..."

"I spoke to Darcy before he left. I am the nearest relation he and Georgiana have in the world and am entitled to know all his dearest concerns. Of course, you might say I am not entitled to know yours; still, I hope you will be as honest with me as you would be with your own mother or aunt so this can be resolved in the happiest possible way."

"Of that, you should not doubt. Is there something your ladyship wishes me to do?"

"Well, *that* you must decide for yourself. My nephew's departure is certainly related to you—there is no debate there. And it is obvious that his absence troubles you more than his presence did, just as I am certain he is more distressed being away than he was being here. I cannot question his intentions, so I must question yours. Is there something you intend to do?"

Her amazement grew, and she could hardly find words. "I do not know what I should do...what I could do..."

"Elizabeth, you must know that my sincerity and frankness are greater than my diplomacy. Be warned that I may ask questions you might choose not to answer, but I will insist nevertheless."

"I will answer any of your questions. After everything that has happened in the last few days, there are no secrets left."

"Very well. I know you refused Darcy last April, and I find it admirable that a woman has the strength to reject a man she does not consider worthy; although, I dare say in this particular case, it was rather a silly decision," Lady Hardwick said, half in jest. She sipped some tea and continued.

"I can well imagine the two of you—both quick tempered, hasty in judgement, proud, and prejudiced—having an argument and heating it until it burned you both. But the past is gone. Please tell me: What are your feelings towards my nephew at present?"

Elizabeth's astonishment at such a direct question matched her turmoil in groping for a precise answer. How could she put into words something she did not understand?

"I was indeed hasty and prejudiced in judging Mr. Darcy in the past. But my opinion of him has changed completely; I—"

"My dear, I am not asking about your opinion of him but about your *feelings*—about how you breathe when you are in his presence, how your heart beats when he is near you, what you sense when he touches your hand. Compare all these things with your feelings in similar situations—with other gentlemen like my nephew Lord Mowbray or Colonel Fitzwilliam—and tell me. Is the answer so difficult?"

Elizabeth stared at the countess, blinking rapidly to stem her tears, recollections spinning in her mind and shaking her.

"No...the answer is not difficult," she murmured, her voice barely audible in her distress.

"Oh, my dear, it gives me great hope to see you so troubled," the countess said with a smile. "But I confess I hardly needed your admission. I have long noticed the sparks between you, although I was not certain of their cause."

"Have you?" Elizabeth replied incredulously.

"Of course, I have—even before we started our journey to Pemberley. But I confess I was rather worried, as I believed it to be the mutual attraction of a gentleman and a young lady. I have seen such situations before, and I feared it might become improper and harmful for your reputation, which could also affect Georgiana. I said nothing because, once we arrived at Pemberley, I did not see either of you attempt to place yourself in private situations. You were always with Georgiana, and Darcy rather avoided your company. Of course, I could not imagine the story behind these observations."

"Oh...I did not know...I was hardly aware myself...I was so confused and..."

"Yes, I can easily guess your confusion, my dear. But now you should decide what you wish then gather your thoughts and strength and find the best way to achieve your desire."

"Lady Hardwick, I must ask: Why are you so kind and generous to me? Why are you preoccupied with my happiness? Most people in your position would condemn any possible connection between me and Mr. Darcy."

A grin twisted the countess's lips. "Elizabeth, I assure you that I am by no means as generous as you believe me to be. Quite the contrary—I am preoccupied with your happiness because I strongly believe it is closely related to the happiness of my nephew and niece. I confess I first admired you for all the traits that make you distinct from other young women your age. Then I appreciated your extraordinary influence on Georgiana and your genuine affection for her. I also considered for some time that you would be very well suited for the position of Darcy's wife, but I had little hope that it might happen. But since I have discovered the truth, the solution for everyone's felicity seems clear to me."

She drank some more tea, watching Elizabeth closely. "I shall not deny that wealth and connections are important; being born into a family of peers, I would be a hypocrite to claim otherwise. But reaching my age, I have realised that there are few things that truly matter in life. One is the way you use your fortune and your power: the help you provide to those in need and the legacy you leave. The other is the love you share with your family and friends, but most importantly with that one person who makes you complete and enriches your life—if you have the good fortune ever to find that person—the person who is your spouse, your confidant, your lover. The person who, when you hold him in your arms, you feel as if you are holding the entire world and nothing else matters."

As she spoke, the countess's eyes brightened while her face coloured. Her voice became animated, and her smile widened, enhancing her delicate, beautiful features.

"This is what I want for my nephew, Elizabeth. And I am confident that, once he experiences all these things, he will help Georgiana to obtain them too."

Elizabeth listened and watched completely mesmerised, each word stirring her mind and melting her heart.

"And I believe you, Miss Elizabeth Bennet, can be that person to Darcy. But that may happen only if his holding your hand makes you feel as you never have before with any other man…"

"I am…he is…I never…if I could only…" she whispered, overwhelmed by the strength of what she suddenly understood. Tearful, she rubbed her hands as she struggled to speak.

"Mr. Darcy is truly the best man I have known. It is true that his behaviour was wrong and his manners unacceptable, but I did reject his marriage proposal, and I offended him in the worst possible manner. I am not certain what his feelings are now. But I know that no man would ever forget or forgive my offenses. No man would propose again after such a disappointment. And no man would connect himself to a family where, to every other objection, would now be added an alliance and relationship of the nearest kind with Mr. Wickham, the man whom he so justly despises."

To Elizabeth's turmoil, Lady Hardwick answered with another grin. "Indeed, I am amazed at how well you know without a doubt what a man —any man!—would do and not do. And you pretend that my nephew is arrogant?" she mocked a distressed Elizabeth. "Even you must admit that, had my nephew been indifferent to you, he would not still be so troubled by your presence, nor would he have kissed you under the bridge, or left his sister and his home before Christmas, simply because your nearness was too painful for him to bear."

"I would have left in his place. I did not want him to separate from his family. If only we could find a way…if I could explain to him…but what to tell him? How could I dare speak my mind? How could I even approach such a subject with him?"

"Dear Elizabeth—when Mist ran and climbed that tree, you found an instant and efficient solution to bring him back when we all panicked and suffered for him."

Elizabeth was disconcerted and puzzled by such a comparison, wondering whether the lady was mocking her.

"Surely, the situations are not the same. I could not—"

"I beg to differ. Just like Georgiana in the park, you are in danger of losing something rare and precious. You may either cry and pine for it, or climb the tree and bring him back."

Elizabeth's astonishment left her speechless while the countess discreetly poured herself a little port to calm her nerves.

"You should go to Georgiana now," Lady Hardwick said. "I have something to finish, and I will join you soon."

Elizabeth walked away, abashed and silent; from the doorway, she turned and said, attempting a weak excuse. "Lady Hardwick, Georgiana misinterpreted what she saw. Mr. Darcy did not kiss me under the bridge…"

"Well, my dear, then you had better do something to remedy that!"

Once Elizabeth left, Lady Hardwick filled her glass again and started to laugh. Then she sat at the small desk, took paper and pen, and wrote:

Darcy,

You are expected home without delay. Miss Bennet and Georgiana agree with me that your absence is most disturbing. As for Lord Mowbray, I shall write to him myself. Neither Miss Bennet nor I feel that he should make the long journey to Pemberley in this bad weather.

Do not bother to send an answer to this letter. You are expected to deliver it personally before Christmas.

ELIZABETH'S AFTERNOON WAS A STORM OF AGONY. THE CONVERSATION with Lady Hardwick, the suggestions and encouragement offered by the countess, and the exhilarating thought that Darcy might still have feelings and desires for a future with her were enthralling. The extraordinary picture of a perfect match with complete happiness that Lady Hardwick drew for her was so wonderful that she feared it was unreal—even impossible.

The countess made her see the truth so clearly. Indeed, she had never felt anything close to what she felt when she was near Darcy. Even in the early stage of their acquaintance, when his manners were despicable and she believed him guilty of countless faults, his presence always disturbed her. And during their dance at Netherfield, the feel of his hand holding hers aroused a sort of chill different than she had experienced with any other partner. Even as they argued, his touch was thrilling, and only now did she understand it properly.

She still did not know what she should do—what she could do. But there was hope—reasonable and fair—that filled her heart with joy.

She joined Georgiana and Lady Hardwick at dinner and was delighted to see Mr. Slade there too. She was still restless, and she followed the conversation in silence, glancing from one to the other absently. She saw Mr. Slade and Lady Hardwick speaking animatedly while Georgiana laughed at something. Suddenly, she rose from her seat, all the weight vanishing from her shoulders and her mind instantly freed from its blinding confusion.

"I beg you will excuse me for a moment; there is something of great importance I must do without delay. I will return shortly, but please continue with your dinner; do not wait for me."

"Lizzy, are you unwell? Shall I come with you?"

"No, dearest, I am perfectly fine. I must write Mr. Darcy a letter."

"A letter? Why? Is something wrong?"

"Everything is fine, my dear. I must climb the tree of my fears, and I do not have an instant to lose. I will explain later," she replied lightly, noticing Lady Hardwick's broad smile. Then she hurried out, ignoring the two perplexed blue-eyed gazes that followed her and the countess's elegant laughter.

A week after he left Pemberley, Darcy arrived in London.

The journey went smoothly, but it tired him as never before. He was without purpose—isolated and lonely—and for the first time in his life, the loneliness was unbearable.

His tours of the estates proved to be useless and even ridiculous. His appearance in the middle of winter, close to Christmas, surprised and worried the stewards and housekeepers. He had kept close correspondence with each of them, and he already knew things to be in order. Therefore, he only stayed one night.

He had no patience to stay longer; he felt welcome nowhere.

With every mile, the distance between Elizabeth and him grew, but that brought him no peace. His thoughts remained with her—as did his heart. He wondered every moment what she was doing—how she was bearing his departure. Her presence had been a distraction, but her absence was a torment. Added to everything else was a sharp pain that had gripped him since Lord Mowbray asked him to send Elizabeth his regards. The earl never even attempted to conceal his admiration for her—why would he? Only he, Darcy, was the fool who did that for months.

The Bingleys should arrive in Derbyshire in three days' time. Elizabeth would surely be happy to see her sisters again, and so would Georgiana. They would spend Christmas in joy, he hoped. Without him. Would Lord Mowbray visit them after all? He passed on his question, and it depended on Elizabeth. Lady Hardwick might easily write to him. He felt jealous and fearful that she might become more partial to the earl. But why would she not? She surely deserved to be happy.

He knew she could be happy with him—happier than with anyone else. Because no one else would love her as he did. If he only had a chance to tell her as much—if he could only be certain that she was willing to listen. If only her feelings would change enough to allow him to make one more attempt to win her heart.

Darcy sat in the library that had been his refuge for months. Memories returned of those dreadful days spent in darkness and solitude, nurturing his anger and resentment against himself and against Elizabeth. He had come so far in only five months; his life—their lives—had changed because of her. Everything was because of her.

Town was animated, but he was in no mood to leave the house. Yet, he would have to. He had sent a note to his uncle Lord Matlock to announce his arrival, and he immediately received a demand to join them for dinner. He accepted it as he truly missed his relatives; even more, he hoped the time would pass more quickly in company.

He went to his apartment to change. Watts already was there, arranging his belongings.

"Sir, there is some correspondence on the desk. It arrived before we did; forgive me for intruding, but as I organised it, I noticed a letter from Miss Darcy."

"I will look through it; would you leave me a moment, Watts? I will ring for you."

"Yes, sir, of course."

The valet left, and he searched through the papers eagerly. He was curious to see what news Georgiana had sent him. Were there any hints, any details about Elizabeth?

Near Georgiana's letter, he found one from Lady Hardwick. He wondered which he should open first, and while he hesitated, his eyes fell on a third one. He touched it, then picked it up and looked at it. He did not recognise the writing, and it was not signed outside. His heart raced with hope while his reason told him such anticipation was absurd. The letter could be from anyone. If she wished to tell him something, she would put a note in Georgiana's letter. But surely, she would not tell him anything directly —much less write to him. Then why did that piece of paper trouble him so?

"Oh, this is ridiculous; I am behaving like a lunatic," he said furiously and quickly opened the letter. He unfolded the paper and saw the date: it was from Pemberley, five days ago. Slowly, his eyes ran down the page, and the revelation took his breath away. There were only three lines.

Mr. Darcy,

In vain have I struggled. It will not do. You must allow me to tell you how greatly your presence is missed and how ardently we await your return to Pemberley.

Elizabeth Bennet.

Three lines—more powerful than a hundred volumes, more important than all the books he had ever read. He looked at the paper again, astounded, incredulous, his heart bursting with joy and trembling with fear of its being a dream. Three and thirty words and her beautiful name added at the end—words that changed his life in an instant.

Chapter 28

The days that followed Elizabeth's brief moment of courage—her letter to Darcy—were not in the slightest easier to bear than those that came before. Embarrassment and uncertainties troubled her as she wondered whether he had received the letter and when. What would he think—and feel—about it?

She also slept as poorly at the night as she had before. During the day, her effort to appear cheerful for Georgiana and Lady Hardwick's sake was even more of a struggle.

Three days before Christmas, late in the afternoon, Elizabeth had the joy of welcoming her sisters and new brother to Pemberley.

The reunion brought tears to Elizabeth's eyes as she embraced Jane—more beautiful than ever on her husband's arm and blissfully gleaming—and Kitty and Mary, who stared about them in silent, astounded admiration.

Georgiana's genuine delight and warm behaviour towards her guests melted Elizabeth's heart. Miss Darcy's manners were no different at Pemberley than they had been at Longbourn, and that helped the guests to slowly feel more comfortable.

"Upon my word, every time I see Pemberley, it looks even more beautiful," Bingley declared, caressing his wife's hand on his arm.

"Miss Darcy, I have never seen such a splendid place. How can we thank you for your kind invitation?" Jane said.

"The pleasure is ours, I assure you, Mrs. Bingley. I am so glad you arrived safely. I hope you travelled comfortably."

"We did, thank you. It is such a pity that Darcy is not here," Bingley continued. "I have never been here without him."

"Indeed. We all share your feelings, sir. Now please allow me to show you to your rooms."

"Oh, well, I still hope I will see him soon. Miss Darcy, I presume my old chamber is assigned to me?"

Georgiana blushed slightly and glanced at Elizabeth.

"No indeed, sir. I discussed this with my aunt and Lizzy, and we decided you and Mrs. Bingley should stay in the emerald apartment in the west wing."

"Emerald apartment? I do not remember even seeing it before."

"That is because you have never been married to this beautiful lady before and in obvious need of privacy," Lady Hardwick said, approaching slowly.

Kitty and Mary immediately curtseyed to the countess while Bingley bowed. Jane coloured and, in her embarrassment, almost forgot her manners. The countess laughed.

"Come and let me embrace you. How are you all? You had a safe trip, I hope?"

Once the guests were settled, Elizabeth had the pleasure of spending some private time with Jane while she helped her accommodate to the new apartment. She happily heard good news from Longbourn and Meryton, struggled to provide lighthearted answers to Jane's questions about her visit to Pemberley, and listened with enchantment to her sister's praise of her husband and her new life.

"Dearest Lizzy, if I could only see you as happy as I am! There is nothing else that I want in the world. For myself, I dare not pray for more as I feel as if I am in a dream."

"My dear, *your* happiness is enough for me." Elizabeth embraced her tenderly. "I missed you so much, Jane! There was not a single day I did not think of you."

"I missed you too, my dear...but I confess I did not think of you as often as I used to when we were separated," Jane teased her then blushed and smiled at her sister.

"To be honest, I hoped as much," Elizabeth replied in the same manner.

"But, my dear, how is Mr. Darcy? How is your relationship with him now?"

Elizabeth hesitated to answer. "Mr. Darcy is kind and amiable and an excellent host. Since I arrived here, I have been treated no differently than the family. He is careful and generous. And...oh, there are many things that I have to tell you, my dear, but not now. We have plenty of time. You should rest; I will see you later at dinner. I hope the apartment is to your liking."

Jane looked around. "It is truly wonderful, Lizzy! Perfect!"

"I am glad you like it. You can easily imagine that all the rooms at Pemberley are splendid, but Lady Hardwick suggested this one for you. She said it was proper for a newly wedded couple. Mr. Bingley's old room was too small."

Jane hesitated a moment, then blushed even more, and averted her eyes. "Oh, I doubt that...we do not need too large a room. At Netherfield, we never use both of the master suite's chambers at the same time. One of the beds is never disturbed."

Elizabeth stared at her sister in disbelief at such a confession, then her cheeks coloured too, and she chuckled. "Upon my word, Mrs. Bingley, what have you done with my sweet, shy, proper, and restrained Jane?"

Her elder sister embraced her again. "She mostly disappeared on her wedding night, but only you know that, dearest Lizzy. I would never dare to confess that to anyone else."

THAT EVENING, DINNER WAS BRIEF; THE GUESTS WERE TIRED, SO MR. AND Mrs. Bingley retired early, followed by the countess.

However, Elizabeth and Georgiana, together with Kitty and Mary, moved to the music room and remained there until late, talking and playing the pianoforte.

"I am glad Mr. Bennet allowed you to come," Georgiana said animatedly.

"Oh, we were so excited when Papa told us about Mr. Darcy's invitation! We could not believe his generosity! Lady Lucas and Mrs. Philips pretended something was strange about that, but Mama said they were only jealous because they would never see Pemberley."

"There is nothing strange, I assure you. My brother is the kindest and most generous man. I hope you will have a pleasant time with us. So please let me know what you wish to do."

"I just want to stay here at the piano to play...and to read," Mary declared.

"I want to do anything you want," Kitty replied, much to Georgiana's amusement.

Elizabeth watched her sisters and her friend in contentment. The girls seemed perfectly at ease with one another, enjoying every moment spent together. At least for them, she had no reason to worry.

The next day started pleasantly and continued the same. The guests went for a walk—it was not warm enough for horseback nor cold and snowy enough for a sleigh—but every moment outside was a delight.

The evening found them in excellent moods and was among the most joyful that Pemberley had hosted in quite some time, the countess declared. Mr. Slade was invited, and his addition was as impressive as it was delightful to everyone. Bingley's admiration for the gentleman was obvious as he related to the ladies a variety of stories about Mr. Slade's courage, learnt from Darcy and Colonel Fitzwilliam. The gentleman, however, denied them humbly and vehemently.

After the first course, conversation engaged everybody. So caught were they in their discussions and laughter that they completely ignored the new arrival looking at them from the doorway.

"Upon my word—welcome home, my friend," Bingley cried and jumped from his seat, immediately followed by Georgiana.

Sitting with her back to the door, Elizabeth did not dare turn—or breathe. Silence fell in the room for a moment, then Georgiana's joyful voice and a hoarse one, made Elizabeth shiver and froze her in her place.

"What a joy to see you all here. I could not hope to return home to better company."

Then steps sounded sharply in the room, and Darcy stopped at the head of the table and bowed to them. She ventured a brief look at him and met his gaze. His eyes glistened with mirth, and his face—although betraying his fatigue—was brightened by a smile that twisted the corners of his lips.

Kitty and Mary seemed too intimidated by him to do more than nod to him, but Jane and Mr. Slade greeted him happily.

Lady Hardwick raised her eyebrow. "Well, well—look who has returned. Have you increased the income of our estates, Nephew?"

"I am happy to see you, Aunt," he responded, kissing her hand. Then he bowed to Elizabeth, who remained silent.

"Miss Bennet…"

"Mr. Darcy…"

Nothing further was said as he excused himself to change from his travelling clothes. In his absence, dinner was interrupted and his return discussed, but Elizabeth was too discomposed to engage in any discussion. She was furious at her silly behaviour, and that made her even more restrained.

He had returned as she hoped. He appeared pleased to be home and to see her. But that was all she knew for the time being. She was still uncertain whether he had received her letter and—if he had—what he thought of it. She felt the scrutiny of Lady Hardwick and Georgiana, and she forced herself to project calmness she did not feel, doubtful of her success. The thought that Darcy would join them at dinner in a few minutes thrilled her, and he did so less than half an hour later, completely changed and refreshed. He took his usual seat at a distance from Elizabeth.

"Darcy, I am quite excited that you returned. I was just telling the ladies yesterday that Pemberley is not the same without you—still beautiful, but different," Bingley said.

"Indeed, everything is different without Darcy," the countess added. "And yet, he thought his absence would be helpful in some way."

"I did, but I am ready to admit my fault," Darcy replied. "And as soon as I understood that my decision was wrong, I admitted it and acted to remedy it."

"It is proof of worthiness that a man can recognise his errors and correct them," Mr. Slade offered.

Darcy responded with a trace of bitterness. "Of course, it would be an even greater proof for a man to closely analyse a situation and judge it properly before making the erroneous decision—especially ones that might affect those closest to him."

"True," Mr. Slade replied. "Except that no man is perfect; so all we can do is accept our errors and make amends."

"I agree with you. I also notice that men are more foolish and make more errors when they are in love. At least I did. However, I was fortunate to love someone who had the heart of an angel and forgave me." Bingley smiled at his wife and kissed her hand tenderly.

"I believe you are too severe on yourself, Charles." Jane blushed at her husband's compliment.

"I must agree with Bingley." Darcy cast a glance at Elizabeth then turned the conversation towards the three puzzled girls listening to them. "Miss Mary, Miss Catherine, I hope you enjoyed your first day at Pemberley."

The girls were so intimidated by his direct attention that they struggled to answer; fortunately, Georgiana came to their rescue and told her brother what they had done that day.

For the entire evening, conversation flowed in the same manner, with Elizabeth being more silent and restrained than ever.

After dinner, the gentlemen chose not to separate from the ladies, and they moved together to the music room. Georgiana offered to play, and she was immediately joined by Mary, who promised to turn the pages for her. Lady Hardwick sat on a sofa with Jane, the gentlemen in chairs in one corner, and Elizabeth with Kitty on the settee.

The music flew enchantingly, and everyone listened with admiration. Then, from the corner of her eye, Elizabeth noticed Darcy walking towards her. Kitty observed him too and immediately rose and moved next to Jane. Embarrassed by her sister's withdrawal, Elizabeth forced a smile. He asked whether he could sit; she agreed, although she could barely understand what he was saying.

They sat near each other, but neither said a word, paying complete attention to the pianoforte. When the music stopped for a couple of minutes, he leant towards her. "I must thank you for the letter. I did not expect it, but I most certainly needed it."

She gathered her courage to look at him, and her eyes lingered on his only a moment before the music continued.

The evening ended when the ladies retired to their chambers, although the three gentlemen remained to enjoy drinks and conversation. On the way to their rooms, Georgiana held Elizabeth's arm.

"Lizzy, I am so happy that my brother is home."

"I know you are, my dear."

"And you, Lizzy? Are you happy?"

"I am," she said, then embraced the girl and wished her good night.

She was happy indeed. Happier than she had been in a long while. He had not only come home, but he let her know that he received her letter and that it was the reason for his return. They spoke little, but that was understandable since she behaved like a simpleton. She barely looked at him and addressed him only to answer his questions. Such behaviour was laughable.

ELIZABETH PREPARED FOR THE NIGHT, WORRIED ABOUT WHAT SHE SHOULD do the next day—Christmas. Could she hope for the gift of a few minutes of private conversation? But what should she say to him? And what could he tell her? Did he return with intentions? Did he have plans? Were his intentions clear to him? Would he share them with her? Or perhaps he wished to renew their acquaintance and develop it gradually—perhaps to court her? She felt her face flush as she realised he had proposed to her but never courted her—at least, she had not recognized it as such.

To avoid more useless and distressful musings, she went to bed, but only a few minutes later, she woke and paced the room. She lit two candles: one near the bed and one on the small table by the window. It was dark outside, the stars and the moon hidden by the clouds. She attempted to read but with no success as patience for that eluded her. Restless, she heard steps in the main hall—stark, slow, and determined. She knew it must be Darcy; there was no one else in the family wing. Of course, it could also be his valet or another servant; she scolded her silly assumption. Unconsciously, she moved closer to the door, taking the candle with her, and listened.

The steps moved forward then back, forward and again back. Her heart beat so loudly that she feared it could be heard through the door. She heard the steps again towards the end of the hall; then a door opened and closed again. It was surely him, and he had entered his apartment. She was about to return to bed when a quiet knock startled her, and she dropped the candle, extinguishing its flame. She ignored it to open the door—only to face Darcy, looking at her through the darkness. The only light came from the fireplace and the weak flame of the other candle. With embarrassment and surprise, she turned to pick up the fallen candle. He entered to help her, and their fingers touched; both rose and stood, inches apart. No words were said, but he apparently awaited a sign from her, so she moved to close the door, assuring them privacy for their conversation.

He followed her hesitantly. She sat on the bed; he stood by the fireplace. They could barely see each other, which was best since their eyes dared not meet.

"Miss Bennet, I beg your forgiveness for this improper intrusion. I saw the light from under the door and supposed you were still awake. I shall disturb you but a moment."

"No apologies are necessary, sir. You could not possibly disturb me more than I already am," she whispered.

A moment of silence, then he answered, his voice so low that she barely understood him.

"You surely cannot be more disturbed than I am…"

For a time, the only sound was the burning logs in the fireplace.

"Will we then argue over the greater part of disturbance that troubles each of us, Mr. Darcy?"

"I hope not…I hope we will not argue over anything for a while, Miss Bennet. We have argued so many times over so many things…too many."

"Do you plan to argue again in the future, sir?"

"I hope not. I hope many things for the future. Your letter taught me to hope as I never dared before…if I understood it correctly. What did you want to tell me, Miss Bennet?"

"What is it that you wish to ask me, Mr. Darcy?"

He moved only a step closer to her.

"I have so many questions—and one more important than all the rest. But I dare not ask. I am afraid I might upset you and make you run from me."

"I am not the one who runs away, sir. And since you do not dare ask, allow me to do so. Why would a gentleman simply leave instead of staying to overcome past faults and clarify painful misunderstandings?"

"Perhaps, he felt that his affection was not shared or desired and that his absence would bring more peace and comfort than his presence."

Their troubled gazes met.

"How many times must a man be at fault before he stops presuming? Why is it easier for a man to fight a battle than to speak his mind and ask the questions that disturb him?"

"That I cannot tell. I have had to carry on many battles of all kinds, but I was not disturbed until I met you last autumn. And I have been ever since. That became the hardest and longest battle I ever waged, and I am not certain I have won it. I pray that you will help me succeed."

He sat beside her and took her hands in his, his grip loose so she could withdraw whenever she wanted. She did not. Her fingers moved shyly within his large, warm palms.

"Shall I dare tell you why I have been so distressed, Miss Bennet? May I finally speak my mind and ask the questions that have tormented me all this time?"

"Please do…"

He touched her face as gently as a breeze. Her eyelids trembled, and her eyes sparkled.

"Because I fell in love with you more than a year ago, and my love has deepened and grown stronger ever since. I loved you when I was near you and when I was miles away; I loved you even when I thought I resented and hated you. My anger, my pain, my turmoil, my longing, and my sorrow only fed my love and made it more powerful."

She listened to him, mesmerised, her heart aching and her mind still doubtful. She wished to answer, but her whole being shivered, and her soul, tormented and filled with affection, was released in the tears rolling down her face.

He lifted her hands to his chest and held them with one hand, then gently wiped her tears.

"You see? I made you cry...my fault again." He smiled.

Her eyes sparkled. "My tears are just the words of tenderness that fill my heart but my lips cannot speak."

His thumb brushed her lips, slowly, gently. She sighed; spellbound, she waited, prayed, yearned, and it finally happened: the touch of his lips on hers, as soft as a fantasy. Tender, sweet, loving, patient. Her first kiss.

He withdrew slightly and whispered endearments while his fingers glided towards her nape and entwined in the hair falling freely on her back.

Her eyes searched for his, and her right hand tentatively touched his face, as he did to hers a moment before. "I do not know when I fell in love with you. I cannot fix on the hour, or the spot, or the look, or the words that started it. I believe I was in the middle before I knew that I had begun."

Their left hands were still clasped together.

"It could not have been a long time ago...I imagine your opinion of me started to change only when Bingley returned to Netherfield."

"No...once I left Rosings, I began to consider more thoroughly my knowledge of you. I suspected Wickham's falsehoods, and I was ashamed for trusting him. Then in London, I was grateful for your help, which I honestly did not expect. When those rational feelings turned into something more, I could not say. But when we were at Longbourn, I longed for your presence. And by the time we began the journey to Pemberley, my heart was half lost."

His surprise was apparent, and he turned to kiss her palm that was cupping his face.

"So in the last three months, all my torment was for nothing? I could have held you in my arms all this time? Why did you not say a word to me?" he inquired tenderly.

Her eyes were still tearful. "Why did you not ask?"

"How could I dare ask when I did not know your feelings had changed?

If you had given me but a little encouragement…"

"How could I dare give you encouragement when I did not know your feelings had *not* changed? You avoided me. You were always grave and silent. You could have talked to me more!"

"A man who felt less might. But I was so embarrassed by the strength of my feelings and desires…"

Her lips and eyes laughed at him while her hand caressed his face again, daring to move lower along the line of his jaw.

"How unlucky that you should have a reasonable answer to give and that I should be so reasonable as to admit it! But I wonder how long you would have gone on if you had been left to yourself! I wonder how long you would have wandered around the country if I had not written to you! And I only did that after a harsh and entirely improper conversation with Lady Hardwick! What becomes of the moral if our present happiness springs from a breach of decorum? This will never do."

He laughed and suddenly covered her face with small kisses. She chuckled and turned away, falling back on the bed, pulling him with her. He stopped and again withdrew, fingers replacing lips in his soft caress of her face.

"I would have spoken—eventually. By the time I reached London, I knew that my departure was useless. I only suffered more—from longing and jealousy. Have I mentioned that I am jealous of Lord Mowbray? And of my cousin? And of Wickham back in Hertfordshire last autumn."

Lying on the bed, she was trapped beneath him, his body only supported by his elbows and almost brushing against hers. She stared in complete disbelief. The dangerous closeness seemed to trouble him even more, so he rose and gently pulled her up with him.

She continued to stare at him, as if to puzzle out his words.

"You were jealous of them? But I never…" She paused then added, "I was jealous of Lady Emmeline. And of all the other young ladies who might capture your attention in Town."

His smile broadened. "No other woman ever caught my attention as you did, Elizabeth. No one ever touched my heart in such a way, and nobody ever made me lose my reason and self-control as you did."

He slowly moved closer to her. She closed her eyes, eager to sense the heart-melting feelings one more time. His lips caressed hers again, as gently as before, then tasted them. She moaned and stopped breathing at the new sensation. She parted her lips, without knowing why, and circled her arms around his neck. Her body and her mind soon were lost in a rapture that became intoxicating. The kiss deepened and left her breathless. She needed air, but she needed him more, so she allowed herself to be trapped in the sweet torment until he put an end to it.

"If you only knew how many times I have dreamed of you, Elizabeth…" he said as he tenderly caressed her face.

"Then tell me…how many times?" she whispered.

"Too many to remember…every night…and every day…every moment since that evening at Sir William's when you refused to dance with me…"

"You must have been upset with me then. Your dreams could not have been lovely…" she teased him.

"Quite the contrary. They were…lovelier than I could dare tell you now… perhaps one day…after we marry. But not as lovely as the reality. Your scent is more exhilarating and your skin softer than I imagined…and your eyes sparkle more brightly…and your lips are so delectable. I was starved for them when I believed my hunger would ever be sated."

Elizabeth shivered under the power of his fervent words and hoarse voice; his passionate confession overwhelmed her senses, and she found no strength to reply.

"My love, I should leave now," Darcy said. He rose to stand, holding her tightly so that she remained in his arms.

"Yes, you should."

"But I wish to stay…more than I ever wanted anything before…"

Her eyes smiled at him shyly. "As do I. And I believe you have an excellent reason to remain longer, sir. You still have not asked me…"

He seemed puzzled, and it was several moments before he understood. Her beauty glowed under his passionate gaze as he took her hands in his, bringing them to his heart.

"In vain have I struggled. It will not do. My love cannot be repressed. You must allow me to tell you how ardently I have dreamt of you every single day and every single night of the last year, and I beg you to make my dreams come true by agreeing to be my wife."

Her mirth combined with tears of happiness, and she replied with trembling voice and laughing eyes. "I do not know the established mode to express my acceptance in such cases as this. But I know there is nothing in the world I want more than to be your wife. Such happiness I did not dare to dream after everything that has happened, after the objections against my family with Lydia's marriage and—"

She was silenced and imprisoned by another tempestuous kiss, so passionate that it conquered her senses and her thoughts. He wished to hear nothing more, and she wished to feel nothing but the delight that had built a fire inside her.

"I must leave, my love. I must leave now," he repeated decidedly. "I will see you again in the morning. Please think of when you prefer to have the wedding. We will inform the others…and then I will write to your father. But I must leave this very moment, or else I shall not leave at all."

She was slightly puzzled by his sudden haste and embarrassed by her desire to keep him longer. She then felt ashamed by her lack of gratitude. Only a few hours ago she was tormented as much by his absence as by uncertainty for the future, and now she had everything she prayed for—and still wanted more.

"I will see you in the morning, my love," she whispered while he kissed her hands again and left, closing the door quietly behind him. Amazingly, it was the same door she opened earlier, allowing him to enter and bring happiness to her life—in the middle of the night—as in all dreams.

Torment and struggle had ruined Darcy's sleep for more than a year, and now happiness and the fulfilment of his wishes left him equally restless.

He had actually run from Elizabeth—again—when he feared he would lose his self-control. She agreed to be his wife. She had loved him and longed for him for months. She received his profession of love and offered hers in return. More than her words, he could see the love in her eyes and recognise it in her restrained, timid passion. But he could not permit more to happen.

She was a guest in his house and his sister's friend. She would become his betrothed as soon as Mr. Bennet gave his blessing and be his wife the day of their marriage. Until then, he still had to be cautious and wait.

He had waited many months; surely, he could bear it a little longer.

Or not.

Chapter 29

The first morning of his new life—one free of turmoil and self-reproach, without fears or inner battles—found Darcy zealous and unsettled, his heart filled with a kind of joy he never knew existed. He —a private and restrained man who rarely spoke of his feelings—was desirous to share his felicity with everyone. Most of all, he was impatient to see Elizabeth. The thought that everything was now clear between them, that each knew of the other's feelings, that they could make plans for the future was tremendous.

Three days ago, he was alone in London, feeling lost and useless. A week ago, he left Pemberley, hoping to give Elizabeth the peace he believed she wanted. Two months ago, he journeyed to Pemberley, carrying the burden of Elizabeth's agonising presence. Five months ago, he was in Town, his days spent in seclusion and darkness at war with his memories, resentment, anger, disappointment, and regrets. Eight months ago, he had presented himself before Elizabeth, claiming her hand in marriage with arrogance and conceit, and she taught him a severe yet well-deserved lesson. And about a year ago, he had left Hertfordshire, striving to put as much distance as possible between him and Elizabeth Bennet—the woman who captured his heart and tormented his soul. Back then, he was certain they would never meet again under any circumstances. He was completely wrong then—as he had been before and would be later.

Lost in these musings, Darcy went to the library, asked for coffee, and considered the letters he had to write. Around eight o'clock, the door opened, and Elizabeth entered, closing the door behind her. She stepped towards him, a broad smile brightening her beautiful face, her eyes glowing with joy. He hurried to her and took her hands.

"Good morning, Mr. Darcy," she whispered with a mischievous smile.

"Good morning, my love," he replied, stealing a kiss—still amazed that he could do that. "Did you sleep well?"

"Not at all; I had too much on my mind and in my heart to sleep."

His fingers traced a soft line down her face then brought her hands to his lips.

"I did not sleep either, but I am more rested than I have been in months. Come, stay with me. Would you like tea?"

"Yes, thank you. It is so strange to be here with you…alone…without distress or awkwardness."

"I know…I spent so much time and effort to avoid being alone with you when all I wished was your company."

He sat in a chair in front of her to better see all of her. Her face coloured from pleasure under his intense look.

"What should we do today?" she asked. "Shall we tell the others—and how?"

"You may decide. I intend to write your father immediately to inform him of my proposal and to ask for his blessing. Have you decided upon a wedding day?"

"Of my father's blessing you should have no doubt. I believe he will be happy with the news. And so will my mother. As for the wedding…do you have a suggestion? You are the one who excels at making plans, Mr. Darcy," she teased him.

"I do; if it were up to me, I would like to marry tomorrow," he answered in complete earnest.

Elizabeth stared at him in astonishment. "Surely you jest!"

"Not at all…" He leant to whisper as he was afraid someone might hear them. "Last night I felt heartbroken that I had to leave you. I wish that to end as soon as possible. I have been away from you too long."

She swallowed the sudden lump in her throat and nodded. His whispers warmed her ear as his lips touched her skin. He continued, turning his head enough to steal another kiss from the corner of her lips.

"But I wish you to decide; therefore, we have two choices. I might procure a special licence so we could marry in less than a week, but it would mean that neither your parents nor the Gardiners would likely be able to attend. Or we could wait a few more weeks and invite them all here—or return to

Longbourn for the wedding. You decide, and I will make it happen."

"I…it is all so astonishing that I find it difficult to think clearly. But everything has happened here at Pemberley, this is your home, and it will soon be mine; so, this is where we should wed. But when—I am not certain. Perhaps my parents would like to attend. Should we ask Papa?"

She appeared suddenly uncertain and slightly overwhelmed. His lips brushed over hers again.

"I will apply for a special licence, so we could marry in a week. I shall also write to Mr. Bennet and Mr. Gardiner today, and we will make our final plans about the wedding day as soon as we receive the answer from Longbourn. Do you agree?"

Her eyes brightened. "Yes—it sounds like a perfect plan. I find it so remarkable that you always take everything into consideration."

"Hardly," he said with a laugh, and he moved next to her on the settee, placing his arm around her shoulders. "I am doing everything out of my usual selfishness. I want to ensure a short engagement so I can have what I most desire: you."

"Your selfishness is sometimes adorable, sir," she replied, moving closer into his arms.

"Will you continue to call me 'sir' on our wedding night?" he teased her.

"No indeed…but I need time to accustom myself to all this novelty…to a new you. Please do not rush me, sir…I mean Fitzwilliam." She chuckled.

He kissed her temple. "I shall not rush you in anything, my love. But I have longed to hear my name on your lips."

"As I have longed to hear you call me 'my love'…Fitzwilliam. That is your name, is it not? Although Georgiana calls you 'William.'"

"Yes and yes." He smiled. "When she was very young, she struggled to pronounce the entire name, so I encouraged her to use the shorter one, and that is how it remained for her."

"And what are you called by the others in your family?"

"'Darcy.' Or 'young man' and 'dear boy' by Aunt Amelia, depending on her disposition." Her laugh was suppressed by another kiss, and the softness of his lips became more important than any word or name.

"And what of our family? Should we tell them today or wait?" he eventually asked, his fingers playing with a rebellious lock of hair on her neck.

"I see no reason to wait. I desire no more secrets or pretended indifference.

Besides, Georgiana and Lady Hardwick would notice immediately that something is different."

"I agree." He laughed, his lips pressing her hair.

They stole another moment of shared tenderness before the door opened, and Georgiana barged in.

"Brother, do you know where Lizzy is? Nobody can find her—"

Georgiana stopped, astounded, as her eyes fell upon them. They drew apart and attempted to rise, but the girl allowed them no time to recover before she ran to them.

"Oh, dear Lord, you are engaged!" she cried. "Are you? I hope you are! I cannot believe it!"

"Yes we are, dearest," Elizabeth answered, tearful at the girl's enthusiasm.

"Oh, Lizzy, I am so happy," the girl said, embracing her tightly. "Does anyone else know? Have you told Aunt Amelia? This is so wonderful!"

"Nobody knows yet," Darcy said. "I will write to Mr. Bennet immediately to ask for his consent, and we planned to inform the others at breakfast."

"Brother, I am so happy for you!"

"I am very happy too, my dear. Let me embrace you."

They continued to talk and share their joy for a time. The ladies enjoyed more tea while Darcy attended to his task of writing to Longbourn and Gracechurch Street. He knew he owed letters to several others: Lady Catherine, Lord Matlock, and Colonel Fitzwilliam. But those would have to wait for Mr. Bennet's response.

Breakfast began animatedly, and Bingley inquired of the plans for the day.

"I first have an announcement to make," Darcy declared, gaining everyone's attention. I asked for Miss Bennet's hand in marriage, and she accepted me. I also sent an express to Mr. Bennet, requesting his blessing."

A heavy silence fell on the dining room. Lady Hardwick had a great smile of contentment, but the others looked at Darcy then at each other, astounded and perplexed.

"Which Miss Bennet?" Bingley asked incredulously. Kitty and Mary glanced at each other with concern as if it referred to one of them.

"Miss *Elizabeth* Bennet," Darcy explained with a tender glance towards his chosen one.

"Miss Elizabeth? But...how? When? I was not even aware that you were courting her!" Bingley continued to express his disbelief.

"I did not...that is...we had some misunderstandings that have now been clarified. But I have admired Miss Bennet since last autumn in Hertfordshire. My affection for her has grown since then, and I was fortunate to win her esteem."

Mary and Kitty were so surprised that neither dared to speak; instead, bewildered and worried, they looked at their sister as if she were in some danger. Elizabeth laughed as she intervened to calm the situation.

"I imagine this is a surprise for my sisters and my brother. Mr. Darcy and I had a rather harsh and arduous beginning to our acquaintance. But understanding between us improved recently, and I assure you that, for the two of us, this engagement was not unexpected."

"Well, it has come as a shock to us!" Bingley concluded. "Oh, and I am sorry that I cannot be at Longbourn to see Mr. and Mrs. Bennet's reaction."

"Oh, Mama and Papa will be happy," Jane offered kindly.

"I agree, my darling," Bingley addressed his wife. "They will be happy but perplexed—unlike my sisters, who will be equally perplexed but less happy."

The rest of the day was spent in discussion of the startling news. Lady Hardwick congratulated them with all the warmth and affection they could hope for while Georgiana expressed her delight countless times.

When Mr. Slade heard the news from Darcy himself, the gentleman said little except, "I am pleased that you listened to your heart, Mr. Darcy. I have rarely seen a more perfectly suited couple in character and spirit. Is it not astonishing that Storm felt the depth of your affection before either of you recognized it?"

"You think Storm felt the bond between us?" Darcy inquired incredulously.

"Why else would he accept Miss Bennet from the first moment he saw you together?"

"It is laughable that I have been such a fool, is it not? Even my horse mocked me."

"What is remarkable is the strength with which you eventually recognized the truth and brought happiness into your life. You should think only of the past as its remembrance gives you pleasure, sir; I learned that philosophy many years ago."

"I shall try; your advice has always been wise and valuable to me, Mr. Slade. But it will be some time before I reconcile myself with the past, as painful recollections often intrude."

"Few men easily reconcile with their past, Mr. Darcy. Painful recollections intrude for all of us. A man is fortunate to find a present and future that are worth the effort; it is sad when he does not."

"With that, I cannot argue, Mr. Slade."

ELIZABETH AND DARCY HAD NOT A SINGLE MOMENT OF SOLITUDE DURING that day or those that followed. They usually had a few private minutes in the library early in the morning, in which they talked and became more familiar with each other. At night, Darcy avoided visiting Elizabeth in her room again while he awaited Mr. Bennet's answer. He felt uncomfortable at the thought of betraying the gentleman's trust, and his duty and honour managed to keep his desires—also shared by Elizabeth—under good regulation.

The reply from the Gardiners arrived with congratulations and regrets for not being able to travel in the winter. Mrs. Gardiner also wrote to Elizabeth to express her delight and pride in her on not less than two pages.

Three days after Christmas, an express from Longbourn was handed to Darcy. It contained two letters: one for Darcy and another for Elizabeth. Eagerly, Darcy opened his, anxious to read the reply on which depended the most important event of his life.

Dear Mr. Darcy,

I must begin by telling you that I have never been so surprised in my life as when I read your express, and I doubt I will recover from the perplexity anytime soon.

I cannot understand how you and Lizzy progressed from enemies to spouses, but I could not be happier if your mutual affection is genuine and has a strong foundation. My Lizzy is truly a remarkable woman, and I would be pained to separate from her for anyone less worthy.

My admiration for you is as deep as my gratitude, and I should never dare refuse you anything you condescended to ask. But I also give you my heartfelt blessing, praying that your unexpected marriage with Lizzy will be to the advantage of both and raise everyone's admiration.

As for your wedding date, you may fix it at your and Lizzy's convenience. It is fortunate that her sisters are there to be by her side. Mrs. Bennet and I cannot possibly travel to Pemberley until Easter, as much as we would like to. Mrs. Bennet insists on your marrying as soon as possible with a special

*licence. I believe she is worried that you might change your mind if you delay
any longer, as she cannot believe you truly proposed to Lizzy.*

*We eagerly await a detailed report of your wedding, including the
number of courses at the wedding breakfast, a description of the ladies' dresses,
and the dimensions of Lizzy's apartment so Mrs. Bennet can share them
with Mrs. Philips, Lady Lucas, and the other four and twenty families
in Meryton.*

Darcy read the letter with equal amusement and gravity as he could guess
Mr. Bennet's concern for his daughter's felicity. He began his reply immediately with further details and assurance to put Mr. Bennet at ease. While
he was writing, Elizabeth entered. He handed her the letter, as well as the
one addressed to her, still sealed.

Elizabeth sat near him, delighting herself with her father's words. Then
she opened the second one, curious and impatient.

My dearest Lizzy,

*I shall not deny that the news of your marriage to Mr. Darcy surprised
me exceedingly. I never suspected such inclinations from either of you, and
I am rather worried. I have confidence enough in you both to hope that you
made the decision based on solid reasons. However, there is something you
must know of your future husband. I might be considered to be breaking a
promise, but I believe it will help you to better know the man you decided
to marry.*

*Mr. Darcy's assistance in arranging Lydia's marriage to Wickham
was not limited to finding the couple. Darcy paid all the debts, procured the
commission, and negotiated with that scoundrel. Everything that was needed
he did of his own will. We argued and refused to allow him to bear all the
expense, but he would not be contradicted.*

*Why he made such a sacrifice we could not possibly imagine then; but
now, it becomes apparent that his affection for you must have been strong
even then and induced all his actions.*

*I hope you are already aware of your betrothed's generous character, but if
not, this knowledge will surely be another proof.*

*Be happy, dearest Lizzy—may this marriage fulfil your dreams of felicity.
I shall see you for Easter at Pemberley.*

Elizabeth put the letter down, incredulous, dismayed, and soulful. She looked at the man she believed she had come to know as if she were seeing him for the first time.

"My love, we will marry in a week. Can you believe it? Only one week. Are you not pleased?" he asked, concerned with her lack of response.

"Papa wrote to me…he told me what you did for Lydia and Wickham. Why did you not tell me?" she whispered.

Surprise darkened his countenance. "I am exceedingly sorry that you have ever been informed of what may give you uneasiness. I did not think Mr. Bennet was so little to be trusted. I asked him specifically not to share this secret with anyone."

"Please do not blame Papa; his intention was good. I believe he fears that my decision to marry you is based on my admiration of Pemberley. He never knew of our past dealings, and he did not suspect any affection between us; he wished to provide another proof of your generous character."

Darcy moved near her and held her hands. "You are troubled and pained."

"How could I not be? You went through so much trouble, you wasted so much effort and money to repair my sister's foolishness…Papa told me then that it was around ten thousand pounds. Was it?"

"My love, this discussion is useless. I did what was necessary to purchase Wickham's debts, and he is now in my power. I do not know whether my affection for you was any inducement for my decision. If so, it was unconsciously done because, at that time, I was angry and resentful and wished never to see you again. Then I met your father; I witnessed his despair, and I remembered my own feelings when Georgiana almost eloped. I knew it was my fault for not exposing Wickham, as I should have done years ago. And I was aware that your father could not provide what Wickham demanded, so my decision was easily made. I did not want you or anyone else to know because I do not deserve gratitude."

"You do deserve it…" she whispered, caressing his face. "Gratitude and so much more. How can I repay you for helping me when I knocked on your door? Your generosity was stronger than your anger and resentment. You put everything aside, ignored the offence I wrongly gave you, and offered your help when you easily could have refused it."

He put his arms around her and pulled her onto his lap; she released a small cry of surprise then circled her arms around his neck.

"Marry me in a week," he whispered. "Not from gratitude, not for anything I did, not for the past, and not for Wickham or your sister. Let the past go, once and forever. Marry me because I desperately wish you to become my wife—to be mine."

"I will not...at least not for that reason. I will marry you because *I* desperately want to be *yours*," she whispered. She was so close that her body pressed against his. His hands stroked her back, and his eyes looked deeply into hers. Small kisses caressed her neck, throat, and chin until his lips captured hers, which parted for him.

"Somebody might come in and see us," she said before her lips were completely captured.

"I care not; I have your father's blessing, and I have the licence. We can marry tomorrow." The kiss became more eager, more demanding as he pulled her even closer. "Then why wait a week?" she replied a moment before his lips conquered her senses.

MR. DARCY'S WEDDING TO MISS ELIZABETH BENNET WAS SETTLED TO TAKE place the first week of the New Year. Four days before, Lady Hardwick asked the couple for a private meeting.

"My dears, I have news for you. I spoke to Georgiana and Mrs. Bingley. After the wedding, we will all move to Tidestone for a few weeks. It is a lovely place, and I am certain they will enjoy it."

Elizabeth's surprise was great. "You wish to leave? Why?" she inquired with concern. To her astonishment, the countess smiled while Darcy seemed perfectly composed.

"Because you should be alone in the first weeks of your marriage. Your engagement has been a rather hectic time for both of you. Now you need complete privacy and comfort. We will be only twenty miles away if you wish to visit."

"I do not know what to say," Elizabeth replied, and her cheeks coloured.

"It is a considerate gesture, dear Aunt; I am grateful for your care." Darcy bowed. "Have you made all the arrangements?"

"Yes—Mr. Slade will come with us if you can manage without him for a couple of days."

"Mr. Slade is our friend, not our employee. He may go and return whenever he wishes. I am content that he will join you, so I know you will be safe."

"You must not worry about us; we will be perfectly fine," Lady Hardwick said with a smile. "It is time for you to be selfish in your happiness and indulge yourself in your wife's company."

Darcy took Elizabeth's hand to his lips. "Of that, you must have no doubts, your ladyship."

Chapter 30

The wedding of Mr. Darcy to Miss Elizabeth Bennet took place on a freezing but sunny morning in January. The beginning of the New Year marked the beginning of their new life. The ceremony took place at Pemberley's chapel in the presence of Lady Hardwick and Georgiana, Mr. and Mrs. Bingley, Kitty and Mary, Mr. Slade and Colonel Fitzwilliam, and several of the tenant families and Lambton inhabitants.

Talk and rumour were aroused by the sudden event, as nobody had noticed a preference of the master for Miss Darcy's friend since she arrived in Derbyshire. But no flaws were found in Miss Bennet, whose pleasant, unaffected manners and amiable disposition had been admired from the beginning. Miss Darcy's close friendship and the support openly showed by Lady Hardwick proved to any sceptics that Miss Bennet was worthy to occupy a position that would affect the lives of many.

During the wedding ceremony, Miss Bennet's beauty shone from obvious happiness, and Mr. Darcy looked more handsome and less severe than he had been seen in a decade.

The wedding breakfast lasted until late afternoon, and Pemberley was filled with more joy, liveliness, and laugher than anyone could remember.

The sun had set before silence returned to Pemberley. The last to leave was the extended family that, with a warm and tearful farewell, departed for Tidestone under the strict supervision of Lady Hardwick and Mr. Slade.

In the midst of a large, quiet, and lonely room, the just-wedded couple suddenly found themselves more alone than ever before.

They gazed at each other and their hands entwined, but words remained lost. The silence was so complete that each could hear the other's heartbeat.

Still wordlessly, Darcy placed his arm around his wife's shoulders and took her hands in his other palm, slowly guiding her up the stairs towards their apartment.

They had taken the same path countless times in the last three months; everything was the same except their feelings and the realisation that, the next time they walked down the stairs, they would be different people. There would be no *he* and *she* anymore but *they*—complete as one being.

At the door of the master suites, they stopped. Elizabeth had visited the mistress's apartment several times in the last fortnight. But that was Miss Bennet. Now, Mrs. Darcy was entering, ready to start a new life with her husband.

Darcy opened the door and looked at her. Her uneasiness met his comforting smile, and she was prepared to walk in when his arms lifted her as a cherished treasure and carried her inside.

He put her down on the bed then sat next to her and took her hands into his, just as he had the night of their confessions and comfort.

"What is it, my love?" he whispered.

"Oh, nothing—I am so ridiculous." She struggled to laugh. "Forgive me —I will call for Sarah. It will not take long."

"Elizabeth…" His hands cupped her face, and his thumbs gently caressed her. "My love, nothing that troubles you is ridiculous. Just tell me…and there is no hurry…we have a lifetime together."

"I know…nothing troubles me. Do not worry…I mean—yes, it does, but it is a good trouble…"

"I am glad to hear that." He smiled and placed a tender kiss on each of her eyelids.

She moved a little, allowing their lips to meet briefly, then pushed him away gently.

"Leave now, Mr. Darcy. I must prepare, and you are detaining me."

"I would by no means want to do that, Miss Bennet…forgive me —Mrs. Darcy."

He reluctantly separated from her, kissing her hands once again, and closed the adjoining doors behind him.

Once alone, Elizabeth glanced at her spectacular apartment. The glamour, the tasteful blend of colours, the impressive furniture—everything spoke of the importance attached to her new position. She glanced at the table, and her eyes were drawn by something that had not been there before, something that told of her husband's love and passion and of his promise for their life together: a bouquet of red roses, fresh and vivid in the middle of winter. She brushed her fingers along the delicate petals and smelled them; her heart raced, and a shiver ran along her skin.

She rang for Sarah, wondering whether he had mentioned when he would return. Should she hurry or take her time and let him wait? She then scolded herself for such thoughts. Whenever he came, she would be ready for him; she had been ready for him since the night he returned home.

Almost an hour passed while she was bathed and changed for the night. The time seemed to fly, and Sarah was suddenly moving very slowly—slower than ever before. When the maid finally left, Elizabeth gazed at her image in the mirror. She did not have time to order a special nightgown, so Jane offered a new one from her trousseau. Elizabeth blushed as she considered that, strangely, her sister seemed to have a great number of nightclothes since she married.

She stepped to the window, gazing outside. In the room, light came from two candles and the fireplace, but outside, a full moon shone over Pemberley.

She startled when she heard the door and turned just enough to see him. Her eyes remained fixed on his intense gaze. She had seen him informally attired before, but his appearance in only trousers and a shirt made her shiver, and her lips suddenly became dry.

He moved closer, and every step made her tremble. She licked her lips and turned to the window again. His arms closed around her from behind and she leant back against him.

"Is there something interesting outside, Mrs. Darcy?"

His lips fondled her ear while his whispers made her quiver.

"Yes…I just noticed that the view from this room is the same as the one from my previous chamber."

His lips lowered to her neck and tasted her skin.

"Yes…that is why I insisted you choose that particular one. I knew that you would have exactly the same view as if you were in this apartment —where you rightfully belonged from the beginning."

His hoarse voice and his scent became intoxicating. She turned in his arms, her body brushing his, and their lips met.

"I thought you suggested that choice for my benefit," she murmured.

"Not at all, Mrs. Darcy—mostly for mine. You should know by now that I am a very selfish man."

He suddenly withdrew from her and distanced himself enough that he could see her. The nightgown caressed her figure, exposing her curves to his greedy eyes.

She was the one who took the first step towards the bed; but there, she stopped. He embraced her again then laid her down.

"I shall blow out the candles," he said, and she nodded. He did so and returned but sat on the edge of the bed.

"You shiver, my love. Are you cold?"

"No…"

He took off her robe and tossed it away; then his eyes deepened into hers as he gently glided the gown from her shoulders, now covered only by her silky hair. He lowered the fabric even more, and she closed her eyes. Slowly, he covered her face with countless, small kisses then traced a warm path along her throat. His hands stroked her bare skin through the thin fabric, lowered along her body over her ribs then on her hips, her thighs, down to her ankles, and held her feet in his palms for a moment. She relished the feeling and moaned, her eyes opening to meet his. But his gaze was now greedily admiring the beauty he had only dreamed of. With torturous slowness, his lips returned to capture hers while his hands finally rested upon her heart.

His kiss became more demanding while his hands cupped her breasts and his fingers traced tingling circles around each of them.

A small cry escaped her captive mouth and another followed as the gown fell away completely. A consuming fire burned inside her, and her back arched towards him.

She felt him pause, and her skin longed for his touch. She opened her eyes and saw him remove his shirt. She gasped for air, seeing his bare torso; shyly, she stretched her hand to touch him, but he impatiently kissed her again while his body brushed over hers. His hands moved even more daringly along her body, now fully exposed to his passionate exploration.

Then his urge seemed to subside; he allowed her a moment of rest as he removed a few strands of hair from her face.

"You are so beautiful, my love…so beautiful…"

She only smiled and licked her suddenly dry lips; his thumb gently brushed over them, and he leant atop her again.

"Let me know if you wish me to stop," he whispered.

She felt him remove his trousers; then his caresses conquered her body again.

"Why would I want you to stop?" she asked, uncertain whether the words were spoken aloud or only in her mind.

He freed her from the nightclothes; then, carefully, his body covered her as he pulled a sheet up to cover them. There was nothing left between them now—skin against skin, heart to heart, passion with passion. The feeling was so intoxicating that Darcy trembled in anticipation, his long-caged yearning screaming for fulfilment. Yet, *his* pleasure meant less to him than *hers*. He felt her growing desire and her sweet body craving his touch. Her moans begged for more, and his hunger for her became unbearable. His hands hurried to reveal the last secrets of her body, and his lips readily followed, tantalising the softness of her breasts and tasting their sweetness; her cries of delight pleaded with him not to stop.

He sensed her warmth and wished to touch the core of it, so he gently caressed her hips then stroked her legs; her thighs locked, and he paused a moment until he felt her relax, then his hand continued its conquest. Soon, no opposition remained, and he dared move his fingers a little higher. He felt her shiver and heard her pleas. His mouth hungrily captured her other breast, and she cried again, quivering. It was still not enough for either of them. With an urge he had never felt before and with a hunger growing stronger, he wished to feel and taste every inch of her. So his lips abandoned their sweet captive and followed the trace of his hands, savouring everything he had previously felt until her fingers tightly entwined in his hair and her body shivered in fulfilment.

For Elizabeth, the world vanished when the sweet, unimaginable rapture filled her body. She needed some time before she dared open her eyes and look at him. His gaze was darker and more burning than ever. He covered her face with small kisses as she averted her eyes, not daring to wonder what had happened.

"You smell of lavender and love," he whispered, his lips tenderly touching hers again. "I dreamed of you so many times, but my imagination was poor…"

"I never dreamed of…never…" she whispered.

"Then we shall learn together what we did not dream before, my beloved."

His caresses renewed, and Elizabeth surrendered completely.

This time she thought she knew what to expect. When his hand stroked her thighs again, they parted, and her heart raced with anticipation. She closed her eyes, but his lips tantalised her ear as he begged, "Please look at me, my beautiful wife."

She did so, though her eyelashes felt heavy. He was lying atop her, their faces merely inches apart. Unleashed passion darkened his eyes and made her shiver, but the lust became tenderness as he smiled at her. Elizabeth's body opened to him, just as her heart and mind had done only a fortnight ago. She felt him enter her with a sharp, brief pain and overwhelming desire. The pain soon vanished, but the ardour continued and grew until it overwhelmed her, and together they found fulfilled, blissful happiness.

They remained embraced, unwilling to separate, breathing each other's scent and wondering at sensations new for both of them, although in different ways. They knew there was more to come—more to discover, more to learn from each other and with each other. Together.

Beneath the light of the moon and the stars—after a year filled with restless nights, resentment, anger, and guilt—Mr. and Mrs. Darcy finally fell deeply asleep. No dream bothered their rest as they needed nothing but each other.

And the only thing that interrupted their sleep—quite often that night and in the nights to come—was their unbridled passion.

Epilogue

A large carriage loaded with luggage rode along the path towards Pemberley House. Inside, Mr. and Mrs. Bennet, together with Mr. and Mrs. Gardiner, spoke animatedly while the children looked outside with curiosity and impatience.

"I cannot believe how large this park is," Mr. Gardiner exclaimed.

"It is one of the largest and most beautiful I have ever seen," Mrs. Gardiner replied. "And you cannot imagine the beauty of the house. I have been inside only once, when I was a child, but I never forgot it."

Mrs. Bennet glanced through the window and breathed in deep satisfaction.

"Well, the Collinses and the Lucases keep talking about Rosings Park, to which they are not even connected. Surely, it cannot compare with Pemberley—which happens to belong to my daughter. I cannot wait to tell all this to Lady Lucas!"

"I look forward to seeing Lizzy," one of the children exclaimed.

"As we all do, my dear. We have not see them since they were in Town two months ago. Oh, Sister Bennet, what a wonderful ball Lady Matlock hosted for her and how beautiful Lizzy was. Lady Hardwick was also in attendance; only Lady Catherine de Bourgh was missing from Mr. Darcy's relatives. She and Jane were the most beautiful ladies there—and you must know there were at least fifty people, all from among the ton!"

"Oh, Lady Catherine is very angry with Lizzy and with Mr. Darcy. Lady

Lucas has told me that many times, as she hears it from Mr. Collins and Charlotte. I could not care less for her since my Lizzy is now the mistress of Pemberley. But a ball, dear sister, I would have loved to participate. Sadly, my nerves would not allow me to go by myself, and Mr. Bennet is so opposed to balls that one would think he is a savage!"

"I am not a savage—only a reasonable man who does not travel in the winter through blizzards and snow for a ball. I was perfectly content that Darcy and Lizzy stopped to visit us on their way home, though for only two days."

"Indeed, I cannot understand why Lizzy remained in Town only a month instead of enjoying the entire Season. Even Mrs. Philips declared that it was rather strange."

"They are newly wedded, sister. "It is only natural that they wish to be by themselves. I believe they would never leave Pemberley were it not for the social obligation of introducing the new Mrs. Darcy to London Society."

"I wish that at least one of my daughters would stay in Town for the entire season, and Kitty and Mary join them. Having two such wealthy brothers-in-law and such lovely connections, I am sure they would easily find good husbands. I look forward to seeing them both—I cannot believe they have not been home at all since Christmas."

"Well, they visited Pemberley for almost two months. And now that Jane and Mr. Bingley have purchased an estate in Derbyshire, it is only natural they would help Jane to accommodate, especially since she is expecting her first child," Mrs. Gardiner said warmly.

"Of that, I am very glad," Mrs. Bennet declared. "I cannot wait to visit Jane next week. And I am so happy that Jane invited Lydia and Mr. Wickham too! I have missed my youngest daughter exceedingly. Mr. Wickham, not so much since I know he was ungrateful to Mr. Darcy and Lady Hardwick. I do not need any details to remove him from my heart."

"I wonder whether Lizzy is at home," Mr. Bennet said.

Mr. Gardiner glanced at him suspiciously. "Brother Bennet, you did inform Mr. Darcy that we would arrive a week earlier, did you not? I specifically asked you about that several times."

"Well, not quite. I thought we should surprise them. After all, he sent me the carriage to travel comfortably."

The Gardiners and his wife were all astonishment. "Surprise them? We are four people and two children barging in!"

The gentleman waved his hand. "Do not worry. Darcy told me I might come whenever I want without any special invitation. So I find it only natural to came when he least expects us."

The unexpected arrival of Elizabeth's family took everyone by surprise, but the joy and the warmth of their reception were not lessened in the slightest. Elizabeth and Darcy, as well as Georgiana and Lady Hardwick, were happy to see them. From the first day, Mr. Slade became a familiar presence and an equal favourite of the ladies and gentlemen in attendance. They were soon joined by Colonel Fitzwilliam, and the party was completed by the visit of the Bingleys, Mary, and Kitty.

To everyone's delight—especially her mother's—Elizabeth had planned balls and parties for Easter time. Even Georgiana—comfortable in the midst of the extended family, more self-confident, and wrapped in her brother and sister's felicity—happily took part in all the plans. There was only one exception to the universal excitement—or perhaps two. Mr. Bennet spoke little but paid attention to everything around him. Aside from the beauties of the estate, his heart was touched by the loveliness of his favourite daughter and the special glow in her eyes, enhancements that could come only from happiness. He noticed the way Elizabeth and Darcy escaped the others as often as they had a chance, stealing private moments away from everyone. They were always close so they could touch, whisper, and smile at each other, and their gazes searched for and held each other's across the room if they happened to be apart. The face of the once-aloof and haughty gentleman brightened when he glimpsed his wife, and Elizabeth beamed under the intense stare that bothered her so in the past.

His concerns forever vanished, Mr. Bennet wished little but to be left in the seclusion of the Pemberley library, and his son-in-law joined him whenever he could escape from his responsibilities as host. Neither of them liked large gatherings, and neither enjoyed balls and parties, but both bore everything bravely for the sake of their loved ones.

One day as they hid from the party and enjoyed a drink and a little conversation, Elizabeth entered with a large smile and a playful glance and sat between the two favourite men in her life.

"Have you come to scold us for our absence, my love?" Darcy kissed her hand.

"No indeed; I came to spend a little time with you both. Papa, I hope you are enjoying your time with us. You are always so silent that I am not certain of your thoughts."

"You may be certain, my dear. Can you not see how content I am—and how proud of you? Almost as much as I miss and grieve your departure when I am at Longbourn."

Elizabeth embraced her father and placed a kiss on his cheek. "Papa, I miss you too. Fitzwilliam might tell you that I speak of you constantly. If I had you here with us all the time, I would wish for nothing more."

"You should not say that too often, as I might give you another surprise," Mr. Bennet joked tearfully. "Although I doubt your mother will ever leave Meryton unless she can bring Mrs. Philips and Lady Lucas with us."

Elizabeth stayed with them a few minutes, continuing the same teasing conversations they used to have at Longbourn, then she returned to their other guests. Darcy accompanied her to the door, and before they left, their lips touched briefly in a kiss that Mr. Bennet pretended not to notice. Darcy resumed his place near his father-in-law and poured him a little more brandy.

"You and Lizzy are still a surprise to me, Mr. Darcy. I know you explained to me all the details of your past when you were last at Longbourn, but I still find it hard to believe that you complete each other so well. You have both changed—in a good way. I would dare say you have found excellence in marriage."

Darcy smiled, and a hidden private thought brightened his eyes and softened his handsome countenance.

"I would rather say we found *happiness* in marriage, Mr. Bennet."

CPSIA information can be obtained
at www.ICGtesting.com
Printed in the USA
BVOW03s1028260617
487843BV00001B/18/P